Praise for *Wonders of a Godless World*

'McGahan is a fabulous writer, not only because of the quality of writing but also because of his courage as an artist.'
Sydney Morning Herald

'A ...ively sustained feat of imagination.'
Australian Book Review

'T writing rises to invigorating heights.' *Sunday Tasmanian*

'B ...tly researched and plotted, intellectually stimulating and re ...ding . . . there are also plenty of moments where the reader is nxiously to the page – or more accurately – unwilling to ose the page and so miss the possibilities poised to erupt. Li e thundering volcano that features heavily in the lives of its ch s. *Wonders of a Godless World* is sure to awaken the senses of who cares to dip into its explosive pages.'
Australian Women Online

'I ly swept up by the passion and energy of McGahan's w e hint of something truly profound lurking within the n: . . I'll be recommending it to as many people as possible.'
Canberra Times

'T ok is totally unexpected and you won't be able to put it d .. It's a thriller, an environmental plea, a book about madness, m l control, nature, space travel and just what it means to live fo If you're looking to escape the mundane, I recommend y up a copy of this book and dive into McGahan's aston- is ination.'
Readings.com

'T ory blew my mind. Plain and simple. This book was engaging from start to finish, with twists, turns and a series of intriguing sub-plots. A roller-coaster ride into the imagination.'
The Southlands Times, New Zealand

Also by Andrew McGahan

Praise
1988
Last Drinks
The White Earth
Underground

Andrew McGahan

Wonders of a Godless World

blue door

Blue Door
An imprint of HarperCollins*Publishers*
77–85 Fulham Palace Road,
Hammersmith, London W6 8JB

www.harpercollins.co.uk

Published by Blue Door 2010
1

First published in Australia by
Allen & Unwin 2009

A catalogue record for this book
is available from the British Library

ISBN: 978-0-00-735263-0

Set in Adobe Garamond Pro

Printed and bound in Great Britain by
Clays Ltd, St Ives plc

Mixed Sources
Product group from well-managed
forests and other controlled sources
www.fsc.org Cert no. SW-COC-001806
© 1996 Forest Stewardship Council
FSC

FSC is a non-profit international organisation established
to promote the responsible management of the world's forests.
Products carrying the FSC label are independently certified
to assure consumers that they come from forests that are managed
to meet the social, economic and ecological needs
of present and future generations.

Find out more about HarperCollins and the environment at
www.harpercollins.co.uk/green

1

The orphan knew something was up that night, even before the foreigner arrived at the hospital. It was a warm evening, early in the storm season, and she had been feeling strangely restless all day. More notably, the old doctor had stayed on much later than his usual quitting time, sitting quietly in his office, sipping now and then from a bottle, and listening to the radio. He waited in there all through dinner and past sunset, and even until lights-out in the back wards, by which time the orphan and the night nurse were normally the only ones left awake in the place.

The night nurse was annoyed, because most evenings *he* sat in the office with the radio and the bottle, but now he had to pretend to be working. The orphan wasn't happy either, because the night nurse, to look busy, was interfering with chores she knew perfectly well how to perform alone. And the inmates in their turn, sensing the irregularity, were making all kinds of trouble for her—climbing out of bed, taking off their pyjamas, wandering the halls and pissing in the corners.

Dutifully, the orphan retrieved clothes and dressed bodies and mopped floors, and said no more than she ever said, which was nothing at all. The inmates had plenty to say, of course, but the orphan couldn't understand them in any case. Between the late hour, the heat and the unusual goings-on, the madness in each of them was bubbling up in their throats, jumbling their words.

Her own madness was alive too. She could feel it beneath her feet, trembling and quivering. It was as if, far below in the earth, a giant machine hummed. The vibrations buzzed against her heels, running right up between her legs, and she couldn't decide if it felt bad or if she was half on the edge of an orgasm where she stood. But *something* was about to happen, she was sure. And by chance she was out the front—emptying her mop bucket in the drainage ditch—when the arrival took place.

First, the town's police car came bumping up the track and parked in the dim pool of light outside the hospital's front porch. The orphan had to step out of the way, and into the ditch, to let it by. The police captain was behind the wheel; a short, sweaty man, frowning over the dashboard. His presence in itself wasn't so unusual. The captain was a frequent visitor, if not always so late. But then an old white van drove up and parked behind him, and that wasn't usual at all. And yet the orphan had seen the van before. She strained her memory. Then she had it. Yes! It was the ambulance. It came from the *big* hospital, down in the *big* town. It was used to deliver patients.

A patient! Someone new! Letting the bucket drop, the orphan hurried over to the van's rear doors and tried to peer in.

Nothing. Darkness through the windows. Then the driver was there, shooing her away angrily. The orphan caught a glimpse of herself through the man's eyes. He thought she was one of the inmates—a short, stumpy girl with a shaved head and a hairy upper lip and a hospital dress stretched tight over big floppy breasts.

Ha! She was ugly and a madwoman and he was scared of her. She barked out loud, baring her uneven teeth, but then the old doctor appeared, and the police captain, and the night nurse too, and the doctor was explaining to the driver that the orphan wasn't a patient. As proof, she retrieved her bucket and held it out. But everyone had forgotten her already. The night nurse and the driver opened the rear doors of the van and from the dark interior they heaved forth a stretcher.

A man lay on it, apparently sleeping, covered to the neck by a sheet. His skin was pale, and his face had a raw, scraped look, but there was no other sign as to what might be wrong with him. The night nurse and the driver carried him away inside, but the orphan didn't follow. She lingered instead by the police car, hoping for clues. The old doctor and the police captain were leaning over the hood, talking, and studying a sheaf of papers the captain had spread there. It was not an easy conversation for the orphan to decipher, full of long words and quick allusions she could never hope to catch. But she had known the doctor most of her life, and the captain too. She was familiar with their voices and their mannerisms and their moods, and that was some help.

She gathered, for instance, that the captain was displeased. It was too hot and he was working late because he had been called down to the big town to collect the new patient. He didn't like the heat or working late, and he didn't like the people in the big town. The word he used for them was *devils*, and they had made him sign a lot of papers and take responsibility for the sleeping man. The captain thought he had enough responsibility as it was. He held out a grimy pen. He wanted the old doctor to sign the papers and then the sleeping man would be the hospital's problem.

But the old doctor, who was the cleverest person the orphan knew, didn't take the pen. Instead, he rubbed his chin and asked a very odd question. He wanted to know if the sleeping man had a name yet. At which the captain, odder still, gave him a disappointed look, and then sighed, lowering the pen. No, no one knew the man's name yet. It was a mystery. The authorities had put his picture in the newspaper down in the big town, and even on television, but no one had claimed him, and it'd been weeks now. The only sure thing was that he wasn't local to the island.

A stranger, the orphan noted, her brow furrowed with the effort it cost her to take all this in. A *foreigner*.

The conversation continued. The old doctor suggested that the man might perhaps be a tourist. After all, more and more tourists came to the island every year. And hadn't he been found asleep on the beach? But the captain shook his head. None of the hotels down in the big town knew anything about the man. Neither did anyone at the airport. And besides, he had been in some kind of fire. His clothes were just ashes when they found him. Burnt to rags. The police in the big town thought that maybe there had been an explosion on a boat out at sea. Perhaps he was a sailor.

The old doctor had another question. Why hadn't the man woken up, or spoken, in all the time since? Was there a head injury? The captain only shrugged. He didn't know. The doctors at the big hospital hadn't told him anything. All they had said was that they couldn't keep the man any longer. Perhaps if he had turned out to be rich, or someone important, then they would have let him stay. But it looked like he had no friends or family at all. And no money. So here he was.

The old doctor finally nodded, resigned. It wasn't for him to argue with the big hospital. The captain offered the grimy pen again, but the old doctor, unthinking, took out his own, and scribbled on the papers.

The orphan let out a puff of air and saw spots floating before her eyes. That was that. And yet, did she understand right? The new patient had lost his name? Why, that was almost the same as her! Well, she hadn't *lost* her name exactly. But she could never quite remember it either. Or anyone else's. She knew that everyone had a name, of course—and that other things did too—but try as she might, she could never recall them. They simply refused to lodge in her mind. It was a symptom of her madness, she supposed. Most probably, the foreigner was mad too.

The old doctor was walking back inside, holding the papers, his back bent painfully. He was too thin, the orphan had heard others say. He worked too hard, and was too old. Besides that, she knew, he was ill. The captain, meanwhile, who would never be thin, went to the door of his car. Noticing the orphan there, he winked and asked her a question. She understood him easily this time, because it was the same question people always asked her. He wanted to know if it would rain soon.

The orphan looked up. She didn't need to look, but people expected it, and were even a little unsettled if she didn't. The sky was clear, but the stars were muddied by the humid air, and it certainly felt as if water-laden clouds would form soon, and cooling winds begin to blow, and lightning to flicker. It was the storm season, after all. But the orphan knew better. She could tell that the great eddies in the atmosphere were moving too slowly for now. It wouldn't rain tonight, or the next night.

She shook her head.

The captain sighed once more, and wiped sweat from his face. Then he climbed into his car and drove off—heading, the orphan sensed, not for his little police station in the town square, and not for his home, where his wife and children waited, but instead for the jungle hut where his mistress lived. (The orphan had met both the wife and the mistress, and thought the mistress was nicer.) Shortly afterwards, the ambulance driver emerged and set off on his much longer trip back down to the coast.

Alone, the orphan idled a moment, her bare feet twisting in the sand. She could hear distant noises from the back wards. The inmates would not be settling down any time soon. She stared into the night, restless still, and expectant. Was there something out there in the dark? Not a storm massing, but a subtler thing?

Away below the hospital she could see the scattered lights of the town. They were surrounded by the wide darkness of the plantations. And much further off, in the sky beyond the rim of the plateau, was the glow thrown up by the big town, down upon the sea, where the rich people lived and no one ever slept.

The orphan turned and gazed up, behind the hospital, to the mountain. The jungle on its lower slopes was thick and black and impenetrable, but high above, the peak was a lighter shadow against the stars.

No, there was nothing out of place.

But even as she stared, she felt again the tremble in the dust, felt the thrill run up her bones, making her belly squirm. Oh yes, something was on its way. The orphan smiled her mad smile, then skipped back inside to her chores.

2

Of course, she had not always been an orphan. In fact, she was most likely not an orphan even now. Her mother was dead, but her father was probably still alive, somewhere in the world.

Not that she would ever know. When the orphan was much younger she had overheard a conversation between two pregnant women in the front wards. She had been cleaning nearby, and they had noticed her there and begun to talk about her as if she couldn't hear them. In particular, they were shaking their heads about all the men the orphan's mother had been with, and how she had gone down to the big town, where no decent girl would go, and involved herself with criminals. It was no wonder, the pregnant women agreed, that the orphan's mother had caught a disease. And it was even less wonder that when she gave birth to an ugly little retarded daughter, no man would step forward and claim the child as his own. Why, the father could be anyone.

Young as she had been, the orphan had understood a simple truth—*anyone*, when it came to fathers, meant the same as *no one at all*.

She had long since worked out what *retarded* meant too. Retarded was the same as *slow*, the same as *stupid*. Retarded was another term for *idiot girl*, or for *poor dumb child*, or for any of the similar things she had heard herself called. Retarded was why she was incapable of speech, and why she had so much trouble understanding the speech of others. It was why she couldn't read, or write, or do anything they had tried to teach her back in the horrible few years that she had gone to school.

Indeed, throughout her early childhood, as she had no other name to use for herself, words like retarded and slow were the closest she came to an identity. But not long after her seventh birthday (she could remember numbers better than names) her mother had become even sicker than usual, and had been confined to the hospital. The orphan had nowhere else to go and so had stayed at the hospital too, looked after by the nurses. And eventually, after long suffering, her mother had died.

The next day the old doctor had called her into his office. He had explained that she was now a homeless little girl, but that she shouldn't worry, because everyone was very fond of her, and it had been agreed she could stay on at the hospital. He had said that this was the best she could hope for, because otherwise she was motherless and fatherless and completely alone in the world. She was now, he had announced, an orphan.

An *orphan*. The gravity of the word had impressed her deeply, and she had accepted it as her true identity, above all others.

Of course, she was only a child at the time. She had grown up since then. The day the foreigner arrived was barely a month after her last birthday; the staff had thrown an especially large party, and declared that she was not a girl anymore, but a woman.

She was, they said, twenty-one years old.

•

The new patient, meanwhile, was an enigma.

He was admitted to the front wards at first, so that he could be examined in detail. And although the orphan had initially thought of him as the *sleeping man*, it turned out that often his eyes were open. They were beautiful eyes—wide, the irises a deep brown, the whites unclouded—and yet they were unsettling. There was nothing *behind* them. No awareness. He might have been a dead thing, lying there.

But he wasn't dead. His body was warm and alive. His heart beat. His blood flowed. And, to a certain point, he functioned. It did not appear that he could stand, or walk, but if he was propped up in a sitting position, he would not slump over. If liquid was put into his mouth, or soup, or mashed food, he would swallow it. And if, once a day, he was placed in a wheelchair, pushed to the shower block and arranged on a toilet, he would piss and shit on command. Which was a miracle, from the orphan's perspective. She could only wish that the other patients were all so talented and compliant.

But it was only sleepwalking. There was no consciousness in him. No will. The foreigner never spoke, never looked at anything, never moved of his own volition. Left to himself he would lie motionless on his bed, and seemingly he would do so forever, uncomplaining, until starvation claimed him.

The mystery was, why was he in such a state? The old doctor prodded and probed his new charge, and studied the papers from the hospital in the big town, but found nothing. The man had no infirmities, no diseases, and his only apparent injuries were the burns on his skin. Actually, it was just the one burn, only superficial, and already mostly healed—but it covered his entire body, every crevice, from head to toe. And every single hair had been singed away. He was as naked as a newborn.

What did it mean? How had it happened? The orphan waited, but the old doctor, for all his patience, was unable to solve the riddle, or bring the sleeping man awake. Day after day went by, and he could only shake his head, at first in bafflement, then in frustration, and finally in failure. Of course—the orphan listened to the nurses discussing the situation—if the big hospital with all its experts and machines had failed, what was the old doctor supposed to do, with no money, and no equipment, and so many other patients to care for? Who could expect him to cure the man?

No one. The foreigner hadn't been sent there to be cured anyway. At length, as was inevitable, he was transferred to the back wards.

●

The orphan's home was not in fact the one hospital, but rather two quite separate hospitals in the one compound. There were the *front* wards, and there were the *back* wards, and they were very different places.

The front wards, and the hospital offices, were in the forward section of the grounds, housed in a concrete-brick building. This was where the townspeople came if they had everyday medical problems—if, perhaps, they had cut themselves so badly they needed stitches, or if they had broken a bone, or had a cough that wouldn't go away. It was a free clinic, but it was a long walk from town, uphill along a rutted track through the jungle, so only the common folk made much use of it. Anyone who was well off or important saw their own doctor in town.

The front wards were also where women could come when they were pregnant, to have examinations and, if there were difficulties, to give birth. But it was considered ill-omened by the townspeople to bring a child into the world so close to the demented souls of the back wards, so only the poorest women ever chose to do so. The orphan herself had been born there. A nurse had once told her that it had been a terrible labour, long and bloody and damaging, and the orphan often wondered if perhaps that explained why she was the way she was. Certainly, the pregnant mothers regarded her with suspicion. Sometimes they would hiss curses at her and make signs to drive her away, as if she might spell a similar doom for their own children.

The back wards, on the other hand, weren't for everyday patients. The back wards were where the dying were kept. And the insane.

The building was hidden behind the front wards, an elongated structure of several wings, with stone walls and high ceilings and narrow windows. It was very old, dating from other times entirely, before the hospital was even a hospital. It had been a grand house once, and grand folk had dwelt there. Or so the orphan was informed. But that was long ago, and she couldn't imagine it. Now the plaster was flaking away from the walls and the stone was crumbling and the tin roof was red with rust. Inside, it was a grim maze of long wards and metal doors and echoing hallways.

Many people were frightened of the building alone, never mind the inmates. But the orphan wasn't frightened, no matter how gloomy the wards might be, and no matter how the inmates might scream or yell, no matter even how tangled their hair or bad their breath or shitty their sheets. It was only smell and noise, after all. The building was just a building, and most of the patients were harmless. (The ones who *weren't* were kept in the locked ward, where she wasn't allowed to go.)

She was even happy to work in the back wards at night. The night nurse—coward that he was—was almost too scared to enter there after dark, but the orphan actually preferred it. It was cooler and quieter then, and she was less in people's way. Most evenings—seeing that the night nurse, apart from being cowardly, was also purely lazy—the orphan was the only soul the inmates might see after lights-out. They liked her for that, and she liked them.

She was less comfortable in the front wards. It wasn't just the unfriendly looks she received from the townspeople—worse than that, the front wards were the territory of the surgeon, and she didn't like the surgeon. He was the hospital's only other doctor, much younger than the old doctor, and all the nurses thought he was very good-looking. But the orphan knew that he cut people open with knives, and whenever he glanced at her, his eyes unsmiling, she felt a little afraid.

•

To begin with, they put the foreigner in the *catatonic* ward.

The orphan did not quite understand the word, but to her, these patients were the empty people, the ones with nobody inside them. And of all the back wards inmates, they certainly resembled the foreigner most closely. One, for instance, was a woman who did nothing but sit and brush her hair for hours at a time, staring, even though she had long since brushed herself bald. Another was a boy who rocked back and forth ceaselessly on his bed, his arms clasped around his knees. Others simply slept all day, or gazed blindly at the ceiling, almost exactly as the foreigner himself did.

None of them, beyond the occasional incoherent mutter or cry, ever spoke.

But things changed after the foreigner moved in.

Over the following days, the woman with the brush began to rake her skull so severely that blood was drawn. The boy's rocking gradually became so violent he repeatedly threw himself to the floor. And the others started to moan and shout hoarsely from the depths of their sleep. The nurses were alarmed. What was happening? It was only when they noticed that things quietened down abruptly if the foreigner was removed—when he was taken to the shower, say—that they came to wonder if *he* might be the cause. True, he hadn't moved or spoken in all that time, or done anything blameworthy. But there was something strange about him, they all agreed. Those beautiful eyes . . .

The old doctor scoffed at the idea. He told the nurses that most likely the other catatonics didn't even know the foreigner was there. But if they really wanted to move him somewhere else, then he wouldn't stop them.

This time they put him in with the *geriatrics*.

It was another ward that was usually sleepy and subdued, for only the very old ended up there. Many of the inmates weren't even all that mad, they were just too infirm to survive on their own, and had no one else to look after them. Others, however, had retreated into deep senility. They drooled, they leered, they smiled and laughed, and sometimes they yelled and cried, but mostly—thanks to the pills they were given morning and night—they dozed in silence. The foreigner, admittedly, was too young to belong there. Although exactly how old he was, no one knew. With his smooth, burnt skin, he didn't look any particular age. Not young. But not old either.

In any event, he had a peculiar effect on the geriatrics. One old man complained that he was not getting any sleep because the foreigner was climbing out of bed and dancing all night. Other patients concurred. But the orphan knew it wasn't so. She checked the ward regularly on her evening rounds, and the foreigner never moved. His bedclothes were never even ruffled. Then one morning an old woman, a vague, timid creature who had never made any sort of fuss, was discovered completely naked upon the foreigner's bed, legs astride his hips, shuddering back and forth in delight. When she was dragged away, she insisted that he had lured her there and possessed her with his eyes and that she would love him till she died. But even while she was on top of him, the man had remained as limp and unconscious as ever.

That was enough for the nurses. Clearly the foreigner was a devil (that word again) of some kind. They wanted him shifted once more. The old doctor was doubtful. It didn't matter what the old people claimed, he said. They were mad, they imagined things. But the nurses insisted. Of course, they weren't educated people like the old doctor. They were just working women from the town, full of strange stories and superstitions. But the hospital couldn't run without them, and so somewhere had to be found to keep the foreigner quietly out of their way.

One option was to lose him among the general community, the everyday mad folk who made up the bulk of the hospital's inmates. But those wards were chaotic places, full of yelling and running and wrestling, and in fairness, no one thought they were a fitting home for a man who was bedridden and immobile.

Someone then suggested the locked ward. Usually, only violent patients were sent there, to be kept in individual cells, with barred windows, and with strong male nurses on hand. Still, the foreigner would certainly be out of the way. (Indeed, the orphan would never have seen him again.) But the nurses protested. If he had disturbed the otherwise peaceful catatonics and geriatrics so much, what might result if he was placed in proximity to inmates who were already aggressive and unstable?

Somewhere he would do no harm, that's where he had to go. In the end, they settled on the crematorium.

3

The crematorium was the nicest of all the back wards. It was somewhat separate from the rest, being contained in a thick-walled bunker that was semi-detached from one end of the main building, accessible only through a single passageway. A large furnace had once been installed there to burn the hospital's rubbish—including, from time to time, body parts. The stump of a chimney, its upper reaches collapsed, still rose next to one wall. But these days the hospital waste was taken away by truck and the furnace had long ago been removed. The bunker now hosted a cosy little ward with its own dayroom and two small bedrooms.

Such privacy was a rare thing, and reserved for just four lucky patients. They had been placed in the crematorium, these four, mainly because they were the most stable and reliable of the inmates, and thus could be left largely to themselves. Which was not to say they weren't mad. They assuredly were. It was just that their madness was different. More . . . coherent. Indeed, the orphan had always found that their particular kind of madness reminded her closely of her own. And the word she had heard used most often to describe the four of them was this—*delusional.*

It meant, she knew, they believed things that weren't real. They didn't spit or rave, but nor did they live in the same world as everyone else. There were two men in one of the bedrooms, and two women in the other. The orphan could never remember their names, of course, but she had titles for each of them, learnt from the nurses.

They were: the *duke*, the *witch*, the *archangel* and the *virgin.*

•

Strangely enough, the orphan herself, in her fourteen years at the hospital, had never actually been diagnosed as mad. On the contrary, the nurses had discovered, even when she was a child, that she could be put to good use around the wards. Schoolwork may have been beyond her, but if she was shown how to perform simple tasks, then she was entirely capable. So they had taught her how to mop floors, and how to make beds, and how to bathe the patients and help them change clothes, and how to perform all sorts of other minor but necessary duties about the hospital. The work made the orphan happy, because it was such a relief to be useful to someone at last.

Nevertheless, she knew that there was madness in her.

It wasn't just that she was retarded. Retarded wasn't the same as insane, she was sure of that. Her mind was slow maybe, filled with fog, and understanding always came hard, but that wasn't madness. The madness involved her other senses, her *special* senses. The things she felt and saw and heard that no one else did. The way she could read the movements of the sky, for example. No one else could do that, and it wasn't simply a seeing thing or a smelling thing, it was a kind of reaching out from herself into the air—in fact, a way of *becoming* the air . . . well, she didn't know precisely how she did it, she just knew that she could, and had always been able to.

That, of course, had to be a delusion. There was no surer indicator of insanity than the act of seeing or hearing or feeling things that no one else could.

Except . . . Was it still madness if the supposed delusion was proven real? After all, she genuinely could predict the weather. Everyone knew it.

Ah yes, but there was a madman in one of the wards with an even rarer ability. He could read minds. If someone stood near him and thought of a colour, he could always guess which colour it was. Always. He was never wrong.

But so what? It didn't make him sane. The same man was incapable of feeding or dressing himself. He was a useless oddity, that was all. Perhaps the orphan herself was no better. Perhaps no one was, in the whole madhouse.

•

The duke was a straight-backed old gentleman, and *his* delusion was that he owned the hospital, and that the staff were supposed to take orders from him, not the other way around. He thought he was a rich man. In fact, he claimed to own virtually the entire island, which was why the nurses had laughingly given him his nickname. In reality, though, he was only a poor man. No rich men ever came to the back wards.

The orphan liked the duke very much, for he was always kind to her, and softly spoken. He had been permitted to live unsupervised in the crematorium for years, and she used to wonder why he was in hospital at all, for his madness seemed so benign. But then one day she heard that for the first decade of his confinement, he had been kept in a cell in the locked ward. He had then been considered the most violent and dangerous man on the premises. It was almost impossible to believe, looking at him now. He passed the bulk of his days merely wandering the grounds, or gently working in the gardens.

The orphan too liked wandering the grounds. They were red and bare and dusty in the dry season, and red and bare and muddy in the wet, but still there was a kind of beauty in them. Occasionally she would walk with the duke, and it pleased her that he seemed to see the beauty too, if only through his dementia.

Then there was the witch, who believed that she could cast magic spells. She was a bent old woman, and ugly, and most of her time was spent hunched over her collection of chicken bones, pronouncing curses or blessings upon the world. She wasn't supposed to have the bones, the orphan knew, and now and then the nurses would confiscate her collection, but she always managed to forage more from the kitchen rubbish.

But if it was only a matter of chicken bones and spells, the witch wouldn't have been in hospital, let alone the back wards. The real problem was that long ago in the outside world, as a young woman, she had started to dig up human graves. Apparently, for her purposes, human bones were best. The authorities had committed her, and she had lived at the hospital ever since, nearly as long as the duke.

Some of the staff believed she really did have powers, and went to her for charms. The orphan, however, knew full well there was no such thing as magic—there were only magic *tricks*. She'd seen magicians perform in the town square, and had always been able to detect the sleight of hand by which they achieved their marvels.

So the old woman could glare and mutter and point bones and frighten people all she liked, it was only nonsense. In fact, it made the orphan laugh. And yet, sometimes, when she caught the witch's eye, there was a sly sense of recognition between them, as if the witch knew what the orphan was thinking and laughed in return. That wasn't so amusing.

Next was the archangel. He was a young man, close to the orphan's own age, and very handsome—striking even—if a little too thin. For the orphan though he was a far more alien figure than the duke or the witch. This was, partly, because his madness was so centred around the book he always carried.

The orphan was wary of books. They embarrassed her, for the black marks on the paper conveyed nothing to her mind. Even children's books, which she was told contained pretty things to look at, *simple* things, were impossible to decipher. She could never see the dogs or cats that were supposedly there, she saw only shapeless blobs—and anyway, how could a dog or a cat be flat on a page? Books were an ordeal.

But to the archangel, his book was the most precious item in the world, even though it was worn and battered, its front cover missing, its many pages creased and greasy from where his fingers ran over the lines. The youth studied it perpetually. He prayed a lot too, on his knees. The orphan couldn't quite grasp how prayer worked. There was a powerful being somewhere in the sky it seemed—a *god*—and other beings too, and prayer was how people talked to them. Even normal folk did it. Yet the orphan had searched the sky, many times, and never seen anyone up there.

But that was an old puzzle, and unsolvable. Anyway, the young man wasn't in hospital because of his prayer. He was there because, as a teenage boy, he had begun harming himself. He cut himself with knives. To the death almost. Suicidal, the authorities declared, and sent him to the back wards. Like the duke, he had been placed in the locked ward at first, but the suicide attempts had abated, and now, as long as he had his book, he was no threat to himself or to anyone. He was, indeed, angelic.

He also had a very big penis, which the nurses liked to joke about. Sometimes they flirted with him, but he never noticed. The orphan didn't fully understand the jokes, but she too rather fancied the archangel. And not just because he was so handsome. There was a hunger in him, she saw, a passion in the way he studied his book and in the way his lips moved when he prayed, that made something turn pleasantly in her stomach, imagining what those lips might be like on her own.

But of course he never noticed the orphan any more than he noticed the nurses. Even if he ever did, what would he see? A fat, ugly girl, mopping the floor. No, she wasn't a fool, there was no point dreaming about *that*.

Lastly, there was the virgin. She was not much more than a girl, slender and slight, but the orphan found her the most intriguing crematorium inmate of all. There was an ethereal air about her. When she moved, she *drifted*. Languid. Indifferent to her surroundings. In fact, she barely seemed aware of her surroundings. She might have been blind, and deaf too. She never spoke, and if she was touched, she would turn away with an aloof displeasure, and shift carefully out of reach.

And yet she wasn't really blind or deaf, the orphan knew, because the virgin liked to watch television. There were two sets in the back wards. One was in the main dayroom, placed high on a wall, behind wire mesh, where it was yelled at (or occasionally pelted with food) by crowds of inmates. But the other was in the crematorium, in the little dayroom, where the virgin had it to herself. Whenever it was switched on, a dreamy light would come into her eyes and she would fold her long legs to sit on the floor in front of the screen. She could sit unmoving like that all day, watching.

But if books were a riddle to the orphan, then television was an utter mystery. She knew that everyone else saw something fascinating on the screen, but all *she* ever saw were patterns of colour, randomly swirling. It didn't matter how hard she tried. When she was very young, her mother had often left her alone in front of the television for hours on end. She had gazed at their little set until her head hurt, the flickering light teasing and promising her, eternally on the verge of becoming *something* . . . but invariably she'd had to look away, eyes aching, before she could see what it was.

Nor could she understand the *sounds* a television set made. Or the sounds that came out of a radio. They could be hypnotic, those sounds, rising and falling like peculiar voices, or thumping with rhythms that matched the beat of her heart. But if there was meaning there, it eluded her. So it baffled the orphan greatly that the girl in the crematorium apparently saw and heard so much when watching TV, her eyes fixed, her head tilted in repose, her mouth open in a distant rapture.

The staff called her the virgin out of mockery. There was her hatred of physical contact, for one thing. But it was also because of her only relative—an elderly grandmother who sometimes came to visit. The old woman would berate the girl endlessly for being such a disappointment and a burden. Oh, if the girl had been marriageable, the grandmother would declare to anyone nearby, it might have been different. Once, men had come calling. Men with money, men with fine houses. But a woman had duties, and what man would want a wife—even a beautiful one—who did nothing but watch TV all day, and who would shrink away every time he reached between her legs?

Well, she would find no man now, not in a madhouse. And with that settled, the old woman would be on her way. The nurses would laugh about it once she was gone, but the orphan never did. She didn't know what delusion possessed the girl's mind, but she knew one thing: she didn't like the grandmother any more than the virgin did.

•

The foreigner wasn't like any of these four, and didn't belong in the crematorium, but that was of no importance to the nurses. They never intended that he should mix with the others anyway. He was a devil and needed to be isolated. The crematorium had a storeroom—reached down a short hall from the dayroom—and it was in there, on his own, that they meant to finally settle him.

The orphan herself helped to convert the room into accommodation, and she did not like the feel of it very much. There was barely space to install a bed, with one narrow chair beside it, and there was no window, only a grate that led into the blackness of the old chimney. The room was, in fact, the remains of the original furnace. It was dim and stuffy, and body parts had been burnt there once.

But it wasn't for her to question the decisions of the nurses. And she was on hand again when they transferred the foreigner from the geriatric ward. He was in a wheelchair, sitting up calmly, his eyes open and clear. But he looked neither left nor right as he was rolled through the hallways and then down the passage to the crematorium. The place was empty. The duke, the witch, the archangel, they were all elsewhere. Even the virgin was away from her television. So none of them saw him arrive. The nurses navigated the chair through to the storeroom, and then manhandled the foreigner into bed. His eyes were open the whole time. And they were still open, staring up, the orphan saw, as they closed the door to leave him there, alone in the dark.

4

But even though the foreigner was now safely isolated and confined in his cell, the orphan couldn't put him out of her mind.

Why that should be, she didn't know. For all his mystery, he was just another patient, one of dozens that she had to attend to in her rounds. Among them were inmates she'd known for years, inmates who talked to her and laughed with her; inmates who played hide and seek with her when it was shower time, who loved to play in the mud when it rained, who did a thousand interesting things that the foreigner didn't; inmates she liked and inmates she hated. But at the end of each evening, as she lay in her bed, the only face that came into her thoughts was his.

True, she spent considerable time with him. Someone had to spoonfeed him his mush and give him water. Someone had to change his sheets, and sponge his body down, and wrestle him into a wheelchair for toilet trips. If the nurses were busy—and they were always busy—many of those tasks fell to the orphan. Indeed it seemed that *most* of the tasks involving the foreigner fell to her. But that didn't explain her fixation. She dealt every day with patients who were likewise unconscious, and sad as it might be, such inmates were little more than bodies to her—an anonymous collection of mouths and bowels and bladders that merely needed to be fed and cleaned up after.

The foreigner was different. From the moment she entered his cell, bent on one chore or another, she was aware of him—in the same way that she might be aware of a spider sitting high in a corner, one of the big hairy jungle spiders that came into the wards sometimes. It was not that the spiders were a threat, they weren't poisonous, but they made her uneasy, and she always *knew* if one was there. It was the same with the sleeping man.

He was no physical danger. She'd already proved that to herself. He was naked in the bed, and while changing his sheets she had studied him from head to toe. His body was slight and soft and pale—his new skin clean of blemishes—and quite defenceless. She could do anything to him. She had bent his fingers back until they cracked, she had pinched at his nipples, she had even clutched his hairless balls for an instant and squeezed hard . . . nothing elicited any response. But still, some instinctive part of her remained wary of him, no matter what her reason told her.

And there was another thing. The vibrations had come back— the buzz against the orphan's heels, the machine humming far underground, the same tremors that had first appeared on the very day the foreigner arrived at the hospital. They had faded away again on that occasion, but the morning after he was moved to the crematorium, the vibrations returned. Only subtly to begin with, but as the days went by, they grew ever more intense. And even though she could not have explained how, the orphan was convinced that in some way the foreigner was to blame.

It became so bad she could hardly sleep. Even masturbating did nothing to relieve the tension. Yet she knew too that the buzzing was only imaginary. She studied tubs of water in the laundry, looking for some ripple of confirmation, but the liquid's surface was always smooth. Crockery on shelves didn't rattle, neither did windowpanes. Walls didn't creak or groan. Her bones might twitch, and the earth might feel as if it was crawling underfoot, but everything around her was solid and steady.

So it had to be madness, and only that. And the foreigner could have nothing to do with it. But then one morning, as the orphan worked with her mop, hiding how frantic she felt on the inside, a nurse came to her with a message.

It had been arranged, the woman said, that the patients in the crematorium were to be taken outside, to sit in the sun for a while. It would be the orphan's job, and her job alone, to ensure that the sleeping man joined them.

The orphan leant on her mop and stared. What was this? Yes, sometimes patients were taken outside for an airing. But it was always done in the afternoon, never in the morning. Moreover, it was only done in fine weather, and on cooler days. This particular morning was hot and humid, and heavy showers of rain were crossing over the hospital periodically. Besides, the other four crematorium patients were free to go outside whenever they liked. They were never *taken*. They didn't need to be taken. Who had ordered this? For what purpose? And why had they included the foreigner, when he was supposed to be in isolation?

But she could enunciate no such questions, and the nurse seemed to think the outing an entirely innocent affair. Indeed, ever since the sleeping man had been shifted, the staff were satisfied that the problems with him were over. The odd behaviour in the catatonic and geriatric wards had ceased, everyone agreed. And nothing unusual had happened anywhere else, not even in the crematorium.

That was—thought the orphan—until now.

But she did as she was told. She collected a wheelchair and pushed it through to the foreigner's cell. The nurse was getting the other patients ready; the orphan could hear her snapping impatiently, and the witch shrieking, and the duke muttering in annoyance. This wasn't part of anyone's schedule. But in the little furnace room, cocooned by thick walls, the foreigner waited silently in the dark. The orphan hesitated, feeling the floor buzz under her feet. She could see the gleam of his open eyes.

It *couldn't* have anything to do with him, could it?

She pulled back the sheet, dressed him in pyjamas, then heaved him from the bed into the wheelchair. It was a familiar enough task, and easier than it might have been. He was not a big man, she was a strong girl, and his arms and legs went where she put them and stayed there. But then in the dimness she thought she saw, very faint on his lips, a momentary smile.

No. When she looked properly there was nothing. He was not capable of smiling. He would not even know that he was being moved. She pushed him along the hall and out through the dayroom, following the nurse and the others.

Outside, the latest burst of rain had just passed, and steam was rising from the ground. Blue sky showed through broken clouds. The wheelchair splashed in puddles. They came to an open area next to the laundry, right up against the back fence of the compound, where the jungle reached down from the mountainside, and where a few old wooden benches and chairs were arranged about a concrete slab. It was here that patients were normally taken on fine days, to sit quietly in the sun.

The absurdity of the whole exercise hit the orphan again. The crematorium patients would never sit quietly. And yet to her great surprise the duke and the witch and the archangel and the virgin all suffered themselves to be led to the benches and chairs. The nurse fussed about them for a few moments, and then—after announcing that she would be back in an hour—she made off again to the wards.

The orphan pushed the wheelchair to one end of the slab and set it there so that the foreigner was facing all the others. A hot silence enfolded them. Even the laundry had fallen quiet. This was becoming more and more weird. The orphan could feel the vibrations so intensely through the cement that she had to keep shifting her weight from one foot to the other, like a child who needed to go to the toilet. Why were they there? What were they meant to do? Whose idea had this been?

And then she realised that the four inmates were watching her. No, they weren't watching *her*, they were watching the foreigner, sitting in his chair in front of her. They were doing so shyly, secretly, the witch glancing from under her brows, the duke pretending to study the sky. The archangel wasn't looking in any direction at all, but for once his book lay unopened and unheeded on his lap, his attention elsewhere. And although the virgin's gaze was as blind and indifferent as ever, her body leant forward, as if trying to gauge the foreigner by sound.

It occurred to the orphan that none of the four had seen their new wardmate out in the open until now. He had always been alone in his cell, behind a shut door. Naturally they would be curious about him. But this wasn't natural. She had seen the way inmates behaved when they were curious, especially ones like the witch and the duke. They investigated, they intruded, they intimidated, they poked and prodded and picked fights. They didn't simply watch in this silent, timid manner.

Was there a low throb in the air? An unheard thunder?

And then, at last, she saw it. Off to the side of the concrete was a muddy puddle, and the surface of the water was juddering in a series of tiny waves.

The vibrations—they were real!

But there was no time for wonder, because a rumbling was suddenly audible, like a hundred trucks driving past the hospital. The ground shook and the orphan, startled, looked up, over the foreigner's head, to the mountain. She saw that a giant fist of grey smoke had appeared from nowhere and was rising into the sky, and that it came, amazingly, from a high cleft near the mountain's peak.

Boom! A great, grinding detonation came rolling down.

Linkages flared in the orphan's mind, one after the other. The mountain, that was the answer! That's where the vibrations had come from all along. They had been a warning of this event. But what was happening? What process? What violence within the mountain was driving it? And with that thought—using her new awareness, sharp and alive, and without even knowing how—she reached out and *felt* at the earth.

Sensations filled her head. Pressure. She could detect an awesome pressure, way down below, far beneath the jungle and dirt, deep under layers of rock, at the buried roots of the mountain. Pressure, and heat, and a squeezing, tortured dome of glowing material, boiling and churning slowly. She could picture it down there almost as if the earth was transparent. And above the molten mass were rents and tunnels and cracks in the rock, leading up into the mountain's heart, filled now with surging steam that roared and rumbled and set the ground trembling, far above.

A *volcano*. The word was there inside her suddenly, from where she could not say—a memory, perhaps—but she knew it was the right word for what she saw. Such a terrible thing, and she held it all in her mind, livid and ferocious. Even as she watched, another explosion of steam ripped up through the mountain and blasted, in another boom of thunder, out from the cleft.

The orphan laughed her croak of a laugh. She could hear frightened shouts behind her, and sensed a confusion of people milling out of the hospital, but she didn't take her eyes from the volcano. She wasn't scared. She was exhilarated. All the tension of the last few days was being burnt away. She watched the pillar of smoke rise and rise into the sky. So much energy! So much power! Cracking sounds rang out, and on the edges of the cloud the orphan could see black shapes spinning upwards. Boulders. Chunks of rock. Flying. And people were screaming now.

Why were they afraid? She studied the boulders as they sailed outwards. She read the weight of each stone, the curve of each arc, and knew exactly where each and every one of the rocks would land. None of them would hit the hospital. They would all fall short. There was nothing to fear. Although *one* of them . . .

The orphan ran forward to the jungle's edge, and watched as a boulder the size of a table came tumbling down from the darkness above. It seemed it must hit her, but instead it smashed into the trees just outside the fence, exploding a wet slap of wind and leaves and mud across her, plastering her face and clothes.

Ha! It was wonderful!

But, ah . . . too soon, she could see, it was going to end. The pillar of smoke had already lost its upward thrust. The high levels were growing vague, dispersing in the wind, and the lower levels were collapsing upon themselves. Her acute gaze bore into the earth and saw that the rush of gas was spent. The molten dome remained trapped, far down. There was more energy there, yes, but for the moment the mass had merely let off a burst of steam to relieve itself. She laughed again, sadly now.

The mountain had burped, that was all. It had farted.

She felt the pleasure drain from her body. Smoke was tumbling in a slow, billowing avalanche down the mountainside. The orphan heard more screams, and wondered why people were so dimwitted. Surely they could see, as she could, how fast the energy of the cloud was dissipating, how it was cooling and slowing, how it would barely reach the hospital. There was no danger.

Calm, she watched the grey wall come. The jungle was engulfed before her, and then a cloud of ash and warm pungent air settled over the compound. The last rumbles from the mountain died away. Rain began to fall.

The orphan turned back. The hospital buildings were barely visible through the haze. She could see no one moving there, nor hear anyone. Sounds were muted, by the rain, by the ash. The benches still waited around the concrete slab, and she saw that the duke and the archangel must have both run away. But the witch remained. She was on her knees, staring up towards the invisible mountain, her lips moving soundlessly. The virgin was there too, dazed, crawling on the wet concrete. And the foreigner sat upright in his wheelchair, where she had left him.

His eyes stared placidly.

Something stirred in her. She realised that, inexplicably, it was fear. Now, when it was all over, she was afraid. Not of the volcano, but of *him*. She felt herself drawn reluctantly forward. He had not caused the vibrations, he had nothing to do with the mountain at all. She was certain of that now. And yet . . .

Why did she feel that he had known it was going to happen? Why did she feel that *he* was the one who had arranged it so they would all be outside, ready and waiting for the eruption to begin? It was impossible—he couldn't even speak, let alone manipulate the staff into doing what he wanted. And yet . . .

She stood before him, dripping wet, streaked with ash. He sat immobile in his chair, as wet as her, but unable even to wipe away the mud that was dripping down his face. He was helpless. Dependent.

Was there a hint of a smile on his lips?

The orphan got down on her knees to look directly into his eyes. Did they see her? *Could* they see? She stared into nothingness, then suddenly there was a spark, an instant of connection, and his pupils opened like black pits.

Now you, girl, said a voice, *are a surprise.*

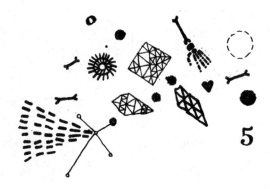

5

She was falling.

Darkness was rushing about her, or perhaps she was moving at great speed through the air, the orphan didn't know and hardly cared. She was too stunned with pleasure, because of the voice. Such a voice.

For the first time in her life she had understood speech instantaneously. Oh, words had always entered her *ears* clearly enough before, but always they had then been waylaid by the fog that enveloped her mind, forcing her to strain to discern their meaning. But just this once—the sweet clarity of language. It had been only a single short statement perhaps, but what a dazzling beam of light, cutting through the mist.

Now you, girl, are a surprise.

It must have been the foreigner. The voice was his, surely. She had been staring at him, and his gaze had come alive, and he had spoken.

Except . . . why hadn't his lips moved?

A doubt rippled through her, and abruptly she wasn't falling anymore, she was standing upright, and she was cold.

The orphan opened her eyes. The volcano was gone. The patients were gone, the hospital too, and the compound, and the jungle. She was standing on the rocky floor of a long and narrow valley. Naked mountains rose steeply on either side, their flanks grey under a night sky, their peaks capped with white. A shallow river ran noisily beside her, and a freezing wind scudded across the stones.

She turned a slow circle, her head tilted to the empty slopes. It was all so alien that she didn't feel afraid. Was she dreaming? Had she fallen over and hit her head? That could explain it. And yet she had never dreamt anything like this before. Her dreams were about the hospital, about places and people she knew, distorted perhaps, and bizarre, but still recognisable. There was nothing she recognised here. She had never known cold like this, she had never seen mountains like these, she had never stood in a landscape so stripped of trees or grass or plantations.

Perhaps it was her madness, then. She knew what it was when people saw things that weren't there. The nurses called it *hallucinating*. But surely hallucinations weren't like this. Not so concrete. She had weight here, the sharp stones bit at her feet. She heard this place, she saw it and felt it and tasted it.

But at the same time there was an unreality too. A distance. She sensed this was not a place that was *now*. This was not the present.

Correct, said the voice.

Her heart lifted. It was the same voice, the foreigner's voice. And he sounded pleased with her, applauding her instinct.

This is the past. This is ninety-two years ago.

He wasn't there. She was alone in the wasteland. But it was him all the same, and once more the sheer thrill of speech elated her. His voice was the most enchanting thing she had ever heard. It came from nowhere, from all around, it encompassed her. She had felt herself falling into his eyes—so was she inside his head now? Held somehow in his mind? In his memory? No, it had to be madness. She was sick. But it felt so good, when he spoke. His approval was as warm as basking in sunshine.

Follow the river, he said.

She walked obediently. He meant upstream, she knew, deeper into the valley, where the mountains crowded together like knives. She waited for him to speak again, but a long time passed and the only sounds were the water and the wind. She tripped on stones, and stared up at slopes so steep and high they made her dizzy. The chill sank into her skin, and slowly, without his voice for company, she did become frightened. How would she ever get back to the green, living warmth of her home?

She trudged on, shivering. A full-moon shone from above, lonelier than an empty sky would have been. But by its glow the orphan saw eventually that she was following a track—two wheel ruts, thinly worn into the rocks, running along the bank of the river. So people did come here, at least sometimes.

Sometimes, agreed the voice. *A very few people.*

He was with her still. She felt better. If he had brought her here, then he could take her back. She pushed onwards, and finally she saw a light ahead. And then another, some distance along the valley. Dim, flickering firelight. And, half-guessed, the shapes of walls and roofs.

It was a village, a handful of buildings huddled up against the foot of a mountain. They were strange houses, made of mud and tiles. The orphan imagined that the people who lived in them must be very poor. Who else but the poor would inhabit such mean dwellings, in such a hard land?

It's better in the warmer season. There is a little grass then for the animals, and the ground thaws for planting crops. But yes, this is a hard land. One of the hardest. It's far from where you live. It's a place called—

The foreigner paused, and the orphan, while delighting in the flood of words, sensed a sudden frustration in him. Of course—it was her inability with names. He must have seen into her mind and realised that, even if spoken by *him*, a name would still slip through her head unremembered and without meaning. He was disappointed, and if the orphan could have, she would have cried out that she was sorry.

It doesn't matter. Look.

She felt her eyes drawn again to the village. A door was flung open in one of the outermost buildings. A smoky light cast out upon the stones, and a man emerged, wrapped in strange clothes and hunched against the cold. He marched down the valley towards the orphan, and she stopped, uncertain, but he hurried by her as if she was not there. His head was hooded, but she caught a glimpse of his face. Young. Bearded. He was singing softly to himself, a formless hum of contentment.

Do you see how happy he is? For a moment the voice seemed to reflect. *And why shouldn't he be? It's not long since he was married, the dowry was a good one, and his wife is already expecting their first child. By the standards of this place, he is a lucky man. He has land of his own, and a small herd of goats. That's where he's going right now, to his barn, to check his flock one last time for the night. Then it will be back to his dung fire and his salt tea and his new wife waiting with her swollen belly.*

Was there something cruel in the voice? The orphan saw that the man had reached a low shed partially dug into a bank of rising ground. She had passed it by in the darkness, all unseeing. He disappeared inside, and she was alone again.

She stared back up to the village. It was a desolate encampment, dwarfed by its own landscape. There were no electric lights, no shopfronts, no cars, no activity. There was only the bitter wind, and the rush of the river in its bed, and the mountain, standing forth from the valley walls to crouch above the houses. Her gaze lifted to take it in. This was no gently sloping cone draped in green jungle, like her volcano. This was a great hump of bare rock, rising cliff upon cliff, rimmed with ice.

Fear and loneliness bore down on the orphan again. And a foreboding too. Something was wrong here. It was an unease she couldn't define, but it nagged at her like the pain of a rotten tooth; an ugly tension that underpinned the whole valley. On some vast level, something, somewhere below, ached.

Soon, said the voice.

A door slammed, and the man reappeared, heading back to his home. Once again he passed straight by the orphan and did not see her. Except, suddenly he paused, and then turned. But he wasn't looking at the orphan—he was gazing up at the mountain behind the village, alerted in some way, frowning.

The orphan followed his eyes up to the sheer face of stone. There came, as if squeezed from the rock, a pale discharge of light—a misty luminescence that played over the entire mountain-side. It shimmered once, again, and then a third time, diffusing into the night sky. Beside her, the man gasped in wonder. It was beautiful. The ground trembled as if in delight, and there was a sound, a single note, soft, and yet profound. The whole mountain rang like a bell. And the young villager laughed out loud.

Dread filled the orphan. The light was a warning, not a spectacle. She extended her senses into the earth, and saw the danger. Deep under the valley, two immense plates of rock, each so big that they extended beyond her vision, and each trying to slide in a different direction, were caught hard on one another, edge to edge. The orphan guessed that they had been caught that way for years, the pressure building remorselessly, the pain of it leaching up through the ground. Until now at last the stress had become unendurable, and in their final agonies the plates were radiating electricity enough to make the mountain glow and sing.

She turned to the villager, even though she could not yell to alert him, even though she knew that she wasn't actually there, that this had all happened long ago. It was too late anyway. The mountain's gentle note faltered, became a groan, and far below the two plates lurched and sprang free.

On the valley floor, the ground kicked hard and the man staggered to his knees. The orphan felt it too, and yet she didn't fall. It was as if she was becoming insubstantial. She was still aware of everything, but she was apart from it too. She watched as the earth jolted and jumped. She watched as the mud walls of the village crumbled and sank. She watched as the man scrambled in the dust, crying aloud in fear.

And then it stopped. The plates shuddered one last time, and locked into a new position. The valley floor ceased shaking. For a moment there was silence, and nothing moved apart from the slow spirals of dust in the air. The orphan watched the villager climb carefully to his feet, his arms held out for balance. His face was white, his eyes black circles. It appeared that every house in the village was levelled.

Then the silence broke, and from the piles of rubble came human cries, and the terrified bleating of animals. But the orphan had ears for only one sound. It was the clatter of small stones and rocks, falling. She looked up at the bulk of the mountain, hanging over the village. Its outline was unchanged to the eye, but she could sense invisible cracks and fissures that had opened deep within the stone, a profusion of them. The ground may have stopped shaking, but those cracks were racing onwards under their own momentum now, this way and that, joining up with others.

The villager was walking in a crazed circle, heading at first towards the ruins of his home, and then turning back towards the ruins of his barn. He was in shock, the orphan understood, unable to choose—and unaware that, very soon, neither choice would matter. He couldn't feel, as she could, the whole forward half of the mountain, with all its impossible weight, pushing and pushing against less and less resistance. The fractures raced and blurred and became one.

The cliff fell. As a single slab at first, and slowly, defying the mind to accept that something so large could move at all. And then, the thunder of its descent filling the air, it dissolved into a black multitude and came surging down.

There was no escape, and hardly even time for fear. The orphan saw the young man take a disbelieving step forward, hands out to stop the cataclysm. Then they were swallowed. The man, the orphan, the village, and the entire valley floor. All of it lost in roaring wind and stone and darkness.

And afterwards . . . quiet.

The orphan drifted, seeing nothing, feeling nothing. Until the voice was there again, the foreigner, calmly observant.

It was one of the largest landslides the earth has seen in its recent history. Quite a famous event, to those who study such things.

It isn't that it killed so many people—only everyone in that tiny village, fifty souls or so. What makes it interesting is that it formed a dam across the valley to the height of six hundred metres, blocking the river. That makes it the highest dam, natural or manmade, that exists anywhere in the world. And in the years since then, the valley behind it has filled with water, over half a kilometre deep.

It was curious and wonderful, the orphan thought. So many of the words he used were unfamiliar to her, she did not really know their meaning, and yet the image was conveyed so easily to her mind. The choked river piling up against the wall of rubble, and all those people, buried forever.

Yes. Buried forever. All of them.

An insinuation in his tone took shape. The darkness solidified around the orphan, and suddenly she was there under the pile of stone, trapped in a coffin of space, an angle between two great boulders, the air clogged with dust.

Except for one . . .

A man was screaming. The young villager, he was in there with her. She could smell his blood and his shit and his pain. She could see—even in the blackness—that he lay between the boulders, half-buried in smaller rubble, one leg caught under solid rock. How long was it since the mountain fell on him? She couldn't tell, but his voice sounded hoarse, at its ragged end, as if he had been screaming for some time.

He was calling for help. At intervals he would stop and listen in the awful silence. Then he would cry out again, his voice growing ever fainter. Eventually he ceased and began to weep. For his wife, for his home, for his goats. And for himself. No one was going to dig down and unbury him. He was going to die.

The warmth of the coffin slowly faded. It grew very cold. The man dozed fitfully, shivering. The orphan slept too—or at least, she lost track of how long they lay there in the darkness. The next thing she knew, freezing water was rising stealthily around them. The villager awoke with a spluttering gasp. Panic took him, and he flailed about the space, arching his back to keep his head above the water.

The orphan could understand none of his cries, but she felt the terror that was unloosed in him, and the horror of the death that was going to be his. And she shared his rage at the trickling water. Rage that the world could kill him in this way—so mindlessly, so indifferently—as if his life did not matter.

Then the water closed over his head and his body was in paroxysms, lungs burning, like there was one great shout of anger left in him, bursting to get out. The orphan heard the cracking of bone as he wrenched at his trapped leg. His ankle shattered, and a sleeve of flesh around his foot peeled away. The limb ripped free. He floundered upwards and found air again, his face pressed to the rock ceiling.

The loathing in him was white-hot now. He was not going to die, he was not going to let the earth kill him, he *refused*. Probing about with bruised fingers, he found a crack above him, barely two hands wide, and, panting with the effort, hauled his body from the bloody water up into the crevice.

The orphan was with him—almost inside him. She had no body of her own, only his. The villager dragged himself along the narrow crack, ignoring the agony of his leg, and ignoring all other pains too, as stones tore at his skin. Sometimes he had to dig through gravel, prying his fingernails backwards until they came loose. Other times there was no room to move any limb at all, and he had to squeeze along on his stomach, the rock scraping welts in him as he went. The earth fought him every inch. And all the while came the hideous drip and trickle of water, rising steadily.

Occasionally exhaustion overcame him and he slept, but the touch of water on his feet would wake him again. A madness of thirst grew in his chest. If only he could reach behind, the water was there! But he was stretched taut. To drink would be to wait until the flood rose to his mouth, and thus to drown. His clothes were gone, he was naked, and the cold was such that even shivering was beyond him now. But still he clawed his way forward. And perhaps even the mountain and the rubble and the river had to admit that there was no crushing his resolve, because finally the stumps of his fingers were clutching open air, and there was no more weight above him.

He crawled forth from the avalanche. The orphan saw that it was night again—although how many nights it had been since the landslide, there was no way to be sure, except that the moon was a different shape now. The villager lay stupefied upon the rubble. It was clear that he had not been buried by the main fall, but merely caught under the apron of the slide. Before him reared a sloping wall of rock and gravel, rising up to nearly fill the valley. And above that, the cloven remains of the mountain itself, a gigantic scoop of pale stone showing fresh on its face.

The man began to climb the wall of debris. It didn't matter that his ankle was broken and that muscle and bone gleamed where his skin was torn away—he climbed. There was no other sign of life. No searchers, no rescuers. The valley was as cold and deserted as when the orphan had first seen it. The wind muttered the same way, the icy peaks of the mountains frowned unchanged. No one cared that the villager lived, no one saw him creep and drag himself, hour by hour, ever upwards.

It was close to dawn when he reached the landslide's crest. In the chill light he looked upon the further side. A moan escaped him, the first sound he had made since emerging from the rubble. There was nothing beyond, only the far side of the fall itself, reaching down again to where the river, dammed now, pooled and spread. There were no survivors, no indication that a village had ever stood there. His wife, his unborn child, his friends, his animals—they were all dead.

But *he* was alive. He had denied the earth.

The villager bared his teeth to the sky. He levered himself upright to see the rising sun, barely recognisable as human, so torn and bloody was he. Not the same man anymore, it seemed to the orphan. He was someone different. Some*thing* different. Stripped down to bone and sinew, then fashioned anew.

And so I was born, said the foreigner.

6

The orphan woke to hands touching her. Fingers. They were exploring her body, probing into all sorts of places, skin upon skin, unhindered by any clothing, as if she was completely naked. In fact, coming more awake, she realised that she *was* completely naked. And the hands kept pawing at her.

She shrugged angrily and the fingers vanished. Her eyes opened. She was in her own room, in her own bed, under the sheet. She was aware of someone hunched by the bedside, but her gaze, blinking and blurred, was drawn to the window. Sky was visible through the glass. Blue, clear of ash or clouds. It felt like early morning, but that didn't make any sense. Had the day gone backwards?

There was movement at the door, a shape appearing. Her vision clarified. It was the old doctor. He bent over the bed, examining her. The truth came gradually—she must have been asleep a whole day and night. Was she hurt? She blinked again, turned her head, and saw the night nurse sitting in the chair by her pillow. He had been there all along, she supposed. And then she remembered—those roving hands . . .

Ha! She was quite awake now, and fixed the night nurse with a stare. His watery eyes shied away, but his hands curled reflexively in his lap. She had never really looked at his hands before. The fingers were long and thin and grubby.

The orphan felt her skin twitch.

Then the old doctor was speaking to her, and she had to concentrate, because she found it unusually hard to understand him, as if her skull was especially dense today. But she gathered that she wasn't hurt. He was telling her not to worry, that she had merely fainted during the fuss with the volcano. He thought it was because of all the ash in the air. But it was over now and there was no reason to be afraid.

The orphan wanted to protest. She had never *been* afraid, let alone afraid enough to do something so silly as faint. But now that she tried, she couldn't really recall exactly what had happened. The mountain had farted, and there were billowing clouds, and people had run away, and then she had turned and seen . . .

Seen what?

The doctor was talking again, but the orphan couldn't focus and didn't understand him. Then, with a last smile, he was gone. The night nurse slouched out too—how ugly he was in the daylight—and she was alone.

She stared at the ceiling, not sure what to do. If she was fine, then she should get up. But she felt drained and sore, and her room lulled her with its comforts. She was very fond of her room. It was in a little hut, off on its own behind the kitchen block. It was actually just an old storeroom, but it had a door that she could lock, and a window, and a cupboard, and a mirror on the wall. And there was a socket into which she could plug her radio—the only object she had inherited from her mother. She liked to listen to it at night, even if the noises it made were meaningless.

She flicked the switch on the radio now, but nothing happened. There was no power. The volcano must have damaged the lines. The orphan sighed, stretched her limbs, and rolled over to peer at the floor. Her clothes were strewn across the concrete. Whoever had undressed her hadn't bothered to fold them or hang them over the chair. She felt sure it must have been the night nurse. She imagined his long fingers tugging at her underwear. Anything could have happened. A whole day and night were lost to her, and there seemed no way to get any of it back.

Except—there was somewhere . . . a stony place . . . cold . . . The memory wouldn't come.

Nor would sleep, no matter how drowsy she felt. The orphan climbed out of bed. Arms stiff, she pulled on her clothes and then went out to her front step, into the sunshine. And stopped short, amazed at what she saw.

Ash. It was everywhere, smothering the jungle, the grounds, the hospital buildings. She remembered the cloud rolling down the mountainside, and then white flakes falling from the sky, mixing with rain and turning into mud. Now everything was blanketed in a thin, gritty layer of the stuff, deadening to sight and sound, and a deep silence had settled upon the world, a hush after the great event.

Presiding over it all was the volcano. The orphan gazed at the rocky profile of the peak. Was the mountain different now? Was it fractured slightly, and slumped in on itself? Empty, that's how it looked. The fires below had gone out. And there were no vibrations anymore, humming under her feet.

Even so, something about the volcano disturbed her. She imagined the upper cliffs bulging forward and overbalancing and toppling down. It was almost like something she had already seen.

And again she seemed to remember a biting coldness, and a grey landscape around her, not of ash, but of rock and ice . . .

A dream? Perhaps. She felt half in a dream even now, her head thick. She stepped out into the ash, and heard it crunch underfoot, a distinct sound in the quiet. She walked around the edge of the kitchen block. A few people were visible—a cook crossing the compound, a woman from the laundry toting muddy sheets—but their movements were somehow muted by the ash, making them seem unreal.

Then she spied the duke, working in the vegetable garden. And at the sight of the old man, a larger fragment of her memory returned. Yes, of course, she had been with him when the volcano erupted. The duke, and the other three patients from the crematorium—they had been sitting in the sun. Then the tremors had started and the mountain had gone up, and the duke had run away. And the others?

Well, she wasn't quite sure about the others . . .

She watched the duke. The garden beds were buried under ash, and he was trying to clear the ash away, but she had to smile because he was using a broom, and what he really needed was a shovel. Poor old madman. The garden was his special pride. It was actually maintained by the kitchen staff, but they didn't mind him helping, even if he sometimes pulled out the vegetables instead of the weeds.

Then she saw that it was *her* broom, and her smile died. He must have stolen it from her cleaning cupboard. And he was ruining it. The ash was still muddy, and it was clogging up the bristles. That wasn't funny at all. She strode up behind him. He was too engrossed to notice her, but when she laid a preventative hand on his shoulder, he whirled about suddenly, apparently enraged, the broom raised as if to strike.

The orphan took an involuntary step back. His eyes! Something blazed in them, and for a confounding moment the orphan felt that she was confronting a different man altogether. Emotions flooded out from him. An immense frustration. Humiliation too, at long-endured indignities. And a fury, normally cloaked deep beneath a mildness so regimented that nothing could break it, and yet burning so brightly now at the old man's core that he wanted to take the broom and—

The orphan blinked, and it was just the duke again, as frail as ever, gentle, his eyes filled with tears. Her hand was out, demanding the broom, and he passed it over. Then, his head bowed in shame, he was hurrying away.

The orphan took a breath. What was *that* about?

She studied the vegetables and plants. His rage was partly to do with the garden, she had sensed that much from him. He thought that it had been befouled and ruined by the volcano. But in fact no serious damage had been done. The ash was not so thick as to choke out growth, nor was it poisonous. Indeed, it was like new soil, fallen from the sky. In time, the garden would be all the richer for it. Couldn't the duke see that? Had his madness blinded him? Fertility still throbbed in the earth. This was no dead landscape, no frozen valley, no . . .

She caught herself, the duke forgotten.

What was it that she was remembering? What *place*?

It slipped away again.

She looked at the broom in her hand. Work! That's what she should be doing! The hallways of the wards would be full of ash. She had been off duty for a whole day and night. There must be all sorts of chaos inside.

She set off towards the back wards, but halfway across the compound she slowed. She gazed about at the grey world. Was she missing something? A nurse passed by and smiled at her. The orphan stared at the woman in confusion. It was the same nurse who had told her to take the patients out into the sun.

Face blank, the orphan turned and made her away around to the rear of the laundry, to the spot where they had all been sitting when the eruption began. The concrete slab with the benches and chairs. Something had happened to her there—not only the eruption, but something else, something important.

All she found now was ash. It was heaped on the benches, and had buried the cement square. And yet—there were patterns *in* the ash. Lines and squiggles and smudges. They meant something, she was sure. Something disturbing.

Laughter startled her. She looked around, but at first could see no one nearby. And then—there, in the bushes by the fence, a huddled, dirty, ash-smeared figure was grinning out at her. It was the witch. Discovered, the old woman grinned wider and laughed again, then came scrabbling out into the open.

Memory stirred once more in the orphan. Yes—that was right, the ash and rain had been falling, and she had turned away from the volcano, and the witch had been there. Of all the patients, she was the only one who hadn't been scared. The duke and the archangel had run away, and the virgin had been facedown in the mud, terrified. But not the old woman. She had been . . . excited?

Now the witch scurried over and knelt at the centre of the square. Several objects were cradled in her hands. She dropped them in the ash, then grinned over her shoulder and gestured for the orphan to come and see.

It was a heap of small dead animals.

The orphan saw birds, their wings crooked out stiffly. And mice, their tiny eyes shut. Even a lizard, shrivelled around its own tail. But all of them had been eviscerated, feathers and skin torn away to reveal their bones. And the witch was crooning happily as she prodded at them, her fingers bloody.

The orphan straightened in revulsion. Why had the old woman caught and killed so many creatures? Normally she was content with bones from the kitchen. Ah . . . but perhaps she hadn't killed them herself. Perhaps she had just found them that way. The orphan looked up at the volcano. Perhaps that was the answer. The eruption had been harmless enough for people, but for smaller animals the rain of ash and mud might have been lethal.

The witch had followed the orphan's gaze, and now the old woman rose to her feet, clinging to the orphan's arm with one withered hand and pointing at the mountain with the other. She was speaking in her low, cracked, spell-casting voice—garbled words, but serious, and terribly eager. Was it some curse she was trying to cast? Some charm? The orphan could grasp no sense in any of it.

She tried to pull away, but the witch clung on. And then abruptly, as had happened with the duke, the orphan was somehow seeing *into* the old woman—indeed, for an instant it was like she occupied the witch's skin. All her own perspectives changed and the world warped subtly into something new. The little pile of dead creatures on the ground—what precious things they suddenly seemed, laden with significance, as if to pick one up and pry at its insides would reveal countless secrets. What a gift they were. What a generous thing the mountain had done, to present them so.

And that was the strangest aspect of all. The orphan gazed at the volcano, and it was transformed now. She knew herself that it was only a thing of rock, lifeless, with no intent, and without thought. And yet through the witch's eyes she saw something else: she saw a *being*. A slow, inhuman, mighty giant of a thing, exhausted after its fiery labours, and resting now, propped on great arms of stone. A giver of life. A bringer of destruction. A titan to be worshipped and feared and thanked.

Madness. It was just a mountain.

She broke free of the witch's grip, and the old woman reared back, offended. They stared at each other. Then the witch tossed her head in dismissal. She gathered up her collection of dead things—already, in the heat, they gave off a whiff of decay—and hobbled away, hunched over her prizes, and scanning the ground for more.

The orphan was breathing hard.

What was wrong with everyone today? What was wrong with *her*? These glimpses, these *emanations* she was receiving, from the duke, the witch—they couldn't be real. They had to be something else, a dislocation in her own head.

She was looking at the ground. She could see the patterns again in the ash. Some resembled scuffed footprints. And there were two strange, straight lines. Then she had it—the lines were made by a wheelchair! Of course. The foreigner—he had been there too. Before the eruption. She had wheeled him out there herself. Why had she forgotten that?

And what had happened to him, afterwards? Someone must have come and wheeled him away to safety. She didn't know who. But studying the ash now, she saw that in front of the point where the lines stopped, there was an impression in the ash that was dimly human in shape. As if someone had lain there for a time, in front of the chair, while the muddy rain fell. And was that another memory? Had she turned away from the mountain, to see him sitting there, unmoving . . .

Why did the thought frighten her?

She glanced at her hands. She was still holding the broom.

Cleaning. Cleaning would make her feel better. She would settle into her chores. She would sweep out the halls and change sheets and carry meals. And she would not—although she couldn't have explained why—go near the crematorium, or the little oven of a room in which the foreigner slept.

7

And yet still the day would not come right.

The whole hospital was busy cleaning up from the eruption, and the orphan joined in, but sweeping, it turned out, didn't help clear her mind at all. Ash was everywhere through the back wards, and no matter how she toiled to shift it, the grains continued to rasp irritatingly underfoot. Dust itched in her nose, and sweat gathered in her armpits. It was so hot. The electricity was still off and the back wards, never brightly lit in the first place, had sunk into an airless gloom.

But worse was the thickness in her head. Faces loomed up at her—nurses and other staff, hurrying by—and the orphan knew them, or at least she knew that she was supposed to know them, but recognition took so much effort. They could have been strangers. And when one of the nurses spoke to her, the orphan could only stare back helplessly. The woman's speech was incomprehensible. The same thing happened when one of the laundry staff accosted her, seemingly to make some urgent request. The words were nonsense. Not just hard to understand, but impossible.

She retreated at last to the kitchen block, and sat in a corner to eat. Normally it was one of her favourite places. Busy. Full of interesting noises and tempting aromas. But in truth, despite not having eaten in a whole day, the orphan was barely hungry. And the kitchen felt all wrong. The smells were bad, the clash of pots and pans too loud, and the yelling of the cooks might as well have been the hooting of animals.

One of the inmates, a young man, was standing in the doorway. The orphan followed his eyes, watching as a cook added salt to a vat of soup. Only suddenly it didn't look like salt, or anything else she could identify. The substance was black and loathsome, and something moved in it, alive. It was a secret poison they added to all the food. It was a drug. It was what made everyone mad.

Then the inmate was gone from the doorway, and the cook was putting the salt away, and it was only salt.

The orphan fled the kitchen.

Where was she to go? Back to her room, back to bed? She knew she would never be able to sleep. Energy ached in her limbs. Yet everywhere else seemed too crowded with patients and staff. It wasn't that they were doing anything objectionable. It was just that she could *feel* them. That is, she imagined she could—their emotions, pressing like heat upon her skin. It made it hard to breathe.

She returned to the main building and found refuge for a while in the catatonic ward. Here at least there was blessed quiet—no minds pushing against her own. There were only the vacant bodies in their beds. It was soothing, at first. She could sweep the floors unbothered as the figures around her stared at nothing. But with time the silence grew deeper. In fact, it wasn't a silence at all. It was an *absence*. It came to the orphan that the catatonics were holes into which life and light and noise vanished. They were emptiness. And such emptiness might be even worse than the crowd. She went back out into the hallways.

And, at length, came across the archangel.

It was the glow of him that caught her attention. He was standing at the far end of a long passage. All around him was shadow, but the archangel himself was positioned beneath a window through which daylight shafted, and for some reason, in the light, his clothes and his face were almost shining.

Reluctant, but unable to resist, the orphan edged down the hall towards him. He was reading aloud from his book, the pages held up to the window, his hollow voice resonating. He was still covered in ash from the eruption, she realised, and that was why he shone—the grey powder flared white in the sunlight. His clothes and skin and hair. He might have been carved from cement.

Madness beat against the orphan's forehead like the wings of birds. The archangel's eyes were closed in some transport of inner ecstasy, but still he read on. His voice rolled over her with a hypnotic authority. Had it always been so deep? He was hardly more than a boy, but with his hair grey and his face mud-streaked he looked much older. So stern, so grave, so perfect. It occurred to her then that, although she knew he had once attempted suicide with a knife, she had never seen a single disfiguring scar anywhere on his skin.

But coming close now she saw that the perfection was an illusion. A muddy sweat had beaded on his brow, and his body was not merely motionless, it was locked rigid. Pain transported him, not ecstasy. Horrified, she realised that the window he stood beneath was shattered, and that broken glass littered the floor. The youth's feet were bare, and as he prayed, he ground his soles against the shards.

And then it happened again. Without volition, she was drawn out of her body and into his. But the experience was more complete this time. She *was* the archangel. She felt the sun upon his face and the book in his hands. She felt his long straight limbs and his broad shoulders. She even felt the fire in his feet.

But she was also in his mind. And in his mind, he wasn't tall and strong at all. He was hideous to himself, a misshapen bag of skin and bones. His head was corrupt with forbidden thoughts, his belly ached with evil hungers, and in his loins there coiled a damp, snakelike thing, insidious. Indeed, his body was his enemy, and he had put it away from him. The orphan had a strange impression of height, and of a lonely room, where he was held safe by the power of his book and his prayers.

But now he was ashamed, for when the earth had shaken and the sky had rained fire, he had forgotten his book and his prayers. Instead, he had surrendered to his bodily fear and run away to hide. The archangel was mortified by the memory. He was supposed to be beyond fear. And so now, through the pain in his feet, borne willingly, and through his prayer, he was seeking redemption. But only blood would be sufficient. He ground his heels down, and the glass bit more cruelly.

The orphan recoiled. The link between them snapped, and she was back in her own head. The archangel faltered. He licked his lips a moment, then drew a ragged gasp, turned a page of his book, and plunged on. Horrible. It was horrible in there. She wanted to flee from him, get as far from his suffering as she could. But she hesitated, torn between pity and disgust. She couldn't just leave him. He would injure himself. He'd done little damage so far, but if he went much further . . .

Blood trickled from beneath his toes.

She drew a deep breath, and lightly took his elbow. This time there was no black gulf opening. The youth shivered, but something in her touch seemed to reach him, because he lowered his book and fell silent. The tension did not leave his body, but he did at least allow himself to be led away from the window.

Slowly, they made their way towards the crematorium. Patients and nurses passed them by, but the orphan avoided their eyes. She could not cope with anyone else. The archangel and his bloody footsteps were bad enough. She would deliver him to his room and be done. Yet with every step, an aversion grew in her. She realised that she was in dread of their destination. Not the entire crematorium, perhaps, but the little furnace room was waiting there, and within it, sleeping . . .

Ripples ran like heatwaves across her vision, but they were waves of cold, not heat, and she was walking, not through the hospital, but down a deep valley of stone, somewhere where it was night, and freezing. And there was a voice, a voice like no other, a voice she could understand inherently . . .

The orphan halted, staring about. No one was visible except the archangel, stiff at her side. She pushed forward, down the last passageway. At its end, all seemed black and quiet. There was something unusual about that, the orphan knew. Then they came to the dayroom, and she realised. Of course. There was still no power. The lights were off. And for once, the television was dark and silent.

Nevertheless, in the dimness, the virgin sat before the screen.

The orphan felt her tenuous grip on reality slipping again. She led the archangel to one of the armchairs, and forced him down. His shoulders were taut under her hands, and immediately he bent himself over his book, his fingers moving across the lines, although surely it was too dark for him to read.

The orphan turned back to the virgin. What was the girl doing?

She *looked* unharmed. Someone had cleaned her up since the eruption, and changed her clothes. And she was merely sitting as she always sat, legs folded, arms resting on her knees, her head tilted towards the television. Yet there was a distress in her so palpable it vibrated through the room like a thrumming wire.

The orphan was helpless to shut it out. She felt her identity melt away, and the virgin's blindness come seeping into her eyes. Darkness closed in, and panic. Except, no, it wasn't quite blindness. It was not a loss of vision, but a *dulling* of it, until everything was pale and distant. The virgin, in her dementia, seemed to be adrift in a world of the utmost dreariness, in which there was no colour or dimension. A flat world. A false world.

But a *real* world did exist, a place of brightness and life, and the orphan knew this because the virgin could see it sometimes, through a special window. A magic window. That world was wonderful, with every shape the most vivid, vibrant hue. Heavenly people moved there, radiant and beautiful and fascinating. That was where the virgin belonged. That was where she went, whenever the window was opened for her.

But something terrible had happened. She had been taken away from the window, and the false world had roared and thrown her to the ground, drenched by hot rain. Then brutal hands had assaulted her, prying and stripping and scrubbing. Finally she had escaped them to return to her window—but to her dismay it was shut, and no matter how she stared with her blind eyes, she could not open it again. There was no colour anywhere, no light, no reality. She was trapped in the false world, and now a frantic terror was rising in her that she could not stop.

The orphan turned away, nearly frantic herself. Madness. More madness than she could bear. Ever since waking this morning, her mind had been wide open to it, leaving her defenceless. The duke and the witch were bad enough, and the archangel worse . . . now this shrilling anxiety from the virgin. What was happening? Where had this hypersensitivity to other minds come from? And why had it occurred with these four patients—these particular four—most acutely?

The volcano, it had begun with the volcano.

The virgin was moaning now, a low, barely audible mew of despair. And the archangel was praying aloud again, fervid, rocking back and forth. He wasn't a figure of stone anymore, he was a boy and he looked like he was about to cry. He needed help. He was suffering. So was the girl. But the orphan couldn't help. She didn't know what it was they needed. But nor could she leave. She felt pinned by their agony and by her own indecision. She was an insect, lanced through by a needle and stuck wriggling to the floor, close to tears, her fists clenched hopelessly.

Take her hand . . .

Had someone spoken?

Take her hand and put it in his.

That voice, she knew that voice from somewhere! Too shocked even to think or question, the orphan obeyed. She took hold of the virgin's hand, and lifted it so that it touched the archangel's fingers where they clutched the cover of his book. A spark of electricity seemed to flash through the room, a stroke of blue light. And in that illumination the orphan saw the archangel and the virgin staring at each other, their eyes suddenly awake, actually seeing, for real, face to face.

There was a heartbeat of all-encompassing silence. Then the room was dark once more. The archangel was muttering his prayers again, and the virgin was slumped back on the floor, blind. Everything was the same—except that something was very different. A searing pain had been removed from the air.

Come here, ordered the voice.

The orphan rose, unhurried. The pin was gone from her back, the strain and the fear and the confusion. She went down the little hall to the door that led into the furnace room. She opened it, and there in the tiny space, unmoving upon his bed, was the foreigner. His skin shone palely in the dark.

She remembered it all then. The cold valley, the huddled village, the landslide, the man buried with her under all those piles of rock, the freezing water rising, and finally his escape, torn and bloodied. Every detail of her dream.

It was no dream, said the foreigner, even though his lips didn't move and his eyes were shut. *It was me. You know that.*

8

Oh, his voice. It was just as it had been in the dream that was not a dream. So clear. So crisp. A cool breath wafting through her mind, delicious.

Come closer. Please.

She complied without hesitation, closing the door behind her, staring at him all the while. His chest rose and fell slightly with his breathing, but nothing about him suggested awareness of her or even consciousness. It was a sign of her own madness, surely, to believe that a man could speak without moving his lips and see with his eyes shut. And yet she had no doubt about where the voice came from. It was the foreigner who spoke, as patently as if he had sat upright and opened his eyes and smiled.

Yes. But only you can hear me. No one else is special enough.

Pleasure warmed her. His wonderful voice—it was for her alone. And he had called her special! Not in the way that others did, where special actually meant stupid. No, he meant it in a good way, in an admiring way.

She took one of his hands in hers, fascinated. She had touched him before, while bathing him or changing his sheets, but he had seemed inert then. Empty. Now she knew that a waking, living presence filled him, and that changed everything. She threw the sheet back and stared, taking in the sight of him, naked and entire. How had she never noticed it properly before? He was quite beautiful. So smooth, so supple . . .

But then she was frowning. In her dream the foreigner had shown her a mountain falling, and a young villager caught beneath it. And she remembered that, afterwards, the foreigner had claimed a strange thing—that *he* was the villager. But when the orphan looked at the figure sleeping in front of her now . . .

I know. I look nothing like that man anymore. But that was me, all the same. The beginning of me, and what I became, anyway.

She believed him implicitly—a voice like his could surely never lie—but even so, a part of her was unsatisfied. The villager had torn his foot away to escape from under the rocks. This man showed no sign of any such injury. Besides, the landslide had been a long time ago. Ninety-two years, he'd said in the dream. That was forever. He should be old. Older than the old doctor even. And yet he wasn't old . . .

Don't worry. I'll explain it all. Eventually.

Again, she could not help but accept this. Somehow, simply, he was young. She had hold of his wrist. She could feel his pulse. It was not erratic or sickly. It was strong and slow and regular. Like his voice. But—another question—why then was he still asleep? His body radiated health, yet it remained limp.

You can ask me directly. I can hear you.

And what did he mean by that?

The foreigner sounded puzzled in turn. *You don't understand 'directly'?*

No, she didn't.

Ah . . . I should've realised. You're unfamiliar with the use of the first- or second-person modes of address. How extraordinary. But then, why should you be familiar? You've never spoken aloud, never had a conversation in your life.

There was an emotion in his words she couldn't quite catch. Was it pity? She was searching his body more closely now, running her hands over his hairless skin, looking for the vital wound that kept him sleeping.

You won't find anything.

Then why didn't he wake up?

I was hurt. Very badly. Not just in one place, but all over. I'll have to stay this way for some time yet. While I heal.

She was confused. Hurt? When the mountain fell on him?

No. This injury was much more recent, and far worse.

Worse? But there were no scars on him. No marks.

You wouldn't understand it.

The orphan withdrew her hands. So he was just like everyone else after all—he thought she was slow. And dumb. Someone to be laughed at.

Regret. *No. I'm not laughing at you. I know you're not slow. On the contrary, you're unique. You have such abilities. It's just that you haven't been taught yet.*

A memory of school flashed through the orphan. Of other children mocking her, of teachers rapping her across her knuckles and shaking their heads in annoyance, of being moved to the back corner of the classroom.

Those people couldn't help. But I can.

The orphan could not stay angry with him. It wasn't just his soothing words, it was the concern in them. She had never felt anything like it before, another person's attention focused so intently on herself. Oh, she knew that the old doctor and the nurses cared about her, but they had never concentrated on her like this, never spoken to her so intimately, and offered . . .

But what was he offering?

You'll see. There's so much I can show you . . .

Like the cold valley of stone? Is that what he meant? She did not want to go back there. And where was that valley anyway? It had felt real, but how could that be? There was no such place on the island, surely.

Again, there was a bemused pause before the foreigner replied, but this time the orphan felt a sharp sensation of exposure. Not physical; it was a thing of the mind, as if the foreigner was peering inside her head, studying her thoughts and her memories, and nothing could be hidden from him.

Oh, child. Is it true? You really have no idea that anything exists beyond this little island?

The orphan bridled. She was no child!

I'm sorry. You're right. And it isn't your fault. How could you be expected to know? Without being able to read, without being able to talk, with even TV and radio unintelligible to you, what could you ever learn of the wider world?

Her anger faded once more, and she was blushing now, ashamed. Child or not, he had seen inside her, and knew exactly how stupid she really was.

He laughed. *I can prove that isn't true. Take my hand again.*

She looked at his expressionless face. But the laugh hadn't been cruel, or pitying, or sad. It was a laugh of . . . promise? She took hold of his hand.

Now, let's see . . . through the door first, I think.

And suddenly, the room was melting away.

No, not melting, but the walls were suddenly insubstantial, even though they were made of solid brick. In fact, the orphan had experienced something like it once before. When the volcano erupted, she had looked down into the earth and *seen* the chamber of molten rock below, as if the layers of stone in between had become as diffuse as a cloud. This was a similar sensation, only much more deliberate. It was happening by choice, not by instinct. It was an act of the foreigner's will.

And they were moving. Without standing up, without walking, they were drifting across the room towards the door. One part of the orphan could feel that she was still sitting by the bedside, and that her fingers were still clasped around the foreigner's passive hand. But another part of her felt cut loose. Weightless. Floating. A shadow self. And that shadow self was being pulled forward by a hand far more compelling. The foreigner was leading her on, a shadow too it seemed, a ghost form with no more substance than mist—but in control of her.

They passed through the door as if it was a film of water.

Into the dayroom. There was the archangel, still bent over his book, in prayer. And curled in front of the dead television was the virgin. The orphan felt a stab of concern for them both, but with one look she could tell that the archangel was calmer, his prayers less fervent, and that the virgin's panic had lessened.

Don't worry. They've discovered each other, those two.

The orphan didn't understand, lost in wonder at what was happening—through walls!—but her guide was already moving on.

And now, he said, his voice smiling, *we go up.*

They lifted, like a gust of wind. The orphan cried out at the thrill of it, and in a blur the ceiling and the roof of the crematorium rushed by, and then they were outside, in blinding daylight, suspended in mid-air, blue sky all around.

The foreigner was laughing at her amazement.

You see what you can do?

She could fly! Or at least, he could, and he was taking her with him, for her hand was still held tightly in his. The initial leap had passed, and they were drifting more slowly now, but upwards yet, beyond the broken crown of the crematorium chimney. For a moment the orphan stared down into its choked funnel, but then they were higher, a whisper of a breeze taking them, and the whole hospital was spreading out below—the back wards, the front wards, the outbuildings, all sleeping dreamily under their grey sheets of ash. A few patients and staff were walking in the grounds, but they were oblivious to the miracle in the air above them, the two impossible birds.

Ha! The orphan was laughing, or crying with joy, she didn't know which. They soared higher, away from the hospital and out over the trees, towards the outskirts of town. And how insignificant the town was from the air, a tiny maze of alleyways and red dirt, dwarfed by the jungle and the plantations around it. And how drab it looked, with its rusty tin roofs and junk piles, and everything dirty with ash.

But they were higher again, and turning away from the town. The orphan realised she could see across a great swathe of jungle —indeed, across a whole flank of the island—and it was clear that the volcano had spewed its debris down just the one valley, and even then the plume had barely reached beyond the town. Past those limits the mantle of ash petered out, and the landscape burst again into vibrant green.

But they were turning further, coming back around over the hospital, and ahead now was the volcano itself, the summit thrust high above them even yet. It was barely recognisable as the same mountain the orphan knew so well. From down in the hospital grounds the profile of the upper peak was stern and unchanging—but from mid-air the mountain was a far more humpbacked thing, its many ridges flung across the island and its high cliffs staring out with a multitude of different faces.

And there! High up on the mountainside was a stony ravine from which a thin smoke leaked. It was the site of yesterday's eruption. But the wind swept them swiftly beyond it. Onwards they rose, to the volcano's summit now, and finally, either by chance, or at the foreigner's choosing, they tumbled a bare arm's reach above the very pinnacle. A single twisted tree grew there, protected and hidden in a hollow. And then the orphan was staring down a dizzying plunge of stone, as the summit fell away again, sheer, into a deep bowl of jungle on the far side.

And still they ascended, the air beginning to cool noticeably and the wind whistling with a keener tone. The orphan felt as weightless as ever—but now, somewhere in the background, she was also aware of an *effort*, either within herself, or within the foreigner, or within both of them, and shared through their joined hands. Somehow, this flight was costing them energy, and that energy was not a limitless thing.

But what did it matter? Even the volcano was dwindling away below them now. And around it, slowly forming itself into a ragged circle of green, the whole island was coming into view. The hospital and the small town were barely distinguishable any longer, lost amid the jungle of the central plateau. But the big town was clearly visible, down on the coast, sitting within its own spider's web of converging roads. Its streets crawled with antlike people and cars, and its harbour swarmed with fishing boats.

It was the island as she had never seen it, a view full of astonishing new things. Not the big town, she already knew about that—her mother had taken her there once, for a day. What truly surprised her now was that she could see *other* towns—places of which she knew nothing. None of them were as big as the big town, and none of them were up on the central plateau like her own, but there were villages all around the coastline, and more farms, and more roads. So many, and she had never even suspected their existence. Why had no one told her before?

But still the foreigner lifted her, and now the circle of land was shrunken, its coastline fringed with white surf and luminescent reefs, outside of which great ships, much bigger than the fishing boats, plied the water, leaving long wakes behind. And then the orphan's gaze went to the horizon, and she saw at last, all around, the glittering green sheet that was the ocean.

So immense, so shining, the waves receding off beyond sight. During that one visit to the big town, the orphan had stood with her mother upon a beach and looked out over the wide water, but she had never conceived, then or since, that it extended so far. Now it seemed that no matter how high they climbed, the ocean would simply unroll forever, wild and deep and dark, and that it was all of the world. But then the orphan caught sight of a shape on the horizon, a smudge of blue. It was an island—*another* island, far away. And staring in disbelief, she saw another, further on, and then, faintly, another still, the three of them in a line.

So high now. Her own island was no bigger than an outstretched hand below, and the air was deeply cold. And it was not only *effort* the orphan could feel, it was something close to *pain*. But she ignored it. A hunger had awoken in her. If there were more towns than she had known about, and more islands, then what else might she see the higher they ascended? It wasn't enough any longer to merely be pulled along by the foreigner, she wanted to soar by herself, faster and further. So despite the cold and the pain, she pushed upwards, and the wind shrieked as they rose.

Sunlight glared at the edges of her vision—but yes, there were more islands out there, and beyond them, a larger, solid mass of land, reaching away unbroken. And something was strange about the horizon now. It wasn't as straight as it had been before. It appeared to fall away. To curve. But how could that be? What did it mean? A revelation seemed almost within her grasp, and she flew, dragging the foreigner behind her, climbing and climbing, until the shriek of the wind scaled upwards out of hearing and faded away. They were beyond the wind now, and the cold was piercing. Fatal, in fact. There was no way they could have survived if their real bodies were this high, instead of sitting safe in the hospital room below. But their shadow selves lofted onwards, through silence and cold and a pain that was close to agony.

But yes! The arc of the horizon grew more pronounced, and suddenly the orphan understood that it went full circle and joined together. Why, the world was an enormous ball! All the great landmasses, all the sparkling oceans, all the sweeping bands of clouds—they were curved into a sphere. And the sphere itself was suspended in a glowing sheath of air, beyond which was only a profound and icy blackness.

Astounding. And beautiful. And so strange that surely no one else had ever imagined it. Oh, but the pain! Its source, she could tell now, was the foreigner. It poured into her through their clasped hands. This was killing him. She had taken him too far, much further than he had meant to take her. They had to go back.

But even then she could not surrender the vision. The sun was behind them, and as she stared at all the lands and seas glowing in the fierce light, she made another discovery—the ball turned! So slowly that it was not even visible, but her inner senses detected it. The vast sphere was revolving there in its void, rotating the lands on its surface from day into night and into day again. And the *weight* of that movement staggered her, so much stone and sea and air in perpetual motion. It was worth the agony to behold it just a moment longer, to feel, to wonder . . .

And then the pain was too much. Someone, herself or the foreigner, cried out in surrender. Something—strained beyond endurance—snapped. The foreigner's hand tore loose from her own, and she was alone. She was falling, in spinning silence at first, then the air was howling around her, and the ocean and the clouds and the sun were all tumbling in confusion as the land rushed up from below.

And then—nothing. Darkness. Heat.

The orphan opened her eyes. She was back in the little furnace room. Her limbs were covered with sweat, her lungs labouring. From terror. From exhilaration. Before her lay the foreigner, his pale skin dry, his breathing calm, his hands folded on his chest. He might have been sleeping as soundly as when she had first entered the room, except that his eyes were open.

His gaze was blank—but the orphan knew better now. She leant over him, her face above his, her mouth close enough to exhale her hot breath onto his cold lips. Deep in his empty eyes she was certain there was recognition of her. Weary. Pain-ridden. Exhausted even. But approving. And proud.

You see? he said. *You see how clever you are?*

9

By next morning the hospital had mostly recovered from the effects of the eruption. The electricity had been restored overnight, the ash had been swept from the interiors and from the roofs, and in the yard the pathways were clear again. The laundry had even caught up with the washing.

It was virtually an ordinary morning, but to the orphan, roaming the back wards, such ordinariness was itself extraordinary. Obviously, no one at the hospital knew what she now knew—that the world was round, that it spun in empty space. They couldn't possibly, because how could people just carry on as usual if they *had* known—if they understood that the buildings they lived in, the ground they stood on, even the air they breathed, was all spinning on an immense, glowing ball?

The orphan hugged the discovery to herself like a treasure. Never in her life had she possessed knowledge that no one else did. Always she was the slow one, the one left mystified. But this—this was a secret greater than any other. The patients would never guess it. It was beyond even the nurses and doctors. Why, if she told them, even if she could find a way, they would think she was mad. Or madder.

But she wasn't going to tell anyone.

You must pretend nothing has happened, the foreigner instructed. He had been too exhausted to speak to her after their flight the previous afternoon, and she had left him for the evening. But, delightfully, he was there in her mind again when she woke at sunrise, quite audible, even though she was in her room and he was all the way across the compound in his. *No one would understand. They'd only be scared of you.*

The orphan didn't think she was capable of scaring anybody, but there was no question of arguing. Not with *him*. So she attended to her usual morning chores as if she was still the same old orphan. As if she couldn't feel the floor moving and moving and moving as the earth revolved beneath her. As if, when she went out into the yard and looked up at the sky, she couldn't remember what it had been like to soar beyond the warm blue air into a pure and freezing and silent blackness. As if the foreigner wasn't with her, hour after hour—no matter where she was in the hospital.

We're connected now, you and I. Distance doesn't mean anything. We'll always be able to talk . . . and do other things.

Other things? Did that mean they would *fly* again?

A rueful laugh. *When I've rested more, maybe.*

She was sorry. She had pushed him too hard and too high.

Yes, you're very strong, and I'm much weaker than normal. But when I'm fully healed, I'll be able to match you. Don't worry.

Wonderful!

But she was aware of a strange frustration. She was so grateful to him, so open to him, so enmeshed with him—quite unlike anything she had experienced with any other person—and yet it seemed that she had no word to define that to herself. No word to identify the sweet uniqueness of him.

My name—that's what you're searching for.

His name! But she could never know names . . .

No . . . but there's no reason that should be a barrier between us. Names aren't the same thing as knowing. After all, you can't tell me your own name, and yet I know everything about you.

Yes, he did, it was true. But what did she know about *him*? Their connection flowed in only the one direction, it seemed. They had soared together, yes, and it was the most sublime moment of sharing she had ever experienced—but the sharing was all on her part. His own mind had remained closed throughout. Who he was, where he had come from, of those things she knew almost nothing.

You will, in due course.

When? Why not now?

More laughter. *Mine is a longer story than yours, and much more complex.*

But that wasn't good enough. She needed to know, because not knowing frightened her. He had been trapped under a falling mountain and somehow survived and that was ninety-two years ago and she believed every word—but none of it made *sense*, and if it didn't make sense, then maybe it wasn't real. Maybe she was imagining it all, making it all up in her head. Maybe it was just her madness.

It's not madness. How could it be? Could you imagine flying? Could you make up the things you saw yesterday?

The orphan wouldn't have thought so. Certainly, she had never before imagined anything so exquisite as the shining world, spinning in space. But wasn't that the cruelty of hallucinations? That they could be fatefully beautiful?

Forget the beauty. What matters is—did it feel right?

And, oh, it had felt *so* right. Indeed, the orphan had recognised the essential truth of what she was seeing even as they first rose above the volcano and looked back down. Those initial, minor revelations—that there were other towns on the island, that in fact there were other entire islands across the ocean—they had all seemed self-evident to her, even at the time. Of *course* there were other towns and islands. It was just that she had never travelled to them, or heard of them before.

And the greater revelations felt just as manifestly true. Why, having seen it now, how else could the world be but round? Yes, it *seemed* flat, but it couldn't actually *be* flat, otherwise it would have to go on forever, a stretched bed sheet that never ended—and a deep part of the orphan's mind rebelled at that thought. Besides, if she stood on a high place, she could see for a long way, but not eternally, no matter how clear the air was. The view had edges. And those edges were simply where the world curved away from sight. The solution was so elegant that the same deep part of the orphan's mind rejoiced in it. This could only be reality.

Even the things she had seen that *weren't* obvious, that indeed seemed the opposite of obvious, did not shake her conviction. There was the mystery, for instance, of how people were held to the earth—despite it spinning—rather than being flung away. She had no explanation for that. But nor did she doubt that it was a natural phenomenon, a force rooted in the fabric of the world. Something in the earth pulled objects to itself, and she and the foreigner had only been able to escape it and fly because they had been in shadow form. Weightless. And even then, it had cost them pain.

No, she could not believe that any of this was madness, nothing she had seen, nothing she had heard. It wasn't in her to create such marvels and puzzles. It was a knowledge that came from outside of her. It was a wisdom.

And it's all ours, my orphan. Yours and mine alone.

Again, wonderful.

Yet questions remained. In particular—was she truly clever now? If she had learnt so much, was she no longer retarded, or stupid? Had the foreigner made her smart?

By mid-morning, she wasn't at all sure.

For one thing, if she was smart, then why was she still having so much trouble understanding people when they spoke to her? The foreigner, oh yes, when he was talking his words fairly hummed with meaning—and she'd hoped that it might be that way when *anyone* spoke now, that the old failing in her mind had been repaired or removed. But it seemed not.

In fact, the problem was worse than ever. In all her various encounters that morning with the patients and nurses, the orphan could not decipher a single word that was said to her. For the most part she coped anyway. She knew her duties well enough to guess what people wanted. But there came a moment when a nurse requested something the orphan could not grasp at all. Nor were there any clues—no patient nearby who needed new sheets, no puddle of urine waiting to be mopped up. The nurse, if anything, seemed to be waving at the empty air.

The orphan was close to panic when—

There's no cause for alarm. She wants you to replace the mosquito coils in the rooms down the hall, that's all. The patients are getting bitten.

The foreigner had come to her rescue!

And why not? He was there in her mind, wasn't he? He could hear everything that anyone said to her. And *he* was not slow. He could understand exactly, and then tell her what was required. How very convenient.

But as she hurried away to the storeroom, the orphan couldn't help noting that she'd been asked many times before to change the mosquito coils, and had always managed somehow to understand. So what was wrong now?

Nothing! And even if there was, what did it matter? The problem might go away, and if it didn't, she was better off anyway with the foreigner there. She wouldn't have to struggle with words anymore; he could simply translate for her.

Except . . .

He wasn't *always* there. Not every moment. Twice more that day he helped her, interpreting instructions from the staff, but a third time, while she was being addressed by a laundry woman, the orphan reached out for his aid and found nothing. She was alone in her head. And she could only stand there, baffled and ashamed, until the laundry woman, impatient, gave up on her and turned away.

I was asleep, was all the foreigner said when he returned.

Asleep? But wasn't he *always* asleep, and yet really awake?

My mind must truly sleep at times. I can't watch you every moment. I'm a man, not a guardian angel.

But couldn't she rouse him? Couldn't she demand his attention? Or was the connection made only when he chose it, and not when she did?

But he was gone again, and didn't answer.

Indeed, he was gone much of the time over the next few days. And for some reason her duties did not take her to the crematorium at all in that same period, as they usually would have, so she was denied even the sight of him.

And other questions arose for the orphan.

Television, for instance. As an experiment, she went and stood in front of the TV in the main dayroom. Half a dozen patients were there, staring up at the wire cage. The orphan studied the screen hopefully, but, as ever, she could determine nothing from the flickering colours. And the foreigner remained absent. He didn't take over her eyes and show her what everyone else in the room, apparently, could see.

It was the same with her radio. She turned it up extra loud, and waited for the foreigner to make sense of the tantalising sounds for her. But he didn't. She even tried staring at posters around the hospital, hoping for the squiggled lines on them to be transformed by the foreigner into messages of some kind. But again, nothing. And when she wondered why this was so—why he either refused to help her, or was incapable of doing so—he offered no excuse and no explanation.

His silences, she began to suspect, could be deliberate. But then she would feel guilty. How could she be so ungrateful, so doubting, after all he had given her?

Finally, late on the fifth night after the eruption, he spoke to her while she was cleaning the old doctor's office in the front wards.

I feel better tonight, orphan. I'm sorry if I've been inaccessible these last days—I was more drained by our flight than I realised.

Oh, he was forgiven, of course. Now that he was with her. Everything was forgivable when he was with her.

Good. There's something I want to show you. It might be useful. There. Do you see it? On that shelf in the corner?

She looked. It seemed that he was talking about an ornament which sat there. It was a multicoloured plastic ball, on a stand. She had noticed it many times before, and knew that it spun if she flicked it with her fingers. But that was all it did, and she'd always thought it odd that the old doctor would keep such a toy.

Really look at it. Does it remind you of anything?

She stared harder, hearing the test in his question and wanting to pass. But the ball was just a ball.

Strange . . . but then I suppose any artificial representation or abstraction . . . the same as it is with names, or pictures . . .

Had she failed him? Disappointed him?

Reassurance. *No. You could never disappoint me. It's just that this . . . globe . . . tells people what the world looks like.*

The orphan studied the ball scornfully. This? This piece of plastic was supposed to represent the majesty of what she had beheld? Impossible. There was no life in it, no momentum or weight, no shimmer of ocean or wrinkle of land, no silver cocoon of atmosphere. Compared to the actuality, it was laughable.

Yes, but it's a sphere, isn't it? And it spins.

Uncertainty seized her. He was right. And that meant that the makers of the toy must have known the great secret about the world. They must have learnt it somehow. But she'd thought that she and the foreigner were the only ones who knew. No one else had flown so high and seen so much. He'd said so!

It's known that the world is round, and that it spins. Everyone understands that—or at least, they think they do, but only because it's what they've always been told. Very few have seen it with their own eyes, and none have seen it the way you and I have. I meant what I said. That experience was ours alone.

Her hurt eased. And it was the thought that he might have been lying to her, rather than anything else, that had been so terrible.

I'll never lie to you.

She was happy again. So—did he have more marvels to show her?

The foreigner's tone was lightly scolding. *Is that what you think this is all about—showing you marvels? It isn't, you know.*

Immediately she was chastened.

You've glimpsed the planet from space, yes, but that's the least someone with your talents can do.

Teach her then! Right now. She wanted to fly again. To circle the world—the *planet*, that was a new word—and absorb its every mystery.

It hasn't occurred to you to wonder why?

What did he mean—why?

Why it is that I'm doing this?

The orphan had no answer. She hadn't even thought!

I supposed as much. Well, perhaps the first thing we should do is go back to the beginning. After all, you wanted to know more about me. My reasons for helping you and the long story of my life are very much one and the same.

She nodded eagerly, her mind wide open.

We won't be leaving our bodies this time, all you have to do is listen, but you might want to sit down anyway. You won't be disturbed?

No, no one would come to the office this late, except maybe the night nurse, and the orphan knew that he was already asleep in one of the empty rooms. She dropped her broom and sat down on the floor.

Very well then. We'll return to the day of my birth.

Ninety-two years ago now . . .

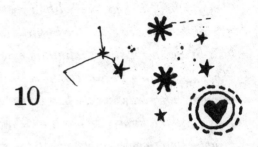

10

You saw me. I crawled out from beneath that landslide, and I was the same man, but not the same man anymore. I stood on top of that pile of stone and there was nothing but frozen mountains all around and an empty sky above, and I knew that I was alone in an inhuman place that was entirely without pity.

I could have lain down and died then, of course. I'd lost enough blood, and I was naked, already suffering from exposure. There was little reason for me to go on living. Everything I had ever known or loved was now under half a kilometre of rock. But I turned and walked away from that place. Exactly why . . . that I can't remember. The things we do, they are decided deep within us sometimes, without our knowing.

And how I managed to walk, when nothing was left of my foot but bone, that I can't remember either. Which is also the way of it. The body—I know this from long experience—doesn't want to remember pain. In any case, somehow I made it all the way down the valley to the next village. It took me a day and a night, without sight of another person, and I really was pretty much dead when I drew near. The first thing I found was a body, a man, in the ruins of a collapsed stable on the outskirts. And the first thing I did was steal his clothes, despite the fact that my fingers were so crippled with cold I could barely strip his corpse.

The village itself was in chaos, the population weeping and wailing. The earthquake had levelled half the houses. At least three days had passed, but the dead and the injured still lay out in the open. Everyone was living on the streets, afraid to enter those buildings left standing. The closest thing to a doctor was the village midwife. She was wise enough in her way, but she had no equipment and no medicine. There was thirst and hunger and soon there would be disease. What frightened people most, however, was that the river had mysteriously stopped flowing. The water was gone. No one knew why.

I could have told them, if anyone had asked, but no one spoke to me. This was a bigger village than my own, and there were so many injured, I was merely one more. The midwife took one look at me, shook her head, bandaged my shredded limbs with a few rags, then left me there on the street with the rest of the dying.

And yet, even then I wondered if there wasn't something else to it. I had travelled to that village before, and was known to many of its inhabitants. But now when they looked, they didn't recognise me. They were in shock, of course. So was I. But in truth, I felt as if I really was a stranger, that there was nothing left of me to be recognised.

A day later, outside help finally arrived.

Now, you mustn't think of ambulances or fire engines, like today. This was a long time ago, and in a remote part of a poor country—even poorer than your little island here. The nearest large town was many miles distant, and the nearest city far, far away. So the only assistance that came up the valley was a small train of wagons, carrying a little food and water, some blankets, and a collection of government officials, there to investigate the damage and to make a count of the dead.

There was no doctor. The midwife debated furiously with the officials, and it was decided that two of the wagons would go back down the valley with the worst of the injured. The midwife walked along her makeshift ward and selected those to go. She looked hard at me, and I knew she was wondering whether I would live long enough to make my inclusion worthwhile. I was sure she would say no—and I was too weak even to argue.

But right then the ground trembled. An aftershock. There had been others, but this was the strongest. People screamed, dust rose, and dread took hold of me. I would be buried again, the mountains would not let me go. All the pain of climbing out from under those rocks and marching all those miles, none of it mattered. The earth recognised no suffering, rewarded no effort. It would kill me as unthinkingly as it had tried to the first time.

The midwife was watching me still, her eyes on mine, and she saw my terror. My anger too. My outrage. And I think that's what decided her—if I was alive enough to feel fear and fury, then I was alive enough to save.

The aftershock passed, and I was put into a wagon. They gave me a mouthful of water and a crust of bread. Then we rattled off down the road. The jolting of the wheels was agony, but I didn't mind—food was warming my belly, and I was propped up so that I was facing backwards and could watch as the village dwindled away behind us. I was going to live. I believed it finally. I was escaping from those cold walls of stone and ice. And I swore that I would never return to that valley again.

A government official was riding beside me. He was writing reports, and in time he turned to me and asked my name, his pen poised above the paper. And in a whisper I told him. A lie. I gave myself a new name—just a made-up name, the first that came into my head. And I gave myself a new home too, a town far away. I was, I said, merely a traveller, a salesman, caught up in the disaster. I knew no one in the valley, had no family there, and had lost all my possessions when the earthquake struck.

He wrote down everything I said and, as simply as that, the person who was me was pronounced deceased—or he soon would be, along with everyone else, when they discovered the fate of my village—and the new me came officially into existence. Take note of that, my orphan. It was my very first death.

Meanwhile, after a slow and painful trip, we arrived in a town called . . . ah well, I'd hoped to show you on the globe . . . it was the closest large town. There I was treated in a proper hospital—although, again, a very primitive place by today's standards. I don't recall much about it. My wounds had become infected, and I grew very sick, lapsing in and out of consciousness. But I recovered—it must have taken some weeks—and when I was finally awake and alert once more, I discovered an amazing thing. My foot had healed.

Oh, it was gnarled and ugly, but there was flesh there, it was a proper limb again, whole and functional. And I remembered—I knew for certain—that I'd ripped the entire thing away, leaving only a stub of shattered ankle. The doctors should have amputated it. A foot could not regrow from nothing.

Yet it had. My whole body, in fact, had seemingly repaired itself. It was crisscrossed with scars, yes, but much less so than it should have been. You can imagine my confusion. Had it really happened? Had I actually been buried by the landslide and then torn myself free of it? Had I perhaps been caught in a smaller rock fall and merely imagined the rest? Might my village still be standing?

But the hopeful fantasy was soon dispelled. I heard other patients in my ward talking. The earthquake was real, and the landslide. Everyone knew now that a village far up in the valley had been buried, and that a giant dam had blocked the river. Fifty-four people were presumed dead. The sum population of the village. Myself included, as far as anyone else knew.

But there I was, not only miraculously alive, but miraculously hale as well. Here was a mystery to ponder. The earth had crushed me, it had declared that I should die, and it was impossible that mere flesh and blood could survive against a mountain. But I had. I caressed the scar tissue of my leg, wondering. What was I to do with this new life, this impossible life, this second life?

I found that one desire burnt in me brighter than all others—the desire to learn. I was, I realised while lying in that hospital, an ignorant man. When I had looked up on that terrible night and seen the face of the mountain fracture and fall, I had felt fear, yes, and anger, but the root of those emotions was confusion. I had not understood what was happening. I was too ignorant. The processes of the earth—even though I'd spent all my short life living upon it, a peasant familiar with the soil—were a mystery to me.

A frightening mystery, as my nightmares attested. Physically I was recovering, but mentally I was still bleeding and broken, scarcely able to sleep for cold sweats and fits of screaming. Paranoias haunted me—that another earthquake was going to strike, that a tremendous flood was on its way, that the ground, if I ever dared venture outside again, would open up and swallow me.

In short, I no longer trusted the earth. I suspected, almost, a conscious malice in it towards my person. And no man can live like that. So I decided I would spend my new life studying the very thing I feared. I would devote myself to understanding the workings of the world. I would learn why the earthquake had struck my valley that day, and why it was that all my friends and family had died.

But more—I would learn about floods too, and volcanoes, and storms. Can you see what I wanted to do? It was the violence of the world that I sought to comprehend. I had to somehow fathom those *moments when the natural forces turn on man and destroy him so casually—because if I could understand what caused those events, then I could strip them of their mystery. And if I could strip them of their mystery, then I could strip them of their terror and their power over me. And end my nightmares.*

Ah yes . . . a grand plan.

Of course, I'm sure I didn't think in those terms while I lay in hospital. I was just a goatherd who could barely read or write. All I really knew was that I never wanted to feel so stupid and afraid as I had the day the mountain fell on me.

So I set out to get an education.

It wasn't easy for someone like me, penniless and homeless. But there were jobs in the cities, and schools and libraries too, so to the cities I went. I worked all day in factories or dockyards—and struggled by night over my books, learning to read and write properly. I hired tutors with my meagre wages. And then, when I was reasonably literate, I spent my evenings in the libraries. And hired more tutors. And passed the basic school exams. And then began to prowl the corridors of universities.

I made note of the fields I would need to study. Geology. Hydrology. Meteorology. Oceanography. Chemistry. Physics. All just words to me then, many of them disciplines in their merest infancy. And all out of reach for a poor man anyway. But then, only three years after the landslide, a great war broke out across much of the world. It lasted four years, and not only did millions die, but revolutions came, and whole societies were turned upside down, including my own. Me—well, all that matters is, again, I managed to survive. And afterwards, all the education that had been denied to me by poverty was suddenly made available, if I had the desire and the intellect to seize it.

I had the desire and the intellect.

So I went to university, and my long study began. And for ninety-two years, it has gone on. Oh, not always as a humble student, no—but the tales of my many careers and fortunes and failures can wait for the moment. All you need know for now, my orphan, is that in one way or another, ever since that landslide, I have been examining this world. And I can safely say that my understanding of the earth is now unequalled. No one else knows nearly as much about this planet as I do. No one else can read its signs or appreciate its subtleties or untangle its complexities as well as I.

And yet for all that, I'm nothing—compared to you.

I sensed it, even as they wheeled me into this place. My sleep was disturbed by a presence. There was someone close by, someone with powers. Comatose, I reached out with my thoughts and went searching among the minds around me, only to discover that I was in a madhouse, and that most of those at hand were insane or catatonic or senile. The mind I actually wanted, for some reason, remained hidden. So I waited. I was sure that the presence would sense me too before long, and seek me out in its turn.

But what irony! My only regular visitor was a retarded girl who came to change the sheets. A girl whose mind, on the surface at least, was blank. A girl I dismissed, summarily, as being of no use to me. What a fool I was!

But meanwhile I felt the earth trembling minutely, and I calculated that there must be a volcano nearby, and that soon it would erupt, in minor fashion. I decided that I may as well be outside to watch. It was no trouble to plant the necessary thought in a nurse's head, hence I was there when it all happened.

And I saw, disbelieving, what you did.

I saw how easily you read the faint vibrations in the earth, long before any machine could have registered them; when even I, for all my expertise, could only just detect the activity. I saw how you knew, *innately, where to look for the source of the tremors, and I saw how your mind pierced the earth to see down to the magma chamber. I saw that you knew exactly what form the eruption would take, how long it would last, and how little damage it would do. I watched you laugh in the face of the blocks falling from the sky, and stand firm as the pyroclastic flow rolled down the mountainside.*

No one else could have done that. Not the cleverest scientist alive today, with all the most sensitive instruments that technology can produce. Even I can't do that. Oh, I can analyse a volcano's behaviour better than anyone . . . but I could never simply glance at an eruption and instantly know its every detail, as you did that day.

And so, as the ash rained down, I finally looked—really looked— inside your head, and discovered the miracle that is there. Such a shock. Like all the idiot doctors and nurses in this benighted place, I thought you were just a simple child who knew no better. When all the time you are a wonder. This world and all its secrets, from the heights to the depths, lie open to you. That's why I want to help you, my orphan.

Because only you can help me.

11

Sunrise found the orphan still awake. She was in her hut, alone. There was no voice inside her head. The foreigner, after his long unburdening, had fallen silent. Exhausted again, perhaps. Either way, she was glad to have her thoughts to herself. Most unexpectedly, his story had disturbed her.

Oh, at first she had been thrilled. A wonder, he had called her. Capable of doing things no one else, not even *he*, could do. And to hear him say that she could be useful to him, that she could help him—why, it was perfect!

Yes . . . but was it *too* perfect?

The very acuteness of her happiness gave the orphan pause, and all the doubts she thought she had banished came creeping back. Was it possible that she wanted this too badly? Was there not a starving part of her that had come awake in these last days, ravenous for exactly what the foreigner was offering? To be admired? To be needed? To be better and cleverer than everyone else?

Was it *delusionally* perfect? Could it be that, in her loneliness and deprivation, she was being deceived by madness after all?

Take the foreigner's tale of surviving the landslide and living all those years since—well, *how* had that happened? What made it possible? How could his foot grow back, or his appearance change? How could he reach into other people's minds? He had explained none of these things. And maybe he couldn't. If this was all made up in the orphan's head, then of course he would have no explanation for his powers, because there *was* no explanation for them. It was a fantasy.

Even the very incident of the landslide. Was there really a far-off valley of stone and ice where, long ago, a mountain had fallen and buried a village? How could she find out? It was the sort of knowledge, she guessed, that might be located in books but that was no use to her. The old doctor might also know, but without speech, how could she even make him understand the question?

There was no way. She was alone with this. If she wanted surety, she would have to find it on her own, her only resources her eyes and ears and the immediate world around her. So, of all the things the foreigner had shown her, was there anything nearby that she could check in person? Something she had not already known, and could not have known, until he had revealed it to her?

She was curled on her bed, staring across the room to the window. Through the glass the upper reaches of the volcano were visible in the dawn, its slopes still mottled with ash, but her eyes were far away, unseeing.

Proof. It was a matter of finding *proof*.

And then suddenly she did see.

She leapt from the bed, went to the window. The mountain! She remembered now. On the day that she had flown with the foreigner, they had soared across the peak, and there, hidden in a crack at the summit, invisible from anywhere else, she had seen a strange little tree. So all she had to do, to prove to herself that she wasn't delusional, was climb to the mountaintop and look. If the tree was really there . . .

Ha. How simple! And why not go right now? What was to stop her? Nothing at all. Grinning to herself—how much better she felt already—she was dressed in a few moments, and then heading through the door.

Outside, it was a warm, hazy morning. A low clatter came from the kitchen, but otherwise the hospital was still asleep. She could be halfway up the mountain before breakfast! Yet she hesitated for an instant, because . . . well, she didn't quite know why. She wasn't breaking any rule. She wasn't forbidden to leave the grounds. She was an adult, responsible for herself. It was just that she'd never gone anywhere on her own before. But then, she'd never had anywhere to *go* on her own before.

Well, now she did. And it was important. Excited again, the orphan walked along the rear fence, past the vegetable garden, until she came to a large hole in the wire. Ducking through it, she tramped across a strip of wasteland, and then she was in the jungle. There was a path there that climbed through the undergrowth. She took it, and after a short ascent she emerged at a grassy height that overlooked the hospital.

This far the orphan had been before, on picnic outings with the patients and the staff. It was a pleasant spot, with a wide view extending over the jungle to the town, and beyond to the plantations. But today she wasn't interested in the view. She was interested in the path. From here, it began to climb the mountain proper, leaving the jungle and following a long ridge that thrust down from the volcano's peak.

That way she had never been. She stared up. It looked an unfriendly route, rocky and bare, and scabrous with ash that had been partially washed away by rain. The slope was steeper than she remembered, too. So steep that the summit itself was hidden. But the path was still discernible. Indeed, someone had walked on it recently—there were tracks trodden into the ash, climbing away out of sight.

Reassured, the orphan started up, her solid legs pumping steadily, her head bent forward to watch her feet. And at first she felt that she was making good progress, rising swiftly along the path. But gradually the incline steepened, and the last greenery thinned away to ash and rock and brown tufts of grass. The sun lifted above the haze and grew hot. The orphan began to sweat and puff. She hadn't thought to bring any water, and there was no breeze. She remembered how, in her flight with the foreigner, it had been so deliciously cool when they were drifting above the island. Maybe it would be the same when she reached the summit.

She paused to gaze up. There was no doubt, the mountain was bigger than she had realised. The peak was still hidden by the slope above, and the terrain had grown alarmingly rugged—what had looked from the distance like mere stones were actually waist-high boulders that she had to either skirt or climb over. Turning back, she was surprised to see that now the hospital and the town were hidden too. She was high on the mountain, but staring out she could see only a haze of blue that might have been sky or might have been the far-off ocean, she couldn't tell which.

Climbing was nothing like flying. There was no freedom of floating above the world. If anything, gasping for breath in the humid air, she felt heavier and more chained to the earth than usual. But she turned and plodded on, and when she looked up again she saw that, at last, the path reached a crest above her. She hurried upwards, but then her spirits toppled as she breasted the rise. Before her the ridge, which from below had seemed to climb all the way to the summit, actually fell away again.

She stared down into a deep ravine cut from the mountainside. Ash lay thick and black about its walls, and its floor was rent by fissures. A pale steam jetted from the ground here and there, hanging like a dirty fog over the stones, and a biting tang assailed her nostrils. She knew where she must be. This was the rift where the eruption had taken place. Only beyond it did the land rise again, springing into rocky cliffs that sheared—straight up, it seemed—towards the final peak, still far above.

The orphan sagged despairingly. Her path had vanished, and even if she made it to the foot of the cliffs, she would never be able to climb them. She had misjudged the mountain entirely, and now it was showing her what a fool she was.

Yes . . . but even so, was her tree up there?

She studied the summit, half-wreathed in shreds of cloud. Was there a hint of foliage protruding just at the pinnacle, from a hollow in the rock? Maybe. Maybe. But it was so far away. It was impossible to be sure. She had wasted her time. Her face felt flushed with embarrassment. She was worse than a fool. She was slow and stupid and should never have come.

And then suddenly she wasn't alone.

The tree is there.

Ah. So he had returned from wherever he had been.

I've been right here. Watching you. To her deep annoyance, he sounded amused by her efforts. *I can't believe you just walked out your door and started to climb this mountain without even a second thought.*

If it was so funny, then why didn't he make it simpler for her—why didn't he fly her, right now, to the top again?

What would that prove? You know that when we fly, our bodies don't go with us. And if your body doesn't actually go to the summit, then whether you see the tree there or not, you still won't be sure it's real.

Then how *could* she be sure?

His tone had sobered. *It's not enough to trust me?*

And how she wished that it was, but the doubt persisted. If he was a product of her madness, then this was exactly what he *would* say.

For a time he didn't answer. The orphan sensed that his mind was roving away from hers, searching for something. Then he was back. *Look.*

Her eyes were drawn into the ashen ravine, and she saw a surprising thing. There were people down there, small figures among the confusion of stone.

In fact, they must have been there for some while, because they had set up tents. They were camping. The orphan knew about camping—how people came sometimes to look at the mountain or to climb it. Occasionally a line of them would walk past the hospital on their way, young and foreign and laden with backpacks. But why would anybody want to camp there now, amid the rocks and smoke? And odder still, some of them were dressed in silver suits, with big masks over their heads. They were clambering all about the place, peering into the fissures.

Do you know who they are?

Of course she didn't know.

They're vulcanologists. They came here yesterday, because of the eruption. It caught them a little by surprise. This mountain has not been active for hundreds of years. Now everyone is worried—will it erupt again? Right now, in fact, back at the hospital, your friend the old doctor is holding a meeting to discuss new evacuation plans, just in case. How does he get all the inmates out, where does he send them, who will pay for it? Oh, a lot of people are waiting to hear what those scientists down there discover.

Fascinated, the orphan watched the figures. Vulcanologists. So were they like her? Could they read the earth's vibrations in their bones?

Scorn. *Not them! They need their instruments to do that, and even then they can't be certain of much. They don't even know if it's safe to be up here right now, or if they might get caught in an eruption themselves. But you know, don't you?*

Yes, she knew. She'd known before setting out. The ground had been quiet beneath her feet. There would be no eruption today.

And that gas coming out of the cracks in the ground—what about that? Is it hot? Is it poisonous? Do they need those silver suits?

The orphan blinked. She hadn't thought about the steam except to note that it was an ugly colour and smelt bad. But now she felt her curiosity bloom. Her inner senses reached forth and she saw, as she had on the day of the eruption, that the mountain was not a single mass of stone, but rather a rough pile of debris, vomited up over ages and jumbled together only loosely. Far below waited the chambers of molten rock that had caused it all. They were in abeyance now, but even so they bubbled and heaved in their prisons, and plumes of gas rose continuously through the earth to emerge from the fissures that riddled the ravine floor.

But no, the steam wasn't dangerous. Most of its heat had been spent as it rose—warming layers of stone down below until they glowed red. And while the fumes at their deep point of origin would have poisoned anyone who breathed them, they were filtered by the earth as they passed through, leaving behind deposits in a multitude of shapes and colours, yellow and green and purple, like noxious forests in the depths. Beautiful. And deadly. But at the surface, harmless.

The foreigner was laughing. *Oh, you're wonderful.*

The orphan could hardly contain herself. She wanted to tell someone what she knew, to run down to the people in the silver suits and make them understand.

Is this proof then? Is this real?

It had to be real. It had to be. But even now, the doubter in her remained defiant. Had she been down there inside the earth? Had she seen those colours with her own eyes, or tasted the poisons on her own lips? Did she know for absolute certain it wasn't the madness putting lies and visions into her head?

Very well. If you need to see something with your own eyes, something you could not possibly have known about, then there's a place I can show you.

Where?

Go back down the path a bit, the way you came.

The orphan hesitated, but there was no way forward in any case. She took a last glance at the peak, then turned away and stumbled down the incline, sending small stones cascading ahead of her. For some time the foreigner did not speak, and the heat grew, and the orphan felt more and more thirsty.

Turn off the path here.

She veered off, skidding sharply down a scree of rubble and ash. Eventually she found herself in high grass. She kept descending, the sun burning on the back of her neck, and then abruptly she plunged into jungle. That was better. It was still hot under the canopy, but there was shade, and the pleasant smell of damp earth.

See, there's no path. Nothing has led you here but me.

It was true. The orphan could see no sign that anyone had ever been there. She was in a steep-walled gully. And what luck—there was a stream trickling along the gully floor. She fell to her knees and drank handfuls of water, only slightly muddied with ash. The foreigner waited until she was done.

Just a little way now, up the gully.

It was simplest to follow the stream. The gully climbed back towards the mountain, the sides becoming more sheer the further she went, until a darkness loomed ahead of her, and the rocky walls sprang up to meet overhead in an arch.

It was a tunnel. Running away into blackness.

You've never seen this before, I know. Neither have those scientists, although they would like to. But you're the first ever to come here.

The orphan stood on the boundary between daylight and dark, fascinated by the shadows ahead, cool and beckoning. What was this place?

It's called a lava tube.

Lava. The orphan did not know the word, but it made her think of something slow and heavy and hot. Yes, she saw it now. The melted, mushed-up stone that churned deep underground—that was lava.

But lava *tube* . . . what did that mean?

Some time, probably many thousands of years ago, this volcano was in eruption. In the process, a flow of lava spilled from a rift higher up the mountain, and flowed down into this gully. It cooled as it went, and the outer crust hardened into rock. Under that exterior, however, the lava kept flowing until it drained away completely and left the crust standing behind in the shape of this hollow tube.

The orphan was still staring in under the arch, her eyes adjusting to the dark. The tunnel was not as smooth as it had first appeared. In fact the walls and the floor were only crudely fashioned, widening and then narrowing again, irregular. Yes. The foreigner's explanation made sense. She could imagine the lava surging and slowing through here, and hardening unevenly, before draining away.

But could she go in?

Well . . .

How odd—was it reluctance she sensed in him? A wariness? Was something wrong? Was it unsafe to enter?

No, it's safe . . .

What then?

It's just that, even now, I still don't like going underground.

Of course! The orphan felt terrible for not realising it sooner. After everything he had been through beneath the landslide . . .

It's a fear I have to live with. Go in, if you want.

Was he certain?

I've been down far worse holes than this, I assure you.

She ventured inwards, stepping carefully because the floor was pitted with holes. Tree roots dangled down from the ceiling and brushed her face. When she looked up she saw that they grew through cracks in the roof, and here and there beams of sunlight stabbed down from the surface. But soon she was beyond the roots and the sunbeams, and only blackness waited ahead.

So why had the foreigner gone into holes, if he was afraid?

His reply was subdued. *There was no choice. I realised it even all those years ago, at the beginning of my new life. If I wanted to understand the workings of the earth, then at some point I would have to go beneath it.*

The orphan advanced. Despite the dark, some part of her mind remained aware of all the edges and pits in the ground, and she did not stumble.

The foreigner's voice dropped lower still. *To have escaped the earth once and then willingly go below its surface again, that was a dreadful thing. My first descent was into a coalmine. The terror I felt! Understand, mines in those days were little better than the landslide itself. Men died below ground by the hundreds. Poisoned by gases, or drowned by floods, or burnt by fires, or obliterated by explosions. But it wasn't those deaths I feared. I feared the collapse. The cave-in.*

I feared that I might be crushed again under a fall, or even worse, trapped on the wrong side of one, buried alive. I knew I could never go through that experience again.

For a moment the tube seemed to grow suffocating and hot around the orphan. It became an airless, lightless prison that she could never escape. Then the foreigner shrugged off the memory, and the heaviness lifted.

How I hated those places. And it turned out they had relatively little to tell me about the earth, anyway. What are mines, after all, but scratches on the surface, two or three kilometres deep? I needed to look much deeper.

This tube, for instance. How far down do you think it goes?

The orphan considered, letting her mind roam forward into the shadows. She could feel the bulk of the volcano rising away to the unreachable peak. And she could imagine the tube burrowing beneath it, all the way to the core, to join with the other fissures, leading downwards together in the twisting throat of the volcano, but descending ultimately to where the lava reserves lay sleeping.

Magma, actually. It's only called lava when it reaches the surface.

The orphan rolled another new word around her silent tongue, thinking that yes, it too sounded right, and *felt* right.

And below the magma chamber? What then?

She frowned. In none of her visions of the under-earth had she thought to go any deeper than those molten pools.

But you should. You've seen that the earth is shaped like a ball—but what's inside the ball? Is there anything at all in there? Or is it hollow?

Which stopped her short. It was true, a ball could be empty, she had seen that herself. The patients sometimes kicked a white ball around the hospital grounds, and it was only plastic, pumped up with air. Oh, but the scale of it! To think that the world might be just a thin shell around a vast empty nothingness.

Who says the space must be empty? Why could there not be an inner sun glowing at the centre of it? And why couldn't the interior side of the shell be populated with lands and buildings and people, all of it upside down?

Which stopped her short again. An *inside* world. The orphan felt an immediate attraction to the idea. Perhaps if she followed this very tunnel she would emerge, wrong way up, into an enormous space within the planet. And in the middle of the cavity, floating, would be another bright sun, illuminating oceans and mountains and plains as great as those outside. It would be a reverse world, the opposite of everything above, where there was no night, where the dumb could speak, where the slow would be quick, and where the mad would be the sane.

Could it be?

Ah . . . but no. Even as she delighted in the vision, she knew that it wasn't right. When she had beheld the planet spinning in the void, she had felt its weight, and the ponderous inertia that kept it revolving. It was not a thin-skinned bauble that could be punctured like a toy. The earth was solid, right through, she was sure of it.

The foreigner projected satisfaction. *Look then. Go as deep as you can.*

She did. She went searching downwards with her mind. But not in one hurried plunge, as she had before, but more deliberately this time, in great descending circles, careful to observe everything around her. Down through the base of the volcano she went, with its familiar rents and cracks, and then down through the base of the entire island, which was nothing but the remains of a larger and older volcano. She was spiralling outwards all the while, until, far down, she was beyond the island's foundation, and searching beneath the ocean floor.

Yes, but you are still only in the crust of the earth's surface, and the crust is at best only twenty or thirty kilometres thick. It holds the entire human realm, true, but on a planetary scale it's no more really than the skin that forms on soup.

And yet already she had found surprises, buried deep. Layers of brightly coloured stone that no sun would ever illuminate. Arched caverns where the air would never stir. Secret lakes of water, so motionless and clear they might have been glass, and rivers that roared and raged beyond hearing. And then there were dry places of a crystal hardness so sharp that even in thought they set the orphan's teeth on edge.

But in other places things *bubbled* down there. Liquids oozed and plopped amid the rock, sometimes in great masses trapped in domes, sometimes in a kind of oily sweat that permeated sheets of stone, black and slick and redolent with decay. There were gases too, greasy and invisible, squeezed into uneasy levels that rumbled with indigestion. Indeed, so much did the underworld squelch with sound and smell, it seemed to the orphan that the crust was not solid at all, but rather a layer of rotting mulch, like the compost heaps in the hospital gardens.

Deeper, girl, you must go deeper.

She went deeper, sinking still in slow spirals. Now she was into rock that was barren and parched, all cracked and folded back on itself in ways too tangled to unravel. Here and there she came across pockets of magma, similar to the chambers under her own volcano. They were like balloons that had ascended from below and were squashed now against the ceiling, trying to squeeze beyond it. From one such balloon, she found a thread of magma descending.

She followed the thread, twisting and turning through the rock, down, and then down further still.

You are entering what scientists call the mantle. And what you see here, far more than anything above, is the true substance of which the world is made.

It was getting very hot, and the rock was now soft and glowing. But more than heat, the orphan was becoming aware of *pressure*. Even as a disembodied mind she could feel the weight from above mounting and mounting. And eventually she was no longer following an isolated stream of magma, it was everywhere around her, mixing inextricably with the stone, until the entire under-level was a congealed, melting, swirling mass of rock that was not a liquid or a solid in any way that she knew.

The mantle goes down to a depth of thousands of kilometres, and the pressure becomes so intolerable that it changes all the rules. The rock here is not liquid, and yet it flows like liquid, it has currents and tides. Above us, the crust floats on those currents, and moves in great slabs, crashing slowly together. And if a crack should open between those slabs, this tortured stone will boil to the surface to explode.

But the orphan was diving deeper. More rapidly now, a plunge not a spiral, because she knew she would not be able to stand the pressure or the heat for long. Faster and faster, and there were no distinct layers anymore, nothing to see, there was only the uniform mush, growing hotter and hotter, and glowing brighter. And then abruptly she *was* in liquid, an ocean of it, infinitely wider and deeper than the seas of the surface above. But not an ocean of water, it was an ocean of *metal*.

This is the outer core. It's made of liquid iron, heated to incredible temperatures. But only a little further down, the pressure grows so indescribable that no matter what the temperature, the iron cannot stay in liquid form.

There! The orphan was at her utmost limit, but at the very centre of the planet she saw something that was indeed like a hidden sun after all, an inner sphere of agonised iron that was hard and huge and white hot, blazing.

And at the centre of that? At the centre of that?

She reached—

But could hold no longer. Her thoughts fled from the heat and pressure, and went tumbling away back to the surface.

The orphan opened her eyes and found that she was standing in the tunnel as before, but breathless now, a sheen of sweat on her skin, her legs quivering. She had been so close! Just a little further down, she was sure . . .

No, it was amazing you got as far as you did.

But she had wanted to see!

Never mind. No one else knows what lies at the very core, either. And for our purposes, it doesn't matter anyway.

The orphan was sucking in disappointed air. The gloom in the tunnel had dissipated—as if, having delved so deep, her eyes had no trouble at all piercing ordinary darkness. She saw now that only a few dozen yards ahead the tube came to an end. It wasn't blocked by some collapse or upheaval, it simply stopped there, and always had. There was no tunnel through to the heart of the volcano, or beyond it to some hollowed interior of the earth. It wasn't a tunnel at all, just a cavity that led nowhere.

Exactly. And what does that tell you?

But she felt too tired now for his riddles. She didn't know what it told her. It was time, she thought, to go home.

It is indeed. But think—if all this was truly a product of your madness, then a hollow earth is precisely the sort of thing you would have found today. Something dramatic, something fantastic. And this tunnel would have taken you there. Indeed, there are thousands of people around the world who believe in exactly such tunnels, and don't even know how mad they are. But you didn't find any such fantasy. You found what's really there—as confusing and complicated as it is. That isn't madness.

No. It wasn't. He was right about that . . .

And if none of that satisfies you, my orphan, then remember the simple fact of this tube's existence. Remember that no one else knows about it. That it's an undiscovered secret—and yet I led you right here.

Isn't that proof enough, finally, that I'm real?

And for the weary orphan, finally, it was.

12

It was a different orphan who arrived back at the hospital. She felt lighter. Cleansed somehow, despite being filthy with ash and sweat. It was relief, she knew. Her doubts had been settled. Now she could trust in the foreigner wholeheartedly; now she could accept, without all the misgivings, the happiness he brought her.

Good. Then we'll continue tonight.

She was standing at the hole in the back fence of the hospital grounds, and the sun was low in the afternoon sky. He had been with her all the way down the mountain, guiding her from the lava tube back to the path, and then home.

But what was it they had to continue?

Your education, of course.

Did he mean that there was still more of the underworld to explore?

Not for now. I have other things to show you first.

What things?

You'll see. Rest now, then come to me later, when everyone else is asleep.

And with that he was gone from the orphan's mind. For a moment she smiled up at the fading sky, as if to watch after him fondly. Then she slipped through the wire and made her way, unobserved, to her little hut. Throwing off her dirty clothes, she put on her bathrobe, went to the washroom and showered.

Then she got back to work.

She was exhausted, yes, but there was no question of her resting. She was too happy for one thing, but more importantly, she had missed an entire day of chores. Already it was time to help serve dinner. And her absence had been noticed. When she hurried into the kitchen, the cooks snapped grumpily at her and shook their ladles. She couldn't understand what they said, but she didn't need to. Where had she been all day?—that's what they meant. What did she think she was up to?

It was the same in the wards. There were certain inmates with whom she usually spent a little time in the afternoons, playing simple games or merely listening to their mad ramblings, but today there had been no chance. In fact, she had to admit that it had been several days since she had really sat with any of them. Now those patients were sulky and withdrawn with her. And the nurses, too, gave her some hard and wondering glances. It was as if she had never been away for a day before.

Well, actually, she hadn't. Never for a whole day. But the orphan found she didn't care. In a way, their puzzled expressions were almost funny. If people only knew what they looked like sometimes, the way their lips and eyes moved. The truth was, nothing could spoil her good mood. It was more than just relief, she realised—it was anticipation. She was looking forward to later in the night, when she could go and be with the foreigner again. Not just mentally, but in person, in his room, by his side.

In the meantime she ducked her head and hid her smile, and once dinner was over and the kitchen clean, she was free to take her mop and venture off into the more remote parts of the hospital, away from everyone else.

Normally she was happiest this way, working quietly by herself into the night—but for once the evening dragged. It was very hot, and the familiar chores were strangely frustrating. As always, she strove to perform them well, but tonight her mop felt stiffer than usual, the grime on the tiles seemed more deeply ingrained, and the sting of the cleaning solution in her nostrils was more galling. What was the point of mopping anyway? The floors would only be dirty again tomorrow.

Her mind wanted to be elsewhere. It wasn't even so much that she longed to be soaring again through the heights, or plunging into the fiery core of the planet, it was just that, after the visions she'd seen, the dreary rooms and hallways around her felt altogether too small. There wasn't an inch of them she didn't know and hadn't cleaned countless times before. How had she never noticed it previously? That for day after day, year after year, she had restricted herself to such tiny confines?

Madness, really. Another kind. But then no one had been able to show her what lay beyond. Not the doctors or the nurses, anyway. They weren't capable of it. It needed a special talent, which only the foreigner possessed. *He* was the real reason she couldn't focus on her work tonight. She was too distracted, waiting until she could go to him. She didn't think she'd ever experienced such an impatience before. Such a dissatisfaction with the present. Wanting time to move faster.

It didn't, of course. It moved slower. But eventually it was long past lights-out and all the day staff had gone home. That only left the night nurse. Normally he would stay in the front wards all night, no bother to her at all. But the orphan decided she should check on him. It wouldn't do if he came wandering.

On any other evening, she would have gone by the covered walkway to the front wards and then clumped noisily through the halls to find him. Most likely he would be in the office. But tonight she didn't want the night nurse to see her; he might assign her some menial task out of sheer mischief. So instead, after exiting the back wards, she left the walkway and circled around to the side of the front building.

In doing so, she became aware that this was another new experience—creeping about in the dark, trying not to be seen. Usually, no one really saw her anyway. But this was different. For once it was her choice to be invisible. The thought made her smile. She felt conscious of everything; the darkness around her, the warm air, the murky stars, the smell of the grass and the jungle, the noises of insects.

The front wards were mostly blacked out, but light shone from the office, and the sounds of a radio drifted through the open window. The orphan edged carefully across a dusty flowerbed and peered over the window sill. The night nurse was there, on the far side of the room, sitting side-on to her, his feet on the desk, his shirt open to catch the breeze from the old electric fan. He appeared to be reading a magazine.

The orphan shook her head. He was so lazy! At best he might rouse himself to stroll through the back wards around dawn, to make sure that all was in order before the day staff returned. Useless. Why did the old doctor even put up with him? The previous night nurse had been a cheerful old man who not only kept a proper eye on the inmates, he had sometimes even helped the orphan with the cleaning. But when he had retired, this sneering, superior youth had taken his place.

She found herself studying his bare arms and chest. He had an ugly face, no doubt, but as much as she squirmed now to remember it, for a few weeks after his arrival she had actually considered him attractive. His body was slim and smooth, after all, and there was a certain languid grace about him. Indeed, she had briefly, alone in her bed at night, fingers between her legs, imagined him there with her.

But all too soon she'd realised that what she'd mistaken for languid grace was actually more a stubborn stupidity, and that there was nothing else to him. He was just a spoilt, selfish, half-grown boy. And how inferior that made him, compared to a *man* like the foreigner. Even helpless and passive as he was, the foreigner radiated such assurance, such maturity. His experiences had honed and strengthened him. *He* wasn't lazy, or selfish. *He* was an adult. And his body was adult too.

The night nurse stirred, glanced around the room quickly, then turned the page of his magazine. The orphan noted that the paper seemed to have no writing on it. It was only colours and shapes. And yet the night nurse studied it intently. Then, after another glance around, he moved his hand down into his pants.

Oh! He was going to do *that?* The orphan couldn't help it—she was too buoyant: she laughed. Right out loud.

The nurse surged from his chair, magazine flying, hands yanking his pants up, his face red as he stared about. The orphan couldn't stop laughing, it was just too funny, she was nearly doubled over, stumbling backwards through the garden. But by then he'd spotted her and was at the window, yelling furiously. In fact, he was climbing *through* the window, his fists clenched like he meant to murder her.

She ran, still laughing. It didn't even matter that he was chasing her. What could a boy like him do anyway? She was tougher than him. In fact, that was part of the fun, running in the darkness, darting under trees and around corners, his angry yells falling further behind. He would never catch her. She was outside herself, floating slightly above, so that the hospital was laid out below. She could weave about the buildings effortlessly. And she could see the night nurse circling blindly in her wake.

She paused in a cranny behind the laundry to catch her breath, and to try to still the gasps of laughter. From the other side completely of the back wards she heard a last frustrated shout from him and, by some fluke, for the first time in days she understood his words exactly. He was calling her nosy and retarded and stupid and a bitch and she better watch out next time—which only elicited a final smile from her.

Silly boy, playing with himself. Ha!

She watched from her mind's vantage point as he gave up and plodded back towards the office. But then suddenly all the laughter was gone, and instead the foreigner was there inside her head, cool and controlled.

It's time, he said.

At last! She hurried off towards the crematorium, wondering at the excitement in her. Was she . . . ? Yes, she was; the chase, the laughing, even the idiot night nurse reaching into his pants—it had all put her in a mood, there was no denying it. She thought of the foreigner's body again, lying there under the single sheet. But that was crazy. He couldn't move, and anyway, something was surely wrong about even thinking—

You seem disturbed.

Mortified, she covered her thoughts as best she could.

Has someone upset you this evening?

No, no . . .

And thankfully, he did not press. She was already inside, and coming down the hallway to the crematorium. All was silent and dark. In the little dayroom, the television was switched off. Good. They would not be disturbed.

Except—

She paused, listening. There was a sound from one of the bedrooms. She was so eager to get to the foreigner that she almost chose to ignore it. But then it came again. A stifled sob, from the men's bedroom. The orphan went to the door and looked in. A pale light came through the window, illuminating the two beds. In one, the archangel slept, stretched out like a fallen tree, stomach down, his book tucked under his chin. The other bed was empty. And in the corner, staring up at the window, was the duke, his mouth a cut of misery, his face glistening with tears.

The orphan stared. What was wrong with the old man? Was he in pain? She approached him, cautious despite her concern. She had not forgotten how enraged he'd been during their last encounter, the day after the eruption. Yet there didn't seem to be any rage in him now. His head was thrown back abjectly and his shoulders shook as he cried.

The foreigner was in her head. *What are you doing?*

Couldn't he see? The duke was distraught about something.

So? He's mad.

Was that all he had to say? The old man needed help!

There's nothing you can do for him.

But a flush of guilt had come over the orphan. In her preoccupation, she had been neglecting people like the duke. Why, she couldn't remember the last time she had walked with him in the yard, and she knew how much he liked her company.

Ah. Well, you must be prepared for that. You'll have less time for him now. Him, and all the other inmates.

But they were her friends. They needed her.

It's hard, I know, but our own business is more urgent.

It was? But why?

You'll understand eventually. Hurry now.

Her eagerness flared again—that voice, so close, so strong, wanting her—but she resisted. She was not going to leave the old man until she had comforted him. In fact, wasn't there something the foreigner could do?

I'm no doctor. Or psychiatrist.

But he could enter people's thoughts! If he would just look in the old man's head, maybe he could see what the problem was.

There came a sigh. *Very well.*

The orphan felt his presence withdraw from her, and she waited. The duke fell silent, his eyes widening in the darkness. Then—

Bring him to my room.

He would help the old man?

If I can. The foreigner sounded oddly moved. *And as it happens, his madness may be instructive to you and me.*

In what way?

Just bring him.

She did as she was told. The duke was still silent and staring, but it was only a matter of pulling gently on his hand to lead him out of the bedroom, through the dayroom, and then down the short hall to the furnace room.

The foreigner lay motionless in his bed, his blank eyes wide open.

Good. Sit him in the chair.

She did so, and the old man sat obediently. He seemed dazed. She wasn't sure he even knew where he was.

She turned to the foreigner. Well?

112

It's curious, you know. The more I look into the minds in this hospital, the more diverting I find it. You, of course, are the miracle. But even this old man . . . He's mad, no doubt, but what strange truths lie beneath his madness.

Now the duke's eyes were moving about the room, as if he could hear voices, but couldn't see where they came from.

Truths? What truths?

For one thing, did you know he really was a duke?

The orphan creased her brow. A duke?

Effectively. He was a very rich man. A great landowner. Or the son of one, anyway. It's all there in his memory. His family used to own half this island. In fact, they lived in this very hospital, years ago, back when it was a private residence.

The orphan stared at the old man. So he really *did* own the hospital, just as he always claimed?

His family did, yes. I suppose hardly anyone else remembers it. Poor old fool. Who would credit it, to look at him now?

But the foreigner could see it, in the duke's head?

Oh yes. It's like a waking dream for him. When he walks around this place, he doesn't see a rotting old hospital. He doesn't see the dark hallways and the little cells. He sees big rooms and polished wood and fine furniture.

The orphan glanced about. The heavy walls of the furnace pressed close, yet even so, she caught a glimpse from the foreigner's words of some other place. As if, fleetingly, all the tattered and tacked-on parts of the building were being stripped away, all the internal halls and wards, to leave a spacious and cool interior, lit by tall windows with white curtains flowing . . .

The old man was gazing at the walls too, smiling now.

The past is where his madness takes him. His youth. He was born and raised here, the oldest son of the family. They were local aristocracy, allied to the old colonial powers. They were exceedingly rich. They owned the entire upland plateau.

What—the plantations? The town? All of it?

There was no town then. Only a village for the family retainers. The view was very different from what it is today.

And this time the foreigner did not even need to speak the words, the vision swirled palpably before the orphan's eyes. The walls of the furnace fell away, and she felt she was sitting in the shadows of a deep veranda, and beyond it was a green garden of grass and flowerbeds and fountains tinkling. And beyond that, where in reality there was now a wall of trees and scrub, everything was cleared and open.

Why, she could see right across the island! But it was nothing like the island she knew. The motley plantation blocks, the patches of scrub and wasteland, they were gone. Indeed there seemed to be hardly any scrub left at all, apart from pockets in the steeper folds of land. Otherwise the rolling uplands were entirely cultivated and ordered. There was no sign of the ramshackle town with all its tin roofs and red dust, there was only a neat little hamlet enfolded by green fields and drainage canals.

And all of it was . . . The orphan paused. For a moment it had felt like it was all *hers*. The sense of possession had flooded into her as warmly as sunlight. All this land, all this prosperity, all this beauty, it was *owned* by her.

The duke was laughing, spittle stringing in his mouth.

The view is deceptive. What you couldn't see from here—what the duke himself never saw—was the big town on the coast.

All was not quite so idyllic there. It was crowded with refugees. The duke's father had spent the previous decades driving all the small landholders off the plateau and down to the slums. He needed their land to grow his sugar cane. It was a common enough pattern in places like these, shifting the population, stripping the hills.

There was resistance, of course, and anger in the big town. But the duke's father had the colonial authorities on side, and armed men to see off the aggrieved peasants. Indeed, the young duke himself was known to smash the heads of anyone who came trespassing. This was his land, nothing was going to change that.

The duke had stopped laughing, uncertainty in his eyes.

But then the colonial powers departed, and there was chaos and revolution. About fifty years ago now, when the duke here was twenty-one—the same age as you—a mob swarmed up the hill and overran the house. The young man managed to hide, but his mother and father and sisters were dragged outside and beaten. Then they were locked in the distillery—it was a big building, where the vegetable garden now stands—and all the molasses and rum stored there was set alight, and them along with it.

The old man had hunkered down now, hands to his ears.

The duke heard their screams as they died, but stayed in his hiding place. And from that point on, he was never quite right again.

The orphan didn't understand. That was when he went mad?

Oh, I wouldn't say mad, not right away. Indeed, after the mob was gone, he was sane enough to fight for his inheritance. He went to the authorities—the new ones—and demanded justice in the courts. It went on for years. But in the end they threw him out and broke up his land and seized his house to use as a hospital. It was only in those later days, and only gradually—homeless, scorned—that he went insane. That's when he started to attack people who were living on his old property. That's when the authorities said enough, and locked him up—in his own house, no less.

And here he's been ever since. He spent sixteen years in the locked ward before anyone thought to let him out, and after so long in there,

*raving and ranting and beating himself senseless against the walls,
well . . . Now he spends his days convinced he still lives in the home
of his childhood. And mostly the delusion is complete enough to keep
him happy. Except, that is, when a volcano erupts next door.*

But why? What was so terrible about the eruption?

*So much quaking and thunder—no delusion could hide that. The
upheaval frightened him out of his dream. But it was the ash that
disturbed him most, raining down over his lovely home and garden.
Ash everywhere, just as there was after the mob burnt his family alive.
That's the memory he is tortured by now.*

The orphan gazed at the duke, curled up with his eyes tightly
shut. No wonder he had been so upset that day in the garden! And
right now they were making it even worse, stirring up his unhappy
history. This wasn't what she had intended, bringing him here.
She'd hoped that the foreigner could *help* him.

I can't effect any kind of real healing. But . . .

A soothing wash seemed to flow through the air, and the orphan
again sensed beautiful rooms around her, and green gardens
outside. The duke's taut body relaxed suddenly, and he slumped
back, groaning in relief.

There. His delusions are intact once more.

The orphan was gratified. Perhaps it wasn't a cure, but nevertheless . . .

Well, I do feel for the old fool. We're kindred in a way, he and I.

Kindred?

*That's why I had you bring him here. I was planning to speak of
such things tonight in any case. For I too was a rich man once, and
I too lost it all through a similar kind of presumption. His story mirrors
my own.*

The orphan studied the foreigner's supine form. Rich? What
did he mean, rich? He had been a poor man. A goatherd. Even in

his second life, after the mountain fell on him and he became a student, he had still been poor.

Good. You remember. A poor student I was indeed. But it's time I took up the tale again, for I did not stay a poor student forever.

Oh, admittedly, in those early days wealth was the last thing on my mind. My studies were all that mattered—my quest to understand the violent workings of the world. I laboured in that cause for many years, and gave no thought to money.

My research took me from university to university, and indeed from country to country, for my homeland was still impoverished, with lesser academic facilities than some, and I felt no particular loyalty to it. I went where the learning was best, and I excelled. I won scholarships. I spoke internationally at conferences. I became known, in academic circles, for my field work, and for the risks I would take to obtain data. Some considered me reckless. Fearless, perhaps.

I wasn't fearless. I still dreaded pain and suffering. It was just that I dreaded ignorance even more. So I tunnelled underground, and climbed over fault lines. I sailed across the oceans, and dived as deep into their depths as I could go. I chased storms across the plains, and huddled on the rims of volcanoes until my clothes caught fire. I stood in the paths of tornadoes, and before the muddy walls of flash floods. I went wherever the world killed people, and I became a master of my field.

And yet after a decade and more had passed, for all my accomplishments, I found myself haunted by a sense of failure. I knew so much, you see, and yet I was still no closer to understanding what had happened to me when the mountain fell. Oh, I had fully grasped the mechanics of earthquakes and landslides by then. But that was no answer to what I'd experienced that day. I hadn't simply been caught in a landslide. I'd been singled out—first to suffer to the verge of death at the hands of the earth, and then, alone of all such victims, I had been singled out to live. No mechanics could explain that.

More disturbingly, I was not sure I cared anymore. As the years had passed, the memory of being trapped—a memory I'd thought would plague me forever—had faded. I began to wonder again if it had really happened. After all, I was alive and healthy, I no longer even had a scar to show for it, so how could it be true? Perhaps it was just a fantasy of my youth, and this whole quest of mine was meaningless.

I looked around me then, full of doubt. I saw that the knowledge I possessed had other uses. Colleagues of mine were being taken up by wealthy companies searching for oil and gas and minerals. There was a growing demand for these things in the more modern countries, and huge amounts of money to be made. And suddenly it seemed idiocy to condemn myself to the sparse existence I'd been living, all to no avail anyway. I decided to stop pursuing an old dream, and to accept cold reality.

I decided I may as well get rich.

I hired myself out to mining companies at first, surveying. I had an instinct about the earth, and an uncanny talent for uncovering its hidden riches. I was paid extremely well for my services, and within ten years of abandoning my academic career—and a full twenty-five years after the landslide—I was so successful that I controlled mining companies of my own. And not only mining companies. I expanded into oilfields and power stations and refineries, too. It was the perfect time for such investments. Another world war was looming, and the demand for resources would soon be insatiable.

In fact, I doubt that I can explain to you how rich I eventually became. You have no way of understanding. But I was far richer than the duke and his family could ever have dreamt. I could buy anything I liked. I possessed enormous tracts of land all over the world, and was free to do anything I wanted with that land. Level hills, dam rivers.

And I would laugh—why had I wasted so much time trying to understand the way the earth worked, when I could control it myself, change it to fit my own desires? Who cared if a mountain had fallen on me, when I could remove mountains entirely!

The duke was sleeping fast now, and the orphan had forgotten about him anyway. In the darkness, the foreigner's pale body had begun to glow faintly, or so it seemed to her night eyes. She felt an irresistible desire to touch him, and knew that it was at his command. She knelt at the bedside and took hold of his lifeless fingers. His eyes stared directly upwards, at nothing.

It was intoxicating, that wealth. I felt invulnerable. Powerful. Virtually immortal. And yet, like the duke and his family, all the while I was courting disaster.

The planet had not forgotten me.

The sensation of rushing through air came to the orphan again, as if a sudden storm was in the room, but silent. The floor seemed to sink away, and she knew the foreigner was taking her somewhere, into his own memories again, as he had when he'd first carried her to his icy valley home.

Not there this time, but to another place, in another country, far from there. And not then, but more than thirty years—a whole lifetime, as I'd lived it—later.

I want to show you the second time I died.

13

She seemed to cover half the globe in a leap.

It wasn't the same as when she and the foreigner flew together, gliding smooth and serene above the earth. This was an incoherent tumble. Nor was the foreigner a shadow shape at her side. Perhaps he could not appear that way in his own memory. But he was a presence in her mind, nonetheless.

The wind rushed around her, and despite her tumbling the orphan glimpsed a sparkling ocean below, and clouds towering. Then, abruptly, she was skimming over land, a great expanse of it, wide and flat and vaster than anything she had seen before, covered with thick jungle and carved by muddy rivers.

And then she was slowing, and descending. The jungle thinned away to scrub and grass, and here and there villages of small huts were visible. Up ahead was a tangle of hills, draped in green. Cattle grazed on the slopes. And cradled in the middle of the hills, surrounded by low cliffs, was a lake.

The foreigner's voice was close.

It all happened shortly after the world's second great war had come to an end. In search of gold deposits, I had acquired the mineral rights to the land you see here. The lake, and the hills around it, with permission, fairly bought, to do as I pleased. This was in . . . well, a wild and poor and somewhat lawless country.

The orphan was drifting now over the surface of the lake. The water was a profound blue, and eerily calm, the surrounding heights seemingly protecting it from any wind. In one direction, however, the cliffs fell away to a valley, a fertile place of villages and fields, where strange-looking people tended cattle.

But the lake, as it turned out, was my downfall.

She was on the ground now, standing at the lake's edge. The water looked even darker from this angle, and the cliffs higher. The orphan was aware of heat and stillness. Cattle lowed from far off, and there was another sound, the clink of tools striking earth. Some distance around the shore, men were at work, digging.

Do you see them? They are labourers in my employ.

The situation was this—my goldmining operation needed water, lots of it, and the only source in the area was the lake. My engineers said that if we cut a channel through the lowest point in the hills, we could siphon off all we needed into holding tanks down in the valley. As a solution it was simple and cheap—and it would lower the level of the lake by only a few feet. Insignificant, I thought.

The natives, though, were alarmed. They warned me that I should not touch the lake at all, that it was cursed, that it had killed people in the past when roused. I laughed at them. They were tribal cattle herders—what would they know? Besides, I owned it, it was mine, even if the natives didn't realise their government had sold it to me.

So I went ahead and cut the channel and began the draining. I wasn't there in person, you understand. I was busy elsewhere, this was just one project among many. But about a week after the channel was opened, I flew in to visit the site. Everything was working exactly as it should. Only, there was something odd about the lake.

The scene altered before the orphan's eyes. The men working on the shore vanished, and now there was a low structure of concrete and piping there. But her attention was drawn to the lake itself. Its colour had changed. The deep blue had been replaced by a milkier shade. And there was a sound. Like the whisper of a far-off wind, even though there was no wind.

What I didn't know—what no one knew at the time, because this phenomenon occurs at only two other lakes in the world—was what lay at the bottom.

The orphan was lifted from the bank and plunged into the water. There was a slap of cold, but it was a distant sensation, only a memory of being submerged. At first it was dark as she dived down, but then, by an act of the foreigner's will, the entire lake became translucent for her. She felt a sudden vertigo, alarmed by the sight of sheer cliffs plummeting away to a jagged bed far below, a great underwater pit.

The lake is four hundred metres deep, which is quite extraordinary. It is, in fact, the crater of an ancient volcano. But there have been no eruptions here in millennia, and there won't be ever again. The danger here is not from an eruption, but from something more insidious. Can you see it, below the ground?

The orphan extended her inner vision, pushing through the crater floor. She was searching for the familiar red-hot regions of magma, but there was nothing—at least, not until she was far, far down, and even then it was only a dimly glowing pool, a magma that was barely molten at all, a chamber that was congealed.

Yes, but look closer.

She did—and then saw it. Leaking up from the magma, insinuating itself through tiny cracks and fissures, came a trickle of gas. Not a rush, nothing that would make the ground rumble or smoke belch forth. Just a trickle. Nevertheless, it worked its way up through the earth remorselessly, and thus emerged at the bottom of the crater, into the waters of the lake. But it didn't then bubble and froth in the water as the orphan would have expected. Instead it simply . . . melted away.

Pressure, that's what's happening. If the lake wasn't so deep, then the gas—it's called carbon dioxide—would indeed foam up to the surface. But under this much weight, it can't form bubbles, so it's forced to dissolve into the water and stay at the bottom. It's the same set of conditions that you would find in a bottle of fizzy drink: as long as the lid stays on the bottle, the fizz stays dissolved in the liquid. Except that this is on a scale billions of times greater. The carbon dioxide has been gathering down here for hundreds of years, maybe thousands, unimaginable amounts of it. Trapped.

The orphan was ascending again, quickly. Towards the surface she was aware of tiny streams of bubbles rising alongside her in the water. Only a few tiny little streams. But then another would appear, and another.

We removed just a few feet from the top of the lake, as I said. But in doing so we released a crucial amount of pressure. And worse, we created currents that swirled down to the bottom, and allowed the first few streams of gas to escape. Those streams created convection currents that increased exponentially, until a flash-over point was reached, and then, in one explosive rush, the whole bottom of the lake—

The orphan broke through the surface and lifted into the air. Below her the lake was now a stark, seething white, and the subtle sound that she'd heard before had become an all-pervasive and vastly frightening *hiss*.

Basically, we shook the bottle, then opened the cap.

She lifted away, towards the lower rim of the crater, where the fields extended down to the villages. Behind her, the hiss became a roar, and then deepened further still, until it was the most awful thunder the orphan had ever heard. The lake was upending itself, but she could not bring herself to look back and see.

I didn't see it either. Oh, I heard it. People heard it twenty miles away. But I was indoors, in an office, down in the valley.

The terrible thunder went on, but the orphan swept downhill and then landed, not far from where a herd of cattle grazed, and where some villagers stood in shock, staring back towards the cataclysm. Beyond them was a complex of offices and sheds, newly built. Dozens of men had come running out. They too were staring up at the lake in awe. And the orphan saw that one of them was . . . yes, the foreigner himself.

He no longer resembled the goatherd who had been crushed under the landslide. He was much older, and more solid. A stronger, richer, more important man. There was no sign at all of the crippling injuries he had borne the last time she had seen him. Nor did he resemble the pale, bedridden figure back in the hospital room. This was a different time, a different life. Yet she would have recognised him anywhere. His expression was puzzled, but quite unafraid as he gazed up at the rim of the crater.

The roaring sound was fading now.

By the time I got outside, the water had fallen back into place and there was only some lingering spray visible. I thought that perhaps it was an earthquake—and I remember thinking how lucky we were that the lake hadn't overflowed.

I couldn't see the gas, of course. Later estimates suggested that as much as three cubic kilometres of carbon dioxide escaped that day. It lifted in a great cloud above the lake. Quite invisible. And it isn't that carbon dioxide is dangerous in itself. It's not a poison. The deadly thing about it in this case is that it's heavier than air.

The orphan finally turned to look. A mist of reddish-white spray was settling back into the lake, but above there seemed to be only empty air. With her other senses, however, she could detect something quite unnerving—an immense dome of gas that had *displaced* the air. And that dome was slowly collapsing. It was heavy, the foreigner had said, and she could see that it was. It reminded her of a bottle of honey, flipped over. It had already filled the bowl of the crater, and now there was nowhere else for it to go. It oozed over the lip, and came advancing down the hill. But no one around her screamed or ran, because no one could see it.

I repeat, humans and animals can tolerate small amounts of carbon dioxide. Even in somewhat larger doses it will only make them ill. But if carbon dioxide replaces the air entirely, and there's nothing else to inhale . . .

Closest to the crater were the cattle. For no apparent reason, they suddenly tottered and dropped to the ground. A flock of birds on the wing—disturbed by the earlier thunder, and still circling above—all stalled in mid-flight and tumbled earthwards. Then the group of villagers who had been watching on—men, women and some children—took a few convulsive steps, knees buckling, and sank as one into the grass.

All of this in total silence.

Suffocation.

Now there were screams. The natives were running. The other men, the miners, were swearing and dashing for their offices, or for their vehicles. But the cries were as much of confusion as they were of fear, for no one could identify the threat. People and animals were falling as if struck by unseen lightning. No one knew where to run, which direction would be safe. Only the orphan could see that in fact nowhere would be safe. The wave of gas was too huge, too high, too wide.

She turned again to look at the man who was the foreigner. He hadn't run like the others. He was staring in what appeared to be rapture at the hillside above him—as if maybe he alone could see what she saw.

No. But I knew, somehow, that there was no escape.

Then the wave was upon them. There was no sensation, other than a tug of warm wind as the breathable air was pushed away, and they were in the gas. To the orphan it felt that an extra layer of humidity had settled over them. Heavy. Clammy. In an instant more the feeling became horrible. Choking. An unreadable emotion flickered across the foreigner's face. And then he, like everyone else, was slowly falling.

Alone, the orphan watched the wave continue down the hill. People still ran before it, and even the cattle had taken fright, but the tide engulfed human and animal alike, cutting them down in rows. Then it piled sluggishly onto the valley floor, filling the depression steadily from end to end. The orphan could count three villages down there, home to what must have been hundreds of people, but there was nothing anyone could do; they died just as the others had, some in the open, some having fled into their huts, some huddled in ditches and some, in vain, climbing trees.

The cloud of gas sloshed back and forth a few times from one side of the valley to the other. Exhausted finally, it pooled and thickened and began to sink slowly into the ground. Equally slowly, the air returned, until the day around the orphan seemed as normal as any other. It wasn't even that long since the surface of the lake had started to bubble; the sun had scarcely shifted in the sky. But now nothing moved anywhere within the orphan's sight, and nowhere in the hills was there a single sound.

The scene blurred and disappeared.

The orphan floated in darkness.

Can you imagine what I felt—the foreigner seemed to be speaking to her from a void, an empty space in his mind, an absence of even the memory of light—*in those few moments as I struggled to breathe the unbreathable? As the world spun and went dark around me? As I realised that I was dying?*

Anger? Oh yes. And fear, and bewilderment. But mostly I felt a piercing sense of awakening, of belated revelation. What a fool I had been to waste my second life. What a fool I had been to give up my quest to understand the mysteries of the earth. And as proof of that foolishness, the earth was killing me again.

The thought came to the orphan—this void from which his voice seemed to originate, was this where people went when they died?

Forty-three mine workers were killed along with me, and over four hundred of the local people. It must have been terrible for the first person who stumbled upon the disaster—so many bodies lying about peacefully, as if asleep, as if slain by the darkest of magic. Indeed, it would take scientists months to figure out what had really occurred. In the meantime, there were all those corpses to dispose of. And that was where I awoke again—it was days later, I don't know how many—in an uncovered burial pit.

So he hadn't died after all?

You don't understand.

The void was suddenly gone, and the darkness became a close, fetid thing, unbearably hot. The orphan felt a weight upon her, fleshy and liquid. It was made up of people. Arms. Legs. Torsos. Decomposing. Heaped about her.

I had most certainly died. Just as I had also, almost certainly, died that day under the landslide, even if at the time I did not recognise it.

She felt her body stir, but her own limbs were rotten. Muscles had turned to mush, sinews were peeling away from bones. To move was agony, all jerking and clumsy. But to stay buried was unendurable, and so she fought against the weight, and great chunks of decayed flesh sloughed off her, reeking horribly.

It was not that I couldn't be killed, as I had once thought. I could die sure enough. I was subject to all the agonies of death.

But the pit was too deep, the bodies too liquefied, she was sinking now, and she could not close her mouth to the vile fluid; her lips had peeled away to naked teeth.

It was just that, afterwards, I was forced to come back.

The orphan was trying to scream, but her throat was clogged with filth and only a strangled moan emerged. But no, the sound wasn't her. It wasn't the foreigner either. And then the pit and the darkness were gone. The orphan opened her eyes and she was back in the furnace room, kneeling at the foreigner's bedside.

But the moaning went on. It was the duke. He was thrashing in the chair, his eyes still closed, but there was no peace in him anymore. He seemed to be struggling with a nightmare, groaning in fear, and the orphan knew instantly that he was the one now buried in the pit, drowning in all the bodies.

She grabbed his shoulders and shook him awake. But when the old man's eyes opened, he only stared at her wildly and bucked against her restraining arms. His terror flooded into the orphan's mind, and for a moment she occupied his nightmare as if it was her own. He didn't know where he was. His safe world of delusion was gone. His lovely house and its gardens had vanished. Instead, he was trapped in a squalid little room.

And there were monsters there. A sweating fat girl with brutal hands and wide, idiot eyes was holding him down. And nearby was a dead man in a bed—all mangled and hideously burnt, but somehow alive. And they were both inside his mind, tearing it, eating it, they would kill him . . .

The orphan pulled back, lifting her hands.

Ignore him. He's hallucinating, that's all.

But this was their fault! Their trip into the foreigner's memory had overflowed somehow into the old man's head.

It won't do him any real harm. He'll forget it before long.

No, that wasn't good enough. The duke didn't deserve it. The foreigner had to put him to sleep again, like he had before.

If you insist. But then there was a pause. *And yet . . . well, why not? Why should it be me? Why don't you help him?*

The orphan stared. She couldn't help. She had no idea how. The foreigner was the one who could alter people's minds, not her.

You won't know if you don't try.

She heard his urgency. This was something important he was asking, some measurement of her he wished to make. She turned to the duke and tried to project calmness towards him, and peace, and safety. And a force did indeed seem to emanate from her, like faint hands, to curl around the old man's head, stroking and soothing. But he only trembled all the more and slobbered in his terror.

That won't work. It's not a matter of comfort—he's too far gone for that. It's a matter of knocking him out, stopping him cold.

Annoyed, she tried to infuse the duke's mind with weariness. Exhaustion. To make the old man go to sleep. But the inside of his head was squirming, and no matter how much she tried to allay his panic, the squirming only got worse.

Pity is no use here. Force him!

And in her frustration she squeezed his mind as hard as she could between her imaginary hands, not caring if it hurt him, only willing him to stop his moaning and quivering, and go to sleep!

And it worked. Abruptly, the old man stiffened, reared up, and then slumped back into the chair, unconscious.

The orphan wiped sweat from her face.

What had she done? What had she been made to do?

How very interesting, was all the foreigner said.

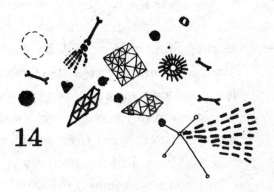

14

Late next morning, as the orphan was sweeping out the covered walkway, the old doctor came looking for her.

She had not yet slept, even though the foreigner had long since withdrawn, leaving her head empty of any voice. She had lain down for a short time before dawn, but sleep had refused to come. Her mind was too full of the night, and her body had seemingly forgotten how to rest.

Now, her eyes red with fatigue, the orphan saw that the old doctor was carrying his black bag, and holding it up for her to see, grinning. Which could mean only one thing—that a whole year had gone by since the last time, and today was the day he was due to go into town to give the schoolchildren their injections.

She felt a dull dismay. Oh, any day but *today* . . .

The old doctor always took her along on these visits. As his assistant. His nurse. It was his special treat for her. Their private game, one she had always delighted in. And his expression now was so expectant of pleasing her—how could she possibly explain that this year she wasn't in the mood for it at all?

She couldn't. It would hurt his feelings. There was nothing for her to do but smile back brightly, nod, and then go and change her clothes.

She made her way to her room. Earlier, when she'd returned there in the pre-dawn darkness, she'd found it in chaos—the mattress flung from the bed, her clothes scattered across the floor. The night nurse's revenge, no doubt, for her catching him with his hand down his pants. But he'd done no real damage, and all was neat and tidy now. She opened the cupboard and took out a white dress, crisp and clean, straight from the laundry where it had gone after she'd last worn it a year ago.

It was a nurse's uniform. The old doctor had given it to her to wear on these very occasions. It was second-hand, but its previous owner must have been short and round and big-breasted, because it fit the orphan perfectly, in a way none of her other clothes ever did. Usually, just putting it on was a thrill. It made her feel so adult. But now, when she yanked off her elastic-waisted pants and shapeless top and wriggled into the dress, studying herself in the mirror, she wasn't so sure.

She noticed for the first time how drab her sandals looked in comparison. Really, she needed a pair of good shoes to go with the dress. And properly grown-up women, when they went out, wore jewellery, and make-up. She didn't have any of that. She looked only half an adult, she decided. And half a silly child.

Then she was frowning at the mirror. Last night, she had beheld herself through the duke's eyes. And he had not seen a child, or a woman, or indeed anything that was properly human. He had seen a squat, malignant figure. A monster. Her.

But that wasn't fair. She wasn't a monster! She was nice, she'd never harmed another person in her life. It was the foreigner who . . . well, what *had* he done exactly? Certainly the old man had not been physically injured. And afterwards the orphan had taken him back to his bed and left him there, tucked in and sleeping peacefully. He would recover, his experience no worse, surely, than a bad dream.

Besides, it was all for the good, it was all for . . .

She faltered. It *was* for the good, wasn't it? That she was learning about the workings of the world? That the foreigner was telling her the story of his long life? Of his *lives*? Of course, yes, it had to be. He couldn't be doing anything wrong, not the foreigner. Not someone so wise, and strong, and beautiful.

The duke was insane anyway. What did it matter if he saw her as a monster? He had seen the foreigner as repulsive and *dead*, and that was ridiculous.

She shook her head at the mirror, smoothed a few wrinkles over her hips, then hurried out to the front of the hospital. The old doctor was waiting for her, and together they set off on foot down the dusty track towards town. Behind them, the peak of the volcano was lost in haze, and around them the jungle steamed as a thousand insects buzzed and droned. There would be a storm by nightfall, the orphan could tell, but for now it was very hot. She was sweating and itching before they were even halfway there, and stains under her arms were ruining her dress.

Then the scrub gave way to naked red soil and garbage piles and huts, and suddenly they were in the town, and people were everywhere. Motorbikes whined. Vans beeped their horns. Static blared from radios, and animals screeched from cages. As always, the orphan fought against a momentary panic, taken back in memory to her childhood, when she had lived here with her mother. Home then had been a bare room above a laundry, with the din of arguing neighbours cutting through the thin walls and an angry landlord always hammering on the door. And out in the streets the orphan had been forever in the way, constantly tripped over and trampled underfoot.

But the unease passed. She was with the old doctor now and everyone made way for him respectfully, allowing her to trail safely in his wake. They proceeded through the market square and came to the school. It was enclosed by a concrete wall, and a gate led through to the yard, a square of hard clay, worn shiny smooth by thousands of small feet. The orphan remembered this too, especially the long moments of standing alone under the hot sun as the rest of the children pointed and laughed.

But today the children were waiting politely, lined up in rows. The old doctor consulted with the teachers, and then set himself up on a bench beneath the playground's one shady tree. The orphan stood at his side, ready with the box of syringes, and that to *these* children at least she was no target for laughter. To them she was a real nurse, an object of some awe. Which had always been part of the fun, in the past. And normally, too, she enjoyed watching the children's faces as they stepped forth to be injected, some of them scared, some not, and some—approaching with tears in their eyes yet offering up their arms anyway—adorably brave.

Today however . . . Maybe it was just that she couldn't understand anyone's speech anymore—not the doctor's, not the teachers', not the children's. But whatever the reason, the orphan felt detached from the event. Even the admiring looks from the children were colourless somehow. She wasn't really a nurse, so it was all counterfeit. She wasn't even needed here. The old doctor could have done it alone.

She watched the back of his head as he worked, her feelings about him suddenly confused. He had looked after her faithfully for years, ruling over the clutch of nurses who had been her dozen surrogate mothers. She had no father, she knew, but the old doctor was the closest thing to it. She was very fond of him, and saddened too these last years as she had seen him become thin and unwell.

But what drew him to her? Kindness and pity, that's what it was. Even these trips to the school—yes, it was lovely of him to let her come and pretend to be important. But it was pity that lay at the base of his actions, and only pity. She would never be genuinely talented or clever or useful in his eyes.

Not like she was with the foreigner.

Ha. Yes. No wonder she was so bored with playing at being a nurse. With *him*, there was no need to play at being anything. He had shown her how worthwhile she was, how important her talents were, and how they were *real* talents, not merely borrowed along with someone else's handed-down clothes.

Ah, but he was asleep now, absent from her, and she was stuck there in the schoolyard. She sighed. The injections seemed to be taking forever. The children were fidgeting and squirming and getting mixed up in their lines, the teachers weren't controlling them, the old doctor was fumbling with the needles, and her dress was too stiff and too hot. She bit her lip, fanned her armpits, and remembered what it was like to fly.

Finally it was all over for another year. The children filed back into class and the old doctor packed up and said goodbye to the teachers. But to the orphan's despair they didn't then go home to the hospital. Instead the old doctor led her to the marketplace. And smiling at her once again—another special treat—he brought out his wallet and gave her some money of her own to spend. They were going shopping.

It should have made her happy. The orphan enjoyed shopping, even if she only ever bought small things. A sweet snack, perhaps some chocolate, if she was hungry. Or the occasional necessity, like some new underwear or a bra, if she was shopping with one of the nurses. Or a few decorations for her room, the most expensive being her bedspread, with its pattern of shiny beads sewn into it. And once she had bought a straw hat with yellow flowers in the band, which she had since lost.

But today she merely followed the old doctor from store to store and held the money scrunched up in her hand. The usual trinkets did not interest her. They all seemed to be made of plastic. Flimsy. Pointless. Stupid. And she kept noticing shops into which she had never been before. In some of them women were having their hair cut, and in others attendants were fussing over women's fingernails. In others again silky dresses hung in rows, or cabinets displayed sparkling jewellery.

But the old doctor didn't take her into any of *those* stores. Why was that? the orphan puzzled. And why had it never occurred to her that if she had no jewellery, and no shoes to go with her dress, that she could buy some? For that matter, why only have a second-hand dress? Why not a dress that was new?

The afternoon crawled on. The old doctor was purchasing dreary things for his office—pens, papers, string—and seemed to have forgotten about her. When he disappeared into another store she lingered outside on her own, very bored now. She was sick of the town. She wanted to be home with the foreigner in his dark, private room. She wanted him to wake up and take her away somewhere, she wanted to tear her hot dress off and—oh, she didn't know what she wanted.

Some women were standing across the street, in front of a bar, and the orphan realised that she was staring at them. They were each of them slim and pretty, and they all wore short skirts and tight, brightly coloured tops. They were laughing and flicking their hair and calling out to passers-by, or to people in the shadows of the bar.

The orphan shuffled her sandals, feeling uglier and stupider than ever. What would it be like, she wondered, to wear bright clothes? To have long hair and put on lipstick? To be thin and lithe and quick? To be pretty?

She would never know. She had never even cared about it before. Ah, but did the foreigner care? He had told her that she was special, and a wonder, and unique, yes . . . but would he ever say she was *beautiful*? Not her mind, not her abilities, but her body? The way she thought *his* body was beautiful?

She sighed once more. No. The idea was nonsense.

What was keeping the old doctor? The afternoon just got hotter and hotter. Her gaze strayed along the street. Three men were heading in her direction, moving at a purposeless amble, staring around at the shops as they came.

They were tourists, she saw. Everything about them was foreign—their clothes, their skin, the idle pace they set. Most likely they had come to the island in one of the big white boats that docked in the harbour. Normally such visitors stayed down in the big town, but occasionally they ventured inland, sometimes whole busloads of them. But these men were alone. Pink-faced. Sweating. Two of them quite fat.

The orphan watched on, curious. Once, she hadn't thought to wonder where tourists like these originated, but now she knew better. She had seen with her own eyes that there were other lands in the world. Why, perhaps these strangers even came from the same country as the foreigner himself, wherever that country was. But then, no, she couldn't believe it. They looked nothing like him. In fact, they were ugly.

But the women outside the bar didn't seem to care about that. They called and waved until the men sauntered over. Within moments the two groups were intermingled, talking and laughing, and drinks had appeared in everyone's hands, although the women hadn't been drinking before. One of the men was even kissing one of the women, right on the lips. And then the orphan understood. She knew what these women must be. She had overheard stories in the past. These were women who *sold themselves*. Who let men touch them for money.

There was a word for that, but the orphan couldn't remember it. Then confusion filled her. Because whatever the word was, the way people talked about such women was the same way that people talked about her mother.

She felt her cheeks burning, not wanting to look anymore. It was so repellent. The men with their sunburnt faces and overloud voices and flat laughs. And the women echoing the laughs, humourless, their eyes watchful amid the layers of make-up. The thought came, hard and horrible, that maybe her mother had been exactly like these women, and that—far worse—maybe her father had been exactly like these men.

Oh no, that couldn't be right. The men were so coarse and clumsy, they didn't belong there; they were ungainly, misshapen outsiders.

But then what was the orphan herself?

Suddenly there was yelling, and a disturbed murmur among the shoppers. The crowd parted and an incredible figure lurched into view. The orphan stared in amazement. It was none other than the duke. What was he *doing*? The old man had never, in all the years she had known him, left the hospital grounds. But here he was, barefoot, still in his pyjamas, shambling towards her up the main street of the town.

The crowd fell back nervously before him, and the orphan finally saw why—the old man had a pitchfork. He must have stolen it from the hospital compost heaps. Its metal prongs were worn to gleaming points, and he wielded it like a weapon, shouting as he jabbed at the air. Unthinking, the orphan stepped out onto the road. But any thought she had of stopping him, or calming him somehow, came to nothing. In a hot instant their eyes met, and the full anguish of his mind overwhelmed her.

He was still trapped in his nightmare, she saw. She had put him to sleep, but it hadn't saved him. He had woken again and found that the horrible dream only went on. He was locked in a dark prison full of grinning faces and mad voices. Someone had ravaged his house and his gardens, and intruders had swarmed over his land. So he'd armed himself and run away from the prison, drawn by something to the town, but at every turn there was ruination and vandalism and mocking crowds.

Now he was in his last extremity of fear, surrounded by a mob intent—he was sure—upon his death. And the tourists in particular, the orphan saw, had attracted his manic eye. If they had appeared ugly to her, they appeared *hideous* to the duke. Swollen, white-pink beasts of men. The worst invaders of all.

He advanced, sobbing, and for a heartbeat the orphan was at one with the old man. Her whole frustrating day—the heat, the school, the laughing women and these horrible men (her father could *not* have been one of them)—rose up in her, and she too wanted to take the pitchfork and stab it in the men's faces, to blind their greedy eyes and silence their awful voices. But then she remembered herself. She pulled with her thoughts, until, abruptly, she was free of the duke's mind.

Too late. People were screaming and cursing, and the duke was flat in the dust, pinned down by a dozen arms. The pitchfork had been thrown clear to land at the orphan's feet. The prongs glistened wetly with dark liquid, and the same liquid had spattered across the front of her dress. She looked up. In front of the bar the women were gone and only the three tourists remained. One of them rolled in agony upon the ground, his two companions hovering above, ineffectual. The man's hands were clutching his head, but for a moment he withdrew them, and the orphan could see the screaming gape of his mouth, and the two bloody sockets of his ruined eyes.

15

It was late afternoon by the time the old doctor and the orphan headed for home. The evening's storm was building behind them. They'd spent several hours at the police station, the orphan sitting in a corner while the doctor argued with the police captain and later with the mayor, who came bustling in, outraged.

The issue—the orphan grasped even without the ability to comprehend speech—was what to do about the duke. The doctor seemed set on taking the old man back to the hospital, but the police captain and the mayor only shook their heads. The orphan could well understand why. The duke as a harmless old madman was one thing. But this *maiming* . . . it would scare people. It would scare tourists especially. And tourists meant money, even the orphan knew that. So it was no surprise that the old doctor was overruled.

The worst thing was that the duke could be heard weeping in the station's cell all the while. The orphan had to block the sound from her ears, or else be sucked again into the misery that was his mind. The poor man still didn't know where he was or what was happening to him. Perhaps he never would again . . .

ANDREW M^cGAHAN

It was a long, hot walk up the hill, back to the hospital. Thunder rumbled distantly. The orphan felt ragged, her dress all wrinkled and bloodstained, her breasts itching. The old doctor was talking as they laboured along, but whether it was to her or to himself the orphan couldn't tell. He seemed tired and in pain, his bag hanging from his arm like an iron weight.

They reached the hospital porch, and he paused a moment to say some last thing to her—a word of comfort perhaps—but his gaze wandered, distracted. It was a relief when he turned and limped away to his office. The orphan herself hurried on to the back wards. She wanted to wash, and change her clothes, but even before that she wanted to visit the crematorium. No, the truth was she *needed* to visit the crematorium.

But when she opened the door to the foreigner's room, her heart jumped unpleasantly, for the bed was empty, the sheets thrown back.

Where was he?! Who had taken him?!

I'm outside. Quickly now. You're late.

She went, confused and lumbering and desperate. She found him behind the laundry, on the cement slab, in his wheelchair. He was all alone, head slumped to one side, blank eyes staring at the sky. The orphan rushed to him and cradled his head in her hands, straightening it, stroking it, and almost, in her eagerness, kissing his lips . . . but not doing so, because there was no welcome in him, no joy at her appearance. His eyes were unfocused, his face as slack and expressionless as ever.

She sat back on her haunches, shielding her disappointment. What had she expected? One day he would be better, he would be able to move and smile and touch her in return. One wonderful day, maybe. But not now.

Anyway, what was he doing out here?

Waiting for you. I had a nurse push me out. A storm is coming.

The orphan glanced at the sky. A hazy wall of blue cloud loomed. But who cared? Storms came every second afternoon at this time of year. What did they matter compared to the awful events in town with the duke?

Yes, terrible. He should not have been allowed to roam loose.

But the old man had never done anything like that before, so how could anyone have known? In any case, why *had* he done it?

He's mad. Isn't that enough?

But he'd never hurt anyone until today. And today was . . .

Today was what?

Today was the day after they had entered the duke's mind and aroused his nightmares. The day after they had made him squirm helpless in a chair, seeing monsters all around him.

The foreigner's empty gaze had somehow become scornful. *You think that's why he did it? That we drove him to it?*

The orphan looked away. Her secret fear was not so much that *they* had driven the duke to attack, it was that she alone had driven him to it. She had been there inside his head as he approached the tourists. She had hated those men with all her being, wanting them to suffer. And obediently the duke had aimed for their eyes . . .

You weren't holding the pitchfork. You can't blame yourself for the way others choose to react to what you say or do. Human behaviour is like the weather. A puff of air from your mouth might result in a hurricane on the other side of the world that destroys an entire city. But that's no reason for you to stop breathing.

Ah, but her loathing for the men had been so strong—it was no puff of air. Who could tell what it had done to the duke's mind? And the orphan didn't even know why she had felt that way. She'd never cared before who her father was. But something about the sight of those men, with their lazy smiles and wandering hands, had revolted her. She couldn't bear to think she came from such alien ugliness.

Except—!

An astonishing possibility struck her.

Perhaps her father really *had* been an outsider. Only not some beery tourist, but a different sort of outsider altogether. Yes, why hadn't she thought of it before? It would explain so many things. Her strangeness, her special abilities. And the link they shared, the remarkable sweetness of understanding. Could it be? Could he have been here on the island some twenty-one years previous, in one of his other lives?

The idea was like a sunburst through clouds, illuminating the orphan's whole life in a new way. Why, his very presence here now might not merely be some accident. It might be a deliberate choice to return and find her. To claim her, to raise her as his own. She dared a glance at the foreigner. Could he hear? Would he answer? She waited, not breathing, afraid of a reply, afraid of knowing for sure either way. But he said nothing. In fact, his head had slipped to the side again, and his eyes were once more gazing away from her, up to the clouds.

She sagged, actually relieved. She needed time to think . . .

Thunder rumbled, louder than before. The orphan looked up and saw that the rain wouldn't be long now. They would have to go inside.

Not yet. The storm is why I came out here. I want to show it to you.

But she knew all about storms! She was the one who could predict them, after all. She had known this one was coming since the morning.

You know a little perhaps. But not enough, if I'm to relate the next stage of my life to you. And explain my next death.

144

Now? He was going to continue his story *now*, with the rain about to fall, and with the blood of the duke's violence still on her dress?

Impatience flared. *Forget the duke. He's no longer relevant. Time is what matters. We have so little of it . . .*

Contrition. She was sorry. Of course she was ready, at any moment that he wanted her. She was his to instruct.

Forgive me. I know you've had a long day. You haven't slept. And it will only get worse for you from here on in. But—

What did he mean, worse?

Never mind. We must continue while we can. All three of us.

All three?!

Laughter. *I wasn't alone out here. I had a companion, at least I did until you came along and scared her away.*

Puzzled, the orphan stared around the yard.

Come out, come out, sang the foreigner, and the orphan, disturbed, realised that he was singing to someone else, not her.

From beneath the bushes by the fence—her favourite hiding hole, it seemed—the witch rose. She was grinning with secret delight, and her eyes were fixed adoringly upon the foreigner. A stab of jealousy went through the orphan. All afternoon, while she had needed him so badly, the foreigner obviously had not given *her* a thought. Instead he had been lolling out here, communing with this madwoman.

Foolish girl, there's no need to worry. This old woman is an interesting specimen—she and her bones—but she is nothing compared to you.

The orphan stared doubtfully. The witch had scrambled out from the bush, her hair full of sticks. Surely the foreigner didn't believe in her magic spells?

Her spells—no. But there's more to her than that.

The old woman was ignoring them now. She pulled out a bone from some pocket—a chicken bone—and scratched at the ground with it. Then she took up a handful of dirt, sniffed it, and finally threw the dust into the air.

Do you know what she's doing?

Crazy things. Pointless things.

She's listening to the earth. In her own limited way, she's as attuned to this planet and its moods as I am. Or maybe even as you are.

The orphan shook her head. The witch was mad.

Yes, but when the volcano erupted she was the only one apart from you and me who wasn't afraid.

The orphan could not deny this. And she also remembered that, the next day, she had found the witch staring up at the mountain with a strange gratitude. As if the volcano had not merely erupted by chance, but had *chosen* to do so.

Aha. There you have it. To this old woman's mind, the world is indeed conscious in just such a way. Volcanoes, if they want, can choose to erupt. And storms—ah, yes, even as we speak—storms can choose to blow.

The first cool gust of air finally sighed through the yard, rustling the trees and skittering dead leaves across the concrete. The dark belly of the storm, which only a moment before had seemed to hang unmoving, miles away, now appeared to hurry forward, dragging curtains of rain.

And yet—why? Why does the volcano choose to erupt? Why does the rain choose to fall? What reason lies behind the choices? That's what the witch wants to know.

The old woman was crooning madly, her dusty hands raised to the black and grey clouds reared above, the chicken bone pointed high. Thunder cracked, close and very loud, rumbling in echoes up against the mountain.

You see? There's her answer.

And what, supposedly, had the storm said?

It says that it blows for us. It says that rain falls and volcanoes erupt to give us life. That's what the witch hears in the thunder.

But that was nonsense.

It's a more valid vision than some. Take the duke, for instance—all he saw when the volcano went up was the mess it made of his precious garden. Not the witch—she saw the gift the mountain had given. Fertile ash, dead animals that would rot. She saw the growth that would come from the destruction. And she was thankful.

The wind gusted again, and the witch was rolling in the dirt now, laughing with pleasure, arms open to the sky.

Oh, she knows the earth is not obliging to each of us as individuals. She knows the planet can kill as easily as it creates. But she trusts that the earth only destroys in a way that provides for life in the longer term. Volcanoes erupt, but they invigorate the soil. Storms blow, but they distribute life-giving water. And so on. Look inside her for yourself, if you want.

Reluctantly, the orphan extended her senses to see, just for a moment, through the old woman's eyes. The storm tumbled towards them, mountains of cloud collapsing upon themselves. The same storm, and yet not the same storm. In the witch's vision it crackled with energy, a vibrant thing, a wild thing, even a dangerous thing—and yet essentially *good*. A positive force, scattering careless fertility in its wake.

Indeed, she sees a planet that is mother to us all, and which convulses itself in a constant labour of birth to keep us in existence.

The orphan blinked and was back in her own head. The wind surged again, and a few large drops slapped against the concrete. The storm no longer looked benign to her. It looked cold and wet. They should get inside.

I told you: not yet.

She glanced at the foreigner. His head was back, and his throat worked, as if he was choking, or laughing, or trying to speak.

Can't you feel it?

And then she could. Her skin crawled, her hair stood on end, and the witch was climbing to her knees. It felt like the air was about to—

Now! the foreigner cried.

A jagged bolt of blue fire seared a line between earth and sky, so close by that the entire world seemed to burn white. For an instant there was only silence, and the orphan waited, eyes shut against the glare, for the thunder to crack and boom directly in her face. But nothing came. She opened her eyes in wonder.

Time had stopped. The rain, the wind, the very lightning—they were all frozen. Beside her the witch was a kneeling stone, her eyes aglow as she gazed up in ecstasy at the lightning bolt. It towered like a split in the sky, its base rooted in the fiery ruin of a tree just beyond the hospital grounds. Outlined starkly against the flames was the foreigner in his chair, his right hand splayed out lazily from the armrest. And by a trick of perspective, the bolt seemed to spring directly from his fingers.

Could he—?

No, I can't call lightning. But it takes no great skill to foresee when it will strike. I know much more about storms than the witch here.

But how had he frozen the world?

It isn't frozen. This is a moment in our thoughts, that's all. And compared to thought, even lightning can seem to creep.

But *why* had he done it?

We're not quite ready for the storm yet. First—

His head had slipped once more, so that he was staring not at the lightning, but at the old woman at his feet.

This pathetic creature here—can you believe that she was just a girl once? Hard to imagine, I know. But I've studied her memories.

The orphan was baffled. What did the witch's childhood matter now?

It matters greatly. It defines her delusion. Perhaps it's true to say that she was born with madness already in her, only waiting its time to emerge, but still, it was events in her youth that decided the intriguing path her insanity would follow.

Take heed of her story, my orphan.

She was raised only a mile from here, in a shack in the jungle. This was long ago, in the years after the duke's property was broken up and given to the poor people from the big town. Like many others, the witch's parents had claimed a plot of scrubland up here to build themselves a house and a new life. Alas, the father was a drunkard and never built more than a hut. What little money he earned, he gambled or drank away. The mother found work wherever she could, but the father stole her savings and drank them away as well. Then, in between his gambling and drinking, he relieved his guilt by beating his wife. And when his daughter was older, he beat her too.

Now, the girl and her mother could bear the beatings, they never lasted long, but the poverty was eternal. Most days it was a struggle just to feed themselves. Their one hope was their garden. Their shack might be falling down, but behind it they had cut out a clearing where they tried to grow vegetables. They worked in that garden day and night, just the two women. And yet nothing ever seemed to grow as well as it should. They subsisted, barely, but for some reason the land refused to give them abundance.

But then one day, when the girl had reached early adulthood and her incipient schizophrenia was just beginning to worm its way into her mind, something quite remarkable happened.

The mother murdered the father.

The incident took place in the garden. The father staggered home from a drinking session late one evening and, inanely, began pulling up whole rows of unripe cabbages. The mother emerged to find him there, and it was too much to endure—that he should ruin the one thing keeping them from starvation. She snapped, as quiet, long-suffering women often will, and attacked him with a trowel. The girl was witness. She saw the blade gash deep into her father's neck, and watched his blood flow into the soil.

Failure that he was, the father did not even have the grace to die quickly. He fought back, and for a long, desperate, sweating, cursing and pleading half-hour, husband and wife were locked together. The girl was paralysed by the horror of it, and could do nothing to help or hinder either of them. But the father was drunk, and the mother had scored the first hit, robbing him of vital fluids, and so in the end it was he who died, slashed in a dozen places, the garden a charnel ground around him. And it was the mother who rose, bloodstained and unrecognisable, to comfort her daughter.

Together they buried his body right there and then, under the garden. No one found out. They had no close neighbours in the jungle, no relatives who ever came to visit, and everyone else assumed that the father had simply abandoned them.

But the real miracle was the garden. Their next season of plantings flourished as never before. Suddenly the two women had as much food as they could want. No doubt it was because of all that blood spread about as fertiliser, not to mention the corpse itself. And besides, there were only two mouths to feed now. But the girl saw it differently. She had watched something horrible, but out of it had come fertility and plenty. Her young mind, already becoming prone to obsession, made a fateful connection.

For a couple of seasons more the garden thrived, but then, to the girl's dismay, the crops began to fail. At about the same time, her mother grew ill, and then finally died. There was only one thing to do. She dug a hole for her mother in the garden. In the process she unearthed her father's bones. They fascinated her. The look of them, the feel of them, the smell of them. They seemed . . . powerful. So after she buried her mother, she kept her father's bones in the hut, talking to them about the garden. And accordingly, as if the bones had answered, the garden was healthy once more.

Thus the cycle was proven in the girl's mind. Death was followed by life. Her father's, and now her mother's. And bones were her magic talismans.

The bounty did not last, of course. A few years later the garden was barren again, and she had no more bodies to bury. She dug up her mother's bones, placed them next to those of her father, and consulted the both of them constantly, but to no avail. What was she to do now? And indeed, she might have gone hunting for fresh bodies, and the town might have had a mass murderer on its hands, and a garden choked with corpses.

But fortunately for the townsfolk, the witch went looking instead for more bones, not more bodies. That's when she started digging in the town graveyard. And that's when she came to the attention of the authorities. She has been confined here ever since, of course. Decade after decade. And it has not been a pretty life. This place has seen dark times. She has known hunger and disease, and, before she became ugly, many rapes. She has been beaten too, and neglected, and forgotten, and treated with scorn.

Even you, my orphan, are guilty of the last. But she deserves this much respect—she has survived it all, still capable of wonder and, indeed, of joy. And it was her magic that got her through. Her silly spells and potions. Silly they may be, but they give her comfort, they let her believe that she has some control over her surroundings.

But most important of all are her bones. Human or animal, large or small—bones are the source of her true power. With bones in her hand, she feels linked to her mother earth, she feels that she is in tune with the cycles of the world, death and life and life and death, just as she was for those few short years when her garden thrived. The bones let her talk to the volcano, and to the storm.

She is convinced therefore of one thing. Just as her father's vicious death brought food, and just as destruction within the world always results in creation, so will the ugliness of her own life one day bring forth beauty. She has hope, in other words.

Poor crazy old thing.

She couldn't be more wrong.

The foreigner paused a moment, reflective.

The orphan was staring at the lightning bolt. By increments it seemed to writhe and prickle all along its length, slowly brightening even further. And right before her face, a raindrop descended, fraction by fraction. But most fascinating of all, a near-invisible wave of force was creeping outwards in every direction from the lightning. She wasn't quite sure how she could see it—a distortion in her vision, a quiver in the raindrops as it touched against them—but she knew what it must be. It was noise; it was the sound of the lightning ripping apart the air. She was watching thunder.

The foreigner woke from his reverie.

But what has any of this to do with our purpose here?

Let us return to my second death, felled by an invisible killer from the bottom of a lake and then thrown into a mass grave. You witnessed the horror of my awakening, and my struggle to climb from the pit. An odious memory that—but eventually I did manage to crawl forth, and then to hide my half-decomposed body away from prying eyes. And over many months, I recovered. I grew muscle again, and skin.

True, my new face was very different from my old, but even so I was myself, reborn yet again.

All very well, but what was I to do then?

Should I simply return to my old way of life, I wondered. There was nothing to stop me. In fact, having survived two fatalities, you might think that I'd pursue my old interests with even more arrogance than before. I might have concluded that I was invulnerable. That I could now treat death with indifference, and treat the earth, which kept failing to kill me, with contempt.

But that wasn't how I felt at all. You have to realise how hideous an experience dying can be. I'm not talking about the physical pain, and the nightmare of the grave, although that was bad enough. I'm talking about the sense of loss. The sense of futility. The sense that all the money and power you have acquired throughout your life have been the most meaningless of distractions. That regret is sharper and more bitter than any bodily agony.

No, I emerged from my second death even more changed than I had from the first. Humbled, chastened, and with a new respect for life.

Life! That would be my passion now. I had no interest in mining anymore, or in dead minerals underground, or in oil refineries. Now I would embrace light and water and air. These were the things that enabled us to exist, these were the truly precious commodities. Yet, when I looked around at what we were pumping into our atmosphere and our oceans—I'd done it myself, after all—I was appalled.

My course was obvious therefore. I decided to devote my third life not to studying the world, nor to exploiting it, but to saving it.

Understand, this was not a popular view in those days. This was over fifty years ago. The economies of the world were booming as never before. No one wanted to slow down and consider the danger, and anyway, the earth seemed so vast and unassailable. It was hard to believe that it could ever be threatened. Still, I was determined to sound the warning. I set myself up in a new country, with a new identity, and got to work.

Money was no issue. In my previous life, I had stashed away large portions of my fortune in hidden accounts. And to access those accounts, I needed only a number, not my old face or my old name. So I was still immensely rich. I published my own magazines and books, I financed academic studies, I lobbied governments and sued corporations. My message was the same to any who would listen—we were treating the world the way I had treated that lake, and every day we were edging closer to the moment when the water would upend itself, and the very air would turn and kill us all.

Now there were some who considered this possibly a good thing. Man might indeed destroy himself, they declared, but in the long run the world would survive, and be better off without him. Man, they said, was the problem. Man was evil.

Some of these folk lived in the wilderness, and invited me to their homes and camps. And when I went to such places, I was indeed struck by the beauty of life on this planet. Untrodden steppes and deep virgin forests and wild cascading rivers. They each had the innate perfection man somehow ruins the instant he intrudes.

And yet as wondrous as such places were, I disagreed with my friends. I didn't think the earth would be better off without man. As I saw it, the beauty of the world was only beauty if there was a conscious mind to perceive it. Man, in fact, created the beauty by witnessing it. Otherwise the world was just chemicals and organisms. Mindless.

Indeed, I argued that humanity was vital to the earth, that we were the whole point of the planet. Obviously we needed to feed and clothe ourselves, and so would always leave our mark on the landscape. But the responsibility of our dominance, of our unique consciousness, was a special one—it was our duty to appreciate the balance of the system that gave us life, and to do our best to preserve it.

In short, we had a deal. If we protected the earth, it would protect us. Oh, individuals would still die by nature's hand. Floods and earthquakes would still kill people no matter how well we treated the air and the oceans. But they would never kill without the saving grace of offering life to the rest of us. They would never kill to exterminate. They would kill only in the grander process of sustaining existence.

That's what I came to believe, my orphan, in those years. Does it remind you of anyone? Perhaps our friend the witch?

Ah, the fatal lure of madness. No wonder I was due to fail, and then to die again. And can you guess what brought my third death upon me? It was butterflies. Yes, butterflies! Frail, feeble, flapping little things. These particular ones had yellow wings, laced with crimson. And they were endangered, on the verge of extinction. In fact, they were very rare to begin with, only inhabiting one small forest in a country far from here. Most of that forest had already been felled by the time I heard of it. There were but a few dozen square miles left, and once they were gone, so would be the butterfly.

Some of my activist friends were planning a campaign to stop the logging. They wanted my help. It seemed a small thing to me at first. Surely there were bigger battles to be fought than saving a few insects? But one afternoon I went for a walk in that forest, alone, and the sun came through the trees, and a warm breeze blew, and the air was suddenly filled with dancing gold wings, so many that they made the whole forest whisper.

I knew what I was seeing. A last flourish before death, a festival of despair, the earth crying out at its loss. And I saw that maybe I couldn't save the oceans or the atmosphere—but these irrelevant little creatures, I could.

What a romantic dolt I was. But I bought the land and preserved the forest. It was not cheap. It cost a considerable part of my fortune. The company that owned it was laughing at me all the while. A fool bankrupting himself for butterflies. But I created a refuge, and in my own mind, I had saved far more than the butterflies. I had saved a piece of my soul. I had upheld my part of the deal with the planet.

And then, one day, a storm came along.

16

Boom! Time rushed on once more. Released at last, the great tower of lightning flickered and disappeared, and the thunder smacked like a hand across the orphan's face. The witch fell backwards, blown by the immensity of sound. A few fat drops of rain spattered down, and the wind rose—yet the deluge proper seemed to hang back. The wind died away again to a calm.

Butterflies, the orphan wondered. And a storm.

Yes, a storm such as this one, such as any of the hundreds of storms that are occurring around the planet at any given moment. Except that the storm I'm speaking of held a secret at its heart. An incredibly rare and deadly secret.

Take my hand now, I'll explain.

The orphan felt a hopeful excitement. Did he mean . . . ? She reached for his hand, and yes, as soon as she took hold of it, there came a familiar tug at her centre, and then, wonderfully, she was lifting off the ground.

Or at least her shadow self was. She was aware of her actual body falling gently to the concrete, and glancing down she could see herself sprawled at the foreigner's feet, stubby limbs outstretched. But the *real* her was rising away, free of weight and flesh. The foreigner was at her side, his useless body also abandoned, his shadow hand clasping hers. They were ghosts now, as light as leaves, and in the still air they drifted out across the jungle, even as the witch goggled up at them in envy.

Of course, this present storm above us holds no such lethal surprise—but it will serve as an example for the moment. First, we need to find our way into an inflow. An updraft. The beginning of the storm cycle. Ah yes, here . . .

They were well ahead of the storm now, and around them the air stirred again. But this was no fitful, cooling wind like before. This was a lift of warm air, a hot breath that smelt as if it had steamed up off the jungle below.

As it has. The sun warms the earth, the earth warms the air, and the warm air expands and rises. This is the basis of all storms.

The orphan and the foreigner rose too. The airflow heaved into gusts, drawing them back over the treetops towards the storm front.

The other crucial thing is moisture. This is wet air, laden with water vapour. That vapour is invisible to us, but we can always feel it—as humidity.

The updraft gusted stronger still. The orphan looked ahead. They were being swept into an overhang of black cloud that extended forward, roiling and seething in apparent slow motion, from the base of the storm.

Now—what's happening around us as we rise?

She dragged her gaze from the spectacle above, and considered the air about her. It was growing rapidly cooler.

Exactly. Air cools as it rises because it expands as it rises. It contains only so much heat when it leaves the ground, but now the same amount of heat has to warm a larger space. It can't, so the temperature drops. And when the water vapour in the air experiences that fall in temperature, it's like steam touching a cold mirror . . .

Ha. Yes! As they lofted up to merge with the rolling underbelly of the storm, the air was magically turning to fog around them.

Do you see? The air is too thin and too cold to hold the water as vapour anymore. It must condense out . . .

She saw. The unseen vapour was abruptly coalescing into a mist of tiny droplets of water. But as the droplets were virtually weightless, they kept surging higher with the updraft, plunging into the base of the storm. Indeed, the point of transformation *was* the base of the storm. The underside of the cloud, the orphan realised, was merely a line of temperature where the updraft changed from invisible to visible.

Yes. You have it. Now—

They lifted on a great gust. The orphan caught a last glimpse, as if between grey cliffs, of the ground below, but then it was lost in fog, and they were plunging upwards into the darkness of the storm's interior.

Notice, the updraft does not falter as we climb. This would seem to defy logic. After all, only warm air rises, but this air is cooling—it should be slowing down. And if the air was dry, the updraft would indeed stall; storms can't develop in dry air. But with wet air, a strange thing occurs. As the water vapour condenses into droplets, it actually releases heat, preventing the air around it from cooling too quickly. The upward push is maintained. In fact, updrafts like this can blast themselves to amazing heights. Ten, fifteen kilometres and more. That's how the great thunderheads are created.

But all the orphan knew now was speed and violence and noise. The updraft felt like a solid thing, a giant hand at her back, and yet it thrummed and vibrated too, it lurched and shuddered, eased for moments, and then slammed into her again. Upwards, always upwards. There was no way of knowing how high. The world inside the cloud had no landmarks, only shades of black and grey, or stark, flaring blue when bolts of lightning set the atmosphere ablaze and thunder cracked loud.

Oh, it was marvellous!

I know, but we are approaching the upper reaches of this draft. Barely nine kilometres high, for the moment. This is no supercell storm, not yet.

But watch now! It's much colder up here, and when the air is this cold, those tiny droplets of fog start to gather together into larger drops. And as the drops get bigger, it gets harder for the weakening updraft to support them.

The orphan sensed a slowing of movement, as if the whole body of air had become confused about its purpose. The push of the updraft faded, and for a time she and the foreigner and the water drops merely drifted, the slightest of winds now urging them sideways. For an instant the world brightened, and the orphan glimpsed a patch of blue high above. And then they were sinking. Back into the cloud. Slowly at first, but then faster. And all around them, the drops of water fell too.

Gravity is winning. The water drops are too heavy. They fall, and they drag the air down with them. The whole mass begins to descend, cold and heavy.

This is now a downdraft, and this is rain.

But note what happens to the temperature. It's the opposite of what occurs in an updraft. Again, we have a body of air which contains a certain amount of heat. But this time the air is descending and becoming compressed, so the same amount of heat has less space to warm. Hence the temperature begins to rise.

Of course, this should slow the downdraft, because the warmer the air gets, the less it wants to descend. But once more the fact that moisture is involved changes everything. Rain is falling with the air, and as the air warms, some of the rain evaporates again, which absorbs heat, preventing the downdraft from warming too quickly. Thus it can maintain speed all the way to the ground.

The orphan was hardly listening. She was transfixed by the dizzying rate of the fall. She was the rain, she was the wind, she was streaking down from the sky, a crazy descent as thunder roared and lightning sizzled about her.

Suddenly they dropped out of the cloud into clear air. There was only rain about them now, in silver curtains, then the ground was spinning up and the downpour slammed into the jungle. Trees bent under the onslaught, and the orphan and the foreigner were thrown up and out and away. When their tumbling eventually stopped, the rain was gone and they were floating free again, in motionless air. The orphan was amazed to see that they had been deposited far ahead of the storm once more.

The foreigner had held her hand throughout. *A heavy shower, that's all that was. But it's via such downdrafts that thunderstorms can produce their worst surface winds—winds that blow down and burst off the ground with devastating force.*

The orphan felt her exultation cooling. It had been a turbulent ride, up and down through the cloud, yet she was aware of a sense of anticlimax . . .

Ah, but that was the mildest of storms. That was but a single cell, destined to rise and live and dissipate in no more than an hour or so. What happens in such a storm is that the downdrafts begin to dominate the updrafts. No more warm wet air gets fed into the base. The cloud starves of fuel and rains itself out.

They were rising again, the orphan noticed.

But if conditions are right, then new updrafts keep feeding into the front of the storm, keeping pace with the downdrafts, and the cycle stabilises—then the storm is free to grow in size and height and intensity for hour after hour.

A breeze stirred—a humid breeze that the orphan could recognise now. A new updraft, being sucked into the storm ahead.

It's too complex to explain exactly, but if a storm grows in the right way, then it becomes a supercell—a cloud system massively bigger than a single cell, and massively more powerful. And the interior of a supercell, well now . . .

Then the giant hand was shoving at their backs again, and they were rushing up into the blackness of the cloud.

The orphan could never judge, later, how long she and the foreigner rode the storm together, or to what size it built. She was not even sure that it was the same storm as the first, or if it was a real storm at all, and not merely something relived from the foreigner's memory. Or a mixture of both. But up and down they went, swapping from updrafts to downdrafts, their ghost bodies drenched by rain and battered by hailstones the size of fists. Winds tore and shrieked from every direction, and vortexes plucked at them from nowhere, spinning them off into oblivion. But what terror and delight there was in the speed and in the wrenching changes of direction. And what splendour there was in the fiery blue latticework of lightning that caged the tumult all about, the very atmosphere stinking of electricity and the din of thunder never ending.

But finally the orphan felt the storm tiring about her. They rode a last updraft as far as it would take them, higher and higher, above any rain or hail, into flurries of shimmering ice crystals. There the last thrust from below died away, and they would have fallen back, but the foreigner took hold now and pushed them higher, until the greyness turned to dazzling white, and then to the deepest blue.

They were out of the cloud and above the storm. The orphan looked down upon a white cauliflower mass that spilled away in the evening sunshine. From its crown streamed a mantle of ice crystals, sheared off by a high, cold wind, and around its base the dark sheets of rain were fading away to wisps.

Yes, said the foreigner, *the storm is dying.*

The orphan noticed something else. She had expected to see her island far below, but it wasn't there. Nor was the ocean. Instead they were over a land of hills and farms and rivers. This was some other place entirely, and some other storm. And she was alone. The shadow shape of the foreigner had left her side.

Yes. This is purely a memory now.

Where were they, then?

This is the site of my third death. My private forest, and my endangered butterflies, are almost directly below us. This is the storm that killed me. But it didn't kill me with rain or hail, or with tornadoes, or with lightning.

The orphan gazed down in bafflement. If it was none of those things, then what could it be? The storm was all but finished, its power spent.

True. This phenomenon can only occur as a storm ends. Observe. The updrafts have ceased, the cell is one giant downdraft now. Normally from this point the storm would dump its last rain and dissolve away. But one time in a thousand perhaps, or one time in ten thousand, a dying storm collides with another weather system. A very particular type of weather system.

Nothing was visible, but the orphan felt it even so. The upper level of the storm was now sailing into a mass of high atmosphere that was unlike anything she had encountered so far. This new air felt . . . old, that was the only word for it. And stale somehow. Dry. Like a forgotten crust of bread in the sun.

The lack of moisture is what's important here. This region of air contains no water vapour whatever. It's a complex phenomenon in itself actually, such dry air, at such a height. But what matters now is how it reacts when it meets the collapsing storm.

Slowly, ominously, the air began to drop. It had been suspended there by some means beyond the orphan's understanding, but now the last downdraft of the storm was opening a vast trapdoor in the sky, through which the dry air could fall.

The orphan fell too.

Faster, and then much faster. But this descent was like no other ride the storm had given. The air about her was clear—it held no rain or mist. It was so dry that it made her shadow skin feel taut. Even the wind sounded different; a drone, rather than a shriek. And as she fell, she felt the temperature begin to rise.

Yes. And that's the dreadful cruelty of it. As the dry air rushes earthwards, it begins to compress, as any downdraft would, and to heat up. But while a normal downdraft is filled with rain which stops the air from getting too hot, this downdraft is utterly parched. This air will simply get hotter and hotter as it falls.

In theory, that heat should stop the downdraft descending. But if it began high enough, as this one did, and gains enough momentum, as this one has, then nothing can stop it. It will hit the ground at high velocity and high temperature. It's the rarest of weather events. But meteorologists have a name for it, nevertheless.

They call it a heat burst.

The orphan stared down at the earth speeding up towards her. She was still very high, but directly below, in the midst of a hilly country that had recently been slashed and cleared, she saw a patch of green forest.

Usually, a heat burst does little harm. The surface winds do not last long, and the air reaches a temperature of only forty or forty-five degrees. Enough to scorch a few plants, enough to be unpleasant to humans, but that's all.

But if the atmospheric conditions all line up in the worst possible way, then the dry downdraft can stabilise. If that happens, then the hot winds will last for hours, and the temperature will go much higher. Officially, the record temperature for a heat burst stands at over sixty degrees. That's dangerously hot. Hot enough to wither crops, kill small animals, and distress larger ones. But severe heat bursts are so rare that very few have ever been measured or studied.

All I can tell you is that this heat burst—the one that hit me and my forest that day—was more intense by far.

The foreigner exerted his will, and the orphan felt herself hurried downwards, moving faster than the dry wind, until she emerged into cool, damp air. She swooped out of the sky, aiming for the little forest. Glancing back, she could see no sign of the beast that was ravening down out of the clouds in her wake.

I was camping in my forest that day, as I often did. I had fallen in love with the place. With its beauty, and its fragility.

And it *was* beautiful, the orphan saw, as she flew low between the hills. It wasn't like the jungle back on her island. This was a sparser, cleaner forest, with tall straight trees and lighter undergrowth. A tangy scent rose up from it, the very embodiment of health. It all seemed so peaceful. The sun was breaking through the clouds, making the hills glow. The air smelt of rain, the treetops glistened. And in a low valley, at the centre of a grassy clearing, there was a tent, and a figure standing beside it.

I'd paid hardly any attention to the storm. Yes, I'd been forced into my tent for a while, but there'd been no hail, no lightning strikes. In fact, I was glad of the storm, for it had been a hot day, and there's nothing so refreshing as a forest after rain.

Small golden shapes, their wings fringed with red, were dancing in the air about the figure, dozens of them.

My butterflies. They had hidden away during the worst of the weather—they can't fly if their wings get wet—but now the sun was out again, and so were they.

But as the orphan slowed and descended to land near the tent, a ghost in the landscape, she saw that the figure standing amid the butterflies was not, as she had expected, a younger version of the foreigner. Instead it was someone else, someone familiar, yet shockingly out of place. It was the witch.

It was me by the tent, don't mistake that. But for our purposes here today, the witch will do just as well, so I've brought her along.

But why? What did the old woman have to do with it?

I've already said. We share a madness, she and I—or at least we once did. I've long been cured of it. Indeed, the events we're about to witness were my awakening.

The witch hadn't noticed them. She seemed entranced, as if in a dream. And perhaps that's all it was for the old woman, the orphan hoped, guessing what was to unfold. A dream where butterflies danced for her.

Look. It's coming.

The orphan gazed up. There was, essentially, nothing to see, but she saw it nonetheless—the downdraft, huge, a cascading mass of air. Unaware, the witch was laughing at the butterflies. The old woman reached out to touch a silken wing, and the orphan would have cried a warning if she'd had a voice.

There were no warnings for me. No time to run.

No time at all. The avalanche of air slammed into the hills on the other side of the valley. The forest there shuddered, and the orphan saw the trees turn almost immediately brown, as if dirtied by dust. But it wasn't dust. Then the winds came roaring across the valley floor, and the oven blast was upon them.

The butterflies were the first to die. They crumpled and disappeared, tossed away like dead leaves. The heat was even worse than the orphan had feared. She knew that she could not be burnt—that she wasn't really there—but even so, she curled in on herself, eyes shut, trying to shield her body from the scorching air.

But notice—no fire. Nothing is alight.

She forced herself to look. The foreigner was right. It felt as if the wind howled at her directly from a furnace—but there were no flames anywhere. The trees writhed and swayed in their distress, but they did not burn.

A fire, in many ways, would have been better for the forest. Fires pass quickly and leave the core of most plants unharmed, the seeds still fertile. But a wind like this—so brutally hot, so prolonged—can desiccate everything completely, slowly sucking out every hint of moisture and destroying life right down to the microscopic level.

Oh, it didn't happen as quickly as I'm showing you now—it took hours to do the real damage, not merely a few minutes. But eventually even the large trees were baked right through. Their sap turned solid inside them, their wood became effectively petrified. They went from living things to being virtually made of stone.

For me, flesh and blood, it was even worse.

The orphan could hear, through the wind, a high-pitched mewing sound. She turned and there was the witch, huddled on the ground.

At first I wasn't really aware of it as pain. It was more that it was hard to breathe. The air felt too hot to inhale, my throat too dry. But there was to be no quick end for me, no merciful suffocation. Oxygen got through. I lived on.

The witch staggered upright. Half-blinded, grimacing bizarrely, she stumbled across the clearing, the wind hammering her to and fro. The orphan drifted in her wake, cutting easily through the heat, untouched and unharmed.

I tried to shelter in the forest.

The old woman reached the cover of the trees at last—but it was no better there. The wind was inescapable. A yellow haze whipped across the ground, as thick as smoke, and the witch went blundering through it from tree to tree.

Eventually my skin turned to leather—cooked, pulled tight, no give at all. It was agony just to bend an arm or a leg. Later my flesh split open, like a chicken's skin roasting in a pan. But the pain wasn't the worst thing, you understand. What was far worse was the sense of betrayal. How could the earth do this to me? That's what I wondered, as I suffered that day. How could the planet inflict such torture upon someone who had done so much to protect it? And why—after I had saved that little piece of forest and those last few butterflies—why had nature itself decided to obliterate them?

The witch was clawing at the ground. She was trying to dig a hole, the orphan saw, but the soil had been baked as hard as pottery. Around her the forest had become a skeletal thing, the trees stripped of all leaves, reduced to dead pillars.

Do you see why that appalled me so? The earth was breaking the bargain I'd made with it. There was no cycle of regeneration here, no life emerging out of destruction. On the contrary, life in this one spot was being made irreversibly extinct. This disaster was going to leave only sterilised dust and fossilised tree trunks.

And for what purpose? For no purpose at all. Thus was the great secret of nature revealed to me. And that secret is this—life doesn't matter to the earth.

The witch gave a despairing cry. She rocked back on her haunches and stared upwards, her ghastly face set like a thick mask. Haze hid everything now, but the downdraft was still an open hole in the sky, and the hot winds still fell from above.

Such is the clarity bestowed to the dying. I understood then, in my last agonies, how wrong I had been. I recognised the randomness of the process that was killing me. I realised that it had no meaning, but was merely the result of gravity and convection. I saw that the earth was nothing but a collection of such systems, and that against such systems life, no matter how beautiful, had no special claim.

The witch cried again, incoherent. She was peering at her arms, at slashes that had opened on her wrists, the skin tearing apart like old cloth. Her insides were already dried flesh, bloodless. And there was bone. Her own bone.

See. She will leave no blood-filled corpse to fertilise the soil of some damp garden. She will become part of no plant or tree, she will not commingle with mother earth. Her hope has been a lie, and her death will be barren and useless.

But the orphan didn't want to see any more. It was too cruel. It was time to let the old woman go, surely.

What—you don't want her cured? This experience will do more to bring her back to sanity than anything the hospital will ever do for her.

No cure was worth this. No sanity either.

But it isn't finished. It took me so long to die. The end only came when my core body temperature rose to fatal levels. I was blind by then, and incapable of movement, my legs and arms locked into place. But I was granted that last hour of consciousness . . .

No, no one deserved such pain.

Did I?

But the orphan no longer cared. She reached out with her mind to the mummified shape of the witch, grabbed hold, and pulled. Away from the wind, away from the hot air, away from the foreigner's pain. And instantly, it was all gone. The forest, the wind, the heat.

Something sharp and cold stung against the orphan's skin. Her real skin. It was rain. She was back in her body, back in her bloodstained nurse's dress, lying flat upon the wet concrete behind the laundry. The rain splattered heavily for a moment, then eased away. Thunder rumbled distantly across the mountain. The orphan sat up. The storm had almost passed by. The sun was setting, a rainbow gleamed in the last shafts of light, and there was no hidden downdraft coming. No burst of heat.

She laughed. None of it was real. It never had been. Beside her the foreigner sat slumped and soaked in his wheelchair, his head askew, gazing at the clouds. And such was the orphan's relief that no actual harm had been done, this time she did grab hold of his face and kiss him, quickly, on the lips.

But then the witch was screaming, and rolling on the ground, and clawing at her clothes and skin as if she was on fire.

17

By the time the orphan had alerted the nurses, the witch had disappeared from behind the laundry. When the old woman was finally located again, hunched in a cupboard, she had shredded her clothes and lacerated her skin all over. Worst was her left arm. She had gouged it open with a sharpened stick. Blood was everywhere and, horribly, the fingers of her good hand were wrapped around the yellow bones of her left wrist, apparently attempting to pry the bones out.

When the nurses tried to take the sharpened stick away, the witch turned wild, shrieking and flailing, and stabbing one nurse's thigh so deeply the young woman had to be hospitalised overnight in the front wards. Mayhem. But at length the old woman was immobilised, and sedated, and strapped onto a stretcher. Then they carried her off to the only place she could be safely held—the locked ward.

The orphan was following behind the stretcher, but past the locked ward's iron door she was not permitted to go. She could only watch from the threshold as the witch was carted down the dark corridor beyond, and listen as there rose, in greeting, a chorus of sobs and moans from the other unfortunates already imprisoned within.

Then the iron door was slammed shut.

All night long the orphan stood vigil outside that door. She didn't even take time to change out of her dress. The old doctor and various of the nurses passed in and out, and she heard the bemusement in their voices as they went, discussing the alarming developments. She knew what they must be thinking. The witch had always been so harmless. What had brought about such a change? Who or what was to blame?

The orphan knew. She should have acted earlier, she should have made the foreigner stop, but she hadn't, she had stood by and watched, too fascinated in spite of the witch's suffering, too interested in what it *meant* . . .

Late in the night, the old woman awoke from sedation and began to rave. Her voice was quite audible if the orphan put an ear to the metal of the door. Up until then, she had been hoping that the witch's condition might be temporary, that she would be better by morning. But listening now, the orphan realised there would be no such recovery. She could hear, beneath the babbled words, how the heat burst still howled in the old woman's mind. The witch remained trapped in the forest.

That was why she had dug into her own arm. She had seen her bones laid bare by the hot winds, and in her madness and terror the witch had reasoned that if only she could dig those bones out—her *own* bones—then perhaps she could make the earth listen to her again, and ask the wind to stop. But now she had been prevented and tied up, and anyway, she had decided that the bones of her arms would never do. They were too thin. They were useless against the furnace wind.

She needed to dig deeper, into her leg, or her chest maybe, to find bigger bones. Stronger bones. If they would only untie her, she would get her stick again and dig, and dig . . . and the orphan couldn't stand it. Towards dawn she shut her mind, and fled to her little hut. Safely inside, she stripped off her nurse's uniform, all filthy with its mud and blood, and kicked it into a corner. She didn't want to wear it ever again.

It was her fault, all her fault.

Hers, and the foreigner's. There could be no argument this time. What they had done was wrong. She had denied it the first time, when they had gone rummaging so disastrously in the duke's mind. The foreigner had calmed her fears about that, distracting her with new wonders, but now, for the second time, they had taken a patient, helpless and old and mad, and destroyed her.

No more denial then. The foreigner was dangerous.

Oh, not to the orphan. She felt no fear of him at all for her own sake. On the contrary, she was at her safest with him. He had a purpose for her that he would reveal one day, and she had no doubt that it would be a *good* purpose.

No, it was just that his singlemindedness could be a problem when it came to others. He hadn't *intended* to be cruel to the duke or the witch, she was sure. They had been convenient tools, close at hand, that was all. But he was so preoccupied with his greater mission that he'd overlooked how vulnerable they were.

So yes, that made him dangerous. But not . . . *bad.* He couldn't be that. Not when he had given her so much joy. Not when she loved him so.

Yes, loved him. There, she had admitted it, and she didn't care how people would laugh—that she, the fat fool of an orphan, was in love with a man. And more, that she dared to hope he might love her back. Why, she had kissed him, hadn't she? Right on the lips. And the truth was, she wanted to do more than kiss him.

But that led her hard up against a wall, and even in thought she could go no further. She had not forgotten the awesome possibility—that he might not be a stranger to her, but someone far closer. And there were things forbidden between fathers and daughters. Even as an orphan she knew that. And right now she couldn't tell what she wanted more—a father she could never touch, or a stranger she could.

But none of that changed the fact that the foreigner had shared the crematorium with four other patients, and now two of them were gone: one to prison, one to an isolation cell—and it was his interventions that had driven them there. That only left the archangel and the virgin. What might happen if the foreigner decided to play havoc with their minds too? The orphan pictured them briefly—the boy and the girl—each lost in their sad manias, and each strangely innocent because of that. A resolve hardened in her. No, it mustn't happen. They must be left alone.

But how to ensure that?

She lay naked on her bed, pondering the dilemma, and watching through the window as the sky turned blue with sunrise. Clanks and clatters came from the kitchen, but she didn't rise to go and help. This was more important. Nor did she stir when the smells of cooking wafted through. She had no appetite. In fact—a part of her noted—she never seemed to be hungry anymore. It was strange, she was a big eater normally—the reason, no doubt, that she was so fat. But lately . . .

She wasn't as tired as she should be either. She hadn't really slept in three nights now, but she felt quite alert, as if there was some independent source of energy—not linked to food or sleep—that was burning within her. She flexed her limbs experimentally. Were they lighter? Stronger? She sat up and stared down at herself, at her breasts and belly. Was it an illusion, or was her squat body becoming leaner somehow?

Impossible. But this feeling too, she was sure, was something to do with the foreigner. And this too she did not want to lose . . .

Well, there was only one thing to try. She would have to go and see the old doctor. She would have to convince him somehow. There was no one else with whom she could hope to communicate.

She rose at once, put on her old clothes, and went out. It was a clear morning, and only a few puddles remained in the yard from the storm. Crossing the compound, the orphan stared up, reading the movements of the air. But although it would be humid and hot later, the atmosphere felt flat, there would be no storm today. And no joy of flying within the thunderheads . . .

Enough! She would not go anywhere with the foreigner again—this was her firm decision—until she could be sure no one else would be harmed.

The old doctor was in his office, drinking tea. He smiled at her over the cup when she entered, but the orphan knew him well enough to see that the smile was strained. He was very weary. He had been up all night monitoring the witch, and that was after his long day in town injecting the children and then dealing with the uproar over the duke. So much bother and trouble for him. But did he suspect the cause?

She had no way to tell him. Not by speech, anyway. But she could *show* him. She went to his chair and took his hand. He smiled again, and said something that she couldn't understand but which she knew was kind, perhaps telling her that he was too busy and had no time for play. But this had nothing to do with play.

She tugged at his hand, serious, and pointed towards the door. He sighed and put down his cup and rose reluctantly, but he allowed her to lead him through the front wards, and then on through the back wards. From time to time he protested, but the orphan ignored his questions. They came at last to the crematorium's little dayroom. Both the virgin and the archangel were there, but for the moment they weren't the orphan's concern. She dragged the old doctor through to the foreigner's room.

He was asleep, serene beneath the sheet, his eyes shut. She reached out with her mind, but felt nothing from him, and heard nothing.

What would he think of what she was about to do? Would he be angry with her? But why? It was no attack on him. It would make no difference to anything he and the orphan might do together. It didn't mean that she loved him any less. But she had other loyalties too. The patients must be protected.

She pointed at the foreigner, and then pointed at the door, all the while staring at the old doctor. His gaze followed her finger, then came back to her, his gentle eyes cloudy with pain and puzzlement. The orphan repeated the gesture, her face set urgently. But still he only frowned at her. Frustration growing, the orphan went to the foreigner's side and, gripping his shoulder, made as if to roll him out of bed.

Understanding broke for a moment on the doctor's face. He saw that she wanted the patient moved. But then he was frowning again, asking a series of questions, none of which the orphan could decipher—no doubt he wanted to know *why* the foreigner should be shifted. Oh, it was so annoying being unable to speak! How to make him comprehend the danger?

Inspiration struck her. She grabbed the old doctor's hand again and took him next door, into the room the duke had shared with the archangel. She pointed at the duke's empty bed. Then she raised a hand to her eyes and grimaced in pretend agony—she was miming the awful moment in town when the duke had impaled the tourist. Then she took the old doctor back to the foreigner's room and pointed an accusing finger.

Did he understand? No, he didn't.

This time she went to the other bedroom. She pointed at the witch's empty bed, then dragged the old doctor through the halls to the locked ward. She rapped her fingers upon the iron door, then pulled the old doctor—she could feel his impatience growing now—back to the crematorium and with an explicit flourish denounced the foreigner yet again. It couldn't be any clearer, surely.

But the old doctor only stared at her thoughtfully. Then he took her by the shoulders and led her out into the dayroom. He closed the door to the furnace room behind him, then pointed at it, wagging his finger back and forth and shaking his head solemnly. This she understood perfectly well. He was telling her to stay away from the foreigner.

The orphan's frustration boiled over. She shook her head, gesturing furiously to the archangel and the virgin. Up to this point, they had ignored all of the comings and goings, the archangel bent over his book, the virgin lost in her television screen. Didn't he see? They were helpless, their minds were wide open! They couldn't be left so close to the foreigner, or they might be next.

In exasperation, she even clutched the archangel's hand, pulling it away from the page of his book, trying to get him to his feet so that she could drag him out of the room. She was saying that if the foreigner was not going to be moved, then the archangel and the virgin should be moved instead.

But the youth merely hunkered lower in his seat, resisting her passively, his lips moving in whispered prayer. And the old doctor, frowning deeply now, turned and disappeared down the hall. The orphan gave up and released the archangel's hand. She watched his finger slide back to the words on the page. But there his finger stopped. She lifted her gaze, and her breath caught—he was looking straight up at her.

The virgin was too. The girl had turned her head away from the television, and was staring at the orphan in silence. Both of them, archangel and virgin, wore dead expressions that somehow didn't seem to be their own. It was as if someone else was looking out from behind their faces. Borrowing their eyes.

The orphan went cold. Was it *him*?

Was he angry after all?

It lasted only a moment, then she could hear the old doctor coming back along the hall. The archangel and the virgin blinked once in unison, slowly, and looked away. The orphan breathed out. But when the old doctor entered, she saw that he was now carrying, of all things, her mop and bucket. Any expectations she'd had of him sank away. He wasn't going to help her. He was as good as telling her that she was overwrought, that she needed to forget the foreigner and get back to her chores.

The fool! If he knew the amazing feats she was capable of now. But then her outrage turned to despair. Amazing feats, yes, but only with the foreigner. Without him she was useless. Indeed, now that she had lost even her limited understanding of speech, she was more useless than ever before. Even to the old doctor. His expression as he looked at her now, despite the kindness, was clinical. Measuring.

The way he would look at a patient.

The orphan felt loneliness freeze her. Maybe the foreigner hadn't glared at her through the eyes of the archangel and the virgin. Maybe he wasn't angry. But she felt she was being taught a lesson by him, even so. *He* was the only person, in the end, with whom she could communicate, and *he* was the only person, in the end, to whom she owed any loyalty. Everyone else was dispensable, innocent or not.

That's what being in love really meant.

She bowed her head, and took the mop and bucket.

18

But how was she to use this new love?

The orphan considered the question as she worked through the morning. If there was no one for her but the foreigner now, then what was she to do in the long hours when he was away from her? How was she to use all this new devotion, and all this new energy? She had so much of both!

Certainly her chores weren't the answer. She stuck it out as long as she could—mopping, carting trays, lugging piles of dirty sheets—but by noon her patience was at an end. She couldn't believe that she had ever been satisfied with such things, or that she had ever thought she belonged there in the wards amid the nurses and patients. She saw now how truly apart from them she was, forever locked out of their conversations and their games and their arguments. Forever isolated.

And worse, some of the nurses seemed to be covertly watching her. The orphan suspected that the old doctor had said something. She caught looks from them similar to his—concerned, but also coolly evaluating. At lunchtime two of the older nurses—smiling and friendly, but resolute—cornered her in the kitchen and made her sit down in front of a bowl of soup. Alarmed, and not in the least hungry, the orphan forced down spoonfuls until the judgement went out of their eyes.

By mid-afternoon she was loitering in the most deserted area she could find, a far corner of the grounds, bare and treeless. It was baking out there, but anything was better than the presence of people. She waited for the foreigner to appear in her head. Why wouldn't he wake up? And what to do until he did?

She stared at the sky, longing for a tempest of some kind to come and suck her up into its depths. But there was nothing, only a thickening haze about the sun as the afternoon lengthened, and she understood enough to know that there was no point merely wishing for something to happen, that there was no consciousness in the sky waiting to respond. The foreigner had shown her—the weather was a matter only of systems, of complicated processes that ruled the behaviour of the air. Not wishes.

But she wondered—could those systems be influenced? It had seemed sometimes that the foreigner could do just that. And yet, while he had taken her to wondrous places and displayed amazing phenomena to her, she could not remember that he had actually *created* any of those places or phenomena. He could explore a storm, yes, if it was already raging, but did he have the power to conjure a storm of his own, here and now, out of the blue sky? Did anyone have the power? Did *she*?

She decided to try.

Oh, she didn't intend to conjure a whole storm—she knew that would be impossible. But what about a cooling breeze? Surely that could not be too hard. And it would be lovely. The day was so dreary and oppressive.

But she would need height, a prospect from which to command the winds. She ducked through the hole in the back fence, and climbed the path through the jungle to the lookout. Yes, this would do. There was little for the casual eye to discern—the view was too hazy, the jungle and the town dozing in the heat, the ocean a distant blur—but the orphan gazed out with her other senses, far more penetrating, and saw.

How intriguing. The air masses weren't as motionless as they seemed. There was movement around her. She couldn't grasp the pattern of it at first, but then . . . yes, suddenly she had it, as clearly as if the foreigner had been there to instruct her. It was so simple. The air above the island was being heated by the sun more than was the air above the sea, and thus the air over the island was slowly rising while, just as slowly, the slightly cooler sea air was drifting in to replace it.

Why, it was almost a breeze already, if only the whole process wasn't so sluggish. All she had to do was speed things up!

She moved to the edge of the lookout and set herself facing the ocean, her legs spread solidly, arms stiff at her sides. She summoned the power within her mind. It was a matter, she knew, of *pushing* the air above. Of making it warmer and lighter. And it was a matter of *pulling* on the dense, cool, salty air out to sea.

She strove. Working by the merest guess, she made herself into a fulcrum and willed the air to move away from her, and towards her, and through her. And it seemed that indeed her mind had engaged with something of enormous inertia, that she strove *against* something. The effort was almost frightening, and yet it was exhilarating too—to feel her own strength, her own resources, extended to full capacity.

And was it working? Was the air above her lifting faster now? Was the sea air, curling so lazily before, rolling in with more purpose? The orphan laughed, despite the strain. She felt that she was shining with energy. She felt lithe and fierce and full of health. Yes, yes she was certain of it. The sea air was coming to her call. It was tumbling over the coast now, and beginning to climb the mountain, like a slow wave breaking over a steep beach. And yet it was so reluctant to climb the hill. And the warmer air above was so reluctant to rise out of the way.

The orphan groaned. Just one touch of the cooler air, that's all she wanted. It was so close. She pushed, and pulled, her arms and legs quivering, her teeth clenched. And just below her, surely, the jungle was beginning to sway . . .

Then her will snapped. She fell to her knees, lungs heaving, and there was no cooling breeze. The jungle below her hung motionless. She had failed.

But when she recovered, and looked out again with her special sight, she wasn't so sure. The air above the island was definitely rising more steadily now, and the sea air was feeling its way more confidently over the coastline. The only question was—had *she* caused it? Or was it a natural thing? The longer the sun shone, after all, the more the land would heat the air, and the stronger the wind from the ocean would become. Whether anyone helped it or not, the sea breeze was in fact inevitable.

So maybe she had done nothing at all. Still, she waited and watched—oddly humbled by the world—until the cool change finally arrived. And then she stayed even longer, watching as the sun slid towards the misty horizon, knowing all the while that it was not the sun that moved, but the earth that was spinning. And when darkness folded over the island and the sea, still she sat there, studying the sky and the air, observing the sea breeze die as the land cooled and the atmosphere calmed.

The night grew deeper. Around her the grass and the jungle came alive with stealthy noises. Creatures moved in the shadows, but she wasn't afraid. What was there to fear in the jungle? It was an insignificant thing, night creatures included, compared to the great movements of the air above and of the earth below.

He had taught her this.

She sighed. If only he had been there today. At the very least, she wanted him to know what she had done, or attempted to do. She wanted to show him what she had learnt. Her gift to him, out of love. She rose and walked back down the hill, stepping lightly along the track despite the darkness. She crept through the fence and across the grounds, into the back wards. No one was about, and when she came to the crematorium dayroom, there was no television flickering, no virgin camped on the floor, no archangel bent over his book. A single bulb burnt dimly.

The hour must be very late indeed, if everyone was asleep.

She opened the door to the foreigner's room, and saw him there upon the bed. And then her heart leapt, for the prone figure stirred, sat up, and in one fluid motion climbed to its feet to stand before her. He had risen! He had been waiting all along in the darkness to show her this miracle. He was properly alive at last!

But then the figure turned in the half-light coming from the dayroom, and she saw that it wasn't the foreigner, and had never been the foreigner.

It was only the night nurse.

Heart pounding, the orphan stared at the empty bed, and all around the room. Then she turned to the night nurse, her face set hard and questioning. Where was he? What had they done with him? But in fact the night nurse was already speaking. His words were incomprehensible, but the tone of them was very strange. He seemed—if the orphan could have believed it—to be apologising to her in some fashion.

He held out a hand. She stared at it, confused. Something lay in his palm, wrapped in paper. A present? From the night nurse? Surely not. It must be some sort of trick. He had played them on her before. But he *looked* sincere.

She took the package. The paper was a plain white page, a little grubby with fingerprints. She unwrapped it. Inside was a brooch. A plastic flower, with a pin at the back. She had seen the same sort of thing in the stores in town. They were very inexpensive. Whatever was he giving it to her for?

He was talking again. Smiling now. Not mockingly, but in a friendly fashion. And then, just for an instant, she caught his meaning. It was about the other night. He was saying he was sorry for making a mess of her room.

She shook her head. She didn't care about any of that! She wanted to know who had taken the foreigner away, and why. Had something happened? Had he been moved to another ward? Had he—and the shock of the thought was like a thump to her chest—been moved out of the hospital altogether?

The night nurse had stopped talking. Now he was just standing there with that peculiar smile on his face. What had he been doing here anyway, lying in the foreigner's bed? Had he been waiting especially for her? And then, more baffling still, he stepped around her and shut the cell door. What was this now? She had to go, she had to search the hospital, she had to find out what had happened. She went to push past him and open the door, but he remained bizarrely immobile, blocking her.

Idiot boy. She glared up at him. But then his hands were on her shoulders, and he was pushing her backwards. The orphan was so dumbstruck she didn't know what to do. The night nurse had never touched her before. Not like this. In moments she was on the bed, and he was on top of her.

What *was* this? Another game of his, some form of punishment? She couldn't indulge his foolishness now, she had to get out and find the foreigner. But the night nurse was tugging at her clothes. He was pulling them *off* her. Her top, and then her pants, and still the sheer strangeness of the situation prevented her from doing a thing to stop him. She was reduced to underwear now, her top wrapped around one arm, her pants around one leg. He had a hand beneath her bra, squeezing and rubbing, and the other, she realised, was tugging his own pants down.

His penis sprang free, erect. And at last she understood.

That. He was going to do *that.*

She was so amazed by the idea that she simply could not make up her mind, right then, whether to resist or not. After all, she had always wondered about it. Not with the night nurse, of course, but if she put aside her basic dislike of him, and the fact that she didn't have the time for this now, the actual physical sensations weren't unpleasant. His palm rasped interestingly across her nipples— he had torn her bra down—and his erection was prodding warmly against her hip. His other hand, meanwhile, had worked its way between her legs.

Spellbound, the orphan let him push her legs open. His fingers slipped in and began to prod and stroke. They were awkward fingers, and it felt nowhere near as nice as when she did it herself, but still, the fact that it was someone else's fingers, there was no denying it made a difference. Warmth and wetness were growing inside her, and if all he wanted to do was give her pleasure, then perhaps there was no harm . . .

But then she opened her eyes—not even realising she had closed them—and saw his face low over hers in the darkness. It was an ugly, pallid face, even more so with his fleshy lips open and his breath panting, but that wasn't what bothered her. Ugliness was no terrible thing. Rather, it was that she could read something mean in his eyes. They were open but they were glazed, unseeing. He was not, in fact, aware of her at all, she could tell. Oh, her breasts, yes, and her cunt too, but not *her*.

This was nothing to do with giving her pleasure. Having barely started, his fingers had already moved away from between her legs, and now he was lowering his hips, the tip of his erection leaving a wet track along the inside of her thigh.

Yuck! The orphan gave a grunt of disgust and, the energy flooding back into her, she heaved the night nurse off her. He yelped in surprise, his head cracking against the wall. She slithered away from under him, until she was crouching on the floor, her bra around her waist and the rest of her clothes in a tangle.

He came up swearing, enraged, but she was ready for him now, and he was far too weedy to overpower her if she was unwilling. Besides, as he struggled to his feet, his legs got caught up in his pants. His erection bobbed in front of her face while he fought for balance, and the orphan couldn't stop herself—laughter burst out of her. He looked so silly, his thing waving about in mid-air.

The night nurse bore the ridicule for a moment or two, leaning over her, his hands clenched into futile fists. But then, spitting out some last hateful word, he turned, flung open the door, and stalked out.

Other laughter, not her own, rang in the orphan's head.

Oh, that showed him!

Relief pulsed through her so intensely it was almost as if the night nurse had indeed managed to bring her to orgasm. The foreigner's voice was clear and strong. Wherever they had taken him, it wasn't far.

No, my orphan. Only to the front wards, that's all.

But he had been silent so long! He'd left her alone all day! Why hadn't he told her? The sight of his empty bed . . .

Regret. *I'm sorry.*

But there was another emotion in him too, heavily repressed. It was a kind of excited triumph. And an image leaked inadvertently from his mind. He *had* been somewhere else, his ghost self at least, somewhere entirely away. The orphan saw a vast and cold darkness. Something was lost in that darkness, or hidden, and the foreigner was searching for it. And then, far off, there was—not a light, but a thing that was less black. It was rushing forward, it was of immense size, and he opened his arms to it in welcome.

A moment, and the vision was gone. Then the orphan remembered she was naked, and was scrabbling to get dressed again.

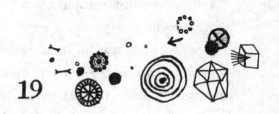

19

The foreigner, it turned out, had suffered a seizure. It had happened while the orphan was up at the lookout, calling to the wind. A nurse had entered his cell and discovered him in convulsions, his whole body taut and vibrating. The episode hadn't lasted long, but they'd moved him to the front wards for tests and then observation overnight. Hence his empty bed. It wasn't until the next morning that he was returned to his own room, and the orphan could finally be with him again.

You mustn't worry, he told her, as she stared gratefully at his body lying in its familiar position. *A seizure is a good sign.*

The orphan wasn't convinced. She'd seen enough seizures in the wards to know that they were never a good sign.

Trust me. It just means that my body is getting closer to functioning again. The nerves are re-forming and beginning to twitch.

So he would be awake soon? For real?

Soon. Be patient. For now, we have more pressing business. Tell me—you suffered no harm from your encounter last night?

No! And the night nurse had not dared show his ugly face again, either. Then she was suddenly alarmed. The foreigner wasn't planning to deal with the night nurse on her behalf, was he? To punish him?

Why not? He deserves it.

Oh, he was just a stupid boy.

He'll hold a grudge, that one.

Even so, there was no need to do anything to him.

Well, if that's what you want. Nevertheless, it was an incident we can't dismiss. Have you considered, my orphan, why that boy was creeping about after you in the first place?

Considered it how? She didn't understand.

You haven't wondered, for instance, why it is that after so many years of either demeaning you or ignoring you he suddenly showed up last night with his pathetic gift and his fake apology and his sad little erection?

The orphan frowned. She hadn't had a chance to think about it—she'd been too worried about the foreigner. And now that she did think, well, it must have been just another of the night nurse's cruel tricks, as she'd first suspected . . .

It was no trick. The boy desired you.

Desired her? No one ever *desired* her!

Laughter. *You haven't seen yourself these last few days, orphan. The way you move, the way you glow. It's no surprise the boy noticed the change.*

The orphan strove to contain a strange joy. So it was real. What she had been feeling on the inside wasn't just an illusion. Her sense of energy, of lightness, of being honed to a fine point—it was visible on the outside too.

Oh yes, you're growing up, little one.

Little one! But she was all grown up already!

In body, yes. But in many ways you still live the life of a child. Don't get angry—it's no fault of yours. But I know, for example, that no man has approached you before as that fool night nurse did last night. Isn't that true?

The orphan felt her face grow hot. It was true. That had been her first experience. And it had been ludicrous . . .

A boy like that is capable of little else. But he's a timely enough reminder—you will have to deal with that sort of thing now.

She did not want to talk about this.

We must. It won't go away. Have you ever been taught how it can be? Has anyone tried? The doctors? The nurses?

No . . . she had never been taught exactly. Oh, when she was younger the nurses had taken her aside and explained about the bleeding every month, but that wasn't what the foreigner meant. He meant *sex*.

I mean even more than that. I can't explain it completely now, but the fact that you're female is not incidental to the special abilities you possess. As compared to my own talents, for instance, which are more in the male domain.

Being a *girl* had something to do with her abilities?

A woman, not a girl. It's a question of maturity too. And the problem is that at the moment you're a woman in age only. An important part of you is dormant. Again, it's not your fault. You haven't been allowed to develop it. But I watched you on the hill yesterday as you tried to summon the breeze, and I can tell you—that's why you failed. Your powers won't ever evolve fully—your kind of powers in particular, so linked to the natural world—if such a potent organic force at your centre is denied to you.

Did he mean—?

You can't ignore your sexuality forever.

She flushed again. But that wasn't fair. She was retarded. She was mad. She was ugly. People like her didn't have sex.

Nonsense. You've dreamt of it, haven't you? Of better lovers than the night nurse? In the privacy of your bed at night?

The orphan squirmed with shame. Yes, she had dreamt. (But could he see her deepest secret? That she dreamt of *him* in that way? He mustn't find out. She had to show him someone else, anyone else, other than himself.)

Ah. I see. The one you call the archangel.

The orphan sighed in relief. Yes. The handsome archangel. Once, she had indeed wondered about him. In vain, of course . . .

Go to him now.

What?!

More laughter. *Don't worry. I mean nothing like that. As you'll see soon enough, it's quite impossible with him anyway.*

Then what *did* he want with the archangel?

Call it your next lesson.

The orphan rose from the foreigner's bedside, but she couldn't hide her deep foreboding. It was just as she had feared. The duke, the witch—the foreigner had used them both in his lessons, to their destruction, and now she had drawn his attention precisely where she hadn't wanted it to go . . .

You're concerned that I'll hurt him?

Oh, not intentionally, but . . .

And hence your silly attempt to have me moved from here.

She hung her head. So he did know about that.

I'm not angry. You have a kind heart, that's all.

She didn't want anyone to suffer! Even so, she would accept the foreigner's instructions, whatever they might be, he could be sure of that. Her loyalties were no longer divided. She had sworn to be of use to him.

Go to the archangel then. I promise that no harm will come to him because of anything I do. In fact, I won't even enter his mind.

The orphan went. She did not have to go far. The archangel was in the little dayroom, sitting on his usual chair. The virgin was there too, as oblivious as ever, her faraway eyes lost in the colours of the TV screen.

The orphan stood before the youth expectantly.

You hear his prayer?

She heard. The archangel was bent over his book, a finger tracing the page, his lips muttering in low tones. Unintelligible.

The words themselves aren't important. It's the noise of them that matters. They fill his head, and drown out the other sounds.

What other sounds?

As I said, I will not enter his mind. But there is no need. You can enter, and see all you need to see, on your own.

On her own? But—

You know you have this ability. You've used it already. And this way, you need not fear that I will somehow exploit or damage the boy.

She should have felt reassured, but all she felt was doubt. What was she to do? And how was she to do it?

Just take his hand. The contact will help.

The orphan sat on the floor. The archangel had so far shown no sign that he was aware of her presence. His right hand moved back and forth across the paper, but his left lay passive against his leg. She took hold of it.

Now, simply open yourself and flow into him.

Eyes closed, she opened her mind—as if there was a door in the front of her skull—and then, so easily after all, she flowed through it . . .

And found silence.

She felt removed from the hospital and its background clatter of activity. The dayroom seemed to have been taken away. No—she was no longer *in* the dayroom. She opened her eyes. She stood in a cool, shadowy chamber. Through wide windows dark clouds were visible, moving slowly. And in the centre of the room, the archangel sat alone in his chair.

He stared at nothing. Calm. Remote.

The orphan looked about. What was there to see here? What was there to learn? But the foreigner did not answer. She was alone in the archangel's head. She walked to the windows. The chamber was high above the ground, she saw, so high that the land below was a formless blur. She was at the top of a tall tower. And all around, the clouds hung, barely moving. And yet they *did* move. And there was something familiar about their shape, something suggestively curved, and coloured . . .

The room trembled, a tremor that came from below, as if a huge weight had shifted, and suddenly the orphan knew that the tower had been built to protect the archangel from something on the ground. There was a horrible thing down there. And it was that horrible thing that the foreigner wanted her to see.

With that thought, she sank through the floor and began to descend. She saw many rooms and levels on her way down, and in some of the rooms she glimpsed the archangel again, only he was younger. She was descending into his memory. And then, abruptly, she was on the ground floor. She was in a little room, simple and plain; far too tiny, it seemed, to support the tower above. It was a child's bedroom.

And there was the archangel. Not a gaunt young man anymore, but only a boy, perhaps nine or ten years old, round-faced still with the last of his baby fat. It was night and it was hot and he was sleeping under a thin sheet. He rolled restlessly, and the orphan could well see why. The sheet was tented enormously over his waist. The orphan smiled. How the nurses would laugh. She knew, somehow, what this moment was. In his dreams, the boy was experiencing his first erection.

Indeed, even as she watched, he woke. He sat up sleepily and looked down at himself, puzzled. Then the sleep left his eyes. He threw off the sheet and stared in amazement. But then the orphan's smile died. The boy wasn't merely amazed by what he saw, he was horrified. He backed away, up against his pillow. And suddenly she saw what *he* saw, there in his groin—nothing natural, but something monstrous, something hideously outsized, as if his penis had become swollen and bloated with poison.

He didn't know what was happening to him, she realised. He had no conception, he had received no warning from anyone about this. And it was so *big*. It seemed impossible to him that his little body could produce something so huge without draining itself of life. And when he tentatively touched the bulbous tip, a pain shot all through him, quivering and twitching, and a white fluid like pus burst forth from within.

It burnt, and the world spun, and he almost fainted. When he recovered, he was appalled to see the mess he had made. He felt sick with embarrassment. It was as bad as wetting the bed. He bunched the sheets up furtively, looking for somewhere to hide them. No one must know the dirty thing he had done . . .

The orphan's heart was wrung. The poor child!

And then she was rising again, through the lower rooms of the tower, and at each level there flickered other scenes, like foundations for the levels above. She saw a crowd of young boys in a dressing shed somewhere, pointing and laughing at the naked archangel as they held his clothes out of his reach. And she saw him in a schoolroom, hunched over his desk, desperately trying to hide the awful bulge in his pants as the teacher waited for him to stand and the rest of the class stared curiously.

And worst of all, she saw a moment when three girls crept into his bedroom one night—they were a few years older than him, one of them his sister—and held him immobile while they hauled his pyjamas down and giggled in disgust at the thing between his legs. The orphan felt his shame as the thing grew and grew when they pinched and pulled at it, no matter how he willed it to stop. And then the girls were shrieking in fury as it spurted out its noxious contents, making a mess of their hands.

Then higher levels of the tower were skimming by, and the orphan watched as the boy slowly withdrew from the world, hiding away from his friends and from his family. His parents did not know what to do. They called in a doctor to examine him, but the doctor found nothing wrong. Not physically. At the sight of the archangel's giant penis dangling long and limp and innocent, the man only winked and laughed, and the boy was too mortified to speak of the terrible things it did.

But he wasn't, the orphan thought, actually mad. He was just confused, and scared, and lonely. If someone had simply explained . . .

But then one day he discovered the book.

She did not see how he came across it, whether someone gave it to him or whether he found it on his own. It was just there suddenly, in his hands, and he was devouring it. And—a marvel!—the orphan could devour it too. The black lines and squiggles, they were transformed through the archangel's mind and entered hers as voices that boomed like thunder and images that blazed like lightning.

So this was what reading was like!

The boy—and the orphan with him—was transfixed. Battles he saw, and blood spilling, and stern-faced men suffering and dying and seeking vengeance, and there were lists of rules and proscriptions and punishments unending, and there were visions of peace and of paradise, presided over by a mighty god.

But as dazzling as all this was, what really captivated him was the recognition he found there of his own condition. For the book spoke too of the evils of the body. In particular, of the evil that dwelt at the core of all men, aroused by the evil that dwelt at the core of all women. It spoke of a *snake*. And at last the boy understood what was wrong with him.

Up through the tower the orphan rose, and now she saw that the walls were made of paper, they were made from the pages of the book, thousands upon thousands of them, read over and over and all stuck together by the moisture of licked fingers. They were a constant warning to the boy to reject the weakness of his flesh, to loathe the baseness of his own desires, and to seek for the purity of the mind and the soul.

And it worked. The more he read, and the higher he built the tower, the further he climbed away from the snake-beast at his waist. And if that beast stirred from time to time, in defiance of all that he had learnt, and if the tower trembled as lust pumped and engorged in his groin, then he knew what to do.

He punished the body.

He took out his knife and cut away at his skin until the pain and the flow of blood soothed him again.

The orphan rose faster now, refusing to watch the knife slice. The last few levels of the boy's life rushed by. At some point the blood of his self-inflicted injuries was discovered by his parents. They sent for more doctors, but it was much too late for that. The cutting continued, and finally he was confined to the locked ward, his knife taken away. But it didn't matter. In isolation, his mind and soul became stronger still, even without the knife. As long as his book was with him . . .

It was over. The orphan was at the top of the tower again. The boy sat in his chair, unmoving. He was fully grown now, and there was no fear remaining in him. His body, and the evil thing that fed on it, had been left far behind. He was a being of spirit now. He sat tranquilly in the cool, calming silence. Not a boy anymore, but an angel.

An *arch*angel.

Except . . . through the windows, the clouds still moved, rolling slowly, fascinating somehow. And the orphan guessed that for all his control and serenity, a part of the archangel wanted to turn his head and look at them.

She withdrew from him, blinking in the dim light of the dayroom.

The foreigner was waiting. *You saw?*

She nodded. It was so sad. When she thought of how the nurses teased him, and joked about the size of him . . .

It's pitiable, I agree. And all so unnecessary. But do you understand? Sexuality is a powerful thing. Denied, warped by superstition, it can deviate mightily.

She had no wish to deny herself. Or to warp herself. But what did he suggest? Should she seek out the night nurse and let him do what he wanted?

Of course not.

Well, who else would have her? (Would *he*?) At least the archangel had found some measure of relief in his tower. It was not preferable to sanity, assuredly, but at least he was free of his shame and misery.

Exasperation. *The archangel is not free! Madness is never freedom! You've missed the point entirely. Those clouds about his tower—*

He broke off. The orphan looked up in the silence. The archangel had paused, mid-prayer. He was staring. As if he heard something.

Ah. It seems you were not quite subtle enough in your investigations.

Had she harmed him?

No. But he is aware of us now.

The orphan stood. The archangel, as ever, paid her no direct attention. But his head was still cocked, searching.

Leave him be and come back to my room. If you've learnt nothing from peering into his god-filled head, then perhaps my own memories, and my own madness, will serve better. It's time, either way, that you heard the tale of my fourth life.

Penitent, the orphan went, and listened.

20

You'll remember where we left me—roasted to death in the forest of doomed butterflies. I came to life again, of course, stark and withered, but there would be no such recovery for my forest. It was now a sterile, silent, killed piece of the world. I couldn't bear to look at it. I crept away and began my slow healing. And, as before, it was with a new face and body that I emerged from the ordeal.

I was a new man within, too. I decided I would have no more to do with defending nature. If the planet itself had no interest in preserving life, then why should I? If mother earth was no more than the empty processes of chemistry, then why find her beautiful? No, I'd learnt my lesson. The only beauty to be found, the only life that offered permanence, wasn't worldly at all. It was consciousness that really mattered. Hadn't I proved that? My mind had survived three deaths now, intact. My body had not.

It was clear then what I had to do—reject the physical world entirely, from the widths of the universe right down to the square inches of my own flesh. I had to concentrate on the only truly meaningful thing. Mind. Thought. Awareness itself.

True, this was hardly an original revelation. History is crowded with religions and philosophies that preach something similar. Oh, they might speak of soul instead of mind, and prayer instead of thought, but at their heart the moral is always the same—the repudiation of the physical in favour of nurturing the spirit.

Indeed, understanding that I was treading a well-worn path, I began to wonder. Was I the first to experience such immortality; the first to go through so many deaths, and yet live? Perhaps all the great prophets and philosophers had been men like me, their beliefs formed as a result of living life after life, and dying death after death.

Were there others out there like me even now? Men and women also on their third or fourth life? Indeed, on their fortieth life? People who had lived not merely hundreds but thousands of years? What would they be like? What would they have learnt? What puzzles might they solve for me, if I could only find them?

Was I, or was I not, alone?

I devoted my new life to finding out. I bought a big house in a big city, and made it my headquarters. I knew that the kind of people I was looking for would hide their immortality, so I hired a team of researchers and investigators to hunt for them. They combed through medical journals in search of miraculous recoveries and patients undying. They posted cryptic advertisements in newspapers around the world, full of hints and clues that might draw someone like me. They travelled from country to country, haunting the halls of philosophy departments and holy places and psychiatric hospitals, searching for the merest whisper of an experience that echoed mine.

They found no one at all, and heard nothing.

But others found me. It was typical of the age, perhaps. The world was going through great upheavals around then. It was a time of new cults and sects, of a younger generation rebelling against the old. And my search had been noticed, rumours about me had spread. Pilgrims *began to arrive at my door. Young people, eager, fascinated. They were not the companions I sought. None of them had died even once, let alone three times. But they were convinced that I knew the secret to eternal life. How I laughed at that. To be accused of concealing the very thing I was trying to discover myself!*

But despite my scorn, the pilgrims kept coming. They turned me into their prophet whether I wanted it or not. They filled up my house and gave me their money and demanded I tell them how to run their lives. They wouldn't go away. And even though they were useless to me, their company was better than nothing.

So I bought a bigger place, a compound, away from the city. More believers came. They requested rituals and rules, and I obliged. I taught them that the mind, and only the mind, was important. I told them to reject nature and the human world and even their own bodies. I told them that only the consciousness knows no death.

Why did I do this? Because my search for other undying humans had failed. And I began to ask myself—if there was no one else like me in the world, if I was otherwise fated to be unique and alone among humanity, then was it possible that I could create someone like myself? Could I make others immortal?

I resolved to try. My followers were certainly willing. Indeed, this was the very reason they had come to me. They would do whatever I asked. I had already instructed them to forswear their families, their careers, their society and their country; to forswear luxury and sex, and the false beauty of the natural world; to throw off every distraction, and seek for mind. And they had obeyed it all.

Now, I said, it was time to forswear life. I told them to stop eating and drinking. Consciousness knows no death, I intoned solemnly, and the time had come to shrug off their bodies and die, and then be reborn, just as I had been.

I lost most of my flock right there and then.

Oh, many gave it a passing try, but soon enough the hunger pangs bit through their fervour, and they left. Only one small group remained, determined to see it through. And I could tell that they really meant it. They would die to please me, and to follow my teachings. I could have stopped them as soon as I realised that. I could have ordered them away, told them to go and live their lives and not be fools. But I did nothing. I was becoming desperate, I suppose. I needed to know, just as badly as they did.

And so they starved. Not all of them, it's true. A last few became afraid as they sickened and grew thin, and their fingernails and teeth fell out. They departed, never to return, and I let them go. But three stayed, trusting me, and I let them stay. Indeed, I was so moved by their devotion that I starved with them. I didn't eat for nearly two months. It was unpleasant, oh yes, but I'd survived far worse. Mere hunger wasn't going to kill me.

But it killed my three disciples.

And when it did, I stood watch by their corpses, waiting to see if even just one of them would rise again, like I had.

All they did, however, was putrefy.

And now the loneliness was inescapable.

Only you, my orphan, can appreciate what I was going through. You've experienced it too, I know you have—the desolation of being utterly different from every other being around you. So different, indeed, that even communication with others is scarcely viable, and true understanding impossible. The fear of that loneliness can drive one to do awful things. But finally I saw that I must turn and confront it. After all, I had been searching for years now, and I had found not even the slightest suggestion that there were other immortal minds in the world. Perhaps then the only thing to realise about eternal life was that it was a life alone. In which case, solitude was not to be dreaded.

In fact, perhaps solitude was to be sought after.

So I bought an island.

That is, I leased an island, at great expense, for my exclusive occupation, from a government that had no other practical use for it.

It was nothing like this island, my orphan. There were no plantations, no jungles, no golden beaches or calm blue seas. This was an island in another part of the world entirely. A bare, rocky lump of a place amid a grey, heaving ocean. A sealing station had stood there once, but now humans no longer visited. It was too far from land, and away from the modern sea routes. Nothing was left but an old stone hut, and stairs leading down a cliff to a small jetty carved out of the rock, washed by waves.

It was perfect, I thought. I gathered my supplies and had myself transported there by ship. I instructed that no one was to call for me for at least five years. The people on the boat thought I was mad and that I would surely die. I was hardly concerned by that, of course, and once they sailed away, I was blessedly on my own. I had not even a radio. I was alone in a way that would strike terror into most souls. But I was elated. Five years, shut off from all human contact. I would become pure consciousness, freed from every distraction, a universe of one. I would at last unlock the mystery of my immortality.

And perhaps it might have worked, if I'd chosen some other place for my exile. An empty desert maybe, where prophets and messiahs always seem to go. Or even simply a concrete bunker underground, away from all noise and light.

But I chose an island. All the while forgetting the very thing that defined it as an island. The body that surrounded it . . .

There was a sound at the door.

The orphan, lulled almost to sleep by the foreigner's tale, snapped upright and glanced around. The archangel crouched there, his book clutched in his hand but hanging loose at his side. His dark gaze was locked on the foreigner's bed.

He could *hear*. He too was listening to the story.

It isn't my doing, said the foreigner, and he sounded tired. *I didn't call him, I don't want him, I'm not speaking for his benefit, and yet here he is.*

The orphan went to rise. She would return the youth to his room.

He'll only come back.

But how could he even perceive the foreigner's voice?

Perhaps one madness speaks to the other. What's the difference, after all, between an island and a tower? Let him be.

All her doubts alive again, the orphan settled.

Both of you then, listen.

The sea—that's what I'd forgotten.

Oh, I knew it was there. I was not ignorant of the ocean. In my various lives I had sailed upon it and swum within it and mined beneath it. I knew its chemical composition and its biology. I knew that it enabled life on earth, that nothing—our weather, our food, our selves—would exist without it. I knew too that, for all its apparent size, it was really only a film of moisture on the earth's crust. I knew that all the waters of the world added together would make not even a thousandth part of the mass of the globe.

I knew as much about the ocean as anyone. Yes.

But I knew nothing at all about the sea.

Even on my island, with water all around me, I still paid it little attention. Instead I happily paced out the limits of the rock on which I stood. It was no more than a few hundred steps across, rimmed by cliffs in every direction, with not a blade of grass to be seen. Its very bleakness was what I liked about it. But gradually . . .

It was a tiny thing at first. An uneasiness I could not define. My days were calm and uninterrupted, I had the minimum of food and water and shelter to keep me comfortable, no ship or plane or other human device intruded to disturb me. And yet I could not quite reach a state of tranquillity. Something was unsettling me . . .

Finally I discovered the problem. The island was swaying.

Oh, very subtly. I doubt that anyone but me—or you, orphan—could have detected it. But as I sat upon the rock, my eyes closed in meditation, I could now feel a slow movement, first to one side, and then to the other. Perhaps an inch over an entire day. It was not like any earthquake or tremor I'd known before. It did not seem to be connected to the inner earth at all. It was too rhythmic, too smooth.

I strove to ignore it. But, perversely, the more I emptied my mind of thought the more insistently, and nauseatingly, I could feel the swaying.

I was seasick.

I would have laughed if it wasn't so horrible. And how could it be happening? I wasn't afloat. I reached out in thought, down below the waterline, and for the first time I saw what my island really was—the last upright shard of a long-collapsed volcanic rim: a single fang of rock that leapt up from the deep ocean floor.

In fact, it was little more than a pillar of stone. And all about it, I saw now, the ocean flowed in great currents. All those unimaginable tons of water would press up against the pillar—and tilt it. It was stone, yes, but it was fighting against the weight of an ocean, and inevitably it was the stone that would give, wrested by inches off its true line. And then the current would ease, and the stone would flex back, only to be assaulted from a new direction, as the cycles of the ocean ebbed and changed.

Can you picture it? Here I thought I was on solid earth, that my island was a stable point upon which I could rest, but instead I may as well have balanced myself atop a slender tree as a gale was blowing.

I could find no peace after that. They whispered to me, those ocean currents. They were constant. I felt them tugging not only at the base of my island, but at my mind. They wanted to take me away with them, to carry me off on their far journeys in the deeps. By daylight I could resist. But at night the currents came for me in my sleep, when I was defenceless, and entered my dreams.

I can remember those dreams even now. I would let go of my hold upon the rock and then be swept away, not tumbling along blindly like a pebble in a stream, but soaring high above the ocean floor, a nimble bird in the water. I flew over the great abysses and black chasms of the ocean trenches. I wheeled above the limitless undersea plains, and climbed across the submarine ranges which gird the earth. I circled the tallest mountains known to the world, drowned deep, all of them, except for their island pinnacles.

I dived, with the currents, under the ice caps, where lethal spears reached down from pressure ridges on the surface. I leapt from continental shelves and plunged over cliffs with undersea waterfalls, thundering silently. I fought in canyons, where the currents were squeezed into narrow gaps and the water rushed at terrifying speeds, stripping bedrock away as if it were mud. And I lingered in stagnant eddies, mid-ocean, where the flow faltered and the refuse of all the seas collected, carcasses of ships and trees and waste, all tangled in a sluggish mass, mile after mile, rotting beneath the sun.

I did not want to wake from those dreams. It was no help to tell myself that the ocean was less than one-thousandth of the world's mass. It was still vaster than anything I had encountered before, a wilderness beyond any other. And the pulse of the currents was endlessly hypnotic. Like blood in arteries, like a mother's heartbeat to a child in the womb. I had only to close my eyes at night and I was entranced.

Even by day I was slipping . . .

I lost track of time. I had taken no watch with me, no calendar. I began to count the days by scratching a tally in stone . . . but then I would forget whether I had marked down a day, or marked it twice, and soon I had no faith in the tally at all. It might have been six months, it might have been a year. Time, I came to understand, was not to be marked by hours or days or weeks anymore. It was marked only by the moods of the sea.

Sometimes, for instance, great calms would settle over the waters. The waves, always so wild and restless, would sink away until the ocean's surface became glassy smooth. The winds too would die, and a silence descend. Then, in the stillness, the sea mist would come—a white line forming on the horizon, and advancing slowly towards the island. The first time it manifested I thought it would be like any other fog I'd seen. Fog is only cloud, after all, and as you know, I was more than familiar with the workings of clouds.

But while other fogs rolled along in billows, the face of the sea mist would remain sheer and straight. And its height would become apparent as it approached, like a cliff moving across the water, rising and rising, until it towered so tall I had to crane my head to take it in. In the moments before it engulfed me, I would feel that I stood at the base of some fantastic glowing wall, so large it divided the earth in two. Then it would slide over my island and I would be lost in a dank, grey world. I would remind myself that this was a natural phenomenon, merely the result of temperature differences between water and air. And yet, trapped in that shadowy limbo, it was no comfort.

For the fog was haunted. Shapes moved within it, twisting and curling and almost, but never quite, forming into something real. Or a deeper patch of darkness would seem to loom up, just out to sea, and pass slowly by the island, like some derelict ship drifting, tattered sails *hanging from mildewed ropes. Or perhaps—I would convince myself—it was a real ship, a modern ship, and I would be sure I felt the thrum of motors, and could even catch the ring of a bell or a snatch of conversation from men upon the deck, and I would have to fight to stop myself from running to the cliffs, yelling for rescue.*

On other days there would be no mist at all, but still the sea would lie flat and unmoving, with a sheen like bronze. A shimmering glare would turn the sky white, and the horizon would begin to tremble. Then I would see mirages. Now, any traveller upon the ocean knows mirages. They too are only an effect of contrasting temperatures, of one layer of air being warmer than another, of light refracting at different angles, creating illusions . . .

Ah, but how the horizon danced for me.

Sometimes it would divide in two, one horizon above the other, both quivering madly as if the edge of the ocean was reverberating like an enormous gong. Then the second line would peel away completely, flailing up into the sky and vanishing like flame. At other times great swathes of the ocean would seem to be reflected from above, and I was certain I could see far beyond my own horizon to places hundreds of miles off; I could see cities, and ships steadfastly ploughing their way across the waters, upside down, labouring higher and higher into the air, their wakes like the contrails of jets.

But it was the human mirages that disturbed me more. Figures that strode like distant giants across the horizon, or smaller apparitions that seemed to walk upon the water only a few miles out to sea. First one, then two, and then more, the shapes cavorting upon an ocean that had turned into glowing tarmac, solid underfoot. And sometimes those figures would turn and stare silently at my island, and no attempt at rational thought would help me; I wanted to step out onto that solid sea and run to join them.

And then there was a drowned rock that would appear to rise out of the deeps, draped in seaweed, with the bones of an ancient shipwreck strewn across its back. And terribly there would be one living soul trapped there, a skeletal, long-lost mariner, waving frantically to be saved. But then the shimmers would clear, and I would see that the rock was my own island reflected in a mirrored sky, the ruined ship nothing more than my crumbling hut, and the castaway merely myself, waving at no one.

I can't tell you how long this went on for. Calms and mists and mirages, all of them were mixed in with featureless days of wind and grey clouds and waves tossing. A year, two, three. I don't know. I was confused and bedazzled to the point of stupor.

But then, finally, came the sea monster.

I was huddled inside the hut at the end of a cold and sleepless night, and suddenly I heard an unearthly sound come from out across the ocean. I stumbled outside to investigate. Half the overcast sky was stained a dull red by dawn, but the other half remained dark. And as I stared into that darkness I heard it again, awful, a whistling moan that seemed to make the black waters shiver. And then a greater darkness gathered, and a vast creature rose before me from the sea, white froth fuming at its waist.

Oh, I knew that there were no such things as sea monsters. But I saw, catching the red gleam of the dawn, impossible tentacles. One, then two, then three, twisting and writhing into the sky. Taller than lighthouses, and twice as thick. And in their midst I saw a great bulbous head with glowing eyes and a rumbling, roaring inner breath. For a full ten seconds, perhaps, I knew stark terror. But then, just as the monster heaved itself over the island, and the red tentacles thrashed on either side, the last sane part of me finally recognised the thunder cloud and the three water spouts that danced around it.

Then the storm hit. Having tortured me with guile and trickery for so long, with fog and mirage, the ocean now shrugged off its dream aspect, and revealed to me its true nature. Fury. Oh, the initial squall soon blew over, for all its ferocity, but behind it came scudding clouds, an unceasing hurricane wind, and mounting seas—a true ocean storm that raged unabated into the day, throughout that night, and on to the next morning.

I watched from the cliff tops, awed and exhilarated, especially by the rising waves. They were nothing like you might see from a normal shoreline. These weren't breakers curling onto a shallow beach. My island, remember, was merely a tower set in the sea. I stood in the deeps, among the great mid-ocean waves, the beasts that mount height upon height, and roll unbreaking around the world.

The grandeur of them! I watched as each one reared closer to my cliff-top perch, a trough falling away before it like a valley. And then, so lazily, the water would swell up and slam against the stone, and boom, the ground would tremble and sheets of spray would rocket into the sky, drenching all. And turning, I would see the rest of the wave tumble away from my outcrop, plying onwards to wherever the wind might be driving it.

They were the most beautiful things I had ever seen.

And I wanted to go with them. It was a yearning born of my long-marooned madness no doubt, but it didn't feel mad. The pang inside me was simple and clear. I did not want to be left on that island. I wanted release, I wanted to let go and be overwhelmed by the sheer energy contained in those seas. Indeed, after all my proud boasts about eternal consciousness, I longed for the oblivion the waves offered.

All that second day of the storm they built. They were grey in colour at first, and then a dull green, but by afternoon they had become a shade that only sailors in the worst of conditions have ever witnessed, and few enough have lived to report—an electrically glowing blue. I crouched on the cliff edge, face to the screaming wind, staring out in search of the one titan I knew must be coming.

And in the dimness of evening, it came—a crest way out on the tumultuous sea, lifting and then falling and then lifting again.

I could explain the theories of wave formation to you, orphan, the interactions of wind and water. I could speak of friction and fetch and wavelengths and resonance . . . but what does any of it matter? All that matters is that the wave I saw gathering out there was twice the height of any other, and it was made especially for me.

I stood. I took a last look at my island, all soaked and windblown and deserted. The relief ship, if it ever came, would wonder what had happened to me. They would think that surely no one could simply be washed away, not when the cliffs rose a good fifty metres. They would declare my loss a mystery, another legend of the sea.

I laughed. I turned back, and there was the wave, its crest level with me, even though it was still far out to sea. I watched it come and could scarce stop myself from jumping into the ocean and swimming to meet it. On it came, the crest above me now, all the surrounding water drawn, against gravity, to that one central peak.

The wave didn't break. It simply rose until I was engulfed. I didn't even need to step off the cliff. The water was simply there, lifting me, cold and irresistible. I was swept right across the island, gripped by a force so powerful it could have smashed me to pieces, and yet which wafted me gently, my head above water all the while.

I cried aloud. This! This was freedom. To be washed away, to let the immensity of nature take me and rule me. I could've ridden that way forever.

But the wave reached its climax at last. Unknowing, I stared down from the peak into the misted chasm that had opened in the ocean below. There came a monumental sense of overbalance, of a catastrophic overtopping. And then I was falling, and the black depths opened to swallow me. Thus the wave broke.

And thus, for the fourth time, I died.

21

The orphan came back to herself with a gasp, as if she had been underwater and only just struggled to the surface.

Somebody was in pain.

She leant forward. It wasn't the foreigner. He lay as insensible as ever on the bed, his eyes open but blank. She shook her head to clear it. It felt like hours had passed, and even though she knew she had never left the room, it seemed that the sounds of wind and crashing seas were only just now fading.

The pain continued, waves of it. A moan came. The orphan looked to the doorway and saw the archangel there. He was curled on the floor, his hands covering his face, his book dropped unheeded at his side. She turned back to the foreigner, frowning. He had promised he wouldn't hurt him!

This wasn't my doing. You saw. He wanted to hear.

The orphan stared at the youth. What was wrong with him?

The siren's call. The seas are building. Any moment now, he'll be stepping off into his own ocean, just as I did. You'll see. I tried to warn you.

She didn't understand. He would have to explain.

But now that his tale was done, the foreigner projected merely an aggrieved indifference. *I promised you I wouldn't go into this boy's head, and I won't. If you want to know what's wrong with him, you go in yourself.*

And with that the orphan felt him withdraw. Annoyed, she dared momentarily to chase after him, to see where he went when he left her—but in place of his mind there was now only a forbidding absence, too cold and dark for her to enter.

She shivered, and the archangel groaned.

Now, *his* mind she could feel. It was throbbing with distress. She could no more ignore it than she could have ignored a bleeding wound. The foreigner was right. It wasn't his fault. She was the one who had brought the archangel into this.

Uncertain, she reached out a hand to his shoulder. It was no use. He flinched at the touch and crawled away, back into the dayroom. For a moment the orphan didn't follow—she was staring in alarm at the floor. The archangel had left his book behind. Impossible . . . he was *never* without it. She picked it up, flicked through its incomprehensible pages, and went after him.

It was night, she realised, the dayroom sunk in darkness. (So they had lost an entire morning and afternoon, there with the foreigner on his island. And yet they hadn't been interrupted. How could that be? Had no nurse visited the crematorium all day?) The only light came from the television, throwing blue shadows. The virgin was sitting in front of it, legs drawn to her chest, dreaming in the ever-changing shapes and patterns. And the archangel was now hunched behind her, on his knees.

What was he doing? Was he praying? But no, he was silent, simply staring at the back of the virgin's neck, his hands on his thighs, trembling. And once more, the orphan felt the pain in him, a pressure building and building. Was he going to hurt the girl? Crouching at the youth's side, the orphan drew a deep breath, then slid her awareness out of her own head and into his.

Into the silent chamber at the top of the tower.

Only it wasn't silent anymore. The archangel sat apparently serene in his chair, but a great roaring surrounded the room, and beneath him the tower shook and swayed. Through the windows, the orphan could see that a storm was raging. The wind was tearing away chunks of paper from the walls, and the clouds, so sluggish when she had first seen them, were racing now.

She knew this storm. It was the same one that had assailed the foreigner on his island. But now it was a particularly *female* thing. The clouds formed lurid shapes as they churned—curved clefts, and protuberances like lips and breasts. And far below, in the tower's foundations, a snakelike thing was stirring.

The orphan withdrew from his mind and stared at the archangel. A woman. The youth was tortured by thoughts of a *woman*. Yet he had never even noticed any of the women in the hospital before, no matter how they flirted. But then the orphan was looking at the virgin, sitting oblivious before him.

The *virgin*? That was ridiculous. She would never allow him to touch her. Why, she would never even deign to notice him.

Except . . .

The orphan studied the girl. Was there something unusual in the tilt of her head? The orphan shifted so that she could look at the virgin's face. The girl's eyes were as unfocused as ever, and yet her gaze seemed to be angled slightly away from the television—as if she knew that someone was behind her.

Ah now . . .

The orphan thought back to the day after the volcano had erupted. She had brought these two together then, the virgin and the archangel, and made them touch hands. There had been a reaction, she recalled. A connection like a flash of blue light. Even so, was it really possible that the girl could . . . ?

She opened her mind again, and flowed out—this time, into the blindness of the virgin's world. The orphan had been there once before, and it was as drear a place as she remembered. Looking through the girl's eyes, the room might have been filled with a brown haze that leached everything of brightness and life. It was a world where there was nothing, and no one, worthy of attention.

But the television! How it blazed!

The orphan gazed in sudden comprehension. When she had been in the virgin's head before, the girl's magic window had been shut, and the orphan had only dimly grasped that it was somehow linked to the television. But now she really *saw*. The window was wide open, the screen radiant, and finally the colours and patterns there made sense to the orphan's eyes. They were *people*. Glowing, gorgeous people. More beautiful than any she had ever seen. They moved as gracefully as water flowed. And the *sounds* that surrounded them. How to describe the sounds, pulsing and lilting? It was only through the virgin's mind that a fitting word came to the orphan, a new word—music.

No wonder the girl stared at the TV so. No wonder she thought that this vivid world was where she really belonged. No wonder she was so uninterested in everything else. And yet . . . even in that instant of revelation, the orphan could see that for all its brightness, the television world was far off and small. And cold. No warmth came from the glowing people. No touch. No matter how she stared, the virgin could never go there and be with those wonderful beings. It was a screen, not a window. She would always be trapped on the wrong side of it, in the world of shadows.

The orphan dismissed the television. It was a distraction. The shadows were what mattered. Why had the real world gone so dark and dull for the girl? The orphan peered deeper into the virgin's mind. Expert at this now, she dug away at levels of memory, unearthing year after year of the girl's life. Surprisingly, even as far back as the virgin's adolescence her world was already darkened, her manner already languid and soporific. So the orphan went deeper, into her childhood. And it was only there, when the girl was no more than eight or nine, that the orphan found light and colour again—and, stern in the girl's memory, a face.

It was the girl's grandmother, the one who sometimes came to visit. The woman was younger in the virgin's memory, but still old, and fiercely commanding. There was no mother that the orphan could see. No father. They had disappeared somehow before the girl was even conscious. There was just this old woman. Grim. And poor. They lived, the young girl and the grandmother, in a house that must once have been grand, but which was dark now, empty of furniture or people. Or food.

But men came there. They came to see the virgin. Though still so young, her perfection brought them. The smoothness of her skin. The pure oval of her face. The fullness of her lips. She was famed across the island. And they were wealthy men, men of property and importance, men looking for future wives for their young sons—or even for themselves. The grandmother rubbed her hands at the delightful prospect. A contract of marriage, a dowry bestowed, the family fortunes revived.

But one man wanted to do more than just *see* the girl. He wanted to be alone with her. The grandmother demurred. It was not proper. But the man threatened, and swore he would take his wealth away, and the old woman eventually assented. And the moment they were alone, he lifted the virgin's dress and groped between her legs. The girl did not fight or scream. Her grandmother had ordered her to be nice.

The man came again and again, but he never proposed marriage.

And then other men came who also demanded to be left alone with the girl. To calm the grandmother they brought money with them, and spoke of weddings. But all they ever did with the virgin was strip her and spread her legs and stick their things into her hairless vagina. It hurt, and was disgusting, but the girl, to please her grandmother, never resisted. She simply drifted off into her own mind, away from the loathsome men and their groping hands, and waited for the pain to pass.

She drifted a little further each time, and found less and less reason to return. All she did, between the men's visits, was sit in her room and watch television. Her grandmother—all generosity now that they had money again—had bought the girl her very own set. It had a big bright screen, and everything seemed much nicer there. There was no bad breath on TV, or sweaty, crushing bodies, or pain.

But then hairs sprouted between the virgin's legs, and the men were displeased. They stopped visiting. There was no proposal, no marriage contract. The grandmother blamed the virgin. She beat the girl daily for their misfortunes and renewed poverty. But even when the grandmother finally brought new suitors home to meet her—men who didn't try to reach under her dress—it was much too late. The girl was mad by then, and the suitors all fled from her blind, indifferent eyes.

The orphan swam up through the memories, back to the present, mourning for the girl and sharing her revulsion. (Is that what *all* men did with their penises? Is that what the night nurse had wanted to do with her?) But it was puzzling too. If the virgin had fled into her blindness to be free of the men and their greed for her, and if no one in the shadow world had claimed her attention ever since, then how could she now be aware of the archangel, crouched on his knees behind her?

It must have happened when—

Yes. There was the memory—the moment the orphan had joined their hands, the instant the virgin and the archangel had touched. Lightning had flared in the virgin's dim world, illuminating a boy's face. And looking into his eyes she had found—unlike all other men she had known—not a lust for her, but rather a loathing. Her smooth skin, her oval face, her full lips—they all repulsed him.

The virgin had been astonished. The boy was gone a second later, but ever since then she had remembered him, pondering. He was no threat to her, she was sure, because he wanted nothing from her. Which meant she was free to contemplate the boy himself. And he was, to her amazement, beautiful. The touch of him! She had felt his flesh. Warm. Not remote, like the other creatures she watched through the shining window. He was real. With an angelic face. Her *own* angel, sent down to her.

And now at last he was near again. She could feel him behind her, strong and urgent, promising joy, the light of his arrival blotting out even the brightness of the screen in front of her. And oh, after so long alone in the dark, able only to watch and never to touch, what a store of *feeling* he roused in her. So much desire, unused and unspent. She wanted to empty herself, and give everything inside to him. If he would only touch her, then she would turn from the window and—

The orphan pulled back into her own head, her blood pumping.

The virgin was in love! Who would ever have imagined it!

But what about the boy?

Immediately, the orphan turned and dived into the archangel's mind. The storm howled louder around his high chamber now, and the tower swayed like a drunken thing, but she went searching through his memory . . .

And yes, it was there, the same stroke of lightning, at the same moment. And he in turn had seen the virgin's face illuminated, and been likewise astonished. For he saw—unlike all other women—no temptation in her, no evil succubus waiting to arouse the serpent in his loins. He saw instead that she loathed his maleness, and in particular his horrible organ, as passionately as he did himself. He was safe from her. And free, in that safety, to realise an amazing thing—she was beautiful.

The boy was in love too!

But that wasn't why the storm now raged and his tower shook. That wasn't why he was crouched behind the virgin, his desire threatening to explode. After all, it had been days since that momentous touch, and he had done nothing. No, the orphan could see that his defences would have held against even love . . .

If it hadn't been for the demon.

This very day, the youth had heard a voice speaking to him out of nowhere. It was not human. It was too powerful, too unearthly to be human. And it told him a tale that could have been his own life recounted, a tale of rejection of the world, and of the search for purity on a lonely height, far from other men. An island refuge.

At first he had thought it was an angel such as himself who spoke. But then a storm had come to the island, and great waves, and the voice had talked of surrendering to the sea, of seeking oblivion in submission to desire. So the voice could only be that of a demon. And oh, how the archangel had been compelled and bewildered by that—for what was a demon but a fallen angel?

Even *arch*angels could fall, if they so chose. He had seen the great wave come, he had seen the demon swept away by it, and he had shared in the ecstasy of that surrender. Ecstasy that could be his, too. With the girl. If only he left his tower, if only he went to the window and jumped . . .

(But no, thought the orphan. No, that wasn't right. The foreigner had not been swept to ecstasy. He had been swept to his death.

This wouldn't work, not this way—)

But it was too late. In the high chamber the boy was up and at the window. The tower rocked again, and the foundations cracked and splintered. A great snake was rearing up within. Outside, the orphan could see that the storm had become almost flesh, warm and pink and swollen, female flesh, opening wide to the boy.

He leapt.

The orphan was thrown back into her own mind, and her own body. Somehow, she had ended up sitting slumped against the wall, legs splayed, her hands at her sides, like a broken doll. She couldn't seem to move. And there before her, on his knees still, the archangel lifted his head, his anguish gone. His eyes were blinking as if they had just opened for the first time, full of wonder. And then his hand was reaching out, fingers trembling, to touch the bare skin of the virgin's neck.

The girl shuddered. But not in disgust, it was a shiver of pleasure. Her blind gaze wandered from the TV screen and her hand rose to rest upon the archangel's fingers. He shuddered in his turn, and for an instant they held that position. The orphan didn't breathe. Maybe it was going to be okay. Maybe the virgin would turn and they would stare into each other's eyes and it *would* work.

But the boy kept shuddering, his arm quivering violently, and it was not from excitement—he was like a man fighting to keep his fingers pressed to a red-hot stovetop. He was staring in horror at her hand on his. And then, with a cry, he wrenched his fingers free and fell back from her in agony.

The orphan didn't need to enter his mind to know why. It came flooding out of him. His shock and anger and betrayal. She had *tricked* him. She had seemed so pure. She had appeared to reject the baseness of his nature. But it was a lie. At his first caress, instead of chastely tolerating his touch, she had turned greedily and sunk her talons into his hand. She was like all women after all, hungry for him, and eager, no doubt, to engulf the serpent at his waist. Hadn't his book tried to warn of this? Images rushed up from its pages—devouring females with poisonous tongues; worms of decay crawling beneath smooth skin. How could he have forgotten that woman was a vile thing, her body a deadly pitfall for man, full of lusts that would destroy him?

The orphan bowed her head. Of course. He could not want *her* if she wanted *him*. His awful book still held him locked in paradox. If the virgin was pure she would not desire him, and if she desired him she was not pure . . .

And the virgin herself?

The orphan switched to the girl's mind, and discovered alarm. Where had her angel gone? His hand had pulled away before she'd had a chance to see him. Why was he hiding again in the dark? The virgin had turned from the television and was crawling forward blindly, hands outstretched. Her fingers clasped the air directly in front of the boy's face, but he was backing away, rigid with disgust. The orphan caught more snatches from him, images of blood and boils, and of rats gnawing at his skin. And yet she felt too the strange pain and pleasure of his giant erection, growing ever harder.

Meanwhile the girl's frustration was nearing panic. Why wouldn't he touch her? He was close, she knew, her skin was all aflame, every hair standing on end, shivering to be stroked. How could she force him to come back? How could she show him that she was ready? She raised herself onto her knees and undid the buttons of her pyjama top. And as it fell away, her skin showed pale blue in the glow from the television, her body thin and yet curved, casting shadows across itself. Naked from the waist up, she spread her arms and waited, her head upright, a willing offering.

The archangel stared, also on his knees, his gaze roaming across the forbidden landscape of her breasts. They contained, his madness assured him, only sinew and bile. But indecision beat on his forehead—he had no control left, no refuge, his tower was gone, he was subject to the thing straining hugely in his groin. Slowly, he stood. And as he did so the shadows hardened along the line of his jaw.

The orphan understood—he was forging a new self. If he could not escape from the woman then he must confront her. And his book gave him only the one means. He must become an avenging angel. A visitation, sent to her by his god. He stalked a circle around the kneeling girl. Yes. He had been sent to save her, to punish her weakness. He had come to abject her pride and to exalt her soul; to drive the evil from her female form, by brute force if need be, and fill it with divine grace.

He reached down, trailing a finger along her cheek. In reply, the virgin quivered and moaned. Then quickly he turned his wrist and, backhanded, slapped her hard across the face. She went sprawling to the floor.

The orphan did nothing. She was paralysed, overcome by the wave of sheer joy that burst forth from the virgin, even as the girl fell. His touch! Her angel's touch! The fire in it, the passion in it!

And all of it real, not viewed distantly through a window, but actually happening to her. Sensation was pleasure and pleasure was sensation, and both were a gift from her wonderful demigod. She had even glimpsed his face as he struck her. He was fiery and stern, and indescribably beautiful.

The orphan watched on, disbelieving. The archangel fell upon the girl. Her back was flat to the floor, and he splayed her arms out, holding down one of her wrists and with his free hand pulling away the lower half of her pyjamas. The virgin did not resist. She allowed him to also force her legs apart, and the more he pressed down, the more the joy lifted her up. The orphan, caught in flurries of the girl's pleasure, felt her own body responding, as if it was herself on the floor.

But the orphan was inside the archangel's head, too. He was staring down at the girl's outspread form, submitted utterly to him, and yet it wasn't enough, his fury demanded he force the submission further. His erection was aching, and until he had humbled her fully he could not be delivered from it.

He glanced about the room. There—the virgin's clothes! He took them up, tearing the hospital pyjamas into shreds, his limbs angelically strong. Then he proceeded to bind the torn segments to her wrists and ankles, and the other ends to points around the room—the legs of the old couch, a water pipe that stuck out from a wall—until she was tied fast, unable to move at all, spreadeagled on the floor.

And still the virgin's joy washed over the orphan. Glimpses through the girl's eyes showed the angel working above her, his arms like thin wings, and the more he immobilised her, the more her excitement built. She wanted to be tied, she wanted escape from this beautiful being to be impossible, she wanted to be trapped by him, taken prisoner by him, possessed by him. She wanted every bit of herself, inside and out, to be exposed and available to his touch.

All of which only enraged the archangel more. Every shift and squirm of her body mocked him. Binding her wasn't enough either. He cast about the room again. There. He strode to the television and ripped the power cord from it. The screen went black with a pop, and in the virgin's mind the shining window slammed shut, but she didn't care, she didn't need the window anymore. The angel had become her window. He was a blazing figure in her darkness now. He loomed over her, wielding a flaming whip in his hand, ready to bless her skin with its touch.

The orphan was powerless to look away. The boy raised his arm and snapped the television cord down across the girl's breasts. He grunted with the effort, the virgin gasped in ecstasy, and a red welt flared across her chest. Then down came the cord again. And again. In near silence—apart from the hoarse breathing of the boy as he laboured, and the panting of the girl as every blow struck.

But the archangel could not be sated. The girl's pain did not suffice. That much was clear from the eager sounds she made, and from the way her skin writhed up to meet the whip. And his own body throbbed in response, betraying him, mastering him, in need of punishment as much as hers. He tugged feverishly at his own clothes, ripping off shirt and pants and underwear, and then he stood naked astride the girl, his hateful erection, as giant as a club, jutting out above her.

(And the orphan saw, horrified, the many jagged white scars that ran the entire length of it, on the underside, from the tip right down to the pouch of his testicles—and she understood at last what he had done to himself with his knife, the repeated mutilations that had led the authorities to commit him.)

Again he plied the whip, once to the girl, and then once to himself, across his back. Pain. Pain would save them both. But for the virgin it was only pleasure, more and more pleasure. The welts across her skin burnt like gold, and her shining angel was naked too now. His body, all aglow with his love for her, was the most exquisite thing she had ever seen. He stroked himself with his whip, and then stroked her too, sharing the gratification. And best of all, the blows were moving one by one down her body, from her breasts and her stinging nipples, down over her belly, and almost to between her outstretched legs, where she could feel herself peeling open for him.

The archangel was groaning in frustration. No matter how he slashed at her, and no matter how he slashed at himself, her moans only grew louder, his erection more strained. He fell to his knees between hers, and there her most tender spot awaited him, glistening wet and flushed purple with expectation. With his last strength he plied his whip, cut after cut, to that spot. And every other stroke, he cut at his own genitals, balls and cock, his back arched with the agony. Again. And again. And again.

The virgin cried out in rapture. The archangel cried in torment. The orphan was swept helplessly between the two of them, slammed about by gusts of pleasure and pain, love and hate, mastery and submission, and she thought she must either scream or faint if they did not stop. But then the girl was convulsing, coming, her bruised cunt clasping and grasping at nothing, and the boy was convulsing and coming too, his erection spurting out vast white jets into the air.

Then it was over, a wave collapsing on itself. Spent, the archangel sank full-length beside the girl and lay there like a corpse.

The orphan gasped for breath. She felt tossed aside, thrown out just as the climax was being reached, and denied that climax herself. The wild seas of emotion in the room slowly calmed, ebbing away until she finally felt alone again within her own skull. Movement crept back into her limbs and she propped herself up against the wall. What had happened between these two? What had they done?

The archangel stirred. He reared up on his arms and looked about in confusion. He did not appear to notice the girl. A whiff of some feeling came from him; the orphan could not quite grasp it—was there a tone of disappointment, of something that had not been achieved? He crawled away, dragging his clothes behind him, until he found his book. He took it up and then slumped, vacant, in the corner.

The virgin lay in her bindings, her breathing back to normal, her bliss faded, her eyes restored to their blindness. The sensation came from her, too. Of having reached a peak, yes, but also of having failed somehow.

So was that *sex*? So doomed, so disconnected, the lovers at such cross purposes with each other . . . ? It was not what the orphan had ever imagined. It was awful. This couldn't be what the foreigner had meant she needed to explore.

And yet, her own body and its reactions . . .

She crawled forward and began untying the virgin. And when that was done, she could stand it no more. Empty and cheated and more acutely turned on than she had ever been, the orphan fled to the privacy of her room, where she tore off her clothes, spread her legs, and masturbated until she came.

22

She dozed, languorous, above the sheets.

In her dreams, shapes and colours moved. Warm things merged and parted again. And then a voice was there, whispering up out of the depths.

Orphan . . .

She stretched her limbs. The foreigner was talking in her sleep. How nice. But then a lazy curiosity rose. He had never come to her like this before.

It can't wait.

She was aware that it was still night. She had been in this drowsing state for only a few hours. She was aware, too, that she was naked on her bed . . . but she didn't care. Let him see, even if it was wrong, even if it could never be that way with him. She was barely awake, she could not be blamed.

Time is running short for us, orphan. There has been an accident.

The urgency in his tone reached her dimly. What did he mean? What had happened? Should she get up? Go to him?

No. Don't come here. Not yet.

But he sounded so worried.

We must expedite matters, that's all. I have to tell you about my fifth and final life, right now, while I have the chance.

Was there the time for that? If something was wrong . . .

We have a few hours yet, I think. And it's important that you hear the full story before . . . well, before we go on.

His *final* life, the orphan noted. The life he'd lived before arriving at her hospital. And of all his lives, this was the one she'd been waiting to hear. It would answer her secret questions about where he'd been twenty-one years ago; whether he'd come anywhere near her island before now; or near her mother . . .

But then for some reason she was suddenly thinking about the archangel and the virgin. Why, she had left them just lying there in the dayroom. She hadn't even dressed them. And if the nurses found them that way . . .

They have not been discovered. Forget about them.

Obediently, the orphan forgot. A wave of sleepiness washed over her again, and all sense of urgency faded. It was so comfortable there on the bed. Maybe it was only a dream anyway. But his voice was lovely. She could listen to him forever. To this story, and to any other story that he wanted to tell her.

It won't take forever. And this is my last story.

Now, I drowned, but you know that I did not truly die from the drowning—that indeed I cannot truly die from anything. Nor, when I let myself be swept off that cliff, as insane as I was, did I expect to truly die. I was surrendering to the world, that was all, to its power and its terror. And it was wonderful while it lasted.

But it was only a temporary release, as these moments of passion must always be. And afterwards, inevitably, comes the regret and the dissatisfaction. In my case, it began in the form of a net dangling behind a small fishing trawler. I was dragged up rudely from the depths and deposited on the bloody deck, gasping amid a hundred other sea creatures—a rebirth for me, even as they died. The fishermen were terrified, not surprisingly. I was not pretty to look at. I don't know how long I'd floated down there in the darkness, but it was long enough; my skin had dissolved and fish had chewed away my extremities. I was screaming. They hid me below and made for land.

Once ashore, however, I recovered as I always had before. More slowly than those other times, perhaps, but just as surely. And for a while I let myself be distracted by the healing, and then by all the business of establishing my new identity, and regaining control of my finances. But eventually the formalities were complete, and there I was. Alive again. And that's when the real disillusionment set in.

For what was I to do now that I hadn't done before?

Where was I to go that I hadn't already been?

I'd tried, ever since my first death in the landslide, to come to terms with the earth and what it had done to me. But every time I thought I'd found resolution, an accommodation with the natural world, it had turned on me and destroyed me.

As a simple goatherd, working the earth and minding my own business, it destroyed me. As a delver into the earth and a developer of its wealth, it destroyed me. As a servant and defender of the earth, it destroyed me. And as a hermit, an aesthete, a denier of the earth—again the planet had not let me be. Can you imagine how trapped I felt, looking back over those lives? How hollow and cruel it all seemed, my immortality? How could I ever win? Where on earth—quite literally—could I go to be free? There was nowhere. I was imprisoned within the four walls of the globe.

And then, one night, in my despair, I turned my eyes to the heavens, and beheld a pinpoint of light sailing across the sky. It was a manmade light—not a plane, but something much higher up, beyond the *atmosphere. A satellite. Already a familiar enough sight, even then. This was two years after man had walked on the moon.*

But watching that satellite, I had my answer. If I was indeed a prisoner on this earth, then perhaps I could break out of the prison . . . and go into space.

Are you laughing at me, orphan?

No, of course not. You have no knowledge of mechanical space travel and the difficulties it entails. But you would be right to scorn my presumption, because in that moment I swore I would go into deep *space, beyond the moon, and beyond even the other planets. Out of earth's sight, and out of earth's clutches. Which was ridiculous. At the time, even the moon was scarcely within mankind's reach. The idea of humans travelling beyond it was only a fantasy. The reality lay decades off in the future, at best . . .*

Yes, but remember, what did decades matter to me? I had as many decades as I needed. I could wait. If it took a hundred years for man to range out to the other planets, I reasoned, then so be it. And if it took another century again to go beyond the solar system, well, what of that? I could be there to see it all, if I chose.

I drew up, thus, some very long-term plans. My first step was to move to the country that was most vigorously pursuing space travel—the country that had put men on the moon. It was a place I knew well anyway, from previous lives. Then I returned to university and began a whole new round of studies. Mathematics and aeronautics and biomechanics and a half-dozen other disciplines. It took time, but I had no shortage of time. I was young. My body was brand new, a whole life ahead of it yet.

Nor was I trying to leap into space with a single bound. In those days it was only a chosen few who made it into orbit anyway. For the moment I would be content with a role upon the ground. When my studies were complete, I took up a research position with the national body that oversaw space travel. And there I worked away quietly for the next two decades. Yes, a full twenty years. You see what I mean by long term . . .

My speciality—and this will not surprise you, orphan, knowing my ulterior interest in the whole endeavour—was the question of how humans would survive for the long periods that extended space travel would involve. Not merely orbiting for a week or two, like the space shuttles, but going interplanetary, or even interstellar. Journeys that could take years. Or possibly centuries. To put it in terms of my own situation—how was a man like me to live, once he had succeeded in escaping the earth?

The simple answer is that, to survive, a man must take a little of the earth with him—air and food and water and heat. Which is fine in itself. Spaceships can carry tons of supplies, if needed. The only issue there is one of fuel. But beyond those necessities, our bodies are also specifically adapted to gravity, to certain radiation levels, to magnetic fields—and these things are not so easy to pack into a spaceship. There are sociological issues too regarding the behaviour of small crews isolated on long voyages. Hostility and paranoia can set in. Cabin fever. Conflict. Still, to me, all those problems were essentially solvable. I was more concerned with yet another complication, one more subtle and yet potentially more devastating than the rest, that had arisen during the early space flights.

I called it the separation syndrome.

I knew of it from only a handful of cases, because only a handful of astronauts had gone far enough into space to experience it. I'm talking about the twenty-four men who went to the moon. Even they only hinted at it. But to a specialist such as myself, those hints set loud alarm bells ringing about the psychological hazards of space.

What the astronauts said was this—when they reached the moon and looked back at the earth, they felt one powerful emotion above all.

Loneliness.

Oh, that's not the word they used—it's not a word they were trained to use. But it's what they meant. They looked back and saw how far they were from everything and everyone they knew, and a brief but utterly piercing bout of homesickness took hold of them. They felt small, they felt desolate, they felt alone. And for a few seconds of doubt, in their deepest hearts, they wondered if they might die.

Die!

Now—these were individuals far too disciplined to dwell on their fears, or to allow such intangible phantoms to unman them for long. But they all noted it, in one fashion or another. And yet they had travelled only as far as the moon, only a few days' journey away, where the earth was still visible and bright and blue.

What, I wondered, would happen when men looked back at earth longingly from a month's journey away, or a year's? When the planet was only a speck in space, without dimension or colour? Or worse, when the planet was so far away that it was lost completely, invisible across the void? How piercing would the homesickness be then, how crippling the loneliness, how overpowering the fear?

My modelling—lacking data, admittedly—showed frightening trends. It showed astronauts on interplanetary journeys reduced to acute depression and psychosis, to panic and dysfunction. I began to theorise that perhaps not merely a man's body was dependent upon the earth, but that maybe his consciousness was dependent upon the earth as well. That our awareness was fundamentally enmeshed with the planet. So enmeshed indeed that it might not only be extremely distressing for humans to travel far from earth, it might actually be lethal to us. It might kill the mind and the spirit to be taken too far from home. And if so, then the implications for space exploration . . .

And the implications for me! After everything I'd been through, to find out that my planned escape might be a mortally doomed exercise!

I needed to know more, so I commenced new studies of astronauts. Ideally, I would have liked to observe and analyse crews who were going at least as far as the moon—but alas, those days were gone. The only missions we were sending beyond earth's orbit anymore were unmanned craft, and they had no feelings to report.

Instead, I turned to the crews of the shuttles, and later the space station, and designed physical and psychological experiments for them to carry out. Officially, I was researching the long-term effects of microgravity. But privately—for I had not yet shared my fears—I was investigating the separation syndrome. True, these astronauts were so close to earth that the syndrome was barely in play—only two hundred miles stood between them and the planet—but I had nothing else to work with. Year after year went by and no definitive answer came. I felt I was peering blindly into the darkness.

The turn of the century arrived. In fact, of the millennium. I had lived to see a new age. It was almost thirty years since I'd drowned, and eighty-nine since I'd first died under the landslide. But then something remarkable occurred. My employers came to me and offered me a place on a shuttle flight, to run my own experiments, first hand.

I hadn't expected that. Not so soon. My own plan had been to wait for more advanced forms of space travel. I would feign old age before then, and retire, and move away. I would change my name and appearance, and then return afresh to the space program, unrecognised by anyone. And only then would I fly into space, and search for the stars. The future was what mattered. A place on a shuttle mission served no purpose of mine at all.

Ah, but how could I refuse? You and I, orphan, may have flown beyond the atmosphere solely by our own willpower, but alone I was not capable of such a feat—not then. I had never experienced space, only dreamt of it.

I forgot all about the future, and said yes.

It didn't happen immediately. There were two years of astronaut training to get through first, and then delays with the launch. But finally—only a few short months ago now, and how strange that seems—I found myself strapped to a seat in the crew section of a space shuttle, listening to the last seconds of countdown.

Then came ignition. Then lift-off. And, at last, ascent.

But what a brutal process it was! For all my preparation, I hadn't really understood the violence it takes to rip a craft free of the planet's grasp. All I could do was grit my teeth and endure as the shuttle shook and kicked and twisted, labouring for eight endless minutes against gravity and the atmosphere. There was a small window visible from my seat, and through it I watched the sky outside turn deeper and deeper shades of blue, until finally it was black, and we had broken through into space. Then the engines cut out, and the imaginary hooks that had been sunk into my shoulder blades, hauling me down, finally let loose. And that's when . . . well, when everything changed.

Microgravity is the correct term. But what a heartless name that is for a state so transformative to a human being—for a creature born to eternal weight to suddenly be weightless! Oh, true, others around me, in those initial moments, grew nauseous and faint because of it. But I felt fine. More than fine, I felt exultant. Some would have said it was only the blood rushing to my brain in zero gravity, yet it wasn't that. I was a prisoner tasting freedom for the very first time, I was a bird taking wing.

However, there was no time just then for mere awe and wonder. We had work to do. There were experiments to be unpacked and set up and initiated—the first few hours passed by in a blur. The first few days, in fact. And anyway, I soon learnt that living in a shuttle is hardly as dreamlike as floating free in space itself.

For one thing, it's noisy. There's no insulation around all the valves and pumps that keep the shuttle functioning—insulation would be extra weight—so every clang and gurgle is painfully loud. And it's smelly too. Washing facilities are limited, and yet people sweat and stink the same way they do on earth. The toilet, technical wonder that it may be, is not exactly airtight when it comes to odours—and microgravity plays hell with human digestion, the result of which is farting. A lot *of farting.*

Still, occasionally I found time to float and spin for no other reason than the simple joy of it. And more importantly, I eventually managed to press my face to a window and—for one long uninterrupted hour—stare at the earth spinning below. Now . . . I'd read all the reports of those who had been in space before me, and I was familiar with the emotions that those men and women had experienced when they'd gazed upon the earth for the first time from afar. They always talked of the ethereal beauty of the planet, of its delicacy and uniqueness, of its soft glow and of the gossamer thinness of its atmosphere.

It wasn't like that for me. Looking down I saw beauty, yes, but not the beauty of an eggshell jewel—I saw the beauty of an immensely powerful beast. I saw the hard, carved faces of the continents, and the inexorable currents of the oceans flowing. I felt the atmosphere humming with electricity, and the inside of the planet bursting with suppressed heat. I sensed what a savage thing the world really is—strong, hot, and driven by systems so vast that they dwarf mankind and all his works to nullity.

In short, I saw the monster that has toyed with me these last ninety-two years. But for once I was safe from it. No landslide could reach me up there on the shuttle. No fumes from beneath a lake could float so high. No downdraft could blast me with furnace winds, no ocean wave could mesmerise me and sweep me away. Oh, the earth held me fast in orbit still, it's true, but otherwise, just for once, it could not touch me.

So I felt no loneliness as I gazed down. I felt no hopelessness or homesickness. All I felt was a dizzying relief. That, and the desire to be even further away; to be on a spacecraft, racing to the outer edge of the solar system; to watch the giant globe dwindle to a blue marble, and then to a pinpoint, and then to nothing at all.

From that moment on I scarcely cared about my experiments and tests. What concern of mine was it if other people would have trouble leaving the planet? I knew now that, when the time came, I would have no difficulty. The separation syndrome was a problem for lesser minds, and for lesser beings than myself. Oh, I performed the minimum duties required of me, I ran my tests and recorded my results. But I did no more.

I confess that I became a little strange. A week in, I felt so detached from earth it was a struggle to remember that other people still lived down here. Even video links didn't help—the world they showed seemed too weird. People could not float at will down here, rooms were deformed by oddities like floors and ceilings, and every movement looked heavy and sluggish and wrong. I was so much more at home in space. In my mind it was already my natural environment, and where I would spend my eternity.

But all too soon, the sixteen days were up. My tests were done, the mission complete. I did not want to go. But I comforted myself, as I packed my things away and we manoeuvred for re-entry, that at least my return to earth would be only temporary. I would see space again one day. I had savoured release now, and there was nothing the planet could do about that. Its long dominion over me was broken.

I've beaten you, I cried silently from my seat, staring at the little window. We were descending into the atmosphere, and on the other side of the glass the fires of re-entry were already beginning to glow. I've beaten you!

The glare outside grew brighter and brighter.

And brighter still.

And then . . .

What a shooting star we must have made. One hundred tons of space shuttle, disintegrating across the daylight heavens.

I don't really remember it. The concussion of breaking up at the speed we were travelling was far too severe. I have the dimmest recollection of the shuttle slewing sideways, and then a series of hammer blows and . . . well, then nothing.

I awoke to find myself tumbling through air. If it can be called waking. I was blind, and deaf. I could taste flesh burning, and I knew somehow that a wind was howling about me, but there was no other feeling from any part of my body. Looking back, I can only assume I had no body—that most of it was gone, burnt away even beyond pain. I must have been little more than a charred lump of bone and calcified tissue, a smoking piece of hardened debris arcing down from the main fireball. A human meteorite . . .

Then came another concussion, and I was in water. I tasted salt. It was the ocean. But I had no arms left with which to swim, and no body fat left with which to float, so I continued to fall, sinking into the depths. I didn't mind. The ocean had welcomed me before. But even as I sank, there came a stinging that grew into intense pain. It was my skin, beginning to knit itself anew. My immortality had been strained to breaking point, yes, but my body was already beginning its recovery. I drifted away then, before the agony became too great, and rolled in the comfortable darkness for a time.

When I woke again I had skin, and arms and legs—and although I was otherwise an empty shell, I could feel sunlight on me.

I was lying on a beach.

I was here.

The orphan opened her eyes.

For a moment she didn't know where she was. Then she saw that it was her own room, she was on the bed, and through the window it was nearly dawn. She was wholly awake, after her long dream and the foreigner's tale . . .

A sudden, inexplicable thrill ran through her.

She sat up, stark naked, her body feeling charged with energy. What was it? Why was she so excited? The foreigner's story?

Yes, there was something he'd said, something amid all the wonders of rockets and machines in space and his fiery descent . . .

No, it was something he *hadn't* said!

He had told his tale in full now. The story of all his lives. Every place he had been. And he had *not* been to her island before. Not in his last life. Especially not twenty-one years ago. He had never met her mother.

She leapt up. She had to go to him. She had to be near him now, to touch him. And even as she threw on some clothes, his laughter echoed in her.

Very well then, dear orphan, come if you must. Come straight to me, do not wander. Talk to no one. But you are right.

Whatever else I am, I am not your father.

23

The orphan hurried across the compound. The lower sky was aflame with red, but it was night yet. Nothing around her seemed quite real. The hospital, the jungle, the mountain—they were two-dimensional, pretend things made of paper. It was only the dream world, the foreigner's world, that was vivid anymore.

And ah, his presence was like a ball of heat she could sense even out in the yard, right through the crematorium walls, as if she was freezing and he was the only life-saving fire. He was her bright saviour who had fallen, burning, from the sky to illuminate her. And the excitement in her gut was almost a nausea.

Then she was in the back wards, the darkness no impediment. She came through the dayroom—empty now, the television useless with no power cord—to the doorway of his cell. He was there, alone in the gloom, prone and helpless in his bed. But to her special sight his body glowed luminous beneath the sheet.

He did not speak. She moved to his side, lifted a corner of the sheet, then tugged it away completely. For the first time, she looked upon his naked form with full understanding of who and what he was. It was all so clear now—the delicate, bare sheen of his skin, clean of any hair or mark or scar. It was *new*, that was why. His old flesh had burnt away in the sky as he hurtled down to earth, and this skin was freshly grown, too young to be anything but smooth and pale.

Yet *he* was not young. He was age and strength and wisdom. He had lived so many lives and seen so much. Pain had seared him, yes, but it had refined him down to something sparse and beautiful. She wanted to possess him, to absorb him, to encompass his inner vitality tighter and tighter, until it shone within her too.

But did he feel the same way? Doubt pierced her. There was nothing new about *her* skin, there was no sparse beauty about *her* body.

His laughter was gentle in her mind. *How many times do I have to tell you . . .*

And that only fed the hunger already awake in her. But the doubt persisted. She had seen herself through the eyes of others too many times—patients, nurses, doctors—and beheld the squat, awkward child they all saw.

Look through my eyes then.

Startled, the orphan lifted her gaze and saw that, while his eyes had been closed when she'd entered the room, they were open now.

See what I see.

The offer was irresistible, and she flowed into him. The world spun, and then she was blinking at—herself. The perspective was low, from the bed. *His* perspective. She wasn't fully inside his body—she was still in her own, upright—but it was through his eyes that she saw. And she was unrecognisable to herself.

It wasn't that she was a different shape. She was still square and stumpy, her hair cropped short by hospital scissors, her dour face glowering at the foreigner in stubborn puzzlement. But to *his* eyes, there was no dullness or stupidity in her—there was only strength. And her flesh strained against her drab clothes not because she was fat, but because she was bursting with hidden light and power, more than her body could contain. And the only emotion she could detect in the foreigner was a desire to see that power unveiled, to glory in every inch of her.

Yes. Take off your clothes.

Instantly, everything she was wearing seemed too restrictive to bear. She didn't hesitate. Still inhabiting his eyes, she watched as her hands fumbled to undress. It was confusing, the double viewpoint—to still be inside her body by touch, but outside of it by sight. But soon enough her clothes were gone.

Ah, the foreigner breathed.

She had never stood naked in front of anyone before; she would have been too ashamed. But now it felt wonderful. Cooler, as if the temperature had rapidly dropped, and free, as if she was suddenly half her normal weight.

And, through his eyes, it *looked* wonderful, too. Her clothes had been so ugly. Without the constrictions of sleeves and straps and waistbands, her body had taken its natural shape, and it was *right*. She wasn't square at all. She was round, she was made up of circles—the circle of her hips, the circles of her breasts and, within them, the smaller, protruding circles that terminated in her nipples—all of them proper, all of them in proportion, all of them swollen with a particularly female potency. And all of them, to his gaze, focused around the great orb of her belly, and the mound partly hidden below it, where a whole new world of curves and circles opened . . .

You see?

She saw. And she felt. Her hands were moving over herself, and the sensations were so maddeningly pleasant that it made the world spin again, and then she was back behind her own eyes. The foreigner lay naked on the bed before her, and she was acutely aware of the contrast between her body and his, how angular he was—his shoulders wide, his torso narrowing into his hips—and how particularly *male* that made him.

A shudder ran through her of outright . . . starvation? Yes, it was a physical need, a deprivation. It wasn't like it was when she played in her room alone, just for fun, fingering the little button of sensitive flesh between her legs. That wasn't going to be nearly enough to satisfy what she felt now.

She reached out, finally, and touched him. And yes, she had touched him before, but never like this, never so gently. His skin was cool and firm, and her fingers trailed along his side, defining his chest and his hip and his upper thigh, sensing the muscles there, unused, passive, yet promising so much.

But her fingers wouldn't do. She needed to smell him too, and taste him. She sank to her knees and lowered her head so that her mouth followed just above her roving fingers. And then, right where his hip bone pushed against his skin, she bit him, her mouth opening to absorb as much flesh as she could.

She shuddered again, tasting salt on her tongue, the thrill of consuming him setting her alight down low. He could feel it too, she knew. Excitement steamed from his mind and made the air tingle. And yet his skin did not flinch or quiver or respond in any way. And when she raised her mouth, her gaze fell upon his penis, lying pallid against his leg. It had not stirred since she'd entered the room.

The orphan did not know much about sex, but she knew that if the foreigner was like other men, then his cock—if he was truly aroused—was supposed to be erect. And the peculiar hunger in her *wanted* it erect.

Alas, my orphan . . .

She understood, of course. His body was rebuilding itself. He had told her. Nerves and muscles were not yet connected.

But oh, the disappointment!

What can I say? I'm free to roam with my mind, but to affect reality, to shift flesh and bone, that's not something I can do.

And yet, you . . .

Yes? She stared at his blank face, alert. Was there a way?

When you called to the breeze, up on the hill, you were very close to success. Perhaps, here and now, if you tried again . . .

Ah! Was it possible? Calling the breeze had been a basic procedure, a matter of warming air to make it rise, and she had failed. To do something like this, to influence someone else's body—she didn't know how to even attempt it.

Look within, beyond the skin. You'll find systems and patterns and order there as you would with any natural thing.

The orphan nodded. She swung herself onto the bed, her legs astride his shins, her breasts hanging down over his thighs. She stared at his penis, smooth and pale, and at his balls beneath, as hairless as the rest of him.

How did it all work? That was the question.

Blood. The blood must flow and fill.

Blood . . . Yes, she could see the veins, faint blue, running along the soft tube of flesh. And then, deeper in—there. Tissue. Like a sponge, ready to absorb blood and engorge to hardness. Ha. It was all so simple.

Only no . . . there were nerves too, clusters of them radiating out from the sheathed head, running to his groin and his balls and his spine. Not simple at all, but complex! Those nerves were the key, she saw, for they would send the signals that would make the blood flow. At least, they would in a normal man, where the nerves were connected. But in the foreigner those impulses had nowhere to go. The way was closed.

You will have to move the blood yourself.

The orphan bent low, so that her mouth hovered above his cock, and she breathed warm air on it, preparing it for life. Then she reached out with her mind, exploring the byways of his arteries and veins, and the reservoirs of his heart. His heart, she began there—heating it with her thoughts, and squeezing it, so that it beat deeper and faster. Then she hunted through the tangle of vessels in his groin and found those that needed to be relaxed and those that needed to be tightened until at last the blood was allowed to pump into the waiting chambers of his penis.

The flesh trembled. Shifted against his thigh.

Then, magically, it began to rise.

Yes . . .

Yes! His pale body flushed with colour. Tremors ran down the length of him, his muscles twitching in the sudden surge of heat. He was coming to life, his essence concentrated into his stiffening prick. It had lifted now, so that it almost brushed against her lips—caused by her, existing uniquely *for* her.

Yes . . .

She heard a hoarse edge to his voice that suggested he wanted something more. And so did she—only, what exactly? What was supposed to happen next? She stared in frustration at his erection, straight as a broom handle.

And then she was remembering what she had witnessed in the virgin's memories, the things the men had done when the virgin was a girl. And she was remembering too the night nurse as he had thrust his hips against her. The very idea had seemed so disgusting then, but now, extraordinarily, it seemed the opposite. There was the obvious hardness of the foreigner, and in comparison

her own urgent desire to enfold something, to clutch at something—
something hard. So, what if she . . . ?

The foreigner was laughing softly at her ignorance, but she
didn't care about that. The hunger was too great. In one compulsive
movement she slid up his thighs, her legs spread, and lowered
herself, using one hand to guide him straight into the middle of
her. For an awkward moment it did not seem that it would go,
the angle was wrong, or there was an inner resistance. But in her
mind she was already wide open to receive him, and with a strange
spasm, her cunt suddenly agreed.

He slid in. And in.

A formless sound came from him. The orphan held her breath,
not knowing what to make of the sensation, whether it was pleasure
or pain. But then a delicious warmth grew in her. She felt they
were both rising off the bed. Not their shadow selves but their real
selves—as if his paralysed hips were actually alive and thrusting
upwards, pushing his cock in deeper and deeper, lifting her up and
splitting her apart.

And oh, but it was *nice*.

Then, behind her, someone sniggered. She whirled about and
saw a shadow in the doorway. A mocking face. It was the night
nurse, grinning at her. She caught a vicious glimpse of herself
through his eyes; she was stupid and ugly again, a ludicrous sight,
hunched grossly over the foreigner's body.

The orphan grunted in embarrassment and fury, but the night
nurse ignored the warning, standing there with his eyes roaming
cruelly, until she heaved herself up and off the bed, lunging at him.
His grin turned to a snarl and he yelled something she couldn't
understand. Then he dashed away. She followed him out into the
dayroom, but by then he was already scampering off down the hall

to the back wards, and she paused. She couldn't pursue him naked through the entire hospital.

She gave it up and stood there a moment, feeling angry and excited and cheated all at once. All she had to do was rush back to the foreigner and resume the wonderful thing they had started . . . and yet she lingered, staring about at the darkness, not knowing why. The sweat was cooling on her skin, leaving her cold. And it was so quiet. The whole crematorium might have been deserted of life.

Well, the duke was gone, she reminded herself. And the witch. There were only the archangel and the virgin left. And they would be sleeping. That explained it. Except it didn't. Not the sense of vacancy. Cautiously, the orphan pushed open the door to one of the bedrooms, the one the witch and the virgin had shared. Both of the beds were empty. Frowning, she turned to the other bedroom. The virgin must be in there with the archangel. But that was against the rules . . .

Forget them, orphan. Come back to me.

But it nagged at her too strongly. If the nurses found them that way, there would be trouble. She crossed to the door.

Please. Don't go in there. Not yet.

But she went. And yes, there they were, two shapes in the darkness stretched on one of the beds, the smaller figure cradled in the other's arms.

Only . . . why were the sheets black?

And then she was really seeing. The swollen, battered face, the bloodstains around the mouth and eyes, the bruised throat. The virgin, dead, and—judging by the way the blood had crusted stiff—dead for hours.

And the archangel, rocking slightly as he held her close.

24

All through the morning, the sandy driveway leading up to the hospital was crowded with vehicles. Some of them the orphan recognised—the police captain's car, and the mayor's car. But others were unfamiliar. Especially the vehicles with flashing lights. She guessed that these came from the big town, and that the men in them, uniformed and sombre, were the big town police.

Two vans came also. One was blue, and into it they put the archangel. His hands were bound and he had to be carried out by the police. He was crying and struggling, pleading to the sky, a skinny, fearful youth. The other van was grey, and into that they put the body of the virgin, on a stretcher, wrapped in a sheet.

The orphan saw it all from the front office. She spent most of the morning there, with the old doctor and the police captain and the night nurse. The three men talked from time to time, and even though the orphan couldn't understand a word, she was certain they were talking about her. The night nurse in particular—he was telling the other two about what he'd seen in the foreigner's room, she was sure; about her being naked on top of the patient, and all

249

the while the dead body next door. The old doctor and the captain would listen, and then they would turn and stare at her.

It was frightening.

She could have reached out to the foreigner and asked him to translate what was being said, but she did not want to talk to him. Not yet. She was too unsure. All the previous night, while she had lazed in her hut dreaming on the bed, the foreigner whispering his tale in her mind—all that time, the virgin had already been killed. And he must have known. He always knew everything. But he'd said nothing. Instead he'd let the orphan come to him, and they had done those things together, and ten feet from them the virgin was cold and staring, her blood gone black.

That, too, was frightening.

Late in the morning, after the archangel and the virgin had been taken away, the big town police themselves came into the office. They addressed the old doctor briefly. Then they turned to the night nurse, eyes hardening. He shook his head at their questions, sweating nervously, and finally pointed his finger at the orphan. Then the police, incomprehensible, were asking *her* the questions.

Even then, the orphan didn't call on the foreigner. It was all too plain anyway. The idiot night nurse—she would make him suffer for this. But her anger flared only a moment, then faded. He was scared, that was all. He was the one who would be most in trouble. It was his responsibility to monitor the wards at night. They couldn't blame a poor retarded girl for this—let alone a comatose patient.

So she merely waited, staring at the police blankly until they gave up, foiled by her silence. They turned back to the old doctor, who shrugged. He began to explain—no doubt—that she was only a simple, stupid thing. They conversed a few moments more, then it was all over. The police departed, and the captain with them, and the night nurse too slunk away. The orphan rose to go. But the old doctor held up a finger to her—wait—before he followed the others out. He was back shortly afterwards, and to the orphan's dismay, he was carrying a bowl of soup.

Oh, not this again.

He put the bowl down on the desk and made the orphan sit in front of it. He wanted her to eat. And she took up the spoon, but . . .

She wasn't hungry. More than that, she simply didn't *need* the food. She'd scarcely eaten in days now, or drunk any water, but it was obvious to her that she was not suffering for it. Indeed, she'd never felt so strong and light. Looking at the soup, all she could think of was how heavily it would sit in her stomach, how much it would slow her down, and how it would only make her urinate, and shit . . . and she felt *past* all that, somehow. She shook her head, shoved the bowl away.

The old doctor gazed at her, disappointed. She realised that this was about more than just the food, that it was about her entire behaviour through these last days. But she couldn't possibly explain. She nodded at the door, asking if she could go, and he nodded back, eyes full of sadness. There was a finality about that sadness that disturbed the orphan deeply. But she went anyway.

She spent the afternoon roaming the wards, too unsettled to stay in one place. The hospital was equally unsettled around her. The nurses, the cooks, the other staff—everyone was going about their routines as if it was a normal day. But to the orphan it was all pretence. It wasn't a normal day. She felt that a facade had been fractured. The volcano erupting, the duke's attack, the witch's self-inflicted injuries . . . each of those occurrences had sent ripples of apprehension through the wards—but even so, the hospital had carried on. This death, however, this murder of the virgin, was far worse. This the staff could not deny or explain away.

Something was very wrong. The inmates sensed it. They refused to behave. They left their rooms, they threw away their food, they ripped their clothes, they yelled. The nurses ran to and fro, trying to maintain control. It was the orphan's job to help them, but she did nothing, even when nurses snapped orders at her.

The townsfolk sensed it too. All afternoon a crowd built in the front driveway, people who had walked all the way from town to stare at the hospital. Some were there a few minutes only, some for hours, gathering into groups, muttering. At one point the orphan stood out on the porch to look at them. A dozen faces turned silently to look back at her, and she retreated again, afraid without knowing why.

But the strangest thing of all was that everyone, staff and patients alike, avoided the crematorium. The hallway that led there may as well have been a dead end. As far as the orphan could tell, no one went down it all day. No one, it seemed, cared about the last remaining patient there. No one wanted to attend to his needs, to feed him, or to wash him—or to be alone with him in the darkness.

The orphan did not enter either, not during the day. There were too many eyes about, watching. She went that night, when the inmates were finally asleep and the nurses had all gone home. The hospital was not completely unvigilant even then—the old doctor was still in his office, the lights burning, and the night nurse was sullenly patrolling the front wards—but no one guarded the crematorium.

And what an alien, shadowy, silent place it had become. In the dayroom there was no longer any noise or glow from the television, and from the bedrooms there came no snore or murmur of sleeping patients. It was all quiet and emptiness. And it was only now that the orphan wondered why that emptiness hadn't been filled. Other wards were overcrowded, she knew. Yet no one had been moved here.

She opened the door to one of the bedrooms. The two beds in there had been stripped, but one still bore dark stains on its mattress. She noticed something else in the shadows, an object against the wall. She went and picked it up. It was the archangel's book. The cover felt smooth from the boy's endlessly stroking fingers, but when she opened it, she saw that the pages were matted together with the virgin's blood.

She dropped the thing, and passed on to the foreigner's cell. He was a pale, lonely shape underneath the sheet, and she hung back in the doorway, watching him, trying to decide how she felt. Was she angry? Was that the reason she'd come? To ask him why he hadn't told her what had happened in the archangel's room? Why he hadn't warned her? Yes . . . but it was more than that.

How could he have let it happen in the first place?

His voice, when it came, held no apology or regret. Only a calm air of inquiry. *You think I should have stopped it?*

Yes, of course he should have stopped it!

That would have meant entering the archangel's mind. Taking control of him. Yet you made me promise not to interfere like that again.

Yes, but—

Anyway, he was not controllable by then. His failure with the virgin had fuelled his madness beyond measure. Twice more he assailed her, after you were gone, and twice more he failed, and each time he had to punish her all the more severely for the sin. Until, willing as she was, she could no longer survive the punishment.

And her—floating in her shadows, looking at the world through her little window. She was like me, orbiting in space, safely out of reach. But then she wanted escape from the safety, she wanted to feel a human touch again. She wanted re-entry. The archangel was her atmosphere, and she threw herself into him, too hard, too fast. And so she burnt up, orgasming with the pain even as she died.

Inevitable really. I didn't cause it. And I couldn't have stopped it. Why, then, am I somehow to blame?

The orphan had no answer. She'd been inside the minds of both the archangel and the virgin, and knew he was right. Or that he *might* be right. But to call her here afterwards, to do the things they did, while the corpse was so close by . . .

I know. But I had no choice. I knew if I told you, you would alert the authorities, and then everything would change for us.

And she *had* alerted the authorities—or at least the night nurse—as soon as she'd found the body. But what did he mean? What was going to change?

The world has not been blind to events here. The duke, the witch, and now the archangel and the virgin. It has all been noticed. The old doctor is wondering. The nurses and the other staff as well. The police are wondering too.

Unease rose in the orphan. Wondering about what?

About me. About what's happened in this ward. And you've seen the crowd gathering in front of the hospital? They've been wondering most of all. No doubt the townsfolk have always whispered tales about this place and its inmates, but now they're whispering about one particular inmate. A man who sleeps, but doesn't. A man who has come to their little town and is spreading havoc and death about him, even though he cannot move or speak. They are remembering old stories their grandparents told them, about undead spirits and devils. They are not educated people. Words like comatose won't satisfy them.

Yes! It was true. The orphan had seen it herself, in the eyes of the men and women out on the driveway. The fear. The hostility.

They'll be back tomorrow. More of them. That's why I did not hurry to tell you about the virgin. I knew this would be the result. Those people will demand action. They will make the police, or the staff here, do something.

Unease became alarm. Do what?

At the very least, they will have me sent away. But even worse things are possible. Violence comes so easily when crowds are involved.

And now she was angry. But not at him anymore. She understood why he'd acted the way he had. He'd had no choice. Not if there was a chance they might send him away from her. That couldn't be allowed to happen. That wouldn't be fair. And if they *hurt* him . . . it was too awful to think about.

Yes, but now that there are the two of us, perhaps there are actions of our own we can take. We may not be defenceless.

She stood straighter in the doorway. What kind of actions?

On my own I am helpless. If they came for me now I could not stop them. But you and I together . . . You saw what you did with my body, with my blood. That was your power. And together, perhaps, we could do much more.

Ah, but she wasn't sure. Had she really done it? The blood may have moved in his veins for natural reasons. She couldn't be positive . . .

There's only one way to find out.

What way?

We must devise a test. A test that will leave no doubt, a test that will tell us just how potent you have become, and how well we can protect ourselves.

She moved to his side, staring at his sleeping face, and a now familiar thrill awoke in her stomach. Yes. Her loyalty and her love may have wavered a moment when she was scared, but she reaffirmed them now. Completely. Whatever he wanted her to do, whatever he needed, she was ready for it.

Good. I know just the place.

She took his hand, and they were away.

25

And oh, how marvellous it was. To be soaring again—high in the atmosphere, two shadow shapes, the wind a thin shriek in their ears, their real bodies left behind unwanted and forgotten in the crematorium.

The orphan didn't know how far they had come from her little island, all she knew was that they had flown from night into daylight, and now the world was unrolling below her in all its multitudes of colours and textures. There were the vivid blues of the oceans, the greenish-blacks of the forests, the brilliant whites of the deserts. There were the tablecloth wrinkles of sand dunes, the knife cuts of river gorges, the piles of shattered crockery that were the mountain ranges. There were sheets of cloud that shone like mirrored steel, and other clouds that were monstrous fists, clenched and raised against the heavens. There were great waves out at sea that reared and rolled and crashed without ever coming in sight of a shore. And everything, land, water and air, glowed as if the light came not from the sun, but from some source internal to the planet.

Then they flew into nightfall again, out-racing day. Lights sprang up across the globe, cities and towns that formed spider's webs of orange, surrounded by darkness. Ships moved at sea, their courses marked by lines of luminescence that streaked this way and that across the ocean like foam. Bright flashes brewed and flickered in thunderheads, and above the storms ghostly flares of green and red streamed into space. And over it all, set in a night deeper than the orphan had ever seen, the stars hung unrecognisable, shaded with subtle hues of emerald and ruby and sapphire.

On and on it went. Forever. But this wasn't like their earlier flights. There was still the wonder and the joy, oh yes, but the orphan felt that she was older now, and beyond the simple amazement of those other times. She had been a child then, not knowing anything, not even about herself. But now, even as she revelled in the freedom of the air, she was aware of a deeper, steadier, more fulfilling purpose.

It was because of him, of course. No, it was because of *them*, him and her—the foreigner no longer foreign, the orphan no longer orphaned. They had joined together, physically and mentally, and now they were flying together to face the dangers that threatened them, their fates their own to decide, their defence their own responsibility. That too was a grown-up thing. And a good thing.

Meanwhile, their ghost selves were stark naked!

She'd never noticed it before. On the other flights she'd been too preoccupied to really look. But now she saw that their forms were not merely the amorphous hints of bodies she had supposed. The foreigner was identifiably himself. His face was a dark veil without real features, but his limbs were clearly outlined, glowing faintly, and every inch of him was familiar to her, right down to the wisp of smoke that was his cock. He was beautiful, a *real* archangel, made by no god, and serving none.

And she was beautiful too. Not the slow idiot girl of the earthbound world, but a wraith, streamlined by the upper winds, a shadow that sparkled as if shot through with its own stars. Still herself, still round and short and plump, but free of weight now, free of awkwardness, a goddess of fertility on the wing.

And ah . . . what would it be like to make use of these bodies? Were they capable of genuine touch and sensation? Could they turn to each other, even now, and set each other's shadow nerves afire with pleasure, and in climaxing become a bolt of orgasmic lightning, arcing across the night sky?

The foreigner laughed. *There'll be time enough for that. Later.*

The orphan felt her skin burning in the cold, half from shame, half from a desire that didn't care about shame at all.

We're close now. Look.

They were descending, she realised, and a pang of loss hit her. She did not want to return to the ground. But it was the foreigner's mind that guided them, not her own, and she could sense the resolve in him.

She looked down. They were far from any ocean now; the world here seemed to consist of desert wastes and bleak mountain ranges. Their destination was a tangled region of narrow valleys, where few lights shone in the night, and where, on the higher peaks, there gleamed crusts of ice and snow.

They fell lower, and the dry mountain air felt more chill even than it had high above. The orphan shivered. She knew this place. Ahead she saw one steep valley which seemed to brim with blackness—a long, spear-shaped expanse of icy water.

Yes. She had been here before.

As shadows, they dropped and then alighted on the valley floor. Beside them was a river bed, rocky and shallow, empty except for a trickle. On either side, walls of stone tilted away to frigid heights.

And before them rose an immense pile of broken rock, blocking the valley from side to side. The orphan looked up, remembering, and there above the landslide she could see the great scoop that had been cut from the mountain, seemingly as fresh as it had been that night ninety-two years before.

Yes. It was here that my immortality began.

The orphan shivered again, from dread. How was it possible that anyone could have crawled alive from under that fallen hillside? The weight of it oppressed her even from without. But to be buried there, crushed beneath it all . . .

It shouldn't have been possible. It couldn't have been.

But it was.

She glanced at the ghost beside her. What did he want here? Why had they come to this place, of all places?

To see if, together, we can release the waters.

The shock of it almost made her laugh out loud. He wanted them to try to shift the landslide? To move a whole toppled mountain?

Not all of it. And there was no laughter in him. *You can feel it yourself, the pressure the dam is under. There are billions of tons of water—the whole lake—pushing from behind. If we weaken it enough, the landslide will fall. And if we can do something like this, then we need not fear anyone, or anything, ever again.*

She heard his sincerity. He believed that this was necessary, and possible. But the orphan was not convinced. To call a breeze, to make blood flow, that was one thing. But to shift so much rock, so much weight!

Come. I'll show you.

They lifted once more, soaring up the dam wall, over stone and scree and dark clefts where small bushes grew, until they gained the top. Here the landslide had formed a rampart a hundred yards across, beyond which the heap fell away again. And there, on the far side, was the water—a great lake, wide and black, running away to lose itself in the far reaches of the valley.

Even now, so many decades since the landslide, this lake remains one of the most remote and unexplored bodies of water anywhere in the world. No boats sail here, no people swim, no houses or docks or parks line its shore. There is only my old village here, buried far beneath. And once in a while, a few lonely tourists will come to marvel at the sight. Or structural engineers, to study the dam and to worry.

They descended to the surface of the lake, sank through it, and slid down the wall until they stood again on the valley floor. They were drowned now, encased in silent, unmoving, ice-like darkness—a vast tomb of captive water. And holding it back was the dam. The orphan, her vision piercing the black depths, saw it rise before her, the submerged rocks covered with a slime that somehow survived at near freezing.

You feel the pressure? You feel the water pushing? Does the landslide seem such a big thing now? Does it seem immovable?

It didn't. Even in ghost form the orphan could feel the tremendous potential energy of the lake, all those miles of water behind her, wanting to run free. And all that weight was remorselessly probing and pushing at the jumbled rocks of the dam.

There is a balance, for now, between rock and water. The lake is not rising. Water oozes through the dam to feed the stream on the other side, and that outflow matches the inflows from further up the valley. It all might stay like this for centuries yet.

But if we upset the equipoise . . . Do you see those giant slabs of rock at the base of the landslide? Do you see how much of the heap rests on them? Do you see that if we push hard enough on them, at just the right angle . . .

The orphan saw. The foreigner's mind illuminated the pile in all its complexity, and the lines of stress were as visible to her as the cracks in the walls back at the hospital. If the slabs at the bottom shifted, and the full force of the lake fell upon a point suddenly weakened . . . then, oh yes, it might happen.

Will you help me?

Of course she would. There was never any question. Only, she was afraid. So much water, so much stone, the fury that would be unleashed . . .

It will be glorious. Push now. With me.

How? She had no hands, no arms, they were only shadows.

Just do it!

She tried. Focusing upon the slabs, she desired with all her might that they would obey. She felt his mind in tandem with hers. Together, they *willed* it. Pushing. Clutching. Wrapping themselves around the rocks, compelling them, no matter the weight, no matter the pressure—demanding that they shift.

Nothing moved.

More! cried the foreigner.

The orphan felt that her very brain was contorting with the effort. She heard the desperation in his voice. And it came to her, even as she strove, why it was that he had chosen this place in which to test their powers. Nowhere else but here, she saw, could he hope to extract payment for his many deaths. There was no point in returning to the lake that had suffocated him with its poisonous fumes. That disaster had left no trace of itself, no damage he could rectify. Likewise, he could not return to the thunderstorm that had roasted him with its heat. The lethal downdraft no longer existed and never would again. Nor could he return to the ocean in search of the wave that had drowned him. It had passed away.

And as for his fall from space, and the atmosphere that had burnt him—well, it was everywhere. Always. Beyond challenge.

No, only here was there anything tangible, anything limited, anything of the scale that he could attempt. Only here was there a memorial to his sufferings and indignities. Only here could he act. He had the knowledge to do it. Far better than she, he saw exactly where the force needed to go. If only he had the strength.

More! he cried again.

And the orphan gave it. She ceased trying to push the rocks. Instead, she surrendered herself to him. Out of understanding, out of pity, out of love. She saw his need and, in response, gave him the totality of what she was. He accepted it all. She filled him, and he swelled with her power, and he struck.

The slabs shattered as one.

The foreigner was shouting. He lifted the orphan up through the lake as the landslide cracked and slipped down, struggling for new purchase. They cleared the surface and rose high over the dam. Just in time. Below them, the wall groaned, slumped, and split apart. Almost half a mile high, a deluge of water and rock collapsed outward into the valley.

It seemed to take an eternity to fall. But then the mass hit the ground and exploded up and out and suddenly everything was in motion, the lake heaving all at once into a torrent that went ravaging its way downstream. The orphan had never known such a sound—grating, roaring, it filled the air like a solid thing. But the foreigner had her, and they were swooping through the dust, chasing after the headwaters as they leapt and burst along the valley, ripping entire hillsides away. He was laughing, and the orphan was dragged along behind, lost to amazement.

They had *caused* this. It was dreadful, and exhilarating, and in some strange way it was painful too, as if in breaking the dam they had broken something inside themselves. But what did that matter? They had proven their power. There was nothing they could not do. The orphan laughed too, a savage elation waking in her. She was flying with her lover, racing the thunderous waters. The mountains shook in awe, and the air withdrew in terror before them. She had no need of doubt anymore.

But then she saw lights ahead, in the valley.

It was a village.

No, larger than that, it was a town, spread along the river. The flood was raging towards it, still filling the valley from side to side, still hundreds of metres high, a black, over-towering wall. She was sure she heard screams coming from the town. Thin cries of panic and fear.

The foreigner slowed, letting the surge run ahead of them, pulling her back. She fought him then. She wanted to see—she *had* to see.

No, he said. *Enough.*

His hand held hers too tightly. Straining forward she glimpsed the water devouring the town whole, and the screams came again, men, women and children dying, but then she was hurtling through air, and everything was a blur, and silence fell.

She opened her eyes, back in the foreigner's room.

Enough, he repeated.

The orphan was staring in horror. All those people . . .

She struggled once more to free her hand, and when she couldn't she looked down and saw something impossible. The foreigner himself slept on, but for the first time since she'd known him, his paralysis had broken.

His fingers were moving. Grasping. Clinging to hers.

26

It was what everyone had been waiting for, the orphan knew. The old doctor, the nurses—day after day they had tested the foreigner for signs of life. They had prodded the soles of his feet, they had shone lights in his eyes. They had been looking for exactly this kind of movement. And now it had come.

You must not tell them. If they found out, they'd only take me away to study. No one else must know about this.

The orphan pried her hand loose from his at last, and his arm flopped back onto the mattress. Loathing made her skin creep. Somehow she had never seen anything so obscene as those writhing fingers.

Don't you want me to get better? Isn't it good that my nerves and muscles are finally starting to connect, and to function?

Yes, yes. But her mind was full of horror still. The roar of the water, the lights of the houses vanishing under the black flood . . .

You imagined it.

No, there was a town.

It was an abandoned village, that's all. There were no people. No lights. Engineers decided years ago that the dam was too unstable to be trusted. They evacuated human settlement from the valley as a precaution. No one lives there anymore.

But she'd heard the cries. The screams.

In all that chaos? You don't know what you heard.

An abandoned village. Was it possible? It had been dark, after all, and the noise unspeakable. But she had been so sure . . .

Be sure of our strength instead. Do you appreciate what we've done? And what it means for us?

But the orphan didn't want to hear any of that now. She needed to be alone in her head, she needed time to think.

Time is what we don't have. Those crowds will be gathering in front of the hospital again today. And the old doctor is—

No! She pushed back from the bed, her mind clamping shut. Not now. She turned and strode away through the dayroom. For a few moments she could feel him pressing against her skull, trying to gain entry. But then, mercifully, he was gone.

She emerged into the compound to find the sky pale with sunrise. So, another whole night had flown by. Time. It seemed to move so fast lately. She would slip into the foreigner's world, and the hours would vanish. She stared up at the pink clouds and breathed in the warm air—this was home, this was reality. But it didn't help. In her memory she saw only a frozen valley, and black water crashing . . .

She simply hadn't thought, as they pushed against the dam, that there would be such consequences. That people might die. But what about the foreigner? It was his valley. He must have known that there was a town so close downstream. Had he forgotten? Did he just not care? Or was it true what he said—had she really only imagined the lights, and the sounds of an entire population drowning?

But oh, what if it was real?

And how could she know for *certain*?

She could go back to the valley, perhaps, and see. But no . . . she couldn't fly on her own, and would not know how to find the valley in any case, not without him as her guide. The world was too big, and she knew too little.

Some other way then.

She went to her room and sat hunched on the bed, her brow furrowed. Her glance fell upon her radio. Ah . . .

She switched it on and listened. The device mumbled at her, and the meaning of the sound seemed so close, just a fraction beyond her grasp. But even if she could comprehend—was it likely she would learn anything useful? She understood, at least partly, that normal people sometimes learned of important events in this manner. But would an event so far away, in such a strange land, be talked about here?

She didn't know. She couldn't know. Nor would it do any good to run to the main dayroom and gaze at the television in the cage. The disaster might be portrayed there on the screen—surely, if a whole town had actually died, someone would pay attention—but even if it was, she would never know it.

Proof, disproof, they were equally impossible.

And it wasn't over. The foreigner might have avenged himself upon the landslide, but she sensed it was only a beginning. The destruction of the dam had been but a test—that was the very word he'd used. Not an end in itself, but practice, a measurement of what they were capable of together.

Now that he had made that measurement . . .

Suddenly, someone was knocking on her door.

The orphan shook herself. Had she dropped off to sleep? The light through her window had changed, it was late morning already.

The door opened. It was only the old doctor, his lined face smiling kindly. But he was carrying a tray on which a bowl steamed. She glared at him, and at the bowl. A terrific rage arose in her. Hadn't she made this clear to him yet? She shook her head. And when he proffered the tray anyway, her temper finally snapped. She shoved it away, upending the bowl upon the floor. Soup went everywhere. They both stared at the mess for a long moment. Then the old doctor sighed, and called out.

Two male nurses came bustling in. The orphan goggled at them. They were from the locked ward. She was so shocked she didn't move, even as they grabbed her legs and arms and forced her down on the bed. It was only when the old doctor loomed behind them with a needle in his hand, his expression infinitely regretful, that she started to struggle and scream, and by then it was too late.

•

Wake up, little orphan.

The voice was a prickle on her skin.

Wake up.

Oh, but she wanted to keep on sleeping. So dark, so deep. She had never known a sleep like it, her limbs had sunk right into the bed.

But the voice wouldn't go away, as irritating as an itch. *You must wake up. Now.*

It was the foreigner. She tried to shrug him off, to roll over and return to the depths, but there was a strange resistance from her hands and feet. The lovely darkness was beginning to fragment.

Ugly blurs of light glared through. Her eyes were blinking open. But everything was wrong, everything was—

They've moved you. You're not in your hut anymore.

She saw white walls, and a white ceiling, its cracks thrown into relief by the bar of a harsh fluorescent light. Where was she? She could think of nowhere in the back wards where the walls and the ceilings looked like this.

You're in a room in the locked ward.

What?! But that couldn't be! What was happening? Her memory seemed to reach no further back than the opening of her eyes. But wait . . . there had been the old doctor, with a needle, and she had been fighting . . .

They drugged you.

It all came back. The nurses, the injection. She tried to lift her arm to see the puncture wound, but the limb wouldn't move. It was held, somehow. She raised her head. The room swum dizzily, but she saw. She was tied down, hand and foot, restrained by straps attached to the bed. She tugged at them in disbelief.

Then she saw that a drip had been inserted into her arm.

They're force-feeding you, giving you nutrients through the drip. No one has seen you eat or drink voluntarily in many days now. They think that you're starving yourself. They think that by doing this they're saving your life.

Frustration washed away the last of the orphan's sleepiness. She tugged again at the straps. How dare they! *Nutrients!* She could feel the liquid clogging her veins like slime. It was an invasion. They hadn't even asked her!

They don't feel they are obliged to ask. To them, you aren't capable of granting, or denying, permission.

But that wasn't true! Not anymore. After all she had done, after all she had proven, to be treated like this—it was outrageous.

I know. But your recent behaviour has disturbed them. You don't eat or drink, you've stopped working in the wards, you no longer seem to communicate with anyone else. They think something is very wrong with you.

Nothing was wrong with her! She was becoming something far better than she had ever been. Why couldn't they see that?

They don't have the eyes to see . . .

There was a sound, she noticed. A murmuring. It had been there since she'd woken. She turned her head, and saw her radio. It was sitting on a chair in the corner. Someone had thought to bring it to her, even in the locked ward.

Her anger cooled a little. After all, they weren't monsters, she should not forget that. The old doctor had always been her friend, had always protected her. The nurses too. They would never intend her harm, not even now. They had made a wretched mistake, that was all . . . But then, how could she blame them for not understanding what she was going through? She didn't completely understand it herself.

You mean, it isn't clear to you yet?

Clear? Nothing was clear. Why *didn't* she need food anymore? Why had the lack of it only refined her, and made her stronger?

I've already given you the answer, from my own lives.

His own lives? What did he mean? But then a key rattled in the lock, and hinges groaned as the door swung open. The orphan lifted her head, and saw the old doctor enter. He wasn't alone. A male nurse was with him, and another man too, the sight of whom alarmed the orphan even further. It was the young doctor. What was *he* doing here? He didn't deal with the mad. He was the surgeon, the man who cut people open.

She stared at the old doctor while he checked on her drip, trying to read a message, any message, in his eyes. But he was avoiding her gaze. He turned to the others and began to speak. She couldn't understand a word.

He's talking about you. About how much weight you've lost. But he's satisfied that they've intervened in good time. The idiot . . .

The young doctor was speaking now. Then the old doctor replied. The conversation grew earnest, their voices rising.

Now they're discussing what the night nurse told them. About you and me. About catching you, naked. They're not happy.

Her anger returned. That was none of their business!

They believe it is. They're commenting that you have never exhibited such sexual behaviour before. They think it must be part of whatever else is wrong with you. They think it could lead to dangerous complications.

Complications? What sort of complications?

Pregnancy, among other things.

Pregnancy?! The thought was so astonishing the orphan forgot her outrage. A baby? A mother—her? But that had never been her intention at all.

Nor mine, even if I was capable. But it's not me they're worried about. They're concerned you might interact with the more virile male patients.

The orphan could have laughed, if not for her residual fear of the young doctor. He was gesticulating forcefully now, and the nurse was nodding in agreement. Only the old doctor, it seemed, was doubtful about the discussion.

And suddenly, the foreigner's steady voice was faltering. *My orphan—they are proposing an awful thing.*

Her fear roared back. What was it? What thing?

They—they wish to prevent the possibility of a pregnancy. They don't think you could cope. They think it would be better if you were incapable of conceiving. They say that mere birth control won't suffice. They—

He broke off. The argument between the three men had reached its height. Then, reluctantly it appeared, the old doctor was nodding with the rest, and they all turned to regard the orphan with grave eyes.

—they're going to sterilise you.

Terror took her. She didn't know what the word meant, but she could hear in the foreigner's tone that it was something dreadful. It must be an operation, it must mean that they would slice into her with knives. The doctors and the nurse were talking again, not arguing now, merely discussing.

The foreigner sounded far away. *It will be an operation, yes, but they haven't decided what sort. They're wondering if they should give you a full hysterectomy. They know it isn't strictly necessary—a ligation would do for sterilisation. But they see advantages in removing your womb. They think it might be simpler if you did not have to bother with periods from now on.*

The orphan grasped nothing of this, there was only the fear, and a terrible sense of helplessness, and her anger surging. She did not want to be cut open. She was healthy. She was more than healthy. And it would hurt. How could the old doctor—her lifelong friend and guardian—want to cause her such pain?

It wouldn't hurt; you'd be anaesthetised. But pain isn't the point. You don't understand—there's more at stake here.

Worse than pain?

Do you remember what we talked about? About your physical maturity as a woman, about your powers, about how mind and body are interconnected? These men want to take part of that away, to remove a piece of you . . .

But perhaps it was only a little piece they wanted. Maybe a piece so little that it wouldn't matter if it was gone . . .

If it was a finger, or an appendix, maybe. But this is no little piece. This is part of what defines you, part of what makes you female. You must have felt it yourself, how your instincts, your connection with the natural world, are based in your gut as much as in your head. Perhaps that's why your strength and your abilities are denied to me—perhaps they are a uniquely female thing. I don't know. All I know is that if they do this, if they interfere with you on such a vital level, you will not be the same.

Not the same? Not herself anymore?

On the outside you would seem no different. But inside . . . you might lose your special awareness. The world might become closed to you. And I might become closed to you as well. You might become someone who can't hear me.

Someone who can't fly.

Oh no. Not that. Tears welled up in the orphan's eyes. That was too unfair. They couldn't take that away. That was all she had. She was struggling against the bonds again, and the doctors and the nurse turned to watch her.

They'll make you as blind as they are themselves, that's what I fear.

Yes, they were blind, they were wicked fools, they should not be allowed to touch her. The old doctor was at her side, his hand gently stroking her hair, his voice soft and soothing, but all the orphan felt now was an uncontrollable rage. Her thrashing became frenzied, and the old doctor drew back, perturbed.

No, orphan, you must not give them reason . . .

But the terror and fury were too great. She was bucking against the straps, shouting out in protest, formless and guttural.

They'll only sedate you again.

Indeed. She could already see a syringe; it had appeared magically in the nurse's hand. But she didn't care about that either.

Orphan, remember—we're not helpless. Trust me.

Even strapped down as she was, it took all the strength of both the doctors to steady the orphan enough for the nurse to inject the sedative.

I won't let this happen . . .

But his voice was retreating. He was no longer in her head, he was in the next room, he was on the other side of the hospital, he was a man yelling at her from a hilltop miles and miles off. Her rage lifted and puffed away like a cloud, and all she knew were warm depths, dragging her down.

27

Pain hauled the orphan back. Something was tugging at her vitals. A fishhook, lodged in her belly, pulling only gently for the moment, but pulling insistently, and threatening far worse if that pull was ignored.

The operation! Had it happened? For a moment she swam in visions of blood, of her stomach laid wide open, and of some bright, pulsating part of her ripped forth, leaving a hole into which the rest of her body collapsed, empty.

Calm, orphan. No one has touched you yet.

Gratitude swept the horrible apparitions away. It hadn't happened. It wasn't too late. The foreigner had rescued her. For a while she merely drifted, happy. But the tug in her belly remained. And it was cold, wherever she was. Cold and silent.

Open your eyes, and see.

There was an excitement in his voice quite unlike anything she had ever heard from him before. She opened her eyes. And there was the earth, hanging directly in front of her, shining against a backdrop of pure black.

But it was so small, so far away! Why, if she stretched her arms out, she would be able to encompass the whole world between her hands. A terror rose in her, a wild vertigo. She was falling. The earth was at the bottom of a deep pit, and she had just leapt over the side, and now she was dropping, dropping, picking up speed . . .

You are not falling. Quite the opposite.

She clung to the reassurance, and her panic receded. She focused her senses, and this time saw that the planet, rather than looming up, was actually slowly shrinking. They were moving *away* from the earth.

Yes. At least, our shadow selves are . . .

Nor was she deceived by the slowness. If something so vast as the world had been reduced by distance to a shining bauble, and was visibly dwindling further even now, then their speed must be impressive indeed.

It is. We can go faster still—but already, this is faster than anyone else has ever gone.

How?

We weigh no more than a thought, orphan.

She shivered, uncomprehending, but aware again of the cold, more penetrating than any earthly chill. And the silence around them was more than just the lack of any noise; it was, somehow, the impossibility of any noise.

It's a vacuum. There's no air here.

No air?

We are in space.

Ah . . . The orphan let her gaze stray from the earth, and finally she understood. The backdrop to the shining planet was not merely darkness. It was a gulf, a chasm that reached off in every direction, bottomless. It was space. This was where the foreigner had lived in the weeks before his last fiery death. This was where he had felt, more than anywhere else, at home.

Yes, but we are already far beyond the reach of the shuttles. Indeed, only a few men have been further out than we are now. But they were in small metal capsules, with tiny windows. They were not free to fly, as you and I are free.

She could hear the joy in him, and wanted to share it. This was the escape he so craved—the planet left behind, impotent to pull them back, their ghost selves too strong and too fast. But somehow all she felt was afraid, and cold, and strangely alone, the tug in her belly like an ache of sadness.

He was not holding her hand, she realised. In all their other flights, their shadows had been holding hands, just as their real bodies had been. But now their real bodies were in different rooms. She could not go to him and he could not go to her. Maybe that was why she felt so detached from him. His shape was at her side, a wraith faintly aglow, as beautiful as ever. He held her now by the sheer force of his mind. But it wasn't the same as the grip of his fingers. She missed holding hands.

The earth was smaller still. And even though there was no wind, no feeling of acceleration, she sensed that their velocity was becoming tremendous.

Where were they going?

There is something out here I want to show you.

But what about her operation?

It is not going to take place right away. The surgeon is a busy man. He cannot fit you in until a week from now. So you have time, a little at least. Alas, I may not have as long. The crowd in front of the hospital will not wait forever.

So they weren't safe, and this flight was only a reprieve, no better than a dream from which she would wake, still strapped to the bed.

It's no dream. Only wait. You'll see soon.

But with that he fell silent, and the orphan could sense his intense concentration. The earth had become no bigger than a melon, swirling blue. They were flying backwards, she realised, facing the planet but moving away from it. Towards the sun. She did not dare turn to look, lest she be blinded, but she could feel it over her shoulder. An inferno, unshielded out here by any atmosphere, hideously bright.

But now—how bizarre—something white and huge was looming over her *other* shoulder. She turned to it, stared in wonder.

It was the moon!

But so gigantic! So wide and round, etched hard against the blackness. It had never occurred to the orphan that the moon could possibly be so large. It had always seemed such an ethereal thing. Yet here it was, not ethereal at all but brutally solid, and seemingly as massive as the earth.

And yet it was nothing like the earth. There was no blur of air to soften its edges, no swirl of clouds, no shimmer of water. Its surface was a wasteland of monochrome grey, shattered into craters or pulverised into dusty plains. A lifeless veneer. And the orphan could tell there was no life *below* the crust, either. There was no hot magma pulsing, no iron core spinning, no warm magnetic heartbeat. The moon was tepid rock right through. Not even a volcano would ever be born there.

She hated it immediately.

But up it rushed, as if they must surely crash into it headlong. It was only at the last moment that they veered slightly, and instead went swooping across the moon's face, hugging the surface in an arc from horizon to horizon. And so astonishing was their speed that in less than a second they had crossed the entire hemisphere and were shooting off into space again at a new angle. The orphan barely registered the transit—a flicker of white, and of stark black shadows—and when she looked back, the moon was already shrinking behind them, a ball hurled away over a cliff.

The foreigner was laughing, but she felt none of his elation. The dead moon, the pale earth, the silently roaring sun, from out here she could sense that they were all in motion, circling each other in some perpetual dance of the spheres, another wonder—but it was too forbidding, too inhuman in scale. It filled her only with dread. Life was unwelcome out here. She felt it as almost a personal hostility. *She* was unwelcome here. She had a rightful place to belong, and empty space wasn't it.

But her rightful place had diminished now to no more than a small blue marble, the details of land and sea lost. The tug in her gut had become sharp enough to be painful, and at last she knew what it was. Her body missed the earth. It was rebelling against being ripped from its proper environment. It wanted to go back, and the ache in her would only increase with distance. But they were accelerating still.

She looked at the ghost flying at her side. Didn't he feel the pain too? But no, he had talked of this—of the affliction that struck down space travellers when they were taken from earth, the loneliness. But it hadn't affected him. He'd been glad to be rid of the planet. And now he was stealing her away too . . .

There's no need to be afraid. We'll return quite safely.

But it hurt!

It's an emotion, not a physical pain. Look away from the earth now. Look away from the moon. Look ahead. Look out into the universe.

She felt her shadow body revolving. The earth, with its moon shrunk to a dot, shifted from her field of view. For a moment she was dazzled by a glimpse of the sun, a ferocious glare, but then it was gone and she was facing forward into darkness. The cold seared her eyes and she wept. The sun, the earth, the moon—everything she had ever known was behind her now.

Yes, but out there . . .

Out there were the stars, a multitude of blurred pinpoints through her tears. But as her vision cleared she saw just how brightly those pinpoints blazed, not merely hinting at colours but boldly shining out red and green and blue. And space itself was not black—between the stars it was dusted with sheets of pink, and with clouds of faint silver, twisted in ribbons and blown like the thinnest gauze. So much colour, so many stars. What were stars anyway? She had never thought of it before. They had seemed such tiny things from the earth, so twinkling, so delicate. But out here they were fierce and hard and frightening. They did not seem tiny, they only seemed far away. And then there were the great wheels and discs of brightness that she intuited were made of even more stars, further off.

The foreigner spoke as if it was something wonderful. *They are suns, all of them, like our sun.*

A kind of horror filled the orphan. Suns? They were all suns? It was too much, it was too dizzying. Was there no end to it, no edge, no finality? She would be lost out here, with no way home. They had gone too far already.

Not far enough yet. Nor fast enough.

He was pushing them even harder. But the velocity that had come so effortlessly before was costing him severely now. There was no longer the sensation of simply flying or falling, now it was like fighting forward into something, as if the structure of space, empty as it might appear, was beginning to resist.

Not space exactly, but the law of relativity . . . His voice was taut with effort. But still they accelerated.

And now everything was turning strange. The stars had begun to spiral inwards to a central point directly ahead, their colours shifting. How was that possible? And the orphan's shadow body, always so weightless, was becoming somehow solid and heavy. Suddenly space was like a gale into which they leant.

Almost . . . almost . . .

And then time stopped.

At least, *something* stopped, and the orphan had no word for it other than time. It was as if they had run full tilt into a wall, even though they were still moving so fast that the stars ahead of them had been stretched into an elongated warp of light. An extremity had been reached. A boundary. A limit. And the pain! It ignited in her gut, an agony of separation as they raced away from the earth as fast as the universe would allow. For a timeless heartbeat they held there, then for another . . .

Then with a cry the foreigner released his grip, and their speed was tumbling downwards from the ultimate, the stars were unwinding, and both of them were sobbing—she with relief, and he with vindication and exhaustion.

Was that it? the orphan wondered, dazed. Was that what he had brought her out here to experience? Could they go home now?

No . . .

He had stopped pushing, and for a time they merely coasted, slowing steadily all the while, the pull of the sun at their backs dragging on them like an anchor. At length, however, he recovered, and spoke again.

Well done, orphan. We have now travelled almost forty million kilometres. Most of it in those few moments at light speed. That's a hundred times as far as the moon is from the earth. At this point, in fact, we are halfway out to the next planet in the solar system.

But where were they?

Nowhere. The end of our journey . . .

But what had they come here for?

Ahead there. Do you see it?

The orphan looked, saw only the stars and the depths of space, normal again, unwarped, now that she and the foreigner had slowed down.

There was nothing.

He laughed wearily. *Look again.*

And then, there it was.

28

At first she thought it was only a trick of her vision, a dark wrinkle caught against the background of the universe. But then she saw that something was rushing towards them, a blackness that blotted out the stars as it came. Quickly it swelled in size, and then a shape was hurtling by them, monstrous, and yet so dark that it defied the eye. Instantly it was gone again, diving towards the sun.

But then the foreigner set off in pursuit, the orphan with him, and as they caught up with the object it was outlined briefly against the sun's glare. The orphan saw a blunt, elongated mass. Awed, she understood that it was a chunk of rock they were chasing, as immense as the entire island on which she lived.

It's bigger. Official estimates have it as roughly fifty kilometres long, and about thirty-five kilometres across.

But what was it?

A comet.

Satisfaction radiated from him. But the orphan was cold and aching, and saw little to like in a pile of black stone plunging blindly through space, whatever its dimensions.

It isn't plunging blindly. It's following its orbit, at over one hundred and ninety thousand kilometres per hour. And it isn't just stone. It contains ice, too.

But ice was white and gleaming . . .

True. But this body has been gathering dust and debris for millions of years, far out on the rim of the solar system. Its frozen elements are buried deep. They are black creatures, comets. Blacker than soot. It isn't until they approach the sun—when the ice inside them melts and streams out into space—that comets shine.

His mind showed her what he meant, and she saw a fuzzy nub of light with a fanned tail sprawling out, spectacular, big enough to dwarf any planet. And yet tenuous, a wisp of cloud blown by an airless wind.

Some of them are famous. They're given names, and come and go every few decades. But this one has no name, and will not come this way again for thousands of years. It's what's known as a long-period comet—so small, so dark, so far out at aphelion that it's extremely difficult for astronomers to detect. In fact, they discovered this one only a few months ago, when it was already well on its way in. I remember. I was on the shuttle at the time.

The orphan studied the dark mass. If it really contained the sort of life he was describing, then it defeated her sight. It seemed just as dead and hateful to her as the moon had. She lifted her eyes to the sun, rising like a miniature dawn over the comet's jagged horizon. Bright, painfully bright. But turning her eyes well away from it, she saw, out in the blackness, a blue dot. Ah, and how the beauty of that dot pierced her. She thought of warm breezes on her skin, of the smell of dirt, of a hazy sky that softened the sunlight . . . and pain bit at her insides.

The foreigner was still glorying in his prize. *Bear in mind, the announcement of the discovery drew little attention. As comets go, this one is quite unremarkable, and on its inward fall will pass no closer to the earth than eleven million kilometres. But for some reason—a premonition, perhaps—I took note. I studied its orbit. And even through my fiery death, I remembered.*

So I knew where to find it out here.

The orphan fought against irritation. This ugly lump excited him more than anything else about their venture into space. But why? It could affect nothing back at the hospital. So what were they *doing* here?

We're here, my orphan, because if you and I so decide, we can alter the path of this thing. It's only a matter of giving it a sustained push.

A push? But it was *huge*, it was—

We've already tested the sort of power we can command. We were strong enough to throw down the landslide. This comet is far bigger, yes, but if we want to, we should be able to alter its trajectory. Just sufficiently.

She still didn't understand. Even if it was possible, what would be the point? How would shifting this rock's course help anything?

Because then the comet wouldn't miss the earth by eleven million kilometres. Or even by one. We can make it hit the earth head-on.

Shocked, the orphan tore her gaze away from the comet to look at him. In the cold sunlight his shadow self appeared to glow like flame.

What did he mean, hit the earth?

I mean—save ourselves. From all those who want to cut you open and ruin the astonishing thing that you are. From all those who are afraid of me and want to move me away from you. The doctors. The townspeople. If we could change this comet's course, it could free us from all of them.

But how?

By clearing them out of our way. Oh, I don't pretend that we could aim this rock so accurately as to hit your island directly, but we don't need to. All we have to do is make it impact somewhere in the surrounding ocean. The wave created would be titanic. It would sweep your little island bare in moments.

What?! The old doctor, the nurses, the patients, all those people in the little town and the big—they would die!

They are lesser beings, orphan, and will die soon enough anyway. In ten years or twenty or fifty. What does it matter if it comes a little sooner?

It would be murder! And they were her friends!

Friends? They have you strapped down and are about to mutilate you in the worst possible way. They are not your friends. They pity you, they dismiss you, they have never appreciated you properly. And even if they did grasp just how wonderful you really are, they would only hate and envy you and want you destroyed.

Emotions of every kind battled within the orphan. What he was saying was far too cold and cruel. And yet certain parts of her rebelled in wild agreement, a kind of wanton liberation from everything else she believed or thought right. Because they really could do this. They actually had the *power.*

Oh, but it was nonsense. If the comet's giant wave swept the island clean, then they would die too, she and the foreigner.

Have you forgotten? I wouldn't die. I would be injured, yes, lost again in the ocean, this body wrecked . . . but I would survive, as I always have.

Ah. Yes. She *had* forgotten. But had he forgotten in turn? That she wasn't like him? That if the comet struck, then *she* would die . . .

His low laugh turned all her certainties to ash.

Little one . . . you won't die.

Do you think for an instant that I'd risk you? Don't you see? This is what your special abilities really mean. This is why you don't need food or water or sleep. This is why you have only become stronger and more beautiful without them.

Orphan, you are as immortal as I am.

And there it was. The orphan found she was staring at the sun, only it seemed black now, surrounded by a halo that writhed in slow tendrils. She would not die. She would live on and on. She could be with him forever.

I don't say there won't be pain if we do this. I know—who better?—how terrible even temporary death can be. But at least this way—if we use this comet to set ourselves free—we will both be reborn. Then the earth and the solar system and the universe can be ours to explore together, for as long as we could ever need.

But if we do nothing, and they cut you open, if they mutilate you in that particular way, then we lose each other forever. Our one chance would vanish. You would return to simple stupidity, and I would be as I was before—alone in the world, wandering only in my mind, limited, chained to the planet, and powerless.

The orphan finally looked away from the sun to the comet. It was revolving slowly, she saw. Subtle shadows played across the deep blue that was its day side, and then disappeared into its night-side flank. The giant rock was *tumbling* towards its solar target. But it would never get there, she could determine that now. On this path it would miss the sun and swing around behind and be flung back out into space, so hard and so fast and so far that it wouldn't be seen again in an age.

Or, if they merely nudged it a little . . .

To never die! To live as the foreigner had, through life after life, experience after experience. To leave the hospital, and the small town, and the whole island, and to discover existence all anew. To be reborn into another body, perhaps one that was beautiful, and quick, and clever. One which could hear properly, and speak. How marvellous that would be. And it *could* be.

Only, the cost . . .

And yet what choice did she have? They were going to ruin her. They were going to condemn her to the body she had now, to being slow and stupid and capable only of drudgeries. That was as good as killing her. It didn't matter that they did so out of misguided kindness, it was still wrong. And if, in self-preservation, the only way to stop them was to do what the foreigner asked . . .

Exactly! This would not be an act we perform with any pleasure. It would be a reluctant choice, forced upon us by necessity.

Yes. Forced. But doubts still clutched at her. She cast her gaze back to the blue dot. Could she really send this hulking monster to smash into something that seemed so tiny and so fragile, and so alone?

The earth is not tiny or fragile. It's the comet that's tiny, in comparison. It's big enough to sweep clear your island, but no more.

But did they have to do it this way? With all their abilities, wasn't there something else they could do? Some other means of escape?

What do you propose? You're bound to your bed, behind locked doors, and I'm unable to move to help you. And even if we could somehow flee the hospital, where could we go on that island of yours? You are known. The authorities would never let you be. They see it as their right to order your life for you.

No, we cannot remove ourselves from the situation, so we must remove everyone else. Only a cataclysm can do that. And it must happen soon, before the doctors perform their butchery and damage you. That's the beauty of this comet. Redirected, at its current acceleration, it could reach earth in just six days.

Six days! The orphan stared, but the comet's speed was imperceptible. And silent. Somehow, it didn't seem right to her that something so huge, so dangerous, should hurl onwards with such stealthy, utter quiet.

But only if we start today, orphan. Only if we start now.

But that was too soon! A choice so immense, of such consequence—she needed longer. She needed to go home to her room and think, away from this horrible place. She needed to be somewhere warm, where there were walls to block out infinity.

But there was no such patience in the foreigner. *Do you think diverting a comet is something we can do in a few minutes? This will be immeasurably harder than breaking the dam. It will take at least several extended sessions of pushing, and we have to begin while the angle of change is still a small one. If we wait too long that angle will become too great and we won't have the strength or the time to swing the comet into the right orbit to intersect with the earth.*

She saw the truth of what he was saying. The comet dwarfed the landslide a thousand times over and far more. And while it apparently floated free in space, in fact it was locked into its path of descent, almost immovably so. A single nudge would not change that. It would need prolonged force. But still doubts tortured her, and not only because so many people would die. Despite the conviction in the foreigner's voice, somehow she could not fully trust in him. His haste, his anger, his demand that she choose *now*. Something else was happening here . . .

They had soared out to one side of the comet.

I've already done the calculations. I know in which direction and how long we have to push. You just have to follow my lead.

She could feel the foreigner's mind reaching forth to embrace the mass, ready to apply pressure. And at the same time he opened himself to her, inviting entry. She knew what he expected—that she would lend him her strength again, as she had at the landslide. As ever, the knowledge and the execution would be his, but the power he needed, the raw ability, would have to come from her.

Now, my orphan. Now.

Ah, but at the dam she had given her strength out of love for him, out of concern for him. Now she was too confused to know what she felt.

We must do this.

But by chance, as she looked across the shoulder of the comet she saw again the blue spark of earth, shining forlornly, as if it was already lined up for the blow. She knew it wasn't that simple, that the comet's path would not be a straight one. And yet nothing else crystallised so well the action they were about to take.

No, she couldn't do it—not this way, not now, not yet. The power wasn't in her to give to him, not for a motivation so selfish and destructive.

She was sorry, but—

Very well. His voice had gone cold. *I was hoping it wouldn't have to be this way, but if you won't help . . .*

And to the orphan's horror, he simply *took* her power.

Against all her will, he reached into her, located the strength she was refusing to give him, and ripped it from her as easily as if from a baby's arms.

It was the worst violation she had ever experienced. All that was special about her, everything that the foreigner had said he so cherished, he was stealing away, and she was powerless to stop him. She hadn't known, had never suspected it was possible. It couldn't be happening. But it was. He swelled up, bright against the void, filled by her. Then he turned, and thrust all that energy against the comet.

At first, nothing happened. Undaunted, the foreigner called for more power still, and the orphan was incapable of refusal. It was sucked out of her in torrents.

It's working!

And it was. The comet was shuddering now, its trajectory shifting by the tiniest of increments against the stars. The foreigner was livid with exertion, a newborn sun, his hoarse cry strained to the utmost. But still it wasn't enough, and so much was being torn from the orphan that she felt there would be nothing left of her, that she was becoming a hollow wisp. There was a limit, surely, to how much could be taken from her. There had to be a point of ultimate depletion, short of death.

And something strange was happening to the comet. Squeezed and pushed, caught between the grip of the foreigner's mind and the relentless pull of the sun, the stone was rippling and convulsing like hot tar.

Too much, too much . . .

Suddenly the comet's surface seemed to crack in a thousand places, and brillance erupted all around, explosions of steam, jets of white in the chill sunlight. After a stunned moment, the orphan understood what was happening. The comet's internal ice had vaporised in the heat and turmoil of the foreigner's assault, and now the gas was bursting forth to encompass the great rock in a dazzling cloud.

The comet had begun to shine.

In surprise, or exhaustion, or both, the foreigner let go.

Enough . . . enough for now.

Had he failed? the orphan wondered. Had he destroyed the comet in his attempt to redirect it? But no, she could see through the jets of vapour that the core of rock remained intact, as solid and massive as ever.

And the foreigner's tone was satisfied despite his weariness. *We've made a good start. The out-gassing would have happened soon anyway, the closer the comet got to the sun. It makes no difference.*

The orphan found she was herself again, released. She withdrew from his voice in loathing, but he addressed her regardless.

It's all for the best, little one. We'll go home and rest now, but in a few hours we'll return and work on it again. Two more long pushes, perhaps, will do it.

No, she would not come back here with him!

Disinterest. *You won't have any choice.*

Despair swept up on her. He was right. Hadn't he just shown her? He could use her as he pleased. And so easily . . .

They were moving, passing swiftly through the glowing gas around the comet, back into the emptiness of space. Ahead of them the blue dot glinted. And somehow they were accelerating again to tremendous speeds, although she was sure the foreigner was exerting no effort anymore. Something else was pulling them back.

Perhaps, she thought, it was the call of their abandoned bodies, hungry for the return of their souls. But then fatigue was claiming her, and there were no more stars, only the unrelieved blackness of unconsciousness.

29

She hung poised in space. Alone.

In reality, the orphan knew, she was asleep. In reality, she was still tied down to the bed, in the locked ward, the drugs stupefying her. In reality, the foreigner was recuperating in the empty crematorium, and there was no way she could have travelled into space on her own. This was only a dream.

But she knew too that it was more than that. It was something that was going to happen. For real. Somehow, she was seeing into the future. *Six days* into the future. She was floating in the void, and had been so placed as a spectator, safely out of the way, but with a perfect view. For here it came—the earth. There had been a time when she'd thought it merely spun fixed in space, but now she knew that it sailed in a great orbit around the sun, serene, and yet with implacable momentum. And from the opposite direction, coming to meet it, equally serene, was the comet.

But not as she remembered it. It was no longer just a naked nub of rock. The foreigner had set free its icy interior, and the jets of vapour and particles had been gushing out for six days since, the cloud ever expanding, so that now the corona was a truly vast thing, thin as mist, but glowing bright; a sphere that seemed to rival the earth in size. From the orphan's vantage point, indeed, it seemed that, rather than a mere rock plunging into the earth, two very planets were about to collide.

In dread, she considered the world. The sun was at her back, so it was the day side she faced. She saw blue ocean, and the tan spread of a large continent, and sprinkled nearby, just coming out of night into dawn, a cluster of island chains, vivid and green. Her own island was down there somewhere, and it was in the surrounding ocean that the core of the comet would hit. All those people, in the towns, in the hospital. What would they see if they looked to the sky? The sun would be on the horizon, but overhead would be a shining white portend of the end, terrifying.

She could not help them. This vision of the future did not allow it. She could only watch as the earth and the comet crept nearer and nearer. So slowly—such was the scale of each body that, even at their momentous opposing speeds, they might have been merely drifting together. Until finally the forward edge of the comet's cloud seemed to merge with the sheath of the planet's atmosphere.

Fires ignited. Scintillating flashes at first, bright even in the daylight. The orphan had seen a fireworks display once, and there had been rockets that exploded into masses of shimmering sparks, lingering. Now it was as if those rockets were detonating all through the earth's upper airs. A random few initially, then increasing in number, and eventually a continuous fusillade of them.

She knew what was happening. All the gas and dust in the comet's corona was slamming into the earth's atmosphere and burning up in countless tiny streaks, as surely as the foreigner himself once had. And over the minutes, as more and more of the corona mashed up against the planet, the sparkling immolations increased until nearly half the earth appeared to be wrapped in sheets of argent flame.

Spectacular. And harmless, the orphan recognised. The wisps of the corona could no more damage the earth than could a shower of rain. But at the centre of the cloud waited the hub, not dust or gas, but a rock bigger than a mountain. And as she watched, the tumbling giant swept on through the fires of its own presaging, parted the planet's atmosphere in a single second, and struck.

There was no sound because there could *be* no sound, but there was light—unbearable, shattering light that seemed to fill space. Even in ghost form, the orphan was burnt by heat and had to look away. And she knew in that moment that the foreigner had lied to her. He had promised that the comet would merely splash down in the ocean and drown only her island, that the damage it caused would not be fatal to the earth itself. And not a word of that was true . . .

But it was some time before the fireball faded, and she could look. Even then, much of the planet remained hidden by glowing clouds of ash and smoke. And the fireworks still blazed too, as the rear half of the comet's corona, only partially shredded, plunged on in. To her special senses, however, everything was clear.

The comet had not splashed into the ocean; at the point of impact it had vaporised the ocean in an instant, miles deep, and slammed directly into the earth's crust. In that same instant it had obliterated all the nearby islands—her own included. Not merely flooded them, but wiped them from existence.

The resultant shockwave had then flattened everything in its path across a whole hemisphere, the air superheated enough to set entire landmasses ablaze. The seas had boiled and reared into vast inundations that were still spilling across the coastlines. Earthquakes, too, were vibrating all around the world, a resonance that was toppling mountains and opening cracks and awakening dozens of erstwhile sleeping volcanoes. And finally, the impact had thrown up a plume of smoke and debris with such force that it was reaching back out into space.

All this, the orphan observed in total silence. But then, feather-light, she felt the touch of another mind. *His* mind. From a vantage point like her own, watching on. And he was happy, she could sense. Pleased by the display.

The touch revolted her. She shut him out, and descended, anguished, towards the planet. The last vestige of the comet's corona had been consumed at last, leaving the earth to convulse alone in its agony. And she could see now that, in some ways, the damage might have been worse. The impact hadn't knocked the earth from its orbit, or made it falter as it spun on its axis. Nor had it fractured the earth's core. The deepest levels of the planet held firm. Oh, but the damage otherwise . . .

She entered the atmosphere, and *now* there was noise, even high up, where the air was thin. It was an echo of the great collision—a tumult of fires burning and winds howling and waves thundering. And there was an awful metallic stench. It was the smell of the innards of the planet, spewed unwillingly forth.

On she glided, down through the fireball's massive plume. It was spreading out now, borne by disturbed winds. The ash up high was as fine as powder, but there was so much of it, the orphan guessed, that eventually it would cloak the planet in a thick cloud. And lower down she found the heavier ash. It was raining back to earth in a deluge that would bury houses even half a world away from the impact.

She dropped closer to the surface and saw the levelled cities, the farmlands scorched grey, the stumps of incinerated forests. Already millions, billons were dead. But that was only the beginning.

The plume of ash was, in fact, a shroud. Because of it, the ground would be smothered, the oceans choked, the skies blotted black. The earth would become a sunless realm, and any survivors would not endure long. They would starve and freeze in the dark. Yes . . . this was the true injury the comet had inflicted. Not to the earth's structure, but to its ability to support life.

And the wound was a mortal one, the orphan could feel. She sailed through a muddy rain of ash, towards the centre of the blast, and all around her there was a lessening, a fatal withdrawal of energy. The loss stung her. A crucial thing was departing from the world—not only life, but the *possibility* of life. The great glow of existence that had wrapped around the planet was fading, and at the same time the orphan felt her special awareness also diminishing, dwindling into everyday blindness.

It was a surprise, that blindness. She had come to think that she was in tune only with the inanimate world—with the wind, and the rain, and the inner earth—and that her mysterious powers came from there. It had never occurred to her that her abilities might in some way be connected to the *living* world.

But to know the truth of it, she had only to look down. The point of impact was still far ahead, but even here the earth had been ravaged and burnt and left sterile. Immense forces were at work; lava gushed from clefts, steaming oceans surged and smashed against cliffs, whirlwinds of hot air howled and beat at the sky. It should have terrified and thrilled her, but it didn't. Instead it all seemed as meaningless to her now as the patterns on a television screen, or squiggles in a book. Her unique insight was blinkered. Because in all this wonder, nothing was alive.

What, then, would be the good of them surviving the comet's cataclysm, her and the foreigner? They would be alone amid all this ruin. Immortal, maybe, but trapped on a dead world, a wasteland without purpose. Trapped forever, for without life around her the orphan would be shrunken and weak, with no power to lend the foreigner, and thus there would be no escape for them to explore the cold marvels of the universe.

Better to not survive at all! So why had the foreigner done it? It was no accident, of that she was sure. He must have known. He was far too clever to miscalculate the kind of damage a comet of such size and speed would cause. He had *wanted* this to happen. Indeed, she had felt his joy as the comet struck.

So his lie had been deliberate. But what about everything else he'd told her? What about the threat of her surgery, and of the mob waiting to attack the hospital? Was any of that true? She had only his word to go on, she hadn't heard herself what the doctors were discussing, or what the crowd was muttering. Had there really been an urgent need to defend themselves? Or had he just made it up to frighten her into obeying him?

Perhaps even his greatest revelation—that she was immortal, like him—was a lie. Perhaps once he had made use of her, she was meant to die in the conflagration along with everyone else . . .

She had risen again in the choked air, and now—after skimming over a range of jagged mountains, newly formed by the shattering of the earth's crust—she found herself above the crater of the comet's immolation.

And what a hateful place. It was so large that, even through gaps in the smoke, she could not see the other side. There was no sign of the ocean that had once rippled here, or of the islands that had protruded above the water, let alone her own island, and its towns, and its hospital. Instead she looked upon a vast sunken plain that was seething with flame and steam and mud.

And yet from somewhere she felt again the touch of the foreigner's mind, watching on. He was closer now, his emotions more evident. And to him, she sensed, the crater was beautiful, a matter of deep satisfaction, of justice . . .

And all at once, finally, she understood.

The heat seemed to be stinging her eyes. Or perhaps she was crying. Everything was blurred now. The light was changing. And suddenly the noises and smells of the crater were gone. She woke to the soft crackle of her radio. The white ceiling, the white walls. Her hands and feet tied to the bed. She was back in the locked ward. Those six days had not yet passed, and the comet had not yet hit.

She blinked away the last tears. There was so much mourning in her, over the depth of his betrayal, but more for the loss of his love. Even if it had never been real, it was the only love she'd ever known. But there was no time for self-pity. The comet had not yet hit, it was true, and indeed it was not yet even on the right path to hit. But all too soon the foreigner would come for her. He would spirit her back into the iciness of space and begin to push upon the rock again until its path *was* right.

She could resist him, perhaps, while she was wide awake, but when she fell asleep, or when she was drugged again, she would be helpless. He could take her then, and use her power however he wished. That could not be allowed.

The strange thing was that, even as she'd woken, she'd seen the solution there in her mind, in all its fitting cruelty. And it was the foreigner himself who had shown her. Long ago now, it seemed. When he was trying so hard to prove that he was real, and trustworthy. Maybe that was another reason for her tears, and her mourning. She wept a little for what she must do to him.

But she mustered her strength anyway, her vision, her anger.

And then she reached out to the volcano.

30

Of course, her cell had no windows, and she could not simply see through the walls. Nor could she, without the foreigner's help, leave her body and soar from the room. But she still possessed all her old sensitivities, honed now to a finer pitch than ever before, and a thousand telling vibrations came to her from the outside. She knew it must be evening. She felt the cooks clattering in the distant kitchen, cleaning up after dinner. She felt water running in the shower-block pipes as the last patients were washed down before nightfall. She felt the snap in the electrical wires as lights were switched on and off. The hospital fairly hummed to her, crowded at day's end.

Which was perfect. She wanted as many people around as possible when it happened. They would add to the confusion.

She let her unseeing eye slip further away, beyond the grounds, and down into the earth beneath the mountain. There, all was calm. Nothing moved in the chambers that led from the volcano's mouth to the magma reservoirs—the semi-liquid, semi-rock at the bottom was congealed into a turgid mass, a plug.

The mountain slept.

The question was, could she wake it? On her own? She had to believe that she could. The strength had been there before, after all. If the foreigner had been able to exploit it to move something as massive as the comet, then surely it was available for her own use.

She reached down to the reservoirs.

Warm them, that was where she had to start. Warm the magma until it glowed white, until pressure sent it creeping towards the surface. She held the reservoirs in her mind and willed them to rise in temperature. But it was like sinking into mud. Cold, clammy, reluctant. The stone did not want to heat up, or to move. It wasn't possible that a single body such as her own could ever contain enough energy to change that.

Ah . . . but it wasn't just her own energy. The vision of the comet's impact had taught her that much. She had access to something greater, to the aura of life enfolding the whole planet. So it wasn't a matter of squeezing the power from herself, it was a matter of shaping her mind into a conduit through which the energy could pass—and then of inviting the power to flow from the planet's vast supply.

The orphan took a deep breath, considered the magma once more. Then she breathed out, opened her mind, and asked . . .

And the living world answered.

Ha! It was like being accelerated to an incredible speed while standing still, it was like being lifted by a thousand warm hands. It was wonderful. And as the energy burnt through her, she turned it and focused it upon the underground reservoirs. The magma turned to livid gold. And then to white hot, bursting upwards.

Slowly, the orphan reminded herself amid her elation. Slowly. She did not want to blow the top off the mountain, or to bury the island under a flood of lava. She was not like the foreigner, she sought no cataclysmic end here. She had a plan, and for the moment only a small eruption was needed. She eased off, finessing the reservoirs now. Tremors ran out through the ground. The orphan was gratified to hear, even in her room, a low rumbling, and to feel her bed tremble. She wanted a small eruption, yes, but also a noisy one. One that would cause panic.

To that end she chose a single fracture in the upper reaches of the volcano, and directed the uplifting magma along it. There came a booming detonation, profound enough to shake the hospital walls and rattle the roof. The orphan laughed. She hadn't blown the top off the mountain, but she had blown a sizeable chunk from one flank. Outside, she knew, onlookers would be watching a great cloud go up in the evening sky, and red fountains of lava rising from near the volcano's peak.

Indeed, she heard the cries now. Footsteps from the compound and the hallways. People running, shouting. Good. Now all she had to do was keep the volcano bubbling, and the ground quaking, until the staff evacuated the hospital. Someone would have to come to her room then. And remove her bonds.

It was puzzling, though. Here she was, manipulating the earth at will . . . and yet she knew that if she ordered the straps around her arms and legs to untie themselves, nothing would happen. The breeze, the volcano, even the flow of blood in the foreigner's groin—all such natural things she could command. The plastic straps, however, were beyond her. The mystery of that she could not even begin to plumb.

For an hour she listened to the fuss of the evacuation. Vehicles arrived in the driveway, and first the patients from the front wards were hustled out and away to safety. Then the back wards followed, a slower process, and more confused, but at times she sent gouts of flame bursting from the mountainside, just to maintain the urgency. Lastly it was the locked ward's turn, and by now the orphan was tugging impatiently at the straps. Footsteps slapped outside, and a key hit her door.

But when it opened, she had to laugh.

Her rescuer, of all people, was the night nurse.

He didn't look happy about being there. He fumbled with her straps, snarling curses at her, and she should have hated him still, but he was so pale and afraid he hardly seemed worth it. She stared out to the hall. Male nurses hurried by, escorting wild-eyed inmates she had never seen before. The violently mad, loose from their cells. Oh yes, it would be chaos outside. They would never have the time to worry about her. Then finally the straps were gone and the drip removed and she was free.

She rolled from the bed, as stiff and sore as if she had suffered a beating. The night nurse had hold of her wrist and was tugging her out the door. She allowed herself to be led until they left the locked ward and returned to the back wards proper, where people were dashing about in all directions. Then the orphan pulled up sharply. The night nurse was making for the exit, but that wasn't the way she wanted to go.

Annoyed, he tried to drag her forward, and for a moment there was a bizarre tug-of-war over her hand. He was suddenly furious, screaming at her, all his fear and yes, perhaps his shame too, bursting forth. In response, the orphan, in her haste, opened her mind wide and hurled the full disgust she felt for him directly into his own head. He reeled back as if struck, appalled by her, and for an instant she felt ten feet tall, unveiled to the fool boy at last in all her magnificence.

But there wasn't time for any of this. Leaving the night nurse to gape stupidly in her wake, she turned away and forgot him. She strode back through the hallways. The lights flickered on and off, unsteady, and tremors shook the floor. Here and there she passed other staff, and a last few patients being led out, but she ignored them all. Her greatest fear now was that the foreigner might already have been moved, that she would have to search all through the hospital, or outside, to find him.

But no, when she came to the crematorium she found it silent and undisturbed. Darkness reigned in the empty dayroom. And abandoned in his cell, there on the bed, the foreigner lay sleeping, his eyes shut fast. Yes. Of course. In some unacknowledged part of their minds, the staff must have known by now what kind of man he was, and so shunned him. He would be the last to be saved, if they saved him at all.

The orphan quite agreed. But even so, she could not resist—she pulled back the sheet and took one last look. His mind did not stir. He slept in exhaustion still from his exertions with the comet. But his body was so beautiful. And how wonderful it had been to believe that it was hers alone to touch.

A pretence. A trick. All his long courting of her, all the times he had made her feel special, he had done it simply to gain access to her strength. Even their one attempt at sex—she had to admit this to herself now—had been initiated by him for the same cold purpose. All he'd wanted to do that day was awaken her power, using his own broken body, his own useless cock, as the lure and the test.

Enough. A wheelchair was waiting by the bed. She wrapped the sheet around the foreigner, then manhandled him into the seat. His head flopped and cracked against the bedframe, and his eyes opened at last.

As she had been dreading all along, his voice awoke too.

Orphan? What's happening?

It was only a gentle inquiry as he rose from sleep, but already she could feel his mind reaching out for hers, and she threw up barriers to prevent it.

The volcano again? That's strange . . .

His thoughts were roaming, studying the eruption. Then suddenly he was more alert. Somehow he had read the truth in the mountain.

You did this!

She ignored him. She pushed his wheelchair out through the dayroom and into the halls. The lights were flickering again—light, then darkness, light, then darkness—and there seemed to be nobody left but the two of them.

But why? Did you think this would help us escape?

His mind was prying at her own again, trying to find answers. The orphan was slightly amazed at how well she could keep him out—and at how wrong his assumptions were. He thought she was still worried about the surgery, that she was trying to run away with him, that she was still in love with him!

It won't work, you know. We won't get away. There'll be confusion for a day or two—but then everything will be the same again.

No, nothing would be the same again, ever. But he'd find that out soon enough.

They emerged finally to the compound, and a glow in the sky. A rain of fine ash was falling. Figures ran here and there, shouting, but the orphan recognised no one, and in turn no one paid her and the foreigner any attention. She paused to stare up at the volcano. It was only a vague shape through the curtain of ash, but about two-thirds of the way up, a rift was visible where sprays of lava rose and fell.

It was all as she'd hoped. She pushed the wheelchair across the yard, straining, because the ash bogged the wheels.

Where are we going, orphan?

The pressure from his mind was greater now, like fingers probing at her skull, and she could feel his doubt, his frustration with her.

Why are you hiding from me?

She could not prevent some of her inner turmoil leaking through. Her pain at his betrayal. Her anger at his lies.

And now he came wide awake. *Lies? What lies?*

That he had ever loved her!

But of course I love you.

No, he didn't. He was lying again. He had lied about it all—and the comet was the final proof of all the other lies.

The comet?

She showed him the memories of her future vision.

But orphan—that was just a dream! A nightmare. It won't be anything like that. It certainly won't be the end of the world.

No. Every instinct told her the vision was true, she would never doubt that. The planet itself had spoken to her in its own defence.

But why would I do such a thing? Why would I cause such total destruction? Why would I so harm the earth?

Because the earth had harmed *him*, that was why. Time and time again. Crushed him, suffocated him, roasted him, drowned him—five lives over. Hadn't he told her every detail? The earth was his enemy. It was *toxic* to him. Why, even the atmosphere, the very air that gave everyone else life, it had turned into a fiery barricade that burnt and killed him rather than allow him to pass through.

I've suffered, yes, but I've always survived.

Physically, perhaps. But his mind—ah, she should have seen it sooner. But she was so used to other types of madness, and he had distracted her by always *talking* about other types of madness—anyone's madness, except his own. But she could see it now, building through all his lives, through all his failures, until his last death had broken him, and all he could think about was striking back at his tormentor, no matter how blindly, and no matter what the consequences for every living thing on earth.

Hence the comet.

No, the comet is for you, only for you. To save you.

Save her! The orphan grunted her derision as she struggled with the wheelchair. It had nothing to *do* with her. She could guess how it must have been. He'd woken from his fifth death, and in his all-consuming rage at the planet he had chanced upon a girl who had the strength to move mountains—or to move something even more deadly. Everything from that moment on had been about bringing the giant rock down to smash the world. It was never about her. It was only about his hatred.

I don't hate the world.

Of course he hated it! He'd never had the chance to do anything about it before, that was all. He'd been too weak. But he hated, sure enough. From the very first moment ninety-two years ago when the landslide had buried him, it was his fury at being killed that had kept him alive. And it still did.

I didn't choose this immortality!

Did he really believe that? Then he belonged in the crematorium after all. He was more delusional than any of them—the duke, the witch, the archangel, the virgin. Well, he could keep his eternal life. It wouldn't matter soon.

Orphan, you are terribly confused. I was too rough with you earlier, and I apologise, but you have everything wrong . . .

They came to the rear fence of the compound. In the darkness the orphan felt for the gap in the wire, and when she found it, she tugged at it until the hole was wide enough to allow the wheelchair through. She would have to carry him eventually, she knew, but she could push him for a while yet.

Why? Where are you taking me?

And again, she could not completely resist him, enough escaped from her mind for him to grasp at least a little of what she was planning. And he was struck silent—a man who did not fear even death, because he could not die.

But he was afraid now.

Shoving the chair through the fence, the orphan began the long climb.

31

She had expected protests from him. She had expected anger, and some kind of struggle, a grappling for her mind, an attempt to turn her from her course. Perhaps she had even expected pleading. But for a long while, as she heaved and levered the wheelchair up the uneven path through the jungle, he said nothing. His body flopped against the seat, passive, a dead weight. And when finally he did break his silence, it was merely to ask a question. Quietly. Thoughtfully.

Orphan, have you ever wondered if any of this is real?

Real? What did he mean—real?

Well, you live in a hospital for the insane, after all. And you've always imagined strange things about yourself. That you can predict the weather, for instance, and that you can overhear people's thoughts. So maybe . . .

Ha. Was she imagining the volcano erupting?

I don't mean the volcano. I mean you and me. All we've done together. Are you sure any of it actually happened?

The orphan frowned against a sudden chill within her. Of course she was sure. She remembered every moment of it.

But how do you know I'm not just part of some fantasy? How do you know I exist outside your head? How do you know I'm real?

He was real. The weight of the wheelchair was proof enough of that.

Oh, the man in the chair is real. But what proof do you have that he is me? Or that I'm him? All you have is a voice.

She faltered a second—a crevice in the track had caught one of the wheels. Of course the man was the foreigner! His voice had only ever come from the one place. Why, she had been looking directly into his eyes when he first spoke. She had been on her knees before him, that first day, as the volcano erupted.

Ah yes, but maybe this man was just a convenient empty vessel. Maybe your own mind spoke that day, and just pretended to be him?

She was shaking her head. No. It wasn't even just her who had been aware of him. From the moment the foreigner had arrived, the weird happenings had begun, all those disturbances with the catatonics and the geriatrics . . .

Those wards hardly ever see a new admission. This man was a strange face, that was all. He upset the other patients a little.

Well, there was no doubt about what occurred when they moved him to the crematorium. Was he going to deny everything that happened there?

Why, what did happen, do you think?

The duke! The witch! He had rummaged in their minds and aroused their madness and driven them to destruction.

They were mad already, surely. That's why they were there.

But they were fine, until he came along.

You mean they were fine until that first eruption came along—that's when the trouble really began, wasn't it? That's when the duke and the witch changed. But psychiatric patients are always vulnerable to natural disturbances—storms and earthquakes and the like; they read far too much significance into them. Ask any doctor.

For that matter, as you say, it was only after the eruption that you yourself first heard a strange voice talking in your head . . .

No . . . the duke's attack on the tourists, and the witch's self-mutilation—the volcano didn't make them do those terrible things. She had been inside their heads, and seen what the foreigner had done to them. He was to blame.

But who says you were really inside their heads? You can't prove it. Maybe you just made up whatever story suited you?

Oh yes? And what about the virgin and the archangel? Had she made up those freakish acts the two of them performed? Or the fact that the girl was dead?

What—you've never heard of two inmates fucking before? It happens all the time here! And those two in particular had profound psychosexual manias, so it was no great surprise that the end result was a violent one. Distressing, yes, but again, there's no need to conjure some imaginary foreigner to explain it.

The orphan exhaled in exasperation, and stopped pushing. They had emerged from the jungle to the headland that overlooked the hospital. She gazed out at the night. It was too dark to see much—but was the rain of ash beginning to thin? She turned to the volcano. Yes, it was slowly falling quiet, the tremors easing. The path zigzagged away from her up the bare slope, very steep. She would have to carry him from here.

As for his ridiculous claims—well, they were more lies, no matter how disturbing she found it to hear them. Things had never been as bald and simple as he was trying to suggest. Duke, witch, archangel, virgin—their fates had all been intertwined with his.

Everything had been intertwined. All his tales about his many lives and deaths, all his stories about how the world worked . . .

Wait! That was the proof! The stories he'd told her! After all, how could she have discovered so much about the earth on her own? She couldn't have. *He* had taught her. About the forces that made volcanoes, and moved continents. About wind and rain and storms. About the ocean. About space.

Not true. You already knew it all.

Nonsense! She didn't know anything. She'd been thrown out of school, too stupid to teach, and had never learnt anything since. With a heave she lifted his body from the wheelchair and rose with him in her arms. She would not be able to carry him far between rests, she knew. Nevertheless, she started to climb.

You didn't need school. You taught yourself.

How?

By listening to the radio. By watching television.

More nonsense. All radios were incomprehensible to her, he knew that, and she could see nothing on a TV screen.

Consciously, maybe not. That's part of your madness. Unconsciously, however, you've always understood radio and TV perfectly well. Your mother used to leave you in front of the television for days at a time, didn't she? And even now, your radio is almost always on. So you've heard and seen all sorts of programs over the years. Movies, documentaries, news reports. You've absorbed all kinds of information. These stories the foreigner told you—it was simply your own mind releasing that information.

The orphan sagged. He was heavier than she'd thought, that was all. It wasn't doubt sapping her strength. And yet, the radio . . . It was true. She always had her radio on. She liked the sound, even without knowing what it meant.

But was it possible . . . *could* she have known?

She hefted him up again, and trudged on. No. It was all a trick. Another way to manipulate her. This wasn't madness or delusion. This was real. She had flown, she had seen lands she hadn't known existed. She had soared high enough to discover the curve of the earth, and its spin. It was impossible that she could have known things so amazing all along, and yet not known that she knew them.

There's a globe in the office. You've always played with it. So you've always known the earth is round. And that it spins.

But she had been into space!

So has everyone; there are endless TV shows and movies about it. Any child half your age has seen enough of them to imagine what it would be like to visit space. You fantasised the whole experience. You never left the ground.

No, she had done things, changed things, affected reality. He of all people couldn't deny that. It had been his sole purpose in cultivating her. Hadn't she summoned the breeze? Hadn't she made his blood flow?

The breeze would have blown anyway. As for the blood—raising an erection in a man, even an unconscious one, is no miracle!

But it had been her strength that had blown apart the landslide dam and set the lake free, roaring down the valley.

Who's to say there ever was such a valley? Or a landslide, or a dam? Why should any of the foreigner's tales be true?

But the comet! They altered its path!

What comet? There is no comet. You've never altered anything. Don't you see? Even in your madness you know that you can't affect reality, so you conveniently claim to be responsible for things that happen far away, things you can never prove or disprove. That way nothing can ever spoil the fantasy. It's classic paranoid delusional behaviour. Otherwise—you even realised this yourself—you would have removed those arm and leg restraints on your own, rather than waiting for a nurse to do it.

Ah, but she had caused the eruption which had brought the nurse running, hadn't she? The mountain had answered her call.

Rubbish. It was the other way round. You felt the tremors of the impending eruption, worked out what was about to happen—albeit unconsciously—and then invented a scenario in which you were responsible for it. And look, the eruption is almost over. If you were really in command, how could that happen?

Gasping under his weight, arms and thighs singing, the orphan paused again, throwing her head back to stare up at the mountain. He was right. The fountains of lava had died away, and only a dull glow came now from the high cleft. The ash had stopped falling, and the night sky was beginning to clear.

Well, of course the eruption was dwindling, she was no longer stoking it with her mind. All she had to do was call again . . .

Try it then.

And she did try. She reached out, sending her mind down into the ground, searching for the shrinking reservoirs to fire them up again . . . but somehow it didn't work. She couldn't seem to concentrate.

But that didn't mean anything! She was distracted, that was all. His pestering was getting in the way. He could not be telling the truth. Because if it was the truth, then there *was* no 'he'. It was just her own mind. And why would she do that to herself? It made no sense. Why would she create him?

You created him out of loneliness. You created him out of your longing not to be ugly anymore, not to be useless and scorned and pitied. And, dare I say it, you created him out of your increasingly desperate sexual frustration.

And what a perfect hero he was. A wondrous, godlike being who could defy death and triumph over every setback. Even better, you made him fall in love with you, you made him want and need you. You gave yourself amazing powers, even more impressive than his. You made yourself beautiful and immortal. What a contrast to the drudgery of your actual life! What a pleasant dream! What an escape!

Every step took immense effort now, every word of his was poisonous, hurting her. Up above, the orphan could see the crest of the first ridge. If she could just make it there, she would rest a while. With rest she would sort it all out. Because it still made no sense. It didn't. If he was only a delusion whose purpose was to make her happy, then why was he making her unhappy now? Why hadn't he kept loving her? Why had he turned on her, and started using her to do things she didn't want to do?

It's the nature of delusions. They break down when they collide with reality. Your own delusion had made you stop eating, you were losing too much weight—the hospital staff had to take action. And once you found yourself chained to the bed, the delusion was unveiled for what it was. A powerless fantasy. The foreigner could not release you or save you, and so, in your madness, rather than accept the truth, you made him into a betrayer, a liar, an enemy. Indeed, you made him into a world destroyer. Better the earth be ruined by a cataclysm than you having to return to being the idiot girl again.

The idiot girl. No, she could not return to that. Not the dreariness of it, not the dullness. It was too heartbreaking, if that was all she was. The ridge line beckoned. If only her aching legs would push her the last few yards.

And now this—deliberately walking into an eruption zone. It's the last gasp of your delusion. It shows suicidal tendencies. That's bad enough—but you've also involved an innocent bystander: this poor man you're carrying.

The orphan staggered, lurched, and crested the ridge at last. Spent, she set the man—the foreigner, he was the foreigner—down on the ground. She hunched there, gulping for air, her hands clenched in the thin layer of ash. She must not stop. She must go through with it. It was the only way to prevent him.

Oh, but if she was wrong . . . If this man here was really just some catatonic she had fixated upon, if he wasn't the foreigner after all, then what she was intending to do to him, completely undeserved, it was too horrible, it was—

Worse than murder, that's what it is.

Tears stung her eyes. But if none of it was true, then what was the voice in her head? Who had been talking to her since this all began?

The voice was only ever your own madness. But things have gone too far. The fantasy is broken. The foreigner is gone.

Then who was talking to her now?

I'm the last rational part of your mind. I'm trying to save you, and to save this man. I'm trying to prevent you from a heinous act.

The orphan clutched the earth wretchedly. He had won. He was too clever for her. Or her own mind, her own voice, was too clever. She couldn't tell which. And if that was so, if there was no way to choose between right and wrong, madness and logic, then she could not go through with her plan. Even insanity would not excuse her. She would have to turn and carry the man down the hill again to safety.

Despairing, she lifted her eyes to the mountain. It was silent now. She had never touched it, never moved it. And beyond was the night sky, slowly clearing, the ash cloud drifting away over the sea. She had never flown to those heights. She had never soared on the winds, or plummeted through thunderstorms, her every nerve thrilling. She could not fly. No one could. It was time to take the man back down.

Except . . .

There was a cobweb in the heavens.

She stared. It was suspended above the rim of the mountain, a wisp of white gauze fixed among the stars, a pale smudge that had not been there before, an object faint and vastly far away—but which was rushing, nevertheless, towards the earth.

Wild relief surged in the orphan's heart.

It was real, it was all real after all.

Their comet was shining there in the sky to prove it.

32

The voice didn't hesitate.

Even if there is a comet, it doesn't prove anything. You certainly didn't visit it out in space with your imaginary foreigner—you heard about it on the radio while you were tied to the bed in your cell. The radio was going the whole time, remember? There was a news report about a new body becoming visible in the night sky, and from there you invented this whole absurdity about the end of the world. If anything, the comet is only more proof of your delusion . . .

But the orphan could scorn him at last.

Oh, he'd been so smart, he'd almost fooled her; he'd twisted everything inside out and she had so very nearly fallen for it. But that fuzzy dot in the sky had banished all her doubts. It was real, it was coming closer, and he was still trying to gain the use of her power, to bring the rock crashing down upon the planet.

It was clear, then, what she had to do.

No, you're regressing. The comet has nothing to do with you. It's just your paranoia, your delusions of grandeur, your sickness.

His voice was still calm, still arguing rationally—but the orphan could hear the flutter of panic just beneath. He was truly afraid now, and rightly so. He had fallen into a snare of his own devising. After all, it was his own impatience that had made him press the comet too hard, squeeze it too tight, so that its surface ruptured. The telltale corona was his own fault. Otherwise the deadly thing would still be invisible up there, and then his trickery might have succeeded. Well, not anymore. She took his unresisting body and lifted it again, a new strength invigorating her arms and legs.

You cannot do this.

Oh, but she could.

Smiling, she turned to the volcano. With the same ease—the power that certainty gave!—she reached downwards and sent a burst of heat surging through the magma reservoirs. The mountain rumbled and shook, and the orphan laughed. She could tear the whole island to pieces if she wanted.

But all she needed was a flow of lava. She pushed, and sent a pulse of molten stone up through the underground channels, and then out, overflowing from a fissure low on the mountainside. Smoke and ash billowed into the night again, and a glowing river began to flow down the volcano's flanks.

In response the foreigner abandoned words. He knew what the lava was for, and lies had not saved him, reason had not saved him. He had only one resort left. Abruptly, like talons, he was digging into her mind.

And it hurt! It was worse even than when he had stolen her strength to move the comet. Ah, but she had been confused then, bereft in space, her body drugged. She was ready for him this time, and she resisted, her mind as hard and smooth as glass. She could not hope to lock him out forever, she knew. He was too strong, and inevitably she would tire. But she needed only a little longer now.

The night was lit a dull orange by the fires on the mountain. With the foreigner limp in her arms, the orphan turned aside from the path and descended from the ridge, down into the adjoining valley. Soon she was wading through grass, and then she was enfolded by jungle again. Trees and creepers rose around her, and it was very dark beneath the canopy, but yes—there was the little stream.

It was all as she remembered it. All as he had shown her, way back at the beginning. No doubt he would say now that she had always known about this place, that perhaps she'd overheard someone at the hospital talking about it. Or that she'd been very thirsty that day, and had smelt the water in the stream, and so come looking. But she didn't believe any of that. The lava tube had been *his* secret.

He was wrenching at her mind now. Oh yes, he knew where she was taking him, and what she intended. He had called it worse than murder, and it was. After all, there was no point in killing him. He would only come to life again.

She followed the stream as before, climbing up the gully, and finally a hole opened ahead in the darkness. It was an arch of stone, the ragged mouth of a tunnel that led into midnight. The lava tube. The orphan lifted her gaze beyond the entrance and saw, through the undergrowth, the fierce glow of fires. Further up the gully, the jungle was burning. The lava was coming, as she had arranged. It would not come through the tube, of course; the tunnel was long since blocked. No, the molten river would simply flow down the gully, slow and deep, until—

The foreigner's attack broke out anew, a mad hammering at her mind. And the blows told. A certain numbness was creeping over her, a dislocation between thought and action. She was weakening. But she made herself move forward into the tube. It was black in there, yet her eyes could see. She carried the foreigner inwards for a distance, and then set him down on the rocky floor. Fifty paces behind her was the opening, and fifty paces ahead the tube ended in a blank stone wall.

A prison then, with only the one exit.

His assault on her mind abated suddenly, and she stared down at him in surprise—and then in revulsion. His dead eyes were fixed upon her, and his whole body, from fingers to toes, was twitching grotesquely. He was trying to wake up. In his desperation, he was commanding his useless legs and arms to function. But it was still too soon. All he could achieve was a kind of spastic quivering, horrid to watch.

Sickened, the orphan turned and walked away.

She came to the entrance and climbed back out into the jungle. The glow from the fires was bright now, she could hear the crackle of flames and smell burning wood. And there was another, more earthy, metallic smell. Much closer now. Good. She clambered up away from the stream, high enough to be clear of the lava's path. Then she paused, and looked back to the tunnel.

He would not die, she was sure of that, not even a temporary death. The lava would be thick and slow at this point, it would not be fluid enough to roll back down the tube and devour him. It would merely seal the entrance. It would be hot in the tunnel for a while, and the air would be foul, but he had survived much worse.

There would be no death—but he would be confined in there for as long as the mountain stood. A hundred years. A thousand. And even if one day he did contrive to die, and be reborn, it wouldn't matter. He could not shift himself while dead. He would come to life again in the same place. The same dark tunnel. Still sealed in. His body might change, and his face, and he could wait even ten thousand years—immortal.

But he would never be able to leave.

And now the river of lava was drawing near. At its forefront it was all black, a smoking, shoving mass of stone and charred wood, but further back, the flow was white and blindingly hot, even from a distance.

She heard something, over the fires.

A sound—liquid, clotted, awful. It came from inside the tube, weirdly amplified. It was the foreigner, the man in the tunnel, crying aloud. In these final few seconds, he was somehow forcing words from a throat not fully formed. She heard the terror in the sound, and the disbelief. He was pleading with her, perhaps. But she would never know what he said. She was incapable of understanding speech.

Then the fires raged too loud to hear anything else. She watched as the lava, a congealed wave half the height of the trees, rolled laboriously over the mouth of the tunnel. And then she had to turn and run from the heat.

33

But that wasn't the end of it, of course.

She climbed away from the burning jungle, towards the ridge again. And no, that wasn't the end of it at all. She might have trapped his body, but that meant very little when he was still free in thought. He could still, even from his freshly formed prison, reach out with his mind. He could still reach into *her*.

Indeed, as if he'd just remembered the same thing, she felt him come rushing back into her head, as she'd known he would. But she barely recognised him now; he was like a wild thing, a raging animal, grappling brutally at her skull. If she succumbed and let him through, then he could still steal her strength away. And if he could do that, then the tunnel was no prison at all. With her power under his dominion, he need only make the earth quake for him, and the tube would crack wide open.

A deep weariness sank into the orphan. An overwhelming desire to sleep, to which she must not yield. In fact, she could never rest again. Never let down her guard, or he would be there. And that was the crux of it. He would win eventually. As long as she was available to him, then the danger would never go away.

So there was only one answer.

She had to remove herself from him.

She was nearing the top of the ridge, and slowing now, not merely from fatigue. There was a sadness in her too. A reluctance to come to the finish. Because it wasn't as simple as running away. After all, where could she go? She would never be allowed to leave the island, not on her own, not the poor idiot girl. And even if she could, it wouldn't help. His mind was not limited by distance. He would track her down wherever she went, even if it was the other side of the planet.

And so that was the *real* answer.

She had to remove herself from the *world*.

The orphan stood atop the ridge, and gazed across the smoking wasteland to the volcano. Already the lava flows had cooled, curdling into slag on the lower slopes, and their glow now barely warmed the darkness. There was only one more thing she needed from the mountain. A final, very special eruption.

For the last time she reached out with her senses—feeling him fight her at every moment—and fashioned the heat and the pressure in the underground chambers to one single purpose. It was quite delicate, really, and despite everything she marvelled at her own ability. How wondrous it all could have been, such a talent, if things hadn't turned out this way, if it hadn't all been ruined by him.

But it was too late now. She summoned the energy, hurled it into the mountain. There came a single detonation, a profound punch of air. A tight knuckle of smoke belched up from the volcano's peak, but thrown beyond it, shot far and clear into the night, was a lone, black, spinning piece of rock. This time she really had done it—blown the top off the mountain. The very tip, in fact. She watched calmly as it rose. It was a boulder the size of a house, her own miniature comet, with a very specific target. She had calculated the forces exactly, and knew precisely where it would land.

The foreigner's savage attacks reached a new frenzy, but she held him out still, staring up. The rock attained the peak of its arc, and seemed to hang above her. She remembered flying. She remembered soaring over the mountaintop with him on the first flight they made together. She remembered seeing a little tree, hidden on the very pinnacle. She had wanted to look, later, for that tree. To prove to herself that everything was real. Well, if the tree existed, it would be up there on that boulder, right now. But she made no effort to see. The rock began to fall.

There was just one last thing she needed to do now, a final risk she must rule out. Because there was a chance—slim, but undeniable—that the foreigner had not lied to her in one special instance. There was a chance that she really was, like him, immortal. In which case, even this falling stone would not be enough. She might survive despite it, and her power with her, still at his disposal.

So, she did it. With a shrug, she gave the power up.

The power, and any hope of life eternal. In a heartbeat, it all slipped away from her like a bathrobe falling from her shoulders.

Which was the strangest thing of all. That it could be done, and so simply. And yet she knew too that such a sacrifice was permissible only as a final act, a choice to be made in the last moment before death, and at no other time. Indeed, it was the choice itself, she saw, that made death possible.

It struck her then, as the rock crept down from the sky, that in all the foreigner's many endings, he had never *surrendered* his life. He had always fought against dying, always clung so bitterly to survival, as if there was nothing else that mattered. Even now he was clinging on—clawing despairingly at her thoughts—just as he always had. Refusing death, and hating the world that demanded it of him.

It wouldn't change even once she was gone, the orphan foresaw. He would refuse death still. Trapped forever in his lightless cell, he would live on and on, the most hideous existence she could imagine. He would come to hate his very immortality. And yet it would never occur to him—and this was the most ghastly aspect—that he could let it go. That he could just say—as he could have all those years ago, beneath the landslide—*enough*. Enough suffering. Let it end. And thus, truly, die.

But he was gone now. As she cast away her powers, so she cast him away too, moving far beyond his tawdry reach. And in place of all the confusion and weariness and pain, a strange peace and clarity infused the orphan.

How remarkable! Her lifelong madness—it was as if it had vanished. The fog of her thoughts had cleared, the wall around her mind had fallen, and all the things that had been blocked or hidden from her were suddenly free to enter. Memories flooded up, transformed. The boulder was tumbling down, but the orphan felt she had the leisure to relive every minute of her twenty-one years. She felt so aware. So *sane*.

Images, and print, and music; it was as though she'd compre-hended them all along. And speech. A lifetime of speech rushed through her, all those words she'd heard in dumb mystification, she understood them all at last.

And names! She could remember names! Her mother's name. The names of all the nurses and the patients. And the old doctor's name. And more—she remembered the name of her town, and of the big town too. She remembered the name of her island, and of the ocean around it, and of all the other oceans. She remembered the name of every city and country in the world. Endless names.

She even remembered her own.

And something was rising in her throat, pushing against vocal cords that had never formed a word, something incredible.

The rock filled the night sky. She could still step back and let it miss her, she knew. She could still withdraw her choice and return to what she had been. There was still time. Why, everlasting life, if she wanted.

But the thing in her throat was bursting.

'Ha!' cried the orphan, out loud.

And stepped forward.

blue door. home to good writing

The Ballad of Trenchmouth Taggart
Glenn Taylor

"[a] galloping, defiant epic…a virtuoso performance." *Guardian*

Meet Early "Trenchmouth" Taggart, a man born and orphaned in 1903; a one time inventor, snake handler, cunnilinguist, sniper, woodsman, harmonica man, and newspaperman. His is an epic story, a tall tale in the tradition of Mark Twain, chronicling more than one hundred years of exile and outrunning trouble. It is the love song of an outlaw and, like the best ballads, it etches its mark deep upon the memory.

"A defiantly incredible creation…this is a genuine success that admirers of John Irving - and others too - will surely enjoy." *Independent*

"An energetic romp." *Dazed and Confused*

978-0-00-733773-6 • £12.99

The Marrowbone Marble Company
Glenn Taylor

Coming in February 2011, *The Marrowbone Marble Company*: a powerful tale of one man's fight for civil rights during three defining decades of twentieth century America.

978-0-00-735907-3 • £12.99

blue door. be in at the start

blue door

Beautiful Losers
Leonard Cohen

"Gorgeously written…one comes out of it having seen terrible and beautiful visions." *New York Times*

The extraordinary and inimitable singer-songwriter's classic novel, echoing the dark poetry and wry humour of his timeless songs of loss, love, sex and religion.

Not just extremely funny, but an original and explicit examination of friendship, sex and spirituality.

"The most vivid, fascinating and brave modern novel I have read." *Michael Ondaatje*

978-0-00-731838-4 • £8.99

The Favourite Game
Leonard Cohen

"He is a writer of terrific energy and colour, a Rabelaisian comic and a visualiser of some memorable scenes." *Observer*

Lawrence Breavman seeks two things: love and beauty. Beginning with the innocent games of delicious misadventure with first love Lisa and the absorbing wanders through Montreal with best friend Krantz, Breavman's tale is a distant echo of *Catcher in the Rye* and *Portrait of the Artist as a Young Man* – injected with 1960s aesthetics and Cohen's unique poetry.

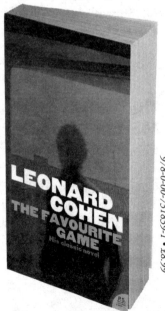

978-0-00-731839-1 • £8.99

blue door. step inside for great books.

blue door

Sixteen Shades of Crazy
Rachel Trezise

"Trezise is an outstanding young writer, with a wonderfully sharp, cynical take on contemporary Wales." *The Times*

Aberalaw, a tiny valley village where nobody ever arrives and nobody ever leaves. With a ban on recreational drugs, the party-loving wives and girlfriends of local punk band, The Boobs, are getting desperate for new thrills: Ellie, factory girl with dreams of a better life in New York; Rhiannon, hairdresser with a taste for violence and designer clothes and Siân, unappreciated, obsessive compulsive mother of three.

Into their lives, enter the languid dark stranger, Johnny: Englishman, drug dealer and shameless seducer. In the space of just a few months, three women's lives will be changed forever.

The long-awaited novel from Orange Futures winner Rachel Trezise dissects the morals and mores of a Welsh village community with a scalpel-sharp pen and an incisive wit.

"Trezise writes with an irresistible self-indulgence… the same complete command of the English language as the heavyweights of contemporary fiction." *Big Issue*

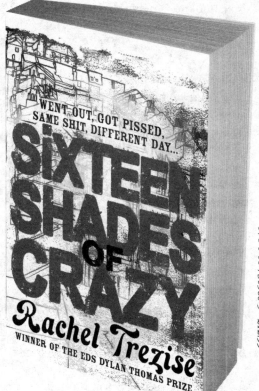

WENT OUT, GOT PISSED, SAME SHIT, DIFFERENT DAY…

SIXTEEN SHADES OF CRAZY

Rachel Trezise

WINNER OF THE EDS DYLAN THOMAS PRIZE

978-0-00-730560-5 • £12.99

blue door. be in at the start of something big.

blue door

Julian Corkle is a Filthy Liar
DJ Connell

"Laugh-out-loud funny and genuinely touching. A magical journey. Julian Corkle is a big fat masterpiece."
Eoin Colfer

Not everyone shares Julian Corkle's dreams of stardom. Television is too much like hairdressing for his father's tastes. A Tasmanian man wants a son for sporting purposes. 'Boys don't like dolls,' he tells Julian, 'They like Dinky Toys.' Not this boy, thinks Julian, who knows better than to tell the truth.

Besides, the family already has a sporting hero, Julian's sister Carmel aka 'The Locomotive'. Julian likes his sister, but knows better than to tangle with her bowling arm. It's the same one she uses for punching.

Julian Corkle is a Filthy Liar is the ultimate feel-good novel, a book that will have the reader laughing out loud on the back of a bus as it follows Julian's bumpy journey through adolescence, fibbing his way through school and a series of dead-end jobs, to find his ultimate calling as creator of 'The Hog'. It's as if Crocodile Dundee has crashed Muriel's wedding and run off into the desert with Priscilla.

"A tour de farce…
This book proves that optimism is not an eye disease."
Kathy Lette

"A genuinely funny book with a great big heart."
Jenny Eclair

978-0-00-733216-8 • £10.00

blue door. step inside for great books.

blue door